The Professional Dominatrix

by

Alexandria May Ausman

Book cover illustration by Alexandria May Ausman
Editor: Jon M. Ausman

Library of Congress Control Number: 2025906287

ISBN: 978-1-963335-42-2 (ebook)
ISBN: 978-1-963335-41-5 (paperback)

Published By:
Ausman & Cousins LLC
1700 North Monroe Street
Suite 11, Box 284
Tallahassee, Florida 32303-0501

For author interviews: ausman@embarqmail.com

Das Kaiser Haus Series

The Rise of the Priceless (Chapters 1 to 10)
Metal Illness (Chapters 11 to 19)
Jonas the Vampire (Chapters 20 to 29)
Prince of the Elders (Chapters 30 to 40)
Leo's Lamb (Chapters 41 to 50)
Mastermind Malfred (Chapters 51 to 58)
Priceless Lost (Chapters 59 to 67)
Broken Silver (Chapters 68 to 74)

The Collar King Series

Return to Das Kaiser Haus (Chapters 1 to 7)
Felicity's Child (Chapters 8 to 14)
Tears of the Violin (Chapters 15 to 22)
The Golden Collar (Chapters 23 to 30)
Rise of the Mortar King (Chapters 31 to 38)
Prisoner of the Stone Palace (Chapters 39 to 46)
Mortar Transformation (Chapters 47 to 54)
Taube Returns (Chapters 55 to 62)
Chocolate Dreams (Chapters 63 to 70)
Pocket Soup (Chapters 71 to 78)
Lucus's Revenge (Chapters 79 to 86)
Night of the Stasi (Chapter 87 to 94)
Revenge of the Mortar King (Chapter 95 to 102)

The Most Brutal Man in Europe Series

Claus's Revelations (Chapters 1 to 8)
Priceless Changes (Chapters 9 to 16)
Silver Well (Chapters 17 to 24)
Book Four (coming soon)

The Psycho Series

Cemetery Kid (Chapters 1 to 20)
Stop Calling Me Psycho (Chapters 21 to 33)
Motor-Psycho (Chapters 34 to 44)
Delusion of the Collar and the Key (Chapters 45 to 53)
Brutality's Prisoner (Chapters 54 to 64)
Aesthetic Akathisia (Chapters 65 to 74)
Metallic Burden (Chapters 75 to 83)

27 Masters Series

Anita the Benevolent (Chapters 1 to 7)
The Beast and the Witch (Chapters 8 to 16)
High Priestess of Schizophrenia (Chapters 17 to 24)
The Professional Dominatrix (Chapters 25 to 33)
Triangle of Trust (coming soon)

Stand Alone Books

The Grannybat's Weird Tales & Gothic Stories Volume 1

Book Four Characters: The Professional Dominatrix

Anita: deceased first Master
Arodia: High Priestess of the Green Ring
Boyd: a deputy sheriff
Carmen: an acquaintance
Christian Axel: secret husband of Psycho/Rachel, trainer and original Master
Christopher: a Dominant
Chuck: spouse of Lisa, member of the Green Ring
Cindy: mother of the sadist Julie
Circe: the third Mistress, a Priestess of the Green Ring
CJ: a college classmate
Commisso, Doctor: state hospital psychiatrist
David: a college student want a be rapist
Debbie: Psycho's sexual psychopathic and sadistic mother
Delilah: niece of Maiden Mary, caretaker of the nursery
Delleh: a High Priestess of the Green Ring, a 5th Level Initiate
Dennis: the county sheriff
Diane: CJ's live in friend
Dude: a command hallucination, an aggressive anger shard of Psycho
Ginger Kirkpatrick: a FemDom, Mistress Ten
Greg: a high school classmate
James: spouse of Tracy, member of the Green Ring
Johnny: a Summoner
Jon Ausman: the current Keyholder

Joyce: a Dominatrix
Julie: a previous Mistress who fled the law
Julius: a funeral home owner
June: a funeral home master embalmer, Mistress Nine, an interim
Kurt: a college student want to be rapist
Linda: a deputy sheriff
Lisa: spouse of Chuck, member of the Green Ring
Looper: a disembodied voice, Psycho's narrative hallucination
Madam Whips: a Dominatrix
Maggie: Matthew's schizophrenic aunt
Marie: Master Seven, an interim
Mary: Maiden to Circe, takes care of Psycho's children
Mary: grandmother of Psycho, mother of Debbie
Mike: a friend of Psycho
Pat: a master mortician
Paul: a California Dungeon Master, Ginger's trainer
Peggy: Master Four, an Interim Master
Psycho: a schizophrenic trying to survive
Randy: a Snake Pit staff rapist
Rebecca: a friend of Ginger
Roary: a High Priest, 3rd Level Initiate, also known as Richard
Ronnie: spouse of Circe, lives with Mary
Shree, Doctor: a professor of psychology
Simon Brag: a command hallucination shard of Psycho, her lost inner self
Stacey: a high school and college classmate

Steve: a college student want to be rapist
Tammy: Master Eight, an interim
Thalia: a Crone of her coven
Tracy: spouse of James, member of the Green Ring
Will: a member of the Green Ring
Zeppelin: a golden fur dog

Preface

Ah, so there is a title worth looking forward to eh? It is about time our life has something new added. The old way was abuse, neglect, cruelty and illegal running rampant. Thank goodness Mistress Ginger has come into our life to fix all this insanity. Sure, she has a heavy hand, but it will take strength to dig us out of the rubble of a world that crumbled long ago. She is here with her tools in hand ready to help us re-build.

However, the glorious Mistress realizes with much disgust, first she must destroy the weak shelter we had tried to construct. We are amazing at using our hands when mending a house but fail when it comes to repairing our heart. This is not something she is willing to tolerate.

With anger and horror we will suffer her kicks, blows, and thuds while she knocks down all our shoddy walls. In order to find true comfort, our Mistress will want to start fresh, and we will learn to please her or suffer the consequences. We don't understand it, but her destruction is for our own good. Our Mistress loves us. The trouble is, we don't really love us. Therefore, she will create something we can accept, and in time, come to adore.

Like Master Marie before her, she will teach us a new dance. The music she plays is one we have heard before and hated it. That is because it was not heard properly. Mistress Ginger will adjust the tempo, bass, treble, and volume. This time, it will sound sweeter to our ears than any melody ever composed. Our feet will begin to tap, our unit will sway captured by the beautiful rhythms of our Red-Headed Goddess on Earth. We cannot help it. It is our nature. The Mistress is everything we need, and we are everything she desires. The dancers are graceful, perfect, and amazing to witness. A perfect union of two into one.

So, ready to get on with the incredible story of Mistress Ginger? Ah! Well, make sure to put the kids to bed early. Close the blinds. Turn down the lights and pour yourself a fine glass of wine. The romantic tale of lovers most unusual and forbidden may titillate your senses. It may even make you question your own understanding of the traditional ways used to heal a broken soul. Sometimes the only way to correct something is to demolish it completely and start from scratch.

Chapter 25: Out with the Old and In with the New Mistress Ginger

"I forgave you that very afternoon Goddess. I know you don't understand, and I can't tell you. Please always remember, no matter where I go, what I do, or who I adore, you are my Goddess on Earth. I worship at your feet till the day I am taken to the Summerlands. Having to see you but never be yours is my punishment for falling in love with you. A punishment I will suffer for eternity."
Psycho to Linda at the Springfields Mabon Sabbat, September 24th, 1994.

Mistress Ginger had originally told me that we would go back to her place so she could enjoy her special privileges of the collar. However, on our way back from shopping she decided that waiting to see her future home was of more importance. I was glad to have the short reprieve. My ass was still on fire from the last thudding I had taken the day before. My mind was whirling, trying to find a way to avoid getting trapped in her bonds at the mercy of her cruel sexual interests.

I had decided to keep her busy by handing over my psychiatric records, important personal papers, and other information about my life as it was at up to that point as she had ordered that morning. I already knew there was a mountain of paperwork she would have to look over. If she did the job of examining them carefully as she had promised, it would be the next week before I had to fear her whip again. There was a ton of this shit is what I am saying.

I had already recognized this Mistress was intelligent, clever and above all trained. Getting around her was going to be quite a task. I was sure I could figure out how she ticked, dismantle her and destroy her but it was not going to be easy. Of that I had no doubt.

Why would I even want to do such a thing you ask? Ah, well you see despite Simon's joy at this Mistress, I hated her. Her whips, and other thudding tools, plus her (what I saw as cruel) cruel ordering me around was simply not okay with me.

I am not a fucking submissive. I am a schizophrenic. There is a God damned difference. Master Debbie and Master Julie had been like this bitch. I had made it my goal to rid the Earth of this type of horrid person. Trouble was, Mistress Ginger wasn't like those two. I just couldn't tell the difference, not yet anyway. To me, a sadist was a sadist. Distinctions were of no interest to me.

The mirroring of this Mistress had begun. Once I had her image well entrenched, I would slowly unravel her from within. I would overtake her world by giving her everything she desired. Then strangle her to death with it.

NOTE: *If you missed it, that is what I do. I destroy those who tried to destroy me. Mistress Ginger had already pointed out that all the abusers of my gifts had not ended up well.*

Guess what? That is what they asked for. I am a mirror and I only gave them what they wanted. Equal service for equal service. When their image was ugly, ugly is what I reflected to them. My Mistress was clever enough to not only discover who I was collared by but learned the fates of those before her. She already had discovered I was not one to be fooled with.

I am intelligent, clever, adaptable, capable of tolerating large amount of pain, and completely insane. A high functioning Schizophrenic with a history of training as a Sadist and an abnormally high IQ. That is a dangerous combination. I am not a sadist. Instead I became a hater of the Sadist. Just like the legends of someone bitten by a Vampire but never turned, if I ran across one like Mistress Ginger, I made it my goal to destroy them. I wanted to make them all pay for one of their kind stealing my childhood and life.

I had decided that everyone who dared to hold my collar was likely a sadist of some level. Professional or just a hateful being, all would pay for being a dark heart. If they treated me with kindness, I would repay their kindness. If they used, abused, and took advantage, well I could just as easily do that one too.

Just as I had warned the beast Keyholder before Circe, 'a pound of flesh for a pound of flesh' is fair. That cruel Master's desires had burned so hot, despite my warnings, it destroyed everything. Seems her desires had set a fire, *snickering*

Once my horror at having been forcibly collared by a professional sadist had cleared, I was now ready to begin the actions designed to take Mistress Ginger out forever.

Remember: "As you wish Mistress. Forever is exactly what I had in mind." Thought that I meant something else didn't you.

I pulled into the driveway of my yellow house. Mistress Ginger gasped, "It is beautiful Psycho. The neighborhood sucks but damn. It is nice. Three bedroom you said?"

I nodded, "It was. I built a fourth off the back of the house. It was a back porch, but I enclosed it and created a ritual room. I had to fix the walls, windows, and floors. I still have a bit of fixing up to finish but it is nearly ready."

She looked at me surprise, "You built a room and did all the work yourself? Well, you are surprising. How did you learn construction?"

I opened my door, "From books Mistress." I slammed my own door going around the car I opened her door to let my Mistress out to investigate her new home.

Mistress Ginger smiled while she got out of her car, "Ah, intelligent too. My, my, I am very impressed. I will start thinking of ways to keep that big brain of yours busy. I will have to remember to keep your mind on a tight leash. Wouldn't want you having too much time to retaliate, now would we?" She walked to the front door.

I stood there in shock. She had figured out I was planning to crush her beneath my feet. Damn. I would have to be more careful. I likely had given her some clue to my plans to pay her back for taking Simon's Key. No matter, in time she would forget I wanted revenge. She would get complacent thinking I was over my anger at her forcing my submission. Then I could strike, and she would never see it coming. I just had to be patient.

I unlocked the house letting her inside. She was immediately struck with awe. I had worked very hard redoing everything inside. It had taken me almost two years, but it was fresh, modern, and new. I had even installed new carpets. I found I had a knack for building and using my hands in general.

NOTE: *This house had been a true pleasure to fix up. I would end up paying around forty thousand in all with the added interest and building materials, but once it was paid off in 1998, I sold it for over ninety thousand. Not only had property values in the area gone up, but I had also made a three-bedroom one bath shit box into a four-bedroom two bath, beauty with a large well-groomed fenced in yard. Doing almost all the construction work myself saved a ton of cash, and allowed me to buy a bigger, more expensive piece of shit, to fix up and sell. As this one, I would choose one in an area set to gain in value. I, of course, chose correctly. I told all of you Psycho was a great real estate prospector and she was.*

"Ah, this is wonderful Psycho. How much longer before it is ready to move into?" She said not even looking at me, while she walked from room to room.

I shook my head, "I am unsure Mistress. I have classes now, and work, plus attending to you and visiting my children. It is difficult to find time to properly attend to the repairs."

Since having been reassigned to June as my Work Master, I was not able to leave to come work as I had been able under Pat. A fact I quickly shared with my Mistress.

"Okay June, yes I know this name," said Mistress Ginger frowning suddenly.

I looked at her surprised. "You know her? She was one of my Interims. The last one in fact, just before you. One that Mistress Circe fooled you and I with."

Mistress Ginger's face twisted in anger which surprised me. "Excuse me Psycho? I was not fooled. Mistress Circe told you that she would auction that Key on September 2nd did she not?"

I nodded completely confused by her strange statement. "She did, but the auction was a lie. She sold my collar to you in June."

"Kneel, damn you Psycho. Now," Mistress Ginger yelled pointing to the floor with a look of extreme anger.

This frightened me quite a bit. I dropped as commanded wondering what just flew up her ass. I didn't have to pontificate long.

"I was not fooled. Nor were you. You had a fucking contract with the old cunt. Like it or not you agreed that she would give you the address of the next to own your collar on September 2nd. She followed that agreement to the letter. I was told you were not available till that time. I didn't ask why, wasn't my business now was it? I knew that when I purchased that collar of yours. I agreed to September the 2nd just like you did. Whatever she ordered you to do during those two months was not my problem. It was, however, your problem. Now I have five fucking women calling my house constantly since yesterday. I have been offered a king's ransom for that Key of mine. I have refused all their offers. I told them all no and hung up on them except for this June person. She reports that you didn't finish your contract with her. Is this true?"

I looked at the floor completely confused, "What? Mistress I don't understand. I did serve her for the time I was there. She is bitching about the days I was kidnapped and hospitalized. June thinks I owed her those days. I couldn't help not being there. The contract ended on September 2nd. I fulfilled that contract. You had my collar and were rightful Master anyway since June. This is stupid."

Mistress Ginger walked over to my unit and told me to look at her. I did as I was told. She at once backhanded the shit out of my face.

"Lower your voice when speaking to me Psycho. You will never refer to anything I have to say as stupid ever again. June isn't claiming you didn't show up to serve. She isn't claiming those lost days you are talking about. She says you refused her special services of the collar and left her home one day early. Is that true?" Mistress Ginger reared back her hand to strike me again if I didn't answer quickly.

I winced but rapidly said, "I did deny her Mistress. I couldn't do it. I was upset by the rape, I left so she didn't repeat the forcing of such services. Please mercy. Don't hit me again."

She struck me anyway this time busting my lip right down the center. Memories of Master Julie filled my mind. I was in big trouble I decided. This Mistress wasn't playing around. I would need to be more careful and watch my manners or suffer more for it.

I dropped to the prostrate pose to hide my face from further blows.

"Get up to a kneel. That isn't going to work. I will correct you how I see fit," Mistress Ginger roared.

I got up quickly but braced for another backhand. However, it didn't come. Instead Mistress Ginger stood there glaring at me with extreme anger. She looked at the ceiling then blew out her breath.

"Shit. Fucking shit," she yelled out suddenly scaring the shit out of me. "You have put me in a bad situation, Psycho. Damn you, why did you deny her what she had earned by contract. She was not Tammy. You punished her for the deeds of someone else. You knew better than that. Did June do her job? Did she?" Mistress Ginger grabbed my collar and shook me.

I nodded while starting to cry at this point. I realized in horror what Mistress Ginger was saying. I had betrayed the rules of the Collar. I never betray my collar. However, I may have hated Mistress June, she had earned the services she was requesting. I had crawfished her on the deal by running off like the loon I am. My contract with her was broken on my side.

"You better cry Psycho. You are a liar and untrustworthy. How dare you dishonor yourself like that. Now what the fuck am I supposed to tell this bitch? My submissive betrayed her. She gave you service and you refused to repay it. A thief is what you are. Why should I trust you. Maybe you will betray me too." She was beyond livid at this point, and sadly correct.

I looked at the floor truly humiliated. She had managed to find a way to get me to feel as close to embarrassed as I would ever get. I had indeed stolen services from June. It may seem wrong of her to demand those services after I had suffered at the hands of Tammy, but I am not a normal. My contract with Mistress June was that of service for service. Mistress Ginger was right. I had punished Mistress June for Tammy's bad behavior by denying her and leaving one day early. I didn't have the right to do that. I had allowed my emotions to override my loyalty to my collar. If this were left uncorrected, I would find it easier to do it again, then maybe eventually disobey every command, contract or order given to me by a Keyholder. Then I would be doomed unable to attend my own best interests.

"Mistress forgive me. I humbly request to leave your side and finish my service to Mistress June. If I don't then I am the thief you call me. I would allow her to correct my bad behaviors, then return to you and submit to your own

11

displeasure at my poor quality of service to you both. There is no other alternative to satisfy the contract with her and still adhere to your collaring. I will need you to lift your demand for monogamy and chastity on the day of her choosing to address this matter." I wanted to barf at the idea of having to sleep with Mistress June after all. Yuck!

However, it was what I would have to do to undo what had been done or not done in this case.

Mistress Ginger's temper appeared to cool as she listened to my words. "Yes, you are damned right you are going to finish this contract. I am super pissed that my collar is going to be in someone else's bed. This is your fault. You never bring the corpse of another Master to the wedding bed of the new. Do you hear me Psycho? You will be punished for this when you finish."

I nodded, "Yes Mistress."

I was still crying at both the horror at having to deal with Mistress June and the righteous anger of Mistress Ginger. The Looper was already having a great deal of fun reminding me what a scumbag I was for allowing this to happen. If I had just done my duty in the first place instead of acting like a normal would, none of this would have happened. I am not a fucking normal, and I don't have choices like one. Now I would be punished severely for forgetting that little detail.

She walked over and sat down in the old rocking chair. "This is never going to do. You have been well trained but apparently hate your nature. I don't care for that a bit. I assumed you were natural, but something is wrong here. I want to see those records of yours. If you are being held hostage due to some fucking symptom of schizophrenia, then I am not sure I want to continue this situation. I know there is a rule about the Key only having one shot but you, Psycho, have now broken your own rule. You tossed Mistress June for no reason at all. I want to consider on this a moment. You will go now and get those records. Bring them to me and sit quietly at my feet while I decide if I want to keep you or send you back to the last one to own that collar, June."

My eyes went wide as I realized what she just said. I couldn't argue. Mistress June had not been allowed to finish her reign. I ran away. Now she technically still owned my collar and Mistress Ginger was poaching it by collaring what was not free yet. Mistress Ginger could if she wished walk away and leave me stuck with Mistress June who literally wanted my ass. I hated them both. A rock and a hard place had been created by this contractual error.

I got up quickly to retrieved what Mistress Ginger wanted. I brought back the huge folder that contained the horror that was my life. Debbie, Julie, all the nightmares were explained in those pages in gruesome detail. My mental and physical health was detailed as well as all prognosis. Even Simon was discussed. Mistress Ginger now had access to my blueprints. I sat on the floor at her feet like I was told feeling I would die from the despair of my stupidity, while my unsure Mistress looked over my history.

Several hours passed while she sifted through the mess of my world. She often gasped, groaned and even would lean back her head appearing disgusted. I just sat there waiting patiently for her judgement. There was nothing I could do, and nowhere to go if I did do anything. As usual, I had no good choices. It was best just to wait and see what the Gods wanted. They would make sure I always got exactly where I was meant to be.

Finally, she appeared satisfied she had her answers when she told me to kneel again before her, "Psycho, I was right. You are not a natural submissive. This history of yours turns my fucking stomach. No wonder you gave me so much shit. You are well trained, gifted, and angry as hell about both. I won't say that I blame you one bit. You have the right to be pissed off. It is a wonder you haven't murdered half the world by now. However, angry or not, it is what you are. Do you know why?" She looked at me hard.

I shook my head no, "I don't even understand what you think I am Mistress much less understand why I would be angry about it."

She chuckled. "Well you are honest I will give you that. You are a victim is what you are Psycho. You are a victim because you have allowed others to convince you that you are. You, my dear Psycho, are not a natural submissive. However, you appear to live like one. You walk the walk; you talk the talk, but your heart is not in it. I don't want something like that. You were raised to answer, scrap, kneel and serve. You have been forced the whole way. I see hundreds of rapes, beatings, assaults and even attempted murders at the hands of the ones who made you into what you are. I thought your refusals yesterday were just what

14

turned you on. You see some submissives like to play the role of 'unwilling.' I was an idiot not to check to make sure that it was not just an act. I now realize those tears were real. You deserve them too. With this history babe, I am sorry I ever struck you even just for pleasure. You don't need more terror. I am not a monster, Psycho. I love what I am, and if you cannot love what you are, then I must release you and keep looking. You are not the lover I thought I was getting."

I looked at the floor feeling even more confused than before. This Mistress was apologizing to me for thudding me? What?

"Mistress, I don't understand. You bought my collar fair and square. I need the help or I will die. I follow my Key…" I was interrupted by her silence hand signal.

She reached out and grabbed my chin, "Look at mem Psycho. You need protection and a lot of help that is true. These records told me what they did to you. I now know about the brain damage, the disease, and the results of the poisoning. I have seen it firsthand remember? You are forever disabled it says. You need to be in an institution where loving people can keep people like Julie, Circe and all these other monsters away from you. You are not able to help yourself no matter how smart you are. I am truly sorry. There are no words strong enough for what I feel about what I have read here, but babe, I can't help you. Your answer to stay out of care is surface only. If you fake and don't feel, then you are going to just be further victimized by my choice of lifestyle. I won't do that to you. Do you understand now? If you can't find pleasure from my adoration of you, then you will never adore me back. Who wants that kind of love? Not me."

She let my chin go as she teared up looking at me with true sadness. I was now unsure what to think. "Are you saying you are going to toss Simon's Key because I don't want to be thudded or bonded?"

She laughed. "Yes Psycho, which is what I am saying but so much more. Are you listening to me? I am going to have to let you go because I want to adore you and I want you to adore me back. You are only doing what you are told because you fear punishment and pain. Not because you love me for it and want to please me. I can't love you because I know you will never love me back. Your appearance of love will always be true terror and despair wrapped in bullshit."

I sat back hard. "Then this is goodbye then? I suppose that is the right thing to do. I will never be able to be the masochist you ask me to be Mistress. I do apologize but that is something you are born to be, you don't learn it. I tried that once, failed miserably."

She laughed hard. "Oh, you are talking about this Julie bitch I read about. What a cunt. Well, she was just a stupid, mean kid. I hope she died of something terrible. No, I am not looking for a masochist. You are correct, those are born not made. Crossed wires somewhere in the brain I have heard. I have dealt with them, and I get real tired of them quick. They want to be hit so they fuck shit up to get a beating. I don't want to spend my life chasing you around beating you so you can fulfill some weird ass sexual needs."

I looked down shocked. "But Mistress, you like to thud. Isn't that what you want? Someone who likes that shit. That hurts. Fuck that."

She smiled. "I like it that you feel that way. If you wanted it, it takes the fun out. I don't thud to injure you, just enough to cause some pain. Your fear, and pain turns me on. Your frustration does too, and your humiliation. Perhaps if I explain why you will understand why that is? I have read your history; would you like to know mine? It is only fair."

I admit I was interested to know why she seemed to be so turned on by hurting me. I nodded then tried to sit comfortably. I assumed it was going to be a bit. Mistress Ginger surely had a tale to tell.

THE STORY OF MISTRESS GINGER THE MAKING OF A DOMINANTRIX

She never took her eyes off me while she told the story of her acceptance of her nature: "I grew up in a beautiful home with loving, kind parents. Until I was fourteen years old no one would have ever guessed the dark path I would end up taking. There was no reason to suspect that things would go so wrong.

I wasn't super popular at school, but I had several close friends and a good-looking boyfriend. I belonged to a few clubs and my grades were slightly above average. I can say that is what I was, average. Nothing about me stood out Psycho, nothing. Or so I thought.

I was walking home from high school minding my own business one day when my life changed forever. I noticed a van but ignored it thinking it was just like any other van in the neighborhood. It pulled up next to me and the fellow inside told me my mother had sent him to find me. She had been hurt and needed me. I didn't know this guy, but he seemed to know my mom. He said her name, my address, and his credentials seemed honest. I was a bit from home, so he offered me a ride. Like a trusting fool I got inside.

It seems silly to have to tell you that he, of course, didn't take me home. This man took me to a secluded spot and raped me for hours. In every way, he took advantage of me. I was a virgin, but no more. Worse than what he did to my flesh is what he did to my mind. I was so afraid Psycho. I cried and he would hit me, I struggled, and he would force me. I was terrified he would kill me when he was done humiliating me. Instead, he threw me out of his van, naked, bloody, crying and broken. The guy sped off, and to this day has never been caught for what he did to me. I walked through the woods until I found a house. The occupants took me in, covered me up and called the cops.

The police and the doctors at the hospital made me feel stupid for having gotten into that van. Turned out he was stalking me for weeks. The van had been spotted hanging around my house, but back then no one would have just assumed he was up to no good. In the end I felt such a fool, and everyone from the police to my parents helped me believe I had been one. I got the 'you should have known better' talk hundreds of times. Instead of holding my hand understanding my pain, they acted as if I asked to be raped. I fell into a deep depression.

Worse, I began to believe them. I felt I got what I deserved. I began to hate myself. Then I started to cut on myself. It was punishment for being so stupid, you know. That wasn't enough. I started to become loose at school. I would sleep with any boy who was nice to me or suck his dick. Then I would start rumors on him, call his girlfriend or mom to give blow by blow descriptions of what I had done with their 'little man.' I did it because I wanted to make every male pay for what that guy and all the police did to me. Even though these guys were innocent, I decided if you had a dick, you were a creep and had it coming. I was in a full-on war with myself and every boy. Still I wasn't satisfied.

My mom and other women had made me feel small too. So, I hated girls just as bad as boys. I would fight with a female, steal her boyfriend, start lies, even rob them. I was out of control. I started to shoplift, and even began to make myself throw up after eating tons of food. Drama and chaos followed me everywhere I went. I left a wake of broken men, women, lovers and friends behind me. Soon, I was the most hated person at my high school with the worst reputation. All of this was to punish the world for what this man did to me.

He didn't just rape me Psycho, he took my power away. Since I thought I could never get it back, I was going to steal it from anyone else stupid enough to try to like or love me. The half-ass suicide threats began around that time. I had quit school and was doing drugs. I cut, did drugs, drank, fucked, trying anything I could think to do to end the

19

numbness. I felt like there was a war inside my head. I wanted to straighten up and have what I used to have, but the anger, fear of abandonment and unstable emotions kept me constantly struggling within.

Then one day I ran into this guy named Paul at a dude's house that I had slated for my latest drama play. Paul was so handsome, and calm. I decided to destroy this cool customer instead. Paul ignored my attempts to get his attention. He turned down my offers for sex saying he didn't like easy pussy. Now that pissed me off big time. He became my obsession. I had to destroy him.

Yet, Paul could not be taken down. Finally, one day after tossing me off his jock for the hundredth time he told me he was sick of my "Borderline Personality Disordered" ass always bothering him. If I wanted to be with him, I had to follow him to his club. He said then he would sleep with me. So, always up for a challenge and believing I had beaten him I followed him.

It was of course a BDSM club. Once there Paul introduced me to several Dominatrices. He left me with these cunning ladies to visit while he went to get a drink and prep a room in the back so we could fuck. I was totally blown away by the power these women had over several men they had on collars there. I watched in amazement thinking I had just died and landed in female heaven.

Paul returned and pulled me away from my newest obsession. He took me to a back room and started to tie me up. I went berserk. I told that rat bastard to fuck off. I was not there to be treated like his slave. He was supposed to be mine. Paul laughed then untied me. He told me that I was using my pain to hurt people who didn't deserve it. He also pointed out that I hated myself for something that was not my fault. I didn't have to tell him someone had hurt me, he just knew, you know?

He asked me if I was tired of the self-abuse. He told me if I was ready to take back my power and deal with my personality disorder in a way that was not destructive, then he could help me. Otherwise get out and finish killing myself because everyone was tired of the drama. I was so super pissed, but not because he told me to go kill myself. I was mad because he was right. I was self-destructing. It was because I felt powerless. I was angry and hateful. I wanted revenge but couldn't get it. I wanted to be loved but I feared abandonment so much, I would hurt people until they left me. I was self-fulfilling my own prophesies. I was a 'I love you, but I hurt you, so why don't you love me back' kind of person.

He told me that if I learned to control my urges, my personality defects I could regain my power, and stop hurting myself. In time, if I worked hard, I could find one who would match my deficits with their own and this 'other half' would be my perfect lover. One that would allow me to hurt them and get my revenge but still love me. The other half would love me despite the fact I did enjoy hurting them. This other side to my coin would be incapable of caring for themselves without the aid of another. They would tolerate my problems because I would fill in their own holes in their soul. All I had to do was learn to control the harm I inflicted on another to safe levels. He said I needed to change my attitude from unconscious revenge to conscious celebration of who I am.

I took his offer. He handed me over to his finest Dominatrix, Madam Whips. She trained me for the next five years. I was only eighteen when I began under this amazing Dominatrix but when she was finished with me, I had a deeper understanding of my personality defect, and why I was such a cunt to everyone. I embraced the Sensual Sadistic Dominatrix I was whole heartedly and never looked back.

When I saw you that day at the Green Temple, unafraid, scared, and strong I was in awe. When I noticed the collar, I couldn't believe my eyes. You seemed to be everything I ever wanted, needed or desired. When I found out your collar was up for grabs, I couldn't believe my luck.

Now I see I shouldn't have believed such luck. You are not what I thought I saw. You are just a schizophrenic with a delusion. You only follow your collar for fear of dying. Psycho you didn't celebrate with me in my bed yesterday, you endured it and likely went home hating me for it. You hate your clothes I bought you because it makes you think of sex, and the lifestyle as something to be avoided not enjoyed. You do what you are told without feeling a thing other than disgust. That makes you cold, impotent, and useless to me.

Those people who trained you, they were wrong to force you into this shit. The lifestyle is meant to be a pleasure, a joy, a wonder, not a terror to avoid. So, now you know, what do you think we should do? I will not take you as you are. That is final."

I gazed at the floor thinking about what she had told me. It was a lot to process, but I finally understood her point. I was not what she was looking for and she sure as shit was not what I wanted. I would need to talk to Simon, but until then my collar would be in grave danger of being tossed back to Mistress June. I couldn't bear that thought.

"Mistress forgive me for saying this, but what if I could learn to be what you want? You learned?" I couldn't believe those words came out of my mouth.

However, I was desperate to buy time to create a plan to escape the greedy Mistress June's collar.

Mistress Ginger laughed hard at that, "Yeah, you are right I did. However, I don't think you can. I wanted to be a Dominatrix. I made the choice to live this way. It was my nature. It took a rape and years of humiliating myself to realize it. You are not a submissive in any way at all. I don't see how I could ever get you to adore me even if I thudded the shit out of you daily. I think I would only make you resent me."

I nodded. "Likely that is true, but there must be some way to work this out? I could try?"

She shook her head. "Well for starters you would have to want to be collared by me. That for sure didn't happen. Second, you would have to trust me. That is never going to happen. Not with a history like you have Psycho. I wouldn't trust anyone either to be honest."

My eyes began to fill with tears. "Please mercy Mistress. You are going to toss my Key without giving me a chance? I know I fucked up with Mistress June, but I can correct that, and you can punish me for it. I won't run away. I promise. Please don't send me to her for good."

Mistress Ginger took out her collar key and undid my collar as I began to cry hard. "I am sorry Psycho, but I just can't deal with this. You should have been willing, not forced. Forcing is against the honor of any true lifestyler. I took your Key and Collar under false pretenses. Now that I have discovered the error, I am the one who is begging mercy. Can you ever forgive me for raping you yesterday? I not sure you can."

I watched as she removed my collar tossing it into the floor at her feet. Terror gripped me when I saw her pull up the Key attached to a chain around her neck. "No Mistress, don't, please Don't toss that. You didn't rape me. I went willingly. It is my job to provide service for service. I am not angry. Mercy, please mercy." I fell to my face grabbing her ankles in full on wailing and begging mode.

If she let the Key touch the ground, she was finished. No one gets a second chance.

Mistress Ginger touched the back of my head while I threw my fit begging her to reconsider her actions. "Psycho, get up please. Now, damn it."

I sat up as I was told still crying hard. "Please let me try again? Don't do this."

She held the Key looking it over appearing to be deep in thought while I sat there blubbering with misery that I was begging a woman I hated to not toss my Key to another woman I hated even more.

"You know what Psycho? You may be right. Perhaps you can learn. I collared you and submitted you under false pretenses. You still belong to Mistress June for one more day. I have now removed your collar and take back the submission, but I will not give back the Key. I will keep that until you come to retrieve it." She looked at me to see if I understood.

"I don't understand Mistress? Uncollar me? Unsubmit me?" This was just not registering in my shattered mind.

She smiled. "Yeah, this could work. You have to go and finish your contract with June. Once you have, then you are free again right?"

I nodded. "Yes Mistress."

"Then here is what will happen. You contact the hag, finish your time. I will consider your collaring and submission null and void, that it didn't happen. If you decide you are willing to submit and be collared by me, you will come back to me on your fucking knees. Otherwise, stand and take back Simon's Key and find one who deserves your hate. Submission to me is a contract of adoration both ways. I will not stand for forcing what you do not want. You will choose me or we are done here. Got it?" She looked at me hard.

I stopped crying realizing this was indeed the perfect solution. I could have time to find someone else but still have Mistress Ginger if that failed.

"Yes, I understand. How long do I have to decide?" I had already started going down my list of people who could possibly hold that Key.

She smiled. "Till next weekend, come get the Key or be on your knees." She stood up and headed for the door.

"Mistress? I need a ride to get my bike." I said still sitting there surprised that she seemed to be leaving me there without transportation.

She turned around. "That is Ginger to you Psycho, and you are no longer my problem. Get your bike by tomorrow or I will have it towed. See you around." She walked out the door leaving me there completely blown away at her sudden change in attitude.

I stood up still stunned realizing I would have to be at the funeral home shortly for work anyway. I could ask Mistress June for a ride to get my bike. I would have to deal with her on both a personal and employment level anyway. I cleaned up my makeup from all my childish tears, locked up my house and began walking to the funeral home.

The whole way to work I watched my back and nearly ran several times when a car drove by too slow for my own comfort. I was still very afraid Tammy was around somewhere. I didn't like feeling so exposed. I cursed Ginger for leaving me in this kind of situation, but that was her right. I was no longer her problem.

I walked in the back door to find Mistress June fuming and tossing things around angrily. I already knew what was up her tail pipe. It was me.

She saw me walking in. "Ah so you are early to work too. No surprise there."

I winced at what I was about to have to say, "Mistress, allow me to apologize for my bad behavior a few days ago. You didn't deserve that. I was wrong to run away before finishing my agreement with you."

She stopped fuming appearing surprised, "Uh, yeah, you screwed me."

I stifled my giggle. "No Mistress, I didn't. That is the problem I believe."

She snorted. "Well, too late now isn't it? Guess you think yourself very clever, huh? I did everything you told me to do, but now I am left without the only service I wanted. I could hire a fucking maid and cook. Psycho, you are a real asshole. I hope your new Mistress watches her back."

I nodded looking at the floor. "I am here to make it up to you Mistress. I do owe you special services of the collar. If you are willing to accept a makeup, I am available at your request to fulfill the desired services."

Mistress June's big eyes almost bugged out. "Are you serious? If you are pulling bullshit Psycho so help me."

I gulped back the bile trying to fill up my mouth, "I am being serious. I owe you a night's service. I will do whatever you ask for that twelve hours. I will offer this compensation only if you are willing to accept it. I expect you to then terminate your complaints that you were not well satisfied that our contract has been completed."

She stood there nodding. "Fair enough."

Mistress June then looked around the room. "There is no work tonight. I already did it all. You will come with me now. I don't trust waiting. You may run away again."

I looked up horrified. I had not expected her to take me up on the offer for a few days. "Now? What if they call us in?"

She laughed. "Psycho don't be stupid. The customer will still be dead when we get to them, now won't they? This is the one job where the work will wait quietly till you come get it. Now march that little ass of yours to the house. I am going to make you pay for leaving me like that the other night. Just so you know."

I nodded angrily. "Yes Mistress, I sort of assumed that much."

She laughed as she walked by slapping my ass. I let out a yelp. It was still bruised from Ginger the night before.

That made Mistress June laugh even harder. "Oh this is going to be so much fun."

I followed the horrible creature back to her house. She groped and pinched me the whole way sending me into orbits of terror and pain. I assumed this would happen. It is why I had run away in the first place. Mrs. Snatchy Grabby was not going to be a gentle lover no doubt.

Of course, I was correct in that assumption. Her seeing the stripes and bruises left by Ginger really worked her into a frenzy. She was a harsh lover, with no respect for my unit in any way. She forced, pulled, slapped, pinched, twisted, and scratched me till I was sure I was going to lose it and beat her half to death.

I could barely stand the minutes ticking by. When my brother finally spilled through her big windows, I couldn't get my clothes on and run fast enough. I tore out her door still buttoning and adjusting my outfit. I didn't even bother to ask her for a ride back to Ginger's place. I just wanted out. She thankfully had fallen asleep, so I had snuck out quiet and quick. No way I ever wanted to see that monster again. I considered quitting the funeral home to avoid any future contact with that nasty bitch.

I had started walking out of town towards Ginger's house wondering how long it would take me to get there when the tow truck passed me hauling my Motorpsycho to the impound. I saw it and began fuming. Ginger had not been kidding. I turned around walking back to chase down my ride. It cost me seventy-five damned dollars to get the old hillbilly to release the metal God back to my custody.

I paid the bill, hopped on the bike and grumbled about the fact that now even my bike had been in jail. I drove right to Maiden Mary's house. She had been very concerned because Ginger had called her to tell her I dropped the collar so she would be returning to the Temple.

"What happened Mother? I spoke to Ginger last night after you got back. She didn't seem like a bad person. She explained to me that she was going to help you with your sickness, and help you get your children reunited. Did you two have a fight?" Mary looked very tired.

I nodded. "Something like that. I had to deal with one of Circe's left-over bombs. It pissed her off. Then she gave me some bullshit about not wanting to collar someone who didn't want to be collared. Who the fuck would want to be told what to do? That is the dumbest shit I have ever been told. I serve for service. I don't have to fucking like it. Apparently, she thought I should love her for beating the shit out of me. What a weirdo." I laughed at that.

Mary sat down at the kitchen table nodding. "Yeah, how could you love someone who is trying to save your life and help you live at home with your kids. That is totally stupid."

That statement pissed me off. "Excuse me? Daughter, did you hear me? Maybe you should listen to my words. Did I stutter? The woman likes to thud. It gets her rocks off. I am not getting involved with that shit." I glared at Mary.

30

She shook her head. "Look Mother I am not condoning that kind of stuff. I don't understand it completely. I mean Ronnie and I have experimented with some light bondage and a paddle, but I believe you are talking about something more than that. I will ask if not Ginger than who will you get to help you do all the stuff Ginger said she was going to do?"

I sat down across from her rolling my eyes. "I don't fucking know. I don't have any good candidates. I suppose I could get my Key and give it to Master Marie. She was nice, or Master Peggy?"

Maiden Mary wrinkled up her nose. "Seriously? You prefer them over Ginger?"

I looked up startled, "They can do the fucking job without beating me half to death."

She laughed, "I thought you have to sleep with your Master?"

I nodded.

Maiden Mary looked at me hard. "It is none of my business Mother, but if I had to choose between hot Ginger and old dried up Peggy or Marie, I would let Ginger stick a fucking fork up my ass rather than munch dust for the rest of my life."

I almost fell off the chair laughing. "Oh my Goddess. You did not just say that Mary."

Maiden Mary chuckled. "Just being honest Mother. You are not using your head. Ginger is very pretty. She is young,

31

and definitely into you. Hell, if I had to sleep with a woman it would be her or you. I would not want to be with an older woman who was just going to keep getting older. You may want to consider that a minute before you make your decision. You have to sleep with the Master, may as well get a view worth having. I mean did you enjoy being with Circe?"

I shuttered. "Hell no."

She shrugged. "That is what I mean. You said that all three of those ladies could do the job. Your only beef with Ginger is her hitting you for fun. Well, if it were me, I would get over that. Besides, I have seen you hit yourself a hundred times and Circe was not too nice to you either but you put up with her. Don't you want to enjoy the sex you have to have?"

I stared at her as if I could suddenly see her third eye popped out on her forehead. "Have fun having sex? Are you serious? Sex is a service Daughter. It is a task, not a pleasure."

That made Maiden Mary gasp. "That is horrible. You mean you don't enjoy sex with any of your Masters or just in general? What about Father Roary? Did you enjoy sex with him?"

I thought on that a moment "No, I guess not. Never considered it before. I just do what I am told, Daughter. If I want to enjoy sex I have it alone. My Priest was a skilled lover so I did find an orgasm with his unit, but I could have lived without it and am happy it is over and done."

She looked at me wide eyed. "Mother, sex is beautiful. It is supposed to be enjoyed not just done like a task."

I giggled. "I told you my Priest gave me an orgasm Daughter. I enjoyed it just fine."

She shook her head. "No you didn't. If you actually did, he would be all you would want or think about right now. I am so sorry that you don't understand what I am telling you. That is tragic. You are beautiful Mother. You are in the prime of your life, and it is passing you by because you have been missing one of the biggest pleasures anyone can ever know. You don't eat, sleep or do anything but work. Now I find out you don't even wish for a real lover. Sex is not just about orgasms; it is about feeling like you are a part of someone else even if only for a few moments. You will only see that person, want that person, dream of that person. Oh unless you have loved someone you can't possibly understand how wonderful it is. I am going to pray that someday the God and Goddess let you have such a blessing as I have found in my Ronnie."

I chuckled. "Okay Daughter. If you say so. For now, I have important stuff to worry about. I have seen how you normals love each other. You can count me out. I am already a slave to a collar and Key. I need no more Master than that." I got up to go find the children.

She yelled after me. "That is why if I were you, I would go and make up with Ginger. You could have your lover and Master in the same person you know."

I snorted but kept walking. Maiden Mary was deluded. She loved Circe's man. I understood love just fine. I loved Simon, my kids and Zeppelin. I sure didn't want to have sex with any of them. Love and sex are two different things. I had had a lot of sexual encounters in my short life. I didn't understand the big deal. You endure the act, get an orgasm if you are lucky, and move on. So much bullshit was spewed over a silly function. It didn't make any sense to me.

NOTE: *The problem here was that because of my traumatic, violent history I had not associated love and sex properly. They were viewed as two separate functions. One did not lead to the other in my mind. In a normal relationship sexual congress is an expression of love, but I had never experienced it like that. So yes at almost twenty-three I didn't understand that sex shouldn't be a forced act. I just assumed it was, and anyone who really loved you wouldn't make you do such a thing. I could now enjoy the act a bit thanks to the Great Rite with Priest Roary, but I still didn't have the mindset that you can have sex with someone because you want to express love, or just plain wanted to have someone you love be intimate with you deeper than a nice long conversation. I had never dated (still never have), kissed, or chased after any one to have sex on purpose. That concept was completely foreign to me. Don't judge to harshly. A lifetime of rape and assault had made the act one of dread, tolerance, pain, and cruelty in my mind. It would have done that to anyone, not just a schizophrenic. Thanks mom!*

I found my kids and spent the afternoon playing with them trying to forget the nasty images of Tammy and

Mistress June forcing their units and lust on mine. Try as I might I could not get them out of my mind. This caused me to become quite agitated. I began to pace the floor, wringing my hands and babbling telling the Looper to 'shut the fuck up.'

Maiden Mary watched from a distance. This behavior was scaring her. I could tell, but I couldn't stop myself. The more I paced the more agitated I got. I called into work sick. I couldn't stand to be anywhere near Mistress June for a while, maybe ever. My job was now in danger thanks to my inability to calm down.

That night Maiden Mary couldn't get me to eat or sleep either. I continued to pace non-stop, even taking off into 'trance dancing' several times. I was headed for an episode. Maiden Mary realized the signs. She finally called Dennis and Boyd when I began banging my head into the trees in the front yard. I had become a threat to myself and likely others. My prodromal was getting deeper and more violent every week. I still had some time, but for that night I would need to visit my Prince Val and be restrained.

As usual, I saw the squad car and took off before it even pulled into the drive. Boyd pulled back out dropping Dennis off for his traditional sprint that would always end with my face eating dirt and his knee in my back while he cuffed my wrists. I tried to kick both officers screaming that I hadn't broken any laws, but they were used to my bullshit. I was stuffed in the back and hauled to cool off my heels in my white padded cell.

My collar had only been off one fucking day, and I was already back to my old tricks of arrest and needle in my ass full of my beloved Prince Val.

Linda had frown at me while she had done her strip search. She saw the healing bruises and strips on my backside and upper thighs from Ginger's 'toys.' She had also seen the deep scratches and cuts from Mistress June's overzealous lust. She didn't say a word because I was too busy yelling off my nut about being 'framed,' and 'targeted' by the 'fucking government.'

Oh yeah beauties, I was having one of my infamous 'everyone is out to get me' blow outs. When I am like that, best to just restrain me and let me cuss it out. I am quite nasty and if you get too close, I will fuck you up. My paranoid is one ugly bitch.

However, once I had calmed down the next morning, she had a lot to say. I was setting up on my cot cursing Circe for the thousandth time when the cell door opened. Linda came inside then told Boyd to give her some time alone with me.

I smiled, "Well about fucking time. I have been trying to get you to do that for ages. So, get on over here and sit on my lap, gorgeous."

She frowned at my teasing banter, "Psycho that is not funny today. I saw the marks. You are beat up again. Who the fuck did it this time? I swear can't you ever find someone who doesn't beat you? I am starting to wonder if…" she trailed off appearing unwilling to say what she was thinking.

I glared at her. "Say it Goddess. Say it and be done with me. I am not going to tolerate much more of your insults. I know you don't understand, so I have cut you a lot of slack, but you keep judging what you don't know shit about, I will eventually hate you for it."

She looked at the floor offering a teary apology over her rash cruel words in the hospital just after my rescue from Tammy. I told her she was forgiven.

"However, you need to stop believing everything you hear," I warned her.

She stepped toward me sending me backing up into the wall in fright. I had never been afraid of her before, but with everyone wanting to fuck or hit me lately I was feeling a bit nervous.

Linda saw my fear. "Psycho, I would love you forever. I could take care of you. No one would ever hit you again. I would kill them for it."

I nodded. "I know you would Goddess. How about my kids? You gonna take care of them too? How about when I get hauled off and hit you in some psychotic fit? Will you be able to stop me from bashing my noggin into trees without beating me down? Or using the cuffs?"

Linda shook her head. "If you let me care for you then you won't do those things anymore. Your kids are of course welcome, Psycho. If you were just treated right you wouldn't be so violent anymore. I just know all you really need is a soft touch. I mean a rough one isn't working that is for damned sure. Look at you. Arrested again, covered in bruises, cuts, scratches. You need hugs not restraints. I am ready to give you the love you need, just say the word."

I smiled at my Goddess. "You are truly from Heaven itself, Linda. What I wouldn't have given to be your girl. You must face that I am violent, and I sometimes need restraint. Sometimes, you have to beat me down to keep me from killing myself or another person. Sometimes I will try to brain myself or cut out my tongue. I am sick Goddess. If you are too nice to me, I will hurt you. I couldn't live with that. I can't hear you if your voice is too soft. If I see you praying for me to stop acting a fool I will crush you beneath my platforms. I am not a normal. I am mentally ill to the hilt. My life is brutal because it has to be. I never ask for this, but it is what it is." I looked at the floor recalling Ginger's words.

I suddenly realized I was a victim and behaved like one. I had lost my power and now couldn't get it back. She had lost hers too but found it by becoming a Dominate. I could not get mine back like she did because I was robbed by a disease not an incident. However, I could pony up with someone who understood what it meant to be powerless. This kind of person would have the knowledge from the time they were me. They would not want to ever put themselves into a relationship that could threaten what they had to fight to get back. Since I could never have power again, I was the perfect match.

I suddenly realized I was continually matching up with those non-empathetic to my helplessness. They were taking advantage of me, because they thought I was like everyone else even when they knew I was mentally ill. They all would unconsciously assume if I wanted them to stop, surely, I would stop them.

Therefore they were able to justify their bad behavior by saying I must love it. That is what Linda was doing just then. She assumed that all I really needed was hugs and kind words. I don't have fucking anger issues. I am not acting like an asshole because I have mommy issues. I am not sleeping with Masters because I have Daddy issues. I am a fucking severely disabled schizophrenic. I do what I must do to survive. I am forever without my own power or ability to stop my bad behaviors. I was and am a sitting duck for those who could never understand or think I can just stop doing this. I need someone to stop me or I die.

I looked back up at my Goddess with tears beginning to fall. "Thank you Goddess for always being there when I need you the most. Stay in Heaven and let me worship at your feet forever. I would like to see Dennis when he is around. I assume they will let me go soon. Tell him to visit me before I head out."

She looked sad. "Psycho, please will you at least consider my offer? It is an honest one."

I shook my head. "I know this will hurt your heart to hear Goddess, but I belong to another. She is a mortal like me. I am simply not good enough for a deity such as yourself."

Linda looked crushed. "You have a girlfriend is what you are saying? Is she the one who marked you up like that?"

I laughed. "Yeah she did. You know red heads. Fiery bitches in the bedroom."

She nodded. "Okay, I understand. If you ever get into trouble, my offer still stands." She left but I could hear her sniffling.

I hated to hurt her like that but I understood what would have to be done. Linda was just not the right one to wield Simon's Key.

Dennis came by to let me know I was released. I asked him to give me a ride back to Maiden Mary's house. I wanted to talk to him about my thoughts and I did trust his judgement above all others. He was a good man and a levelheaded thinker.

He agreed. The minute we were out of the jailhouse parking lot I looked at him, "Dennis I need some advice."

He almost choked. "You are asking me for advice? Since when do you trust me, Psycho?"

I chuckled. "Since the first time you pulled me from the barbed wire in the woods when I ran away from class. You remember that day right? Mary was still my guardian. Damn the only time I have ever outrun you."

He laughed hard suddenly recalling that incident. "Oh yeah. But that barbed wire did my job for me. Tore you to shreds if I remember right."

I nodded. "Anyway, do you think love that is not normal is possible?"

He almost veered off the road. "Uhm, what do you mean? Like same sex love…"

I snorted. "No. I know that is normal for some. I mean really different, like loving someone who hurts you a little so you don't hurt yourself a lot kind of not normal."

I could tell Dennis was significantly relieved I wasn't going to ask how he felt about homosexual love. "Well Psycho, let me say this. Sometimes a parent must spank a child to keep them from getting hurt by say touching a hot stove. That is the kind off love you are talking about, right?"

I nodded. "Yeah, I guess. Sort of? What if the child were grown up and the other grown up is spanking because they like it?"

His eyes went wide. "Oh my, uhm, well, I think if both adults agree this is okay then sure it is possible to be in a loving relationship. It depends on if both people are consenting, I would say."

I thought on that. "But what if one doesn't like it but needs to keep the other happy or they will be unloved."

Dennis growled at that. "Then it is wrong. Just plain wrong. It should be that both are getting something from that kind of behavior. If only one enjoys and the other is putting up with it to keep from being thrown out then it is abuse."

I nodded. "Okay. That is what I needed to know. Thank you, Dennis."

He looked at me surprised. "Psycho, do you need to talk to me about someone? Is someone hurting you again like Julie did?"

I laughed hard. "No. Actually someone realized they were and stopped immediately saying the same damned thing you just said."

Dennis smiled. "Well then there is hope left in the world, Psycho. Sounds like this person is a good-hearted soul. Not too many would care as long as they got what they wanted."

I nodded. "Yeah, I know that all too well. Someone who has that much control is someone who can be trusted I think."

Dennis looked at me. "Yeah. It would seem that way. If they realized they are wrong and ended it, then they are not likely to do it again. Anyone can make a mistake." He said as he pulled into Maiden Mary's driveway to drop me off.

"The mistake was mine, Dennis," I said as I got out. "Thank you so much for the ride, saving my life repeatedly and always being just a tad faster than me."

He chuckled. "Psycho. I noticed no collar. So, did you give up that silly delusion? Can I finally rest easy at night?"

I looked at him smiling. "No, my collar is in the shop. You can rest easy though. This Master knows her shit, Dennis. Everything is going to be okay. I just need to get some re-adjusting done is all." I closed the door leaving him with a look of confusion at my odd statement.

I realized that in the morning, I would have to go crawling on my hands and knees begging Mistress Ginger to allow me to submit to her. Then I would have to suffer another painful collaring. I was ready to stop being a victim. I now understood I could do this by learning how to wield the power of the true submissive.

Tomorrow we dive deep into the world of BDSM with an emphasis on D/s. It is the way it must be if we are to mirror Mistress Ginger properly. She isn't the only problem we have. Mabon is coming and don't forget we must deal with college and the crass Mistress June. Oh so much is on our plate. Will we ever get on a straight and narrow. Of course not. We are not straight, and we are very curvy.

Chapter 26: Almost Honest
Mistress Ginger

This chapter is not for children, so do enjoy or think holy shit, seriously. Either way, we do hope you at least get a chuckle or two out of this fubar that was our second collaring and discussions of other stuff that happened that crazy day in September 1994.

Speaking of honesty, we had a habit of only telling half-truths. In fact, one could say we used to be a liar. We thought we were being completely forthright with everyone. However, Mistress Ginger caught our habit of bending reality to suit our needs. She will not tolerate such bad behavior from us. She will stop our hypocrisy by tackling our defenses. One by one, she will break down our mechanisms designed to keep us from facing horrible facts about ourself. We had become a mirror. However, we needed to clean the surface. We had become grimy with the filth of our dirty past. Our reflection was blurry, and details are hard to define.

Mistress Ginger needs to open our blocked sexual chakra pathway. She loves to be loved. She wants us to be loved too. We have so far only lived to serve, but this Mistress desired we both enjoy delivering and receiving the service. She has a battle coming. Our demons are strong, but she had many weapons in her closet arsenal that she hopes can beat them into submission. We will be held hostage, restrained while she begins her war against the darkness within us. Mistress Ginger will not stop until she gets what she came for, satisfaction.

Ready to take that deep dive into the secret world behind the red and black curtain? Oh boy. Get ready everyone. Don't be ashamed to shed tears if it hurts. That is half the fun. Make sure to bring your patience and cancel all your plans for the next few hours. You aren't going anywhere until Mistress Ginger grants you permission. So, kneel and submit to this wild story of embracing who you are meant to be.

"I can almost feel the anger radiating out of you Psycho. Everyone can. You are justified in your fury. If you don't let me help you identify the real reasons for it then allow me to control it, you will eventually finish what that horrible mother of yours started. It is up to you"
---**Mistress Ginger's warning to Psycho-Second Submission September 1994.**

I rarely ever missed classes, but this September day was a special exception. I had to settle my situation of Simon's Key. If Ginger would take me back, I needed to get her assigned as my guardian quickly. The cruel Mistress Circe had never robbed my checks before. However, she had apparently intended to have me raped then murdered. I no longer was willing to believe she would continue to treat my income fairly.

I had slept in Darlin that Sunday night. When Dennis dropped me off at Maiden Mary's home I went and attended my kids. After I put them to bed, I explained to my Maiden that since I was now unable to control myself, it was safer if I removed my person. I feared what I may do when everyone was asleep.

She of course argued with me, but I assured her it was for the best. It would be better if I got psychotic. I would rather risk bashing my head into a grave marker than come in and kill everyone while they slept. I was no longer sure I wouldn't do just that. There were periods of time where I had no consciousness of what I was saying or doing. I needed a heavy hand if there was any chance of my survival much longer. I informed Mary I hoped Ginger was the one who could do what was needed to keep my mad dog from unleashing its fury on those around me.

Master Peggy had been eliminated from my possible choices because while she was able to do the job, I had been completely residual during her reign. She had not been tested. No way I could chance her failure. This was just too far gone now and once collared there could be no taking it back.

Master Marie had also been eliminated but not for the reasons Maiden Mary thought I should kick her to the curb. I didn't give two shits that Master Marie was older. Male, female, old, young, black, white, other, they all were horrid in my mind. One as bad as another, the fact that I would have to sleep with a Master was never a reason to turn down one who could do the job correctly. I had rejected her based on her affection for me. She was able to push me around and was great at structure and ordering but failed at punishment of my bad behaviors.

My psychotic self only fears pain. Talking to it is like talking to a fire hydrant. Good luck with that. You can yell all you like just as I cut your throat. Only fear works with the bitch I was fast becoming. If I feared the Master's punishment bad enough in residual, then the Master could get the psychotic to back the fuck off. However, you had to make a believer out of me sadly.

Master Marie was too permissive. When I tore shit up, talked back or even came at her, she would run and wait it out. Then she would do some light thudding or something that barely registered on my pain tolerance scale. I had warned her several times and always got the 'I just can't bear to see you cry' excuse.

NOTE: *Oh yeah? Think I cry because you whipped my ass now? Trust me, I will get over the whipping. Hell, I am very used to it. Wait till they tell me I cut you into little pieces while I am serving life in the Snake Pit. You can bet your bottom dollar I will be crying then and you would have too just as I started my chainsaw deaf to your pleas.*

Is it possible that I could be a psychotic killer? Uhm, yeah. I have a history of extreme abuse, deep seated anger and am violent as hell when off my rocker, especially back then. I may be sorry when I get back from Mars, but sorry don't bring back the dead does it? The other possibility is that in an effort not to hurt another, I may take my own life. Remember, I have cut my arms to shit looking for imaginary 'discount radars,' and ask Carmen about my tongue. She has seen the scar. Yep, I almost got that sucker that one time. I can cut my own unit like that without even noticing when I'm psychotic. I am certainly capable of injuring, even killing someone else. It is an ugly truth that I hate. I will do anything to prevent this bad behavior. Even suffer for a lifetime under the crushing weight of a collar.

It is better to get my attention quickly and keep on the pressure. It is my only hope of life outside jails or institutions. Pouring on the control and pain is something Ginger was specially trained to do. Master Marie loved me, but she didn't understand sometimes loving someone means hurting me a little to keep me from being hurt or hurting others a lot later.

In the end, for the safety of my children, my Coven family, and even for Dennis and Boyd's comfort, I decided to turn myself over to the sadistic thud loving Ginger. She seemed capable of knocking the shit out of me when I tried to stand up to her. I would not have fulfilled my broken contract with Mistress June had it not been for my fear of Ginger's punishment. Now, that was impressive. I felt that Mistress June was a stupid bitch who didn't earn the services.

She did earn the special services no matter how much I didn't want to grant them to her. I had convinced myself that she was so nasty she forfeited. That was simply not honest and I knew it but didn't care at that time. I didn't want to sleep with her, so I made an excuse that worked for me. It was a contract and I had stolen services by not complying with her demands.

Ginger was right that I was a thief. Mistress June was righteously angry. However, had I not feared Gingers thudding I would have gone ahead and pretended I did the right thing ripping Mistress June off like that. I know me too well. Once I get something in my head, unless you can scare it out of me, it is the way it will be. Right Master Jon?

The decision was made, and I had heard Ginger loud and clear. If I wanted her back, I had to submit willingly to her. That would be tougher than I ever imagined. Apparently, I had been doing all my submissions unwillingly. I knew that but wouldn't really admit it at the time. Honestly, I didn't know how to submit the way she wanted me to. No worries. Ginger was going to teach me. She was going to teach me a lot of things very soon.

I drove to her trailer as my brother woke up rising to light the world with his smile. The birds were all singing, the breeze was pleasant but had just a hint of the coming coolness of winter on its breath. The trees had all started to adorn themselves with their coats of the reds, tans, and oranges of fall. It was shaping up to be a beautiful day if you weren't me that is.

Unfortunately, I was me. Despite the amazing weather and sights of the rural landscape all around me, I could see only the darkness of abject subjugation in my future. I was convinced that Ginger would only be a sometimes nicer version of Master Julie from so long ago. My stripes and bruises now had turned yellow and grey. They were already healing from her last 'fun' at my expense. I could hardly believe I was actually going to crawl on my hands and knees on purpose to submit to this red-headed demon. I had to be out to lunch.

On at least two occasions I almost turned the bike around to run the other direction. However, I steadied my nerves remembering that in truth there was no other good options. I needed to be put on a leash, like it or not.

I arrived at her long driveway. Before driving down it I stopped the bike and took one last look around me. I closed my eyes feeling the rhythm of the world in motion. For a moment, I could believe I didn't have to be me anymore. I could just scatter into a thousand pieces and join the power grid forever. Then pain, fear, anger, despair would all be a thing foreign to my senses. I really wanted to just never be. I yearned for the dark void of nothingness.

The Looper laughed while it taunted me with the voice of dozens, all trying to remind me that I was sure to fail in my bid to please this new Mistress. Well this time, they would be wrong. I could do this, damn it. I swallowed hard, braced my nerves then started the bike towards my destiny.

I killed the motor, hopped off and headed for her door. I knocked but at first no answer. I had a key but dared not use it without permission.

Then suddenly the door opened. A very angry looking Ginger was standing there glaring at me. She was in a red latex outfit, holding a crop in her hands.

"What the fuck do you want Psycho," she said in a mocking voice.

I tore my eyes from her thudding tool casting my gaze to the ground, "I am here to submit to your collar willingly."

She glared hard. "Are you? Hmmm, I don't think so Psycho. I think you are here because you think you have no choice. I think you are going acute and fear yourself. You are here to use me. I will not allow that. Beat it." She started to close the door.

I yelped then dropped to my knees right there on the steps. "No, please Ginger. I am here to willingly submit, I swear it." I dropped to prostrate assuming this is what she wanted.

She laughed. "Nice try. You are a lying bitch. I am right Psycho. Admit it. You don't want to be in my collar. You are here because you are scared of you. You would run to the hills if you could right now." She kicked me in my shoulder lightly.

I didn't know what to say to that. She was right. Yet, if I said it, she wouldn't accept my submission. She told me it had to be willing and obviously she wanted me to admit I was not willing.

"No, I am willing. Please, mercy. I am here to submit." I started crying and that was no lie.

I was indeed scared. Ginger seemed to be unwilling to take me back. I had not expected this.

"Get off my porch you fucking liar. In fact, get on that bike and leave before I call the law." She kicked me hard enough this time to send me off her three little steps. I landed on my ass when I fell backward.

She slammed the door shut and I heard it locking. I sat there stunned unsure what had just happened. I looked toward my bike then back to the door. There was nowhere to go. I couldn't leave. If I did, I was doomed. I thought she may be calling Dennis and Boyd. She said she would. I couldn't stand another arrest. Anger ripped through me with a force I had not felt so strongly since knocking out Julie's teeth years before.

I stood up and with all that I had started bashing on Gingers door full force. Not just knocking on it, I was kicking it, shoulder and head banging it too. I was getting in her fucking door if I had to break it in. She was going to fucking collar me or else. I wasn't taking no for an answer.

"Let me in Ginger, God damn it. I am here to submit willingly. You wanted a partner that wants you back. Here I fucking am. I will break your fucking door. Open this motherfucking door now," I roared like a beast even giggling wildly with stress.

The door flew open hitting me and once again knocking me backward to my ass. I was less graceful and landed much harder this time. I stood back up ready to tackle Ginger but stopped. She was standing there holding a cat o nine tails in her hands this time. I still feared this instrument of torture. Ginger had read my records and was aware that would get my attention. My anger rapidly retreated to terror. We stood there staring at each other sizing the other up for a few moments.

Finally, she spoke, "You are one ignorant cuss for being so damned brilliant. You will admit to me that you are only here because you think you have no other choice. Admit it and we can start this submission." She growled.

I looked at her hatefully. "Okay, yeah, I admit it. I am only here because I am afraid of me. Are you happy now? Can we just get this over with," I yelled feeling more afraid than angry.

She smiled at that. "So you don't adore me? You would rather be collared by anyone on the planet than me, wouldn't you? I would say you are feeling pretty disgusted with yourself that you are begging me to submit you right, now aren't you? If you lie to me, I will indeed call the police and send your ass away Psycho. So choose your words carefully. Be honest. I mean it."

I shook my head realizing she was stupid to ask me to say it, but I did anyway, "You asked for it. I think you are fucking crazy is what I think. I hate you. I will hate you even more when you put that collar on me. I will spend my days and nights thinking of ways to kill you for it. You are a fucking monster. I would rather suck cock at the Greyhound station than have to provide you any fucking service. Honest enough for you there, cupcake?" I smiled evilly no longer caring that I probably just fucked myself out of this collar.

Ginger dropped her head back emitting a loud laugh. "Ah, now honesty finally. Didn't that feel better, Psycho?

However, you are not done just yet. I know you hate me. That is evident. Now admit you hate yourself more, cupcake." She continued to laugh.

I looked at the ground on that one. "Huh? I don't have a fucking choice, you bitch. You are the monster here. You want to put a collar on me and then beat the shit out of my unit. All so you can feel better about you. Fuck you. You hear me? You are a cunt."

She took a step toward me, I backed up one step. "Oh! I am the monster? I want to put a collar on you, that is true Psycho. But you are here to get that collar put on. It takes two to submit, doesn't it? If I am a monster what does that make you? What about those tears of yours when that collar was locked? What was that about hmmm? Maybe a little bit of feeling like a failure? Maybe thinking what a loser you are that you must put up with monsters like me? How about it Psycho? Am I getting warmer?" She smiled arrogantly.

I felt my chest start to ache. I looked away from her realizing she could see into my mind. She was more than warm, she was right on the money.

She saw my sudden surge of despair. "Oh my. Did I just touch a nerve, Psycho? I bet I did. Ouchy. Does it hurt much? Knowing you are stuck forever unable to care for yourself? Trapped having to sleep with people you hate while they rob and beat you because you can't be trusted to handle a puppy? I bet that must suck. It would make me real mad. Hell, I would maybe hate everyone who put that collar on me. Even if they were only doing what I had asked them to do. I mean hating them keeps me from hating myself, facing my own failure, easy to blame the bitch making me get on my knees than the one who really put me on them." She stared laughing.

"Shut up. Fuck you, Ginger. You don't know what this is like. How dare you? You have a fucking choice. How dare you laugh at me." I took a run at her.

She knew I would do that. She stepped out unafraid swinging the cat o'nine tails at me.

I stopped abruptly falling to my knees out of sheer training right at her feet as she yelled out, "Kneel Psycho."

I looked at the ground trying to figure out why I didn't just keep going. How did she do that? I minded her even though I was full of anger demons. I just followed her orders blindly?

I looked up at Ginger confused. "What just, why? I think maybe you should stop now and just get that fucking collar out of my saddle bags. These games are fucking with my head."

Ginger got down into my face. "No, I will not collar you until you admit that you hate yourself, not me, over having to submit to my authority. It is the truth, Psycho. You are almost honest with yourself when you say you hate me. You don't know me well enough to hate me. You do know you well enough. Your hatred is misplaced. You either put it where it belongs or we are done forever. I will not spend my nights being afraid of my own fucking lover. Hear me?"

I looked at her. "I am not your lover,. Ginger. I will never be your lover. I am here because I have to be here. I already admitted that. You are getting what you want. I am willing to tolerate whatever you do and serve you well. Why are you doing this bullshit."

She smiled. "That is why, Psycho. You tolerate. I want more than that. You will give me what I want and I will give you what you need. You need a lot. You think it is just a guardian and a reminder or two, but you are wrong. You need to have a reason to fight as hard as you do. So, I am going to give that to you. You will repay me by adoring me back. First, you must let go of all that hate. So strip, I want you naked right now."

I looked at her. "Here? Now?"

She laughed. "Did I stutter? Yes, here and now. Hurry up." She stepped back with her arms crossed.

I shrugged. "Okay. As you wish." I stood up then quickly did as she asked dropping my clothing in a pile next to my unit.

She looked over my unit appearing irritated. "You have scratches and bite marks all over you. I didn't put those there."

I chuckled. "I finished my contract with June as we agreed. She is a cruel thing. It is why I ran off in the first place. She only bid for my collar so she could do this to me. Well, she is well satisfied now. Can we please get this submission over with?" I looked around to see if anyone would drive by then call the police at my indecent exposure.

She growled. "Humph. Well I will deal with that nasty bitch shortly. First, you smell terrible, Psycho. It makes me want to barf. When did you last bathe? In fact, when did you last eat? Did you bother to take your medication? Have you even slept in days? You look like shit."

I looked at the ground. "Uhm, no? I don't recall. I am not wearing your collar. I will do those things as soon as this submission is…"

She silenced me with her hand gesture. "You didn't even clean up since June? You nasty creature. I have had enough of this. Liar, thief, filthy. Well, I know exactly what to do with you." She walked over to a garden hose she had laying out that she watered her flowers with.

She turned on the facet. I watched her thinking it very odd she would be watering her flowers this very moment. She turned around smiling as she opened her 'sprayer' full force right onto my naked unit.

The freezing water shocked me into stupid. I let out yelling, swearing, and tried to drop to protect my face from the force of it.

She walked around my flailing unit laughing. "There, now you will at least be clean. I hate dirt and stink. If I am going to live with you and fuck you then you will be squeaky clean. If not, I will provide you with Mistress Ginger's bath service. Got that Psycho?" She kept the cold water spraying harshly onto my skin.

"Yes, Mistress," I yelled, "I with bathe. Mercy, please mercy."

She laughed harder. "Oh I am being merciful. You come to me looking like this again, I will do worse than just spray you with a garden hose. Now, kneel. You will allow me to finish. Stop hiding your head. You are getting this bath. Now."

I did my best to do as she commanded but my reflexes kept causing me to try to cover my face. Every time I did, she would spray harder. Eventually, I was able to just hold still and allow her to spray the unit as she wished. She enjoyed tormenting me a great deal and laughed the whole time especially when she hit my female parts. That water was fucking cold. It certainly made me jump and squeal when she got to that point.

Once she was satisfied, I had been 'washed' enough she threw down the hose. I watched as she gathered up my drenched clothing.

She stood looking very stern over my kneeling unit. "You will stay out here to dry off. I am taking these with me. You may come inside when you are dry crawling on your knees, ready to admit you hate yourself, and only after one car drives by. I want them to see you kneeling here in my yard naked and wet. You come in without one of those three things, and I will make sure to send you back to the hell you came from. Got that Psycho?"

I looked up at her startled. "That could be hours. You are in the sticks. Plus, I don't hate myself. That is a lie."

She growled. "Hours are fine with me. I have nothing else to do. See you around, Psycho. Hope that breeze doesn't pick up. It sure is getting cool these days. Hmmm, seems like jacket weather." She walked into the trailer slamming the door behind her.

I was already shivering. She was right, it was cool as hell. The fall was already on the way, and I was already freezing. I was unfortunately in the shade of one of the trees in her yard. I wanted to get into the sunlight for warmth, but I could see her watching me from her window. If I got up, she may call the cops. I was in no mood for an arrest. So, I pulled my legs to my chest and arms in tight hoping to warm just a little. Truth is I was miserable. I hate the fucking cold.

I sat there thinking about what Ginger had said to me. She was right. I hated myself for having to wear a collar and having to submit to some asshole there only to take advantage of my weakness. I didn't understand why I couldn't just admit that was the truth to her. I suppose it was my way of not giving the Master complete control of me. If they didn't know how much it hurt me to have to be this way, maybe they wouldn't use it to hurt me more? I started to see the wisdom in Gingers actions. She was forcing me to face my truths and stop hiding behind my fake submission. I am not a fucking submissive, I am sick. I knew there was a difference but no one else had ever figured that out. Except Ginger.

Finally, around noon, the postal worker drove up to her mailbox. The fellow was staring at me while I shivered looking back at him. I was kneeling and tucked tight so he could see I was naked but didn't see the view he apparently hoped to. He lingered at the edge of the yard waiting to see if I would stand or uncover myself wide eyed and in shock. I waved.

He realized I was watching him back. My wave woke him from his lustful stupor. His mail truck bolted off in a hurry. I could hear Ginger laughing in the trailer at my strange wave.

I grimaced bitterly thinking, "Crazy bitch."

I almost stood up until I recalled she said I had to crawl on my hands and knees to finish this hideous submission. I looked at the bike wondering how I would get my collar out of its hiding spot.

"You want to leave, go for that bike. Otherwise start crawling Psycho. I have what you want right here." Ginger said from her doorway holding a ring of silver that was much sleeker and pretty than the old one Julie had given me.

I started crawling wondering how I had ended up in this situation. I ran a fucking Temple with almost thirty adults calling me a leader. I had given birth to two children without even a tear. I had survived years of abuse most foul and still lived. I was a college student, homeowner, and full time employed, and crawling like a baby across Ginger's lawn naked as the day I was born. All because someone told me too. Because I feared myself, and because I was unable to care for myself. Pathetic. Pure and simple.

Each inch closer to that red-headed smiling Dominate holding the tool of my humiliation made me hate myself more. By the time I finally got up the steps to kneel in front of a prideful Ginger, I was ready to admit it. I hated myself. Of that there was no longer any doubt. She had ordered that undignified behavior, but I was the one who willingly did what I was told. I had no problem telling her right away that I hated myself.

She smiled. "Yeah, I already knew that. Now you do too. Good to be on the same page you know? This time you submit you will be honest with me and yourself. I don't want almost honest. Are you ready to submit to me of your own free will this time? You always have a choice, Psycho. Maybe not the ones you want, but you are free to choose. You are also wise enough to realize that you had other candidates for this collar. You chose me because I am the right choice, not the only choice."

I nodded already beginning to cry because she was right, and because I was now submitting for real for the first time in my whole miserable life. I finally understood I really needed to trust my Keyholder. I couldn't keep on submitting to those who I could clearly tell were only trustworthy enough to abuse my gifts. I don't recognize my own self, so I can only feel hate for whatever I am. That would allow others to feel justified in treating me less than human. I had just discovered I didn't love me because I can't find me. Weird? Well welcome to schizophrenia.

Ginger would not abuse me. She would thud me, bond me, and enjoy me but she would never take more than her fair share. There is a difference in the types of sadist. Not all of them abuse. Some have found a way to curb needs with another who can trade their own weaknesses equally. Mistress Ginger was one of these types, and so is Master Jon but his is a story for another day.

Through Ginger very seemingly odd punishment I had just learned my first lesson of a healthy D/s relationship.

1. **LESSON:** Ginger was angry because her power was robbed from her. She needed to hurt another to feel empowered and deflect the hurt away from self-destructive abuses. She desired someone to love her despite her need to harm them without abandoning her. I was angry just like Ginger. A disease had robbed me of my ability to love myself. I no longer recognize myself due to brain damage. I am helpless without assistance. The only hope I had was to trade the abilities I still possess. Ginger could save me by giving me the love I could no longer have for myself.

Goals to achieve from this lesson: *Ginger needed to have a partner who loved her despite her need to hurt them and could never leave her thanks to a contract. I needed someone who loved me when I could no longer even understand there is a 'myself.'*

Mistress Ginger went on to repeat all her promises from the first time she had collared me. I listened to her silently weeping. This time I understood that it wasn't my Mistress I feared, it was me. What kind of a monster must ask another person to put a collar on their neck and beg for help? Well, this one does beauties. I was lucky Mistress Ginger was willing to take on the mess that was me. If she didn't abuse her position, I should be grateful by doing whatever I could to bring her joy.

I had been doing my job all wrong. I had always just tried to serve my Master by picking up the slack in their daily tasks. I had done this to buy them time to deal with the drama I would stir up with the symptoms of my disease. That was fine. However, if the Master is worth a shit she or he has done more than just granted their time to me. They have stopped their lives to take on my nightmare. It was something I had never considered. They were agreeing to suffer along with me. I should expect and demand they become as attached as Master Marie had become. If they didn't then they would likely turn on me after a short time due to fatigue at dealing with my disease.

My overlooking the possibility that someone needed to be aiding me for more than just an easy piece of ass never occurred to me. In fact, if they did their job right my ass was far from easy. I was more trouble than most ever imagined.

The only way that my collar was worth having is if I could find a way to make the Keyholder love me the way Simon does. That would require I find a way to love them too or at least be significantly fond of them. Mistress Ginger had to point out I was allowing my hate of my disability to override the natural progression of compassion and care. These things are something that should come with trusting another when I granted them my will. I had just learned my second lesson.

2. **LESSON:** *When someone accepts the time consuming, daunting task of wielding Simon's will, it should be anticipated that a fair amount of adoration and love will or has developed on both ends. If it does not, the Master is not doing their job or I am not doing mine. Only compassion, adoration and love can bind the Key and Collar properly. If we don't enjoy serving each other the match is useless and even dangerous. That is why the other collarings had become one side, and abusive so rapidly.*

I made my promises back to the red-haired beauty. To her joy and surprise I added that I would no longer accept more than three leashes in a single reign. I informed her I wouldn't tolerate her being a part of my Green Temple. Last I promised that if she was able to adore me and I her, then in one year I would grant her my Loyalty for life.

Mistress Ginger readily agreed to my newest stipulations, then I endured the hideous click of her collar closing around the unit. She showed me Simon's Key to bond the collar to her. Now, I was truly submitted and without a doubt belonged to Mistress Ginger. Not just my unit this time. She had possessed my heart and soul. Without her I couldn't exist. She was more than my Mistress, she was my World.

I expected her to want to rush off to her bedroom to consummate the new union. To my surprise, she ordered I fix us lunch, then we would go to the courthouse to transfer legal guardianship. I almost got into trouble for staying in my submission kneel too long while the shock of not being immediately thudded to terror sank into my shattered brains.

I was permitted to get dressed finally. She had already laid out the outfit she wanted me to wear on her bed. It was long sleeved, and high collared, completely black. Though it was skintight almost no flesh showed. She came into the room while I finished dressing. My Mistress watched a few moments then went to her dresser retrieving a back corset and riveted breast harness with tons of D rings. I was instructed to fix my hair and signature makeup 'to my finest ability.'

Once I had finished everything, she had requested she placed two red upper arm cuffs made of a latex material that closed with Velcro. She informed me this was her color that I wore. Though I already wore a collar, the cuffs of her signature red indicated I belonged to her exclusively. I was not up for leash nor was my collar up for bids. From that day forward I was not allowed to wear any other color than black and her color cuffs. The only time this command was lifted was when it came to my circle work as High Priestess. Mistress Ginger intended to control even my choices in clothing. It was her right, but I was a bit unhappy about it.

"Psycho stop pouting. I know you are not really a submissive. However, in the lifestyle world there is no category for what you are. Therefore you will learn to at least look like your role. You are more Dominant than I like. However, in every good submissive there is at least a little Dominant," she said while tightening my corset cords.

I shrugged. "Seems to me Mistress, if I am lucky, I will have a lot of Dominant in me later on tonight."

Mistress Ginger stopped tugging my corset. "Oh my God, now that is fucking hilarious, Psycho." She began to laugh heartily over my off handed foul statement.

I looked at the floor. "I apologize Mistress. Sometimes, nasty things like that just come out of my mouth. I don't know why I say them." I was truly kicking myself for making an inappropriate sexual pass at my Mistress.

She pulled my cording hard. "Did I ask for an apology, Psycho? No. I didn't. Don't ever apologize or make excuses unless I say you can. Got that?" She was breathing in my ear sending tingling down my spine.

I took a deep breath both from the tightness of her pulling my corset hard and from the sudden urge to be involved in sexual congress. I had never been interested more in fact. Her breathing in my ear had sent my drives into full gear. That was very odd to me, so I ignored the signals.

"As you wish Mistress." I let my air out suppressing the urge to beg my Mistress to attend my 'personal' needs. I never needed anyone for that kind of business. I was just fine at handling all of that myself. I only got aid from another when I was being forced to attend them, and they were generous enough to return the favor. Otherwise, I was more than happy to deal without them.

However, as with Master Anita, Mistress Ginger had chaste me (that means no masturbation, how rude eh?). I was

66

no longer allowed to attend my own needs without her permission. That sort of pissed me off, but it was her right to request it. I would just have to lump it and keep my hands doing something else.

Once I was dressed to the hilt, Mistress Ginger had me make our meal. She asked for details regarding my fulfillment of the special services of the collar to Mistress June. I answered her without realizing why she was asking.

"So she didn't return anything? Not a single orgasm for you? No touching or oral?" She stood next to me with her arms crossed while I prepared the food.

I shook my head. "No, she touched me alright. She forced my head to her desires. Then while I attended her she scratched me, bit me and twisted my breasts. But you are right Mistress, she didn't touch me in any way to cause me orgasm. Only to injure my unit." I flipped her grilled cheese sandwich, not sure why this was such an issue.

Mistress Ginger looked shocked. "She forced your head? You mean you refused to submit to her orders?"

I looked up at Mistress Ginger. "Oh no Mistress, I did exactly what I was told to do. I mean that even though I was doing as commanded she grabbed my head and pushed, pulled and held it. She wouldn't allow me to get up, catch my breath or just do my job. She was rough, Mistress. Some of them are like that. It hurts but I deal with it. I suppose they are just into the moment."

She snorted. "No, they are bitches, Psycho. They like to hurt you when they do that. If this had been a man forcing your head on his dick would you have said what you just said?"

I paused to think on that. "I guess not, Mistress. It does seem a bit much since I am already doing my job correctly. I would think I don't need their assistance. Grabbing my head like that hurts the unit's neck, is cruel and sometimes they almost rip my ears off. They will hurt for days."

Mistress Ginger nodded. "That is correct, Psycho. They do it because they are being selfish and cruel. Now, did she say why she didn't return the service?"

I looked at the stove hard. "Mistress, I know you have asked me a question. I know you have demanded honesty, but you will not like what she said about why she refused return. I would beg your mercy to keep that reason to myself."

My Mistress glared. "Mercy denied. Tell me right now, Psycho."

I grabbed the plate for her sandwich. "She said she would get me later while at work. That from now on I had to do what she told me or she would make sure I was fired from my job."

Mistress Ginger roared, "That is bullshit. Why didn't you tell me this. You belong to me, not that sow. How dare she think she can just rape someone by threatening their job."

I fell to my knees immediately frightened that she was going to hit me over this. "You had removed my collar. Mistress, at that time I did not belong to you anymore. I told June I would fight her. She could fire me, but I would never allow her abuse of my unit again. If she had come at me tonight, I would have held her off even if it meant unemployment. I would then return home unmolested. I always honor my agreement of monogamy, Mistress." I looked at the floor waiting to see what Mistress Ginger would do.

She snorted. "Get up, Psycho. I am not angry at you. You are the victim in this situation. However, don't you ever keep shit like this to yourself again. How can I look after you if I don't know what you are needing protection from?"

I stood up feeling very relieved that I was not in trouble over this mess. June was a monster. I had just assumed that after she fired me later that night I would come home and take the beating for losing my job. I certainly wouldn't submit to that nasty woman ever again, so there was no other option. Telling Mistress Ginger seemed like just setting off my Dominant for no reason. What could she do? Nothing as far as I could see it.

I served her on her couch and ate my own meal sitting at her feet like I was ordered. After lunch was cleaned up, I let her into the passenger's seat then took the wheel of her car. I drove her to the courthouse. It was very nice to remove Circe's name officially from my life. I granted Ginger Kirkpatrick my Collar, Key and now guardianship rights over my funds, medical decisions, and all-important life changes.

The ladies at the courthouse stared at Mistress Ginger in her red latex cat suit, and myself in my black outfit complete with bondage gear. We couldn't have advertised our D/s situation louder. Mistress Ginger may as well had pushed me to my knees with a ball gag in my mouth in front of those ogling ladies.

Now you must remember this is 1994, deep in the south, in a town of less than one thousand souls, you can safely say we stood out like a hemorrhoid on a worm. Mistress Ginger seemed to really get a kick out of it. I just sighed realizing at some point the town would rise in mass to come calling with pitchforks demanding our heads.

We left the courthouse. Mistress Ginger demanded that I take her to the funeral home after asking if June would be there yet.

I shook my head, "most likely. She has a funeral tomorrow and Pat is off for the next week on vacation. She will be there prepping the client no doubt."

I pulled into the driveway of my workplace dreading seeing the vicious June again. "Mistress I am not on shift until eleven. It is only three o'clock. It is not for me to question but why are we here so early?"

Mistress Ginger used hand gestures signaling I open her door. "You are correct, Psycho. It is not for you to question my authority. So, remember never to do it."

I went around the car and opened my Mistress's door to let her out. "You will do what I say from here on out without a word or hesitation. If you do either, I will punish you severely. I demand total unquestioning obedience until I say otherwise. Do you understand me?"

I nodded. "Yes, Mistress, as you wish." I followed her inside the back door unsure what the hell was going on here.

June was cleaning up the embalming room apparently just having finished her client for his public appearance the next morning.

Mistress Ginger walked right into the room as if she worked there. "Ah, you must be June. Hello, my name is Ginger. You already know my ward, Psycho, I believe."

June turned around startled to see Mistress Ginger standing there like a Dominatrix nightmare holding out her hand to shake. She looked at me appearing to ask what was going on with her eyes. I cast my gaze to the floor trying to chase off the images of the foul night as a hostage of her lustful abuses.

She shook Mistress Ginger's hand. "Uh, okay. You are not allowed in here, Ginger is it? Psycho should have told you. Psycho, you can be written up for bringing friends into our workstation. You know that." She looked to me.

Mistress Ginger glared at June. "Uhm, Psycho is not allowed to speak. You have something to say you say it to me. She is mine now. Do I make myself clear. June is it," she said in a mocking tone.

June snorted. "Figures. Well good luck with that. As it is the little slut ripped me off. She took off a whole day early. Didn't even let me fuck her. I was surprised since she has already fucked everyone else in town. You got yourself a used-up piece of trash there. Hope you didn't pay top dollar."

I almost forgot myself by arguing with the lying asshole. I did repay my debt to her. My anger began to well up, but I saw Mistress Ginger put up her silence gesture. I fell back as commanded.

"Oh, so you are not only a stupid cunt, shitty in bed, but a liar too. I happen to know Psycho did provide you the service you are now claiming you didn't get. You see June she is my lover now. So, I have seen your handiwork. Apparently you feel like you must beat a girl up because you don't know how to get one off properly. Psycho here is far too advanced for a low-level skank such as yourself. She is not a whore, idiot. She was trained to love-make and has likely forgotten more about fucking than you or I will ever know. However, you are such a dumbass you treated something that rare and beautiful like shit," growled Mistress Ginger to a now very surprised June.

June's face twisted with anger. "Why you stupid bitch. Just who do you think you are? I will see Psycho fired because her owner can't keep her big trap shut."

Mistress Ginger smiled wide. "Go ahead and make that call June. You see Psycho got arrested the other day. They took pictures of your handiwork. She refused to give them the name, but it hasn't been seventy-two hours yet. I am sure she could have a sudden change of heart. Wonder how it would look to have that in the papers? Local mortician beats and rapes mentally ill co-worker in vicious lesbian attack. Hmmm, has a ring to it. What do you think, Psycho?" She looked at me still smiling.

I kept my eyes down. "I think it would end a career Mistress and maybe destroy June's reputation." I stifled a snicker.

June's eyes went wide. "Psycho, you wouldn't do that. You came to my house of your own free will. I didn't rape you. Tell this woman what really happened."

Mistress Ginger chuckled. "Oh she already has told me, June. All of it. Psycho didn't come of her own free will. She came because I ordered her to go fulfill her promise to you. I assumed you would treat my girl right. Instead she comes back bruised, scratched, bitten, and without compensation. Then you try to double dip my property by lying to me about her completing your contract. You further compound this insult by telling her if she didn't allow you to force more deficient sex at your will she would be fired. Tisk, now that is truly low. No one is permitted to fuck Psycho without my say so. Not even Psycho."

June growled. "Oh fuck off Ginger. Both of you get out. I don't need to fuck Psycho anymore. I have already been there. The girl is a dead fuck. Trained my ass. You can have her. I would rather fuck one of these corpses. I would probably get more of a reaction." She started laughing hard at her foul attempt to insult me.

Mistress Ginger started laughing too. "Ah, that is such bullshit. You tell a great yarn, June, but you know I prefer Aesop's fables. Do you remember those from school June? You know what my favorite one is? The story about the Fox and the Sour Grapes. Do you recall that one June?"

June shook her head. "What the fuck do I care about Aesop's Fables you stupid bitch. What the hell are you even talking about."

Mistress Ginger chuckled. "Oh, you have forgotten that one. Well let me tell you the story. I think I will have Psycho demonstrate while I tell it. Come here Psycho, help your Mistress teach June here about sour grapes."

My Mistress hand gestured me to come stand in front of her. I did as she ordered. I was very confused but not willing to fool around with an obviously irritated Mistress. This whole exchange was not making any sense to me. All my Mistress was doing was pissing June off. I assumed I would be fired for sure thanks to this little scene.

My Mistress was much taller than me. She walked up behind me and wrapped her arms around my waist putting her mouth right by my ear then began the fable breathing it with much passion into my overly heightened auditory organ, "A fox one day spied a beautiful bunch of ripe grapes hanging from a vine trained along the branches of a tree. The grapes seemed ready to burst with juice. The fox's mouth watered as he gazed longingly at them."

Mistress Ginger paused her story while she undid the buttons on the front of my pants. I tried to pull away.

She held me tightly. "Be still, Psycho. Just relax. This is my pleasure. You will now serve your Mistress well."

I stopped trying to get away but felt tears welling. Honestly, I was afraid Mistress Ginger was going to remove my clothing and let June have her way with me again. I closed my eyes trying to prepare for that indignity. I really hated my life.

My Mistress didn't remove my pants at all. She slid her right hand into my clothing right there in front of a shocked June. I felt her finger gently seek to find my female organs. She wasted no time working her talent with my most tender spot causing me to heave upward. I tried to grab her arm to pull it out of my pants. My Mistress grabbed my shoulder demanding I let her go. I did as I was told, fearful of what would happen if I didn't let her have her way. All I could do is look at June who was now watching the scene with what looked like shock and disbelief.

Mistress Ginger knew her business. Despite myself I was completely overtaken with pleasure as she increased the rhythm of her stroking my joy button as she continued to breath the Aesop fable while pausing to kiss my neck gently. "The bunch hung from a high branch and the fox had to jump for it. The first time he jumped he missed it by a long way. So he walked off a short distance and took a running leap at it, only to fall short once more. Again and again he tried, but in vain."

Her magic was working me into overdrive. I couldn't stop myself from panting, then I began to moan.

My Mistress quickened her pace. "That is right, Psycho. Demonstrate for June here the fox missing those grapes. Moan for me my love, tell June how much you adore me for this."

"Yes, Mistress, I adore you," I moaned out now about to explode in pure extasy as she continued her efforts to bring me to the brink.

Mistress Ginger chuckled, then breathed faster into my ear as she finished the story. "Now he sat down and looked at the grapes in disgust. What a fool I am, he said, here I am wearing myself out to get a bunch of sour grapes that are not worth jumping for. And off he walked very, very scornfully."

I couldn't hold it back any longer when Mistress Ginger then ran her tongue into my ear just after the word 'scornfully.' I let out a loud moaning yell, while spasming in extreme pleasure.

Yeah, I am a screamer. Too much information but hey, the neighbors know so why not the family too?

I had reached an orgasm right there in front of the still watching June just from a simple hand down my pants by my Mistress. I was now coming back down from my journey to pleasure town, panting, sweating and a lot more than grateful for that fine stress reliever. It had been awhile.

Okay there was a bit more she was doing with that hand down my pants but if I need to describe this in more detail, damn I am sorry but you likely are all ready to blow a gasket yourselves. Go clean your pipes right now, the story can wait. I promise I will be right here when you get back. It is okay. I won't tell anyone. Just be sure to lock that bathroom door.

Mistress Ginger buttoned me back up. She groped my breasts from behind me while saying, "Well, seems that Psycho here is working just fine June. I don't know about you but that was fucking hot. I think I will have her demonstrate more stories, in the privacy of my own room as often as I like, for as long as I like. You see that pretty silver collar around her neck? That is my wedding band. This beauty is mine, June. You will keep your fucking nasty paws off or I will see to it you are sorry you ever met me. As for Psycho being worthless or a dead fuck, now we have witnessed that to not be true. Apparently, you were the one who sucked. Just like in that fable June. It was the moral that mattered. It reminds me of you. You remember the moral right? Oh, let me remind you: ***There are many who pretend to despise and belittle that which is beyond their reach.*** Psycho is too good for a pig like you. Good day bitch. Oh, Psycho won't be in tonight. She will be in my bed, I mean sick in bed." She chuckled evilly as she commanded my now very relaxed unit to follow her.

I saw June's face full of desire, fear and jealousy just when I turned to follow my Mistress. I merely shrugged at the angry woman. That was my way of saying, 'oh well, you had your chance.' She had been shown up for the poor lover she truly was.

The act of causing extasy in your partner can be an act of pure pleasure all its own. Mistress Ginger told me to "put the pedal to the metal" to get her back to her trailer house. Apparently, causing my 'demonstration of the fable' in public had indeed been the aphrodisiac she was looking for.

All the way back she howled with laugher. My Mistress continuously mocked the look on June's face while she was forced to watch her lost prize orgasm at the hands of another. I just rolled my eyes at what I viewed as a gross display of power.

"Mistress, I don't get it. Why did you bother? June is a nothing. I don't care what she says about me. Just because someone says something doesn't make it true. You could have caused me to lose my job. I may lose my job. No way June isn't going to retaliate," I whined feeling a bit sheepish even bringing up the obvious.

Mistress Ginger chuckled. "Boy do you have a lot of growing up to do, Psycho. First of all I wasn't bothered by what that dumb bitch was saying. However, she was talking about my girl. Would you have let that cunt bad mouth me like that?"

I shook my head no. "Course not, Mistress. I would have knocked her teeth out."

And that was the truth. I always defend my Masters. If something happens to them, I am screwed. Plus, it is honor and sometimes it is even love.

She smiled. "Exactly. I will not stand for anyone to talk shit about you. As for her retaliating, nah she is a wussy Psycho. You should have figured that out since you were the one intimate with her. Only someone who has a deep-seated fear of failure or a bully would have behaved the way she did in the bedroom with you. I already can tell you she will run like a scared puppy every time she sees you now. I proved she is a shitty lover in front of you. She won't want to hazard your calling her out in front of others. Trust me will you, Psycho? You really have to try harder to understand that I am here to help you, adore you, make your life worth living not to abuse, use or hurt you."

I winced. "I will try harder Mistress not to question your motives or techniques."

I felt like running for the hills. I knew when we got to her house, my ass was in for a beating. I couldn't help the fear. Years of Julie's and Debbie's abuse had instilled a serious terror at the idea of even being in the same house with the BDSM tools of torture. I really wanted to like Mistress Ginger. After all she had just given me my very first orgasm without me having to provide any service in return. That was my only experience that was one sided in my direction. I could learn to like that a lot. However, now I knew I owed her whatever she wanted in return. I just wish what she desired would not include shit that left bruises and burned like hell. I am like everyone else, most people anyway. I want to scream in a bedroom, but not because someone is beating the fuck out of me with a weapon of torture.

Once back to her place my fear was quickly realized when she demanded I park, let her out then follow her. She of course headed right for her room. I did as I was told but caught myself whimpering as she closed the door going for her closet immediately.

She heard my whimper and stopped, "What is it Psycho?"

I looked at the floor trying not to tear up, "Nothing Mistress. I am sorry was just clearing my throat."

Mistress Ginger glared. "You are going to start the lying again? You sure you want to go there while I am going to my closet? I think you better try that again and thank me for granting you the mercy of allowing a second chance. I should just punish you right now for it."

I felt the first tear spill down my cheek. "Mistress, I apologize for lying. I thank you for your mercy. It is not proper for me to complain about your pleasures. I am supposed to just tolerate whatever you desire. Forgive my moment of weakness. I will try harder to stop acting like a child in the future."

She looked very sad all the sudden. "Psycho, sit down on the bed please. I told you I need you to trust me. I told you I am never going to abuse you or hurt you. I meant that. I don't want you to tolerate things for me. I want you to enjoy them with me. I am sorry that others before me took advantage, but I am not them. You must remember who I am, forget those other assholes. I command you to look at me while I make love to you. I don't want you to close your eyes. Stay focused on who is loving you, and let my face block out the demons that live in the darkness behind your eyelids. We are going to take this slow. In time you will not be afraid anymore. Not of me, my thudding tools or of your sexuality. Do you hear me?"

I nodded. "As you wish Mistress." I tried to stop crying but it didn't work as I saw her take out her crop.

NOTE: *The crop was her very favorite and signature thudding device. She was well trained and enjoyed the cat o' nine tails, the quirt, the brush, various floggers, canes, the paddle, and single tail whip. Her favorite restraining devices were the sleep sack, spreader bar, posture collar, bondage mittens, the straight jacket, rope, and bondage hoods. She also enjoyed using the violet wand and the usual stuff most people have, or should have such as vibrators, dildos, etc.*

Devices she used only for punishment were the vampire gloves, shock collar and leather strap. She made damned sure to keep me terrified of fucking up with those three very nasty devices.

If you don't know what any of those things above are then find someone and make sure they explain what they do specifically. I am not going to waste space here talking about them but will describe and discuss them as they come up in the story where important. Yikes!

She immediately put me into a straight jacket. While she strapped me in, she was telling me how much it pleased her that I was already well trained to handle restraints for long periods of time. Thanks to my disease, and months of inpatient treatments things such as sleep sacks and straight jackets, even rope bondage, didn't bother me much. I still didn't want to be tied up or strapped in but the experience of helplessness, immobility and the patience one must have with both was already deeply ingrained within me by now.

Once she had me completely unable to escape her advances, she began to pleasure me by stimulating with her crop itself. She brought me to extasy using the very tool that normally she would strike me with. She would use this device to stroke the important parts then very lightly strike my thighs with it as I was about to reach the point of no return. She was careful to repeat this pleasure then very mild pain technique before finally allowing me to reach my destination. My Mistress took her sweet time demanding I look in her eyes the entire time. She was trying to demonstrate that I could trust her.

I was screaming, struggling and crying as if she were beating me full force with that crop. This was because the psychological damage done by years of torture with such a device was driving more pain from memory than reality. This was the very nightmare she was up against. It was going to take her almost a full year to stop this overreaction behavior

However, my Mistress was indeed loving and non-abusive. She had seen those horrific records. If she wanted me to stop acting like she was torturing me, she would have to make sure not to be adding any more trauma. She would use this technique with each one of her thudding tools, slowly accustoming me to light striking after much pleasure from the same device. In time she would turn up the striking pressure slowly increasing the pain delivered by each item. Mistress Ginger only turned up the volume on the tool after I had learned to appreciate them for the pleasuring they could also cause. I never would learn to enjoy being struck by them, but I did finally stop fearing the damned things. That was still a long way off, for now she was just taking it step by step.

When she was fully turned on by hearing my pleas for her to stop tormenting me, yeah she tended to make me orgasm till I begged her to please stop, it really hurts trust me, she would order her own pleasures be given. When the entire sexual congress was finished with Mistress Ginger in her bedroom torture chamber, I was often too spent to even consider terrorizing neighborhoods, pacing or threatening the local Freewill Baptist Church. Mistress Ginger was an animal in the bedroom, always ready to give a girl a workout, and then a nice long nap in a straight jacket.

Half-way through her second sexual congress with me I began to feel the tilting of my brain. Thankfully, she already had me tightly bonded in ropes, but eventually she had to wrap me in wet sheets again. It would not be much longer before this kind of psychotic episode would be the rule of the day. She sat with me while I babbled, drooled, screamed and cried. I never asked her, but I am sure it was very disheartening to have to see it take me down like that, and during such a vulnerable act. I spent the entire night at her house that first day of the second collaring. She made sure to keep me restrained while she slept. Mistress Ginger was no fool. I was significantly prodromal now heading right for acute like a speeding silver bullet.

Wow, I need a cold shower after this chapter. Mistress Ginger was hotter than a firecracker trust us. She was fully in touch with her sexual interests and was happy to drag us kicking and screaming (okay and moaning too) all the way. Life under her Vampire Gloved hand was strict, pleasurable and full of adventures most only dream of after popping a bunch of ecstasy at the club.

Chapter 27: Pandering to Baser Instincts
Mistress Ginger

Mistress Ginger's reign was full of sexual energy, both public and private. Hers is the tale of crossing lines. Some of them may be a bit too erotic for sensitive eyes. She only had respect for her own desires. Mistress Ginger didn't let anything or anyone stand in her way of what she wanted, and she wanted everything.

If you enjoy this sort of discussion, do dig in while we explore many aspects of human sexuality. If it is not your cup of coffee, then we ask you to do as we have always done, just endure it. Her time as our Mistress was not much longer than that of the evil Mistress Circe. It will come to an abrupt, mysterious, and ugly end. To this day, we have no answers to many questions left by the disappearance of this most unusual woman from our life.

Oh Stacey. You are so close minded. Why can't you just accept people for who they are. You are not the only viewpoint on earth you know. Maybe what you needed was the sound of more than the voice inside your head to understand others have the right to be different than you. Good thing Psycho has found others who will help you to listen more intently. Your stony heart doesn't have to be what you really are, but it should at least let others who are braver than you be free.

The Festival of Bread has arrived, Blessed Be. The Green Rings are rejoicing at the fruitfulness of their High

Priest and High Priestess. Many children have been born of their magical union. Beltane was truly a time of fertility as Mother Earth is strengthened by the hands of those who love her the most. Roary and Arodia will stand proud parents, but what is this? Their beloved Mother is very weak. The dark half is coming. Oh no. The veil will be thin soon, the Queen is too ill to resist the call of those who are waiting for her in the Summerlands.

The loving duo will need to work together quickly to secure the Covens before Loki and Hel come to reign over the world with mischievous chaos. There is no stopping what will be. The Mother has her coins in hand for the boatman. The people will soon be celebrating the Mothers ascension to the sixth and final level. She will smash the evil Circe's cup, then have her own broken on the hearth to the sound of great wailing.

Ready to take another ride on the wild side? For this chapter leave your morals and judgements at the door. No worries they will be there waiting for you when you are done with this trip. Love comes in so many forms, and guises. Mistress Ginger's belief is one of acceptance of the alternative. Get ready while she expands our minds to the point of explosion. Just be careful not to get too close. We wouldn't want you to get pulled into her world too deeply like we did. Once you get in, it is pure hell trying to find your way back out.

"I don't care what you say Psycho if you fuck a woman you are a lesbian. There is no difference. You are either gay or you are straight period."

Stacey arguing with Psycho and CJ during LGBT Pride meeting- September 1994.

- **Definition of Pansexual:** *"not limited in sexual choice with regard to biological sex, gender, or gender identity."*

- **Definition of Bisexual:** *"attracted to both men and women."*

Pansexual is not Bisexual. A Pansexual will choose sexual partners based on personality traits rather than what is in the person's pants. The Pansexual is sexually interested in all human beings and is not picky regarding race, religion, gender identification, creed, nationality or background. The Pansexual is all inclusive when it comes to attraction with one single exception: If you are an asshole you need not apply. Even we have our limits.

The next morning Mistress Ginger let me out of the straight jacket after checking my mental health. She was concerned about the growing strength of my psychosis. She almost kept me from going to class for a second day. However, with some serious begging I finally got her approval to attend. I hated trying to find people kind enough to share notes with me. I was not well received at college thanks to my odd appearance and strange behaviors. After a full year of being a constant face on campus I still had not managed to make a single friend or find even a weak support system.

In fact, thanks to the rude actions of my previous Mistress I had managed to alienate my only connection: the hateful, homophobic Stacey. She had been calling my Maiden Mary over the past couple of weeks. Thanks to my significant issues with the collar change, I had been ignoring getting back to her. I really had nothing to say. She was a closeminded fool. My lifestyle, even before Mistress Ginger, was chaotic and off the beaten path. Not even my choice of faith was appreciated by this ignorant bitch. I had to fight enough just to survive day to day. I was in no hurry to add a daily battle with someone who was never going to stop judging others for shit that had no bearing on her continued peaceful existence.

Stacey and now Mistress Ginger's demands had been forcing me to examine my own sexual preferences. Stacey had been cruelly arguing with me about my reputation as both a whore and a lesbian. I of course knew I was no lesbian.

I did appreciate the unit of my handsome Priest and other males in my past. Most of my sexual interests had been male in fact: Greg, Mike, Boyd, and Roary. However, I was also realizing my interest in Mistress Ginger and had been in love with Linda for some time already. One would have thought if I were to identify with any group it would be that of the Bisexual since I could find pleasure with either. However, I had discovered earlier in my history that my interest in another person for sexual pleasure went beyond just the parts they possessed. I found that the only thing about a potential sexual partner that truly mattered to me was that they were not an asshole.

Thanks to the horror of my mother's upbringing I had not been allowed to develop "normally" or even choose my sexual partners. For almost a decade starting way too young I was forced into sexual congress with persons of various backgrounds, genders, and tastes. This had destroyed my ability to place boundaries between what I liked or didn't. In fact, what I wanted out of sex or type of sexual partner never mattered, and the sad fact is that it still didn't.

My unfortunate situation of being unable to care for myself without a stable support system then lead to the delusion you are all aware of. Thanks to the changing of my Key from holder to holder, I would never be able to turn my nose up at any lover that possessed Simon's Will. I would not have lasted long if I suddenly got picky or demanded my sexual needs and interests be considered. The reality is that I had to eat, drink, sleep and bathe to survive, but I didn't have to have sex to live till the next day. However, my Masters would value the carnal act with great importance as I had already discovered, some in most brutal ways. I had no choice but to entertain their desires or risk the tossing of my collar and abandonment to face the true horrors of my disease.

This had led to a Pansexual tolerance for anyone who held the Key. It had so happened that all of my Masters had been female to this point. However, that would not always be the case in my future. People who would identify as: male, female, gay, straight, bisexual, lesbian, gender fluid and pansexual would all eventually get a shot at Simon's Key.

NOTE: I have often wondered if I had been given a choice and allowed to explore my own sexuality without being forced into it would I have been pansexual? The answer is very tragically no. I would have been straight, believe it or not.

How can I know that? That is very easy, when Debbie began to rape me when I was little, I hated being with her and not just because she was my mother, the fucking twisted bitch. I hated being with any woman in the beginning. It did nothing for me. My first experience with a male at age eight was very brutal. Despite this viciousness I felt more natural with males than with females. My unit responded better as was demonstrated by the Great Rite during my congress with my Priest. My orgasms come faster, are stronger and I am more satisfied with fewer of them to give you a bit more of the old too much information.

However, my many years of experience with the female form had slowly caused my distaste for it to fall away. Eventually, as with anything you repeat continuously, I learned to appreciate sex with a woman or anyone for that matter if they were kind about it). I had become very talented at it as well, and still am. Sexual congress with a male was much easier to learn due to my underlying original nature of heterosexuality. Plus, let's face it, men are just simpler to please. A woman is a complex creature with many bells and whistles that require years of intense training to understand, master and honestly to even find.

Maiden Mary had called Mistress Ginger's house that morning to inform her that Stacey was once again calling frantically looking to speak with me. She asked me about this girl, and what the nature of the relationship had been. I, of course, told her the whole story as I was commanded to. Mistress Ginger decided the girl was not a threat, and that I should at least meet with Stacey to see what she wanted.

I was ordered to call the dumb bitch and arrange a meeting for that afternoon after classes at Mistress Ginger's house. After what happened with June, I admit I was more than a bit nervous to bring the WASP Stacey to this den of the alternative. However, when your Mistress tells you to do something, you do it or suffer the punishment. Stacey was not worth more of "Mistress Ginger's Bath Service" or a session with the Vampire gloves.

Mistress Ginger insisted I wear the outfits she handpicked each morning. I ended up having to attend classes that day wearing a black cat suit, corset, chest and arm harnesses, with red cuffs and black stiletto platforms. With my usual signature makeup, I was a walking BDSM nightmare. My outfit that day was so obnoxious even though my professors lost their train of thought when they looked my direction during lectures. I was not embarrassed by it. I did think it very silly, maybe even dangerous, to be so obvious about my current lifestyle status. Even though college was comprised of a larger pool of persons from other regions it was still in the south. It seemed to me that Mistress Ginger was putting me at an unnecessary risk for hate crimes.

This was realized that day when groups of so-called religious students paused to scream at me about the "hell fires" I was sure to experience since I was an "unrepentant sinner." Seems they must have missed the day their preachers had taught that little statement in their cannon about "judge not less thee be judged." I just kept walking ignoring their statements of indignation. I always just walk away. No need to argue with someone who has already made up their mind. It would be a waste of my time. I already waste enough in strait jackets and inpatient treatment. Oh well, it sucks to be me.

I was walking back to my metal God when I felt someone tap me on the shoulder. Since it was still far too close to Tammy's little trick, I let out a yelp and took off running.

"Hey Psycho, hey it is me, CJ. I am sorry. I didn't mean to scare you," I heard a female voice yell behind me.

I stopped when the memory of who CJ was finally kicked into my shattered mind. I was nearly to my bike, out of breath and my heart was doing acrobatics in my chest. I turned around to see the girl trotting to catch up with me after my wild run.

"Psycho. Shit. I feel terrible. I didn't do that on purpose. I was just trying to say hello," said CJ as she got into earshot without having to yell to me.

I nodded. "Don't sneak up or ever touch me again," I said feeling mildly irritated.

She smiled. "Yeah got it. Hey, love the look today. I saw you in the hallway and pointed you out to Diane. She wants to meet you. In fact, I have a bunch of people who are just dying to meet you."

I narrowed my eyes suspiciously. "Now why the fuck would anyone want to meet me?"

CJ laughed loudly/ "You are such a riot. You seriously don't know why anyone would want to get to know you chick? My God, you are amazingly beautiful, the top student in our class, and one of us. What is not to want to know?"

I shook my head. "You are talking in riddles, CJ. I don't understand what us is. Look you seem really nice and all but I have places to be. I am already behind. Have a nice day."

I began walking again towards my bike. I needed to get going if I was to beat Stacey to Mistress Ginger's place.

CJ was relentless. She followed me matching my own rapid pace. "Okay, you need me to spell this out? I am the representative of the LGBT group here at school. We are always looking for members. You Psycho are definitely someone we would like to add to our list. You are not hiding like so many of us must do. That shows strength. We need all the strength we can get with the hate crimes against us growing in numbers lately."

I kept walking. "I don't even know what LGBT group means CJ. You have the wrong person if you are looking for strength. As for hate crimes, call the cops. Not interested in vigilant shit, darling. I already have an arrest history that could choke a horse. More trouble I certainly don't need."

CJ laughed. "Oh, okay, I see. Well LGBT stands for Lesbian, Gay, Bisexual and Transgendered. Diane and I are trying to get a chapter started here on campus. We have a pretty large group who have already signed up but we are always looking for more recruits. We don't do vigilante stuff. The group is designed to help people who fall into those categories transition into college and have a place to meet others who are like them. Wait here I have a pamphlet."

I stopped while CJ dug around in her backpack. "CJ, what in the holy hell made you think I was in any of those categories? Hmmm? For your information, not that it is your business, I am not a lesbian. I am not gay. I am not bisexual either. Just because my voice is deep doesn't indicate that I am transgendered. My voice reflects a vocal cord injury when I was younger. So, thank you very much, but no thank you. Good luck with your group. I hope you get your chapter." I took off leaving CJ still digging in her backpack.

I was grumbling all the way home after that little scene with CJ in the parking lot. It seemed everyone was too damned interested in my sexual orientation all of a sudden. Worse still, they were all making assumptions about it that were completely wrong. At that time I didn't understand that LGBT included persons like myself too. CJ had made the mistake of not explaining that this group was fighting for the rights of all alternative types of lifestyles that were not straight, nuclear family oriented. Had she maybe put it to me that schizophrenic, pansexual, D/s persons were also included under their large umbrella, then perhaps that first attempt may have yielded a more friendly response. However, she didn't ask, she assumed. Just like everyone else.

NOTE: *That is because even though CJ identified as transgendered, lesbian, she was still above all normal. That's right. Sexual orientation is useless in identifying a person as non-normal. I should know. If you looked at her life, and didn't look at her sexual situation, you couldn't tell her from Maiden Mary or Lisa or even my Priest.*

She wanted all the same things they did out of life. She had all the same goals too. Marriage, family, a home, a career, someone to love her. Unlike this nutjob who just wanted to spend one year out of inpatient treatment and not be beaten too badly by someone I called Master. I was not interested in marriage ever, my career was only designed to keep me off the streets, my home was for the children Master Anita had forced me to keep, and love? What a joke. That emotion belongs to Simon. So, yes, CJ is normal and I am not. In time, she would discover that. For now, she was still only seeing what she hoped to see. I told all of you I am a mirror. Anyone can see themselves in it. That is my problem.

I got back to my Mistress's home just as Stacey pulled in behind me. Even from my vantage on the bike I could see the disgust on her face while she parked her car. Mistress Ginger came out the door heading my direction.

I quickly hopped off the bike wondering if I was about to get punished right in front of the bully Stacey. She was already getting out of her car as my Mistress approached me. I looked at them both wishing I had just stayed in bed that morning.

"Psycho baby. I have missed you so much." Mistress Ginger said as she grabbed me pulling my unit to hers while tightly hugging me.

I just stood there unsure how to respond. My Mistress began to grope my backside then started kissing my neck passionately. I won't lie, she was turning me on.

Stacey almost hit the ground her eyes going wider than dinner plates at the scene unfolding before her eyes. "Uhm, seems you two are busy. I can come back later."

Mistress Ginger stopped kissing then turned her head but kept me in her embrace. "Oh no Stacey. You must stay for dinner. I insist. I was just welcoming my baby home is all. I will leave you two alone so you can discuss your business."

My Mistress turned back to me and to my absolute horror grabbed the back of my head. She forced my mouth to hers, then her tongue into my mouth deeply French kissing sending the feeling of terror throughout my unit. I felt she may chew my face off. I tried to back off but her grip was very strong. I had to endure her exploration of my mouth as Stacey looked toward the sky appearing to turn green with extreme illness. This was her nightmare come true, and mine too.

96

Finally satisfied she had caused enough of a public display of her affection for me, my Mistress let me go. She smiled at me evilly but said nothing. I watched her shoot a look of arrogance at Stacey. Mistress Ginger then went back inside the trailer leaving me to deal with the homophobic Stacey, alone.

Stacey looked at me still standing there in stunned silence. "Okay, so you are going to still deny you are a lesbian?"

I looked at the ground. "Uhm yeah Stacey I am. I am a lot of things, but I am not a lesbian."

She laughed bitterly. "Sure looked awfully lesbian just a second ago, Psycho. Just saying when you kiss a girl like that, it is pretty obvious you are fucking one too."

That made me a bit angry. "Okay asshole. Whatever, are you here to question my sexual orientation? If so, I think you had better leave now. Otherwise get to your reason for bothering everyone demanding to talk to me. I have more important shit to do."

She shook her head. "Look I need to ask you to come back as my partner sharing a ride. I can't keep on affording the trips back and forth. I don't give a shit if you are fucking half the cheerleading squad anymore. I just need the gas money."

That made me laugh. "Oh I see. It is okay to be a lesbian and a whore as long as I can help you by paying half your freight. Hmmm. I have a motorpsycho. I don't need your money. So, guess that means the answer is go fuck yourself, Stacey."

I started to head back into the trailer after my Mistress. She had me now interested to see if she would be willing to finish what she started.

Stacey ran after me stopping me at the steps. "Psycho, wait please, I need your help. I know I was a mega bitch to you. I had no right to stick my nose into your personal stuff. You were right, who you fuck is not my affair. I judged when I should have just looked the other way."

Her continuing to bother me was getting on my nerves. "No Stacey, I hate you. I have always hated you. My rides to school have never been more peaceful since I stopped having to listen to you five days a week. I have enough trouble in my life without adding your bigoted bullshit to it." I glared while starting up the steps.

She started to cry. "Please Psycho, I swear I will never say another word about rumors or call you a lesbian or a whore. I swear it. I mean what are you going to do when the fall storms come, or the winter. It gets really cold. That motorcycle will be cold and miserable when the weather turns. Give me a chance to prove I can change. What do you have to lose? If you change your mind you can always go back to the bike." She was now acting more than desperate.

I stopped and thought of her words. She was right. The storms and cold of fall and winter were on their way. I was already starting to freeze my ass off on long rides to the college. Her car had a heater and a roof. She had valid points even though I hated to admit them.

I nodded. "Okay, deal. I will try it again but this is the last time, Stacey. I am tired of your shit. You don't get another chance. Fuck with me and I am gone forever. I mean it. See you in the morning." I walked into the house leaving her behind me letting out sounds of relief.

Mistress Ginger was at the window watching Stacey leave when I came inside. "She wants me to share the gas money and ride together to college, Mistress. I told her yes to save money for fixing up our new home."

Mistress Ginger smiled. "Oh, I have a surprise for you, Psycho. I already called in a moving van. We are all going home, you, me the kids, this very weekend."

I was shocked. "But Mistress, the house is still not finished. I have some painting and repairs left."

She lifted her silence hand gesture. "Those are just cosmetic. I can help with them. It is time we made this family whole again. Especially since you are going acute. Those kids need their mother, and I need to have all of us in one spot to manage everything smoothly. No arguments. We are going home. You will help me get settled in. Face it Psycho, you and I are together forever now."

I was even more shocked. "You will never toss Simon's Key? Mistress, you surely are not going to like me forever. I would love to believe you, but I know that is not likely. Everyone tires of my shit eventually."

She frowned. "Psycho, I have told you repeatedly that you are the one I was looking for. You must learn to trust what I tell you. I would punish you for questioning me, but I understand why you have trouble believing me. In time, you will see that I was being honest. We are together forever. You are my girl always, I promise."

I really did want to believe that Mistress Ginger would never leave me. It was not for romantic reasons, though she was turning out to be an amazing lover. I was just so tired of trying to learn a new way of living, new rules and adjusting to new personalities all the damned time. It was nice to think that one day I would be able to have a forever home. However, I already knew Mistress Ginger hated the rural town.

She was originally from, yes you guessed it, California. My Mistress had been working in a BDSM club in Los Angeles when she met a man and fell in love. They had married, and like Cindy, his mother had gotten sick. She lived in the small town where my cemetery home Darlin was located. This man hauled a very unwilling Mistress Ginger from her city of excitement to the middle of nowhere to attend his ailing mom. Unlike in Cindy's case, his mother had died rapidly. Mistress Ginger expected they would then return to her city of lights, but instead she awoke abandoned by this dude. With no money, not job and no connections she had called her Dungeon Master Paul.

Apparently, she was not going to get any help from her BDSM family either. In the end she was left high and dry with only the trailer and her car. She had been trying to sell both. She couldn't just return to her beloved town without funds. Her old job was gone, she had no startup funds. For now, she was trapped in the hillbilly hell of a small rural town.

NOTE: *Now wait a minute…how the hell did she buy my collar? Yeah, you are wondering that too aren't you. That my beauties is only one of the great mysteries that this Mistress left as a legacy. To this day I do not know how, why or what was paid to Mistress Circe. I did ask but I was told that was none of my business. Since Circe is dead, and Mistress Ginger disappeared without a trace in October 1996, I will always be left without an answer to what happened that June in 1994 or in October 1996 for that matter.*

She had promised that when we had saved enough money to start a new life in LA she would move myself and the kids with her. I didn't enjoy my last trip to California but I was more than willing to follow my Mistress wherever she wanted to go. It had only been a few days and I was already starting to bond deeply with her. Except for Simon, Zeppelin, Greg, Dennis, Linda and my kids, I had never felt much for anyone. My feelings for Mistress Ginger were indeed different than any before her. I wanted to be wherever she was, and it was my pleasure to make her happy. She was getting through my icy core and melting my frozen heart. It would not be long that I would be desperately in as close to love as I can ever come with this red-headed beauty.

She wanted to celebrate our upcoming move. So before I went to visit my children and then to work, Mistress Ginger took me back to her room and reminded me why I kept coming back to her with my tail wagging. Her thudding tools were a bit of an issue, but if that is what it took to encourage her to take me to pleasure town, I was ready to sign up for the horror show. She of course, didn't let me down.

As before she used a tool of my worst nightmares to take me to the brink of ecstasy. This time she used the cat o nine tails. I nearly was sent jumping out a window when she picked that one for our afternoon delight. My initial belief was like the day before it would only be her crop. I had not realized yet she was planning on using every one of her thudding devices. Over time she would us one at a time to calm her nervous partner, me, into compliance with her pain driven desires.

I was most unhappy to see that old enemy in her hands. Despite my best efforts to keep my mouth shut I bravely voiced my displeasure with that particular weapon. After demanding I kneel, she used a few well-placed knots in nylon rope around my wrists and ankles. This way the Mistress made me hold still so she could finish her lesson in pleasure and pain. I endured her use of that horrible whip but to this day I still hate it above all other flogging devices. She was completely unsuccessful getting me to change my mind about those damned things. I still hate them above all thudding devices to this very day.

When she was satisfied, I was finally let loose to go see the children at my Maiden's house. I was informed that the next night we would be going out for dinner together. I was really surprised to hear that. My Mistress informed me she wanted to show me off to a couple of her friends. Somehow that didn't sound good, but what Mistress Ginger wanted, she got. I merely agreed I would let my Maiden know I would be later than normal to see the kids the next night. I made a quick meal for my Mistress, then headed off to attend my other responsibilities. That dinner would end up being put off for almost two weeks, but no worries, we will get to that story shortly.

My Maiden was thrilled to hear that in only three short days I would finally have my children home with me, except when I was working. It had been almost two full years since we had all been under the same roof. They had grown accustomed to Mary's home and family. They were safe and stable all that time with a roof over their heads, constant attention, and their own rooms.

I had suffered the homelessness for them by surfing couches, frequent cemetery camp outings, and of course months of sleeping on a cot in the Snake Pit. I was even known for catching a nap on a slab at my funeral home job from time to time. Life had been very hard under the lazy Mistress Circe. My gratitude to Maiden Mary could never be described in words. While it is truth I paid for their keep and care, she did more than just look after them. She loved them like her own. Money doesn't buy that. Maiden Mary had my loyalty for life, if she ever called on me, I would have fought to the death to defend her. There are few that ever walked this Earth as good hearted as she was. Note the word was. Yes, Maiden Mary is no more but that story is many years from now. So, let's not suffer that loss just yet? I don't look forward to reliving that sad day I assure you.

NOTE: *Interestingly, of the original Coven members, only myself, Lisa and Delilah still live. Roary is still around too, but all the rest of them, even Ronnie, are in the Summerlands now. We will deal with each as they happened. It is very odd to realize how many of your associations fell as the years rolled on, but if you live long enough, it happens sadly.*

I headed to the funeral home feeling a bit of fear at what June may do in retaliation for the whole 'sour grapes' situation the day before. It was still blowing my mind that my Mistress had been so arrogant with her belief that I would not pay for that gross display of property rights.

I walked in to find June cleaning up the embalming room feeling a bit of déjà vu. She turned and saw me standing there looking like a ghost had just flew past. No matter how hard I tried I couldn't think of a thing to say. I mean what is there to say to the woman who saw you manually stimulated to the point of orgasm while the Mistress demonstrated an Aesop Fable exactly?

June glared at me. "I guess you think you are clever? You had no business telling your Mistress about our little arrangement Psycho."

I cleared my throat. "Uhm, yeah I did. She ordered I report back to her all you said and did while I attended the left-over contract. You had no business demanding more than was yours to begin with. You want to fire me, go ahead. I will file a complaint of sexual harassment against you. Try me." I couldn't believe those words just came out of my mouth. I just stood up for myself without hitting someone. Bravo Psycho.

She growled. "You would have to prove it."

I chuckled. "Yeah I would likely lose, but not before dragging your good name through the mud. Everyone thinks me a lesbian and whore. I have never complained before, so some will believe me June. Some won't. All will wag their tongues about it. In the end, you will always have a black mark over your name. So, want to hire an attorney or do you want to do your fucking job and leave me the hell alone?"

June looked at the ceiling. "You fucked me over. I saw what that Ginger did. Why didn't you act like that when I had you for myself?"

"You weren't interested in what I wanted. Had you allowed me the choice you would have never even received the service at all. I am not only not attracted to you; I despise you June. I think you are a foul, ugly person and a bully to boot. The only way anyone would ever fuck you is if they were forced like I was. Well, good luck with that. You pull what you did with me on someone else you will eventually get murdered in your bed," I said while smiling evilly at her.

She looked at me anger flashing. "Well I think there is no need for you and I to be around each other any longer. I wouldn't want people associating me with your kind."

I laughed. "Fine by me June. Bye, bye now." I waved mockingly.

She snorted then stormed out the door. From that day forward, whenever she saw me, she turned and went the other way. My Mistress had been correct, June was just a bully. Once we stood up to her, she ran like the chickenshit she was. I was happy to finally have my shift all to myself once more. I hated that June still took a cut of my income, but my clever Mistress would soon put an end to that thievery as well.

Thanks to June's sudden belief that she need not be up my ass constantly, I was able to return to my yellow house and work on it for the three days before the big re-uniting move. I wasted no time even finishing the final touches hours before the wee hours of Saturday morning. That was more than luck. At the time, I was sure it was the Gods letting me know I was on the right track to getting wherever it was they wanted me to be.

Wednesday morning Stacey showed up at Mistress Ginger's to pick me up for class. The first week would go smoothly. She kept her word never mentioning rumors or pushing her belief system on me. It almost seemed too good to be true. It was of course too good to be true. Stacey was always going to be Stacey. I was aware of that. However, the incident that caused trouble the next week between us began over one that happened the Thursday before the big move to my yellow house.

Stacey had parked and we went our separate ways as usual. I had an Advanced Microbiology lab so my walk across campus was much further than hers. She tended to park in front of the building where all her social science courses were located, the lazy bitch. I practically had to run to make it to my lab class on time it was so far away. That morning didn't appear any different than any before it, however, I didn't see the three young males watching my mad dash to my destination.

They had seen me before and noticed the very obvious bondage gear that Mistress Ginger insisted I wear. These fellows were of the mind that perhaps a young lady who advertised such apparel may be up for a bit of forced fun with them. They had waited patiently outside the Science building for my lab work to finish up. I only had the one class on Tuesdays and Thursdays. Stacey had arranged her schedule to also have a morning lecture around the same time.

When I came out to head back to meet Stacey and head home, I was approached by these guys who had heinous ideas on the brain. This time I had noticed them following me keeping pace. I need not say I was nearly running.

The largest of the males rushed ahead and blocked my path, "What is your hurry there beautiful? My name is Kurt, this is Steve and David. We noticed you are alone. Do you have a boyfriend?" He was looking at his friends who had now started to surround me.

I looked around desperate to find anyone to aid me out of this wolf pack situation. People were walking by but none close enough to help.

I tried to move forward and Kurt grabbed my chest harness holding it tightly. "Hey hold on. Where you going? No, no, you are coming with us." He began to drag me by the harness while his friends closed in so no one would notice what he was doing.

I kicked, swung and started yelling with all I had but Steve grabbed my arms and Dave covered my mouth. I bit him but he pulled his hand from my mouth cussed then covered it again more carefully now. They started to haul me toward an alley behind the Science building. I knew if they got me there, I was doomed. It was an off day and early, so very few students were around. It was well known to every female student on that campus that a rape that occurred on campus grounds rarely resulted in serious prosecution. It had been a growing problem for the last several years and still is one to this day.

Each college is a country all its own. They have their own police, and legal proceedings. If a crime was committed, they would reach the scene first. The city cops would only get to see what the campus goons allowed them to have access to. I had heard the horror stories of what happens when a girl tried to get justice for such violence as these three were very obviously about to try to force on me. I struggled with all I had despite being very obviously outmatched.

As luck would have it, my denial of waiting for that pamphlet for the LGBT would come in handy. Often when I am an asshole it comes back to bite me. This time, it saved me. CJ and Diane had come looking for me assuming I would be headed back to the parking lot. They saw the males hauling me against my will towards that dark, secluded place.

The ladies had come running yelling the whole way to "Let her go, you creeps. Someone call the cops. Rape! Rape!"

Kurt, Steve, and David all panicked when they saw the couple running toward them screaming like that. They let me go and ran off fast as their legs could carry them. I fell to my knees nearly pissing my pants in pure terror and relief.

"Jesus, Psycho, are you okay," said CJ as she reached me almost out of breath from her sprint across the campus.

I nodded as the tears began to fall. "Yes. Thank you, CJ. I owe you one." I stood back up dusting myself off trying to shake off the growing terror at what had just about happened.

The memories of Tammy, Randy, so many others all flooding in my head. I couldn't afford a break down, so I took a deep breath focusing on CJ's face. "So you come here often," I smiled through my tears.

She looked sad. "Poor baby. You sure you're okay sweetheart? You need to report those bastards."

"They won't do anything CJ, you know that. Especially since Psycho is dressed like that. They will say she asked for it. Don't even put the girl through the bullshit. I think she's had enough. Oh, I am Diane, CJ's girl," said the dark-haired Diane as she finally caught up to CJ and me.

I shook Diane's hand ignoring the shock of it. These two were my heroes. I would have let them French kiss me had they wanted to. It would have been less than what would have happened had they not been hell bent to get me into their membership rolls.

CJ snorted, "Baby you are right but still. These assholes can't just run loose getting away with whatever they want. Something must be done. Just because we are different doesn't mean the law doesn't apply to us."

I nodded. "Yes, you are right. I seriously cannot thank you enough. However, Diane is right. I will not waste my time reporting it. I would waste the afternoon, get a lecture about how I dress, then sent packing to be attacked later anyway." I sadly realized I would have to start carrying a weapon to defend myself on the fucking campus. Who has to do that.

CJ must have read my mind. "Look Psycho, Diane and I head this way on Tuesdays and Thursdays. We will walk with you from now on to keep those bastards off you. They may come back and try again you know." She looked off in the direction they had run.

I smiled. "I will accept your offer happily, CJ. I thank you both again. I need to get going though. My ride may leave me stranded if I mess around too long. You are more than welcome to tag along."

CJ looked at Diane. "See told you she is cool as hell. Now Psycho, you must become a member of our LGBT group. We are fighting to stop that kind of shit that just happened," she said as w began walking back to the parking lot and awaiting Stacey.

I snickered,. "I told you CJ I am not a lesbian or bisexual. I am pansexual and D/s. I pointed at my collar and chest harness. I don't belong in your group."

Diane looked at CJ then they both started laughing hard. I was a bit miffed thinking they were making fun of me. "Excuse me. What is so fucking funny? I didn't laugh at you for being lesbians."

That made them laugh even harder. Finally, CJ caught her breath. "Psycho, pansexual and D/s are also welcome. We include every lifestyle that is not heterosexual. I guess I should have told you that."

I narrowed my eyes. "Okay fine, but why is that so fucking funny?"

She looked at Diane. "Well, Diane and I were just talking about the pansexual before we saw that bullshit those guys were pulling. It is just weird to meet one. Neither of us have before."

I stopped. "You haven't? I assumed if you have a group that includes them, there should be a bunch of us around here." I looked at CJ hard.

She shook her head. "Nope. We have several bisexuals, even a few that are transgendered but no pansexual people. Until now that is." She smiled as she handed me the signup sheet and pamphlet she had tried to give me the Tuesday before.

I took them politely assuming it was the least I could do after she had literally saved my ass. "Okay, well, what do I have to do?"

She pointed to the paper. "Just sign up and bring me back the sheet. Where it says sexual orientation there is no place for the pansexual so just write in *greedy*."

I broke out in laughter as did Diane. "Damn CJ. Way to not judge there, darling."

She smiled big. "Hey just saying. Pick a fucking team will you."

I smiled big back. "I did. I picked the whole team, oh and the coach too." I winked, which sent them both into riotous laughter.

The three of us were laughing and yapping about the LGBT meetings while we approached Stacey's car. CJ stopped, looking at the ride in pure adoration.

"Oh boy a Z28. I love this car. Beautiful." She made a face of approval.

I could see Stacey inside the car fuming staring at the lesbian/transgendered couple I had just drug along behind me. I smiled at her as I allowed the ladies to give me a hug goodbye. I didn't do that to rub it in Stacey's face I think, but because they had just saved me from being gang raped. I was beyond grateful to my newest buddies, and much needed support system. Besides, I had just found out, I am one of them.

To her credit Stacey said nothing that day or the next day. However, I could tell, it was burning inside of her. She wanted so badly to tell me what a freak I had become. In her mind I was a witch, who lived with a woman, slept with everyone, wore bondage gear to class and now was bringing more of my nasty kind around. It was very clear; this was blowing her small mind right to smithereens. The countdown to confrontation had begun.

That weekend true to her word, my glorious Mistress's moving truck arrived. I aided her and the crew to pack up her belongings. She didn't own a terrible amount, so it only took the morning with a group of five of us boxing and wrapping her stuff. The fellows did raise an eyebrow when they got to her bedroom and began to haul out the boxes of BDSM toys and other gear. My Mistress told me later all three of them had offered both of us their phone numbers. I bet. The idea of a good looking, young, kinky, red-head and submissive blond who were obviously into each other were most fellow's wet dream come true. Needless to say, the boys were left with only their fantasies of what was going on in our bedroom to keep them warm at night.

In reality, it was hotter than hell in our boudoir no doubt. Once the kids would go to bed for the night, Mistress Ginger would pull out all the stops. Now that we were all together under one roof, I got very acquainted with the ball gag, I am a screamer remember, so that we didn't wake the children with our 'fun and games' BDSM style. I still was not okay with her need to thud to get her rocks off, but by now I had started to accept that was just the way it was going to be. My Mistress was good to me in every other way. I had decided if this was the only complaint I had, best to just have her gag me so I kept my stupid mouth shut.

It was wonderful to finally have my children back with me full time. Mistress Ginger was also happy to have little ones around. My daughter was now almost school age and my son was three. They were curious, intelligent, well-mannered and above all my own flesh and blood. We all celebrated with a 'Barney' party. If you don't know who Barney the Purple Dinosaur is then you are one lucky person. I still cringe at that damned icon to this very day. What parents will do for their kids, eh? Mistress Ginger was everything one could hope for in a partner of any kind. A beautiful woman, a strong lover, resourceful, clever, loving mother figure for the kids, attentive to my own shortcomings, and above all structured. That first two weeks went smooth as chocolate silk pie. If my life had always been so peaceful, I would have almost have no story to write today. However, like all good marriages the honeymoon was about to be over.

DISCUSSION ABOUT MY SEXUAL PREFRENCE: *When schizophrenia kicked in my ability to feel true desire was ripped away. It belongs to Simon. Desire is what you beauties feel when you look at someone or something and think I HAVE TO HAVE THAT NOW. It is what fantasies are made of. You don't have to touch a person's unit to cause them to want to desire someone they find pleasing to look at for example. I do not have such a beautiful gift any longer. It sucks to be me.*

114

Left with a sex drive that is set off only by stimulation of the parts (no desire or psychological interest is not fun), there was no longer a true distinction for any gender other than if they could do the job as Master or not. I am a slave to hormonal drives, or like eating, I require reminding to attend to my own sexual needs. So, there it is. I identify as pansexual not because I was born that way, but because I was bent and twisted that way.

PS: One side effect caused by this fact is that I could be with anyone without it bothering me at all. Old, ugly, young, beautiful, kind or cruel, didn't matter, I didn't have desire for any of them. What could cause me to become interested in obtaining more stimulation from them was how they treat me. If they always attempted to get me to ecstasy, I was happy to return repeatedly to their bed. If they do this enough, I will then feel attachment for the person who is as close to desire as I ever get. I can look at a person's unit, male or female, and view it as beautiful in an artistic fashion. That is not the same thing as wanting to sleep with them. I find all of you amazingly beautiful and my Master Jon is very handsome. I even appreciated Mistress Ginger's and Roary's unit as being well lined, but that is fact. See the difference?

The serious issue with the female most males do not require is the high level of psychological affections. That is one area that due to the ravages of my illness I found incredibly hard to provide. I couldn't even find affection for myself, much less for my girl. Mistress Ginger had very harshly pointed this out during her second collaring lessons. She was a very strong-willed woman, but she was

still a woman. Much to my disappointment, she was already demanding I show her outward affection to prove to her that she was my one and only.

Romance was just not my forte beauties. My cold, harsh, and aloof schizophrenic personality would continually trip me up in my bid to try to completely please Mistress Ginger. I was simply untrained in this area. No one had ever asked me before her to love them. This was going to be one uphill battle.

I could not even tolerate kissing due to my tactile hallucination of 'shock.' This experience hurts like hell when another touches my unit anywhere. I could overlook it if the touching was on parts that could set off more powerful experiences, hence I was able to have sexual congress without too much intolerance.

However, to ask me to endure the kind of pain it causes by placing a mouth onto mine was beyond cruel. The very thing that is supposed to be a type of foreplay and allegedly sets off lustful mechanisms does exactly the opposite to me. It feels like someone is chewing off my face with a mouth full of puppy teeth. Yeah that is a perfect analogy. If it felt that way every time your lover kissed you on your mouth, I bet you would say pass just like I do.

Chapter 28: What's My Charisma
Mistress Ginger

In this chapter we will examine the reign of Mistress Ginger deeper than we have thus far. That means you may want to lock the door, put the kids to bed early and remember to expand your mind to its limits. This wild woman didn't respect the laws of physical. She never seemed to know when she had enough nor did she respect when we had reached our limits.

We will have to draw lines in the sand and force our own Mistress to remember her own promises to our collar. This is not something we are used to handling, nor are we in any mood to learn it. Our red-haired Goddess still carried her own baggage from past pains. She tends to point fingers at our hang ups while refusing to acknowledge many of her own. The drama and chaos she will bring into our life is not necessary worth the pleasure she brings us when the ropes come out. Mistress Ginger will soon be forced to recall we are not a submissive no matter how much she would like to believe we are.

Ready to take another trip to 'pleasure town?' Oh, we do hope so. There are so many windows to look through in this village of the forbidden. For this kind of shopping you can leave your wallets at home. We are neither going to buy nor will we rent. This is for the pure joy of visual stimulation only is.

For us, it will be a journey we have already taken and hated. Turns out we still do. Too bad for us, our Mistress doesn't have the same aversions. She will leash us then pull us hard through this most annoying but incredibly sexually charged chapter in our memory. So, you all start on the right of the road, we will be over here on the wrong side waiting for you to catch up.

"Mistress forgive me, but I have to ask you to cut out your bad behavior. You were warned to stay out the business of the Green Rings during our submission ceremony. You agreed to release your control during my religious duties. If you persist in your attempts to butt into a world that is forbidden by our contract, I will be forced to punish you. Neither of us wants that, now do we?" **Psycho warning to Mistress Ginger just after Mabon Sabbat, September 1994.**

The first two weeks under my new Mistress's reign had been a time of awakenings and facing old demons head on. I had finally re-united my family under one roof, and with her help rid myself of the horrid June at my place of employment. Classes had been going well, once again I was demonstrating my prowess as a top-notch student. I had even managed to create a new support system though my association with the power couple of CJ and Diane. My prodromal had appeared to slow down in progression to a baby crawl. My beloved Mistress Ginger had held back the beast of acute by structured, strict adherence to my medication regiment. Things were finally looking up in my life for a change. Even my Coven was doing well.

Everyone was preparing for Mabon and the 'great mass initiation ceremony.' Mother Delleh had cancelled Lughnasah but was planning to repay the Gods by mixing the Festival of Bread with the Fall equinox celebration. At the Green Temple it was all anyone could talk about. My Coven of eight plus its Priestess would soon be full with a membership of twenty-seven. My Mistress had stepped out of her place within the Circle as agree during our submission ceremony. Much to my displeasure, however, she was now hedging our deal by demanding she come to Springfields with me to witness the passing of many white cords. She explained she would not interfere and my 'temporary forgiveness' of submission would still be granted during the Sabbat, but I didn't like it. If she was in the same area with me, my training would almost guarantee a need to 'mind her' commands. For me this was just intolerable, but no matter how much I protested she would not hear me. We were about to end our honeymoon phase and re-enter the real world.

In every relationship no matter normal or alternative, there will be disagreements. Just because Mistress Ginger and I were actively engaging in a D/s marriage of sorts, it did not prevent this human tendency. I am not a submissive no matter how much Mistress Ginger was trying to make me into one. I may mind, but if I am pissed on or off, I tend to make it clear I will obtain retribution in one form or another. Submissive behavior would dictate that I accept whatever the Mistress desired and always submit my reasons to the ideal that she is 'always right.' However, because I am something else this shit doesn't fly with me.

NOTE: *I am a service for service kind of creature. If the service is shit, shit is what you will get in return. Fairly balanced and mirrored. I will mind my Master/Mistress in every way, but woe to the one who demands I do things that are not fair or the one who doesn't hear my warnings. I always tell a Keyholder when they are crossing my lines. If they don't choose to listen, then I don't hear suddenly either. That is just the way this works. Too bad my Mistress never did learn that little fact. She would never accept that she had collared a reflection of her own desires and not a trusting submissive. In the end, it is likely what caused this relationship to dissolve so suddenly despite its initial good tidings.*

PS: The end to my peaceful run of good luck began on a Monday only one week before the Mabon Sabbat scheduled for Saturday. Stacey would begin my week of extreme stressful agitation that would eventually lead up to a Psycho blow up of epic proportions the following week. In this chapter we will examine the reasons behind one of the most violent arrests I'd had to that date. It was driven by extreme stress, purposeful setting off my many triggers by my Mistress, and my weakening mental health. I would like to take just a second to apologize to Dennis, even though he is now in the Summerlands, just in case he is able to see this or knows about it by now. I never told him what happened, but he certainly was the hapless victim of my displaced anger over these next several events. So on to the story as I can recall it.

Stacey pulled up and picked me up from my yellow house. Mistress Ginger was going to watch the children while I attended my classes. She had decided to play the role of the stay at home partner for now anyway. My Mistress knew if the kids got to be too much, Maiden Mary was always happy to take up the slack. For now, this was Mistress Ginger's way of trying to save money for our future move back to her home state. I just shrugged when she told me she was capable of handling two little ones under the age of five. It seemed out of character for my tough and sexually charged Mistress. However, who was I to question what hidden faucets to her personality I had yet to witness. Maybe she did have a softer side. I did doubt it, but she wanted to tackle this problem, and it was her right to try.

I had made it clear that while I was not against corporal punishment, I did not employ it myself. My inner anger was too significant to ever dare raise a hand toward my children. I had made a promise to myself and Simon that I would never touch my kids in any other way then loving. As for the use of spanking for my Mistress, since my young were separate from my key and collar, she was to mind my wishes regarding their treatment and upbringing. I would not allow her to use such methods to correct poor behavior.

Maiden Mary had managed to get them to behave without such brutal force, and my Mistress would do the same. If she couldn't follow my instructions, then I would remove them from her presence. She may have been a liar in most other areas, but my Mistress was honest when it came to my son and daughter. She didn't break her promise to punish without anger or laying a hand on them her entire reign. Good thing for her.

Stacey started the ride quietly. Since we had started riding together again, she had thus far kept her promise to mind her own business. However, after witnessing two full weeks of my hanging out with the likes of CJ and Diane who now walked me to the car almost every school day, she was becoming fed up with holding her tongue.

"Psycho, why are you hanging out with that dude woman and that lesbian? It looks really bad you know," she said while clearing her throat trying to appear calm.

I snorted. "I was nearly raped on campus, Stacey. That dude woman and lesbian saved me from a horrible situation. For your information, they are both lesbians and together. So, I would appreciate your watching your mouth about shit you know nothing about."

She shook her head. "If you wouldn't dress like a, uhm, that, the boys wouldn't have assumed they could have their way with you Psycho. Start dressing normal and you won't have to hang out with the likes of them." She wrinkled her nose as if she smelled something bad.

Now I was angry. "Excuse me? Do you hear yourself, moron. It is okay for boys to rape a girl in a pack just because she dresses in a certain way? Exactly who decides what is 'rapable' attire, smart ass? You? Them? Who, Stacey."

She sneered, "You know damned well that shit you wear is just asking for trouble. Plus, you are fooling around with other women in public. What does your girlfriend think of that Psycho? If I were her I would be watching you like a hawk."

I widened my eyes at that, "Seriously? You are the worst kind of woman on earth. Do you know why men think they can treat women like shit, Stacey? Because your kind sit around justifying their bad behaviors such as isolating their female partners and feeling entitled to injury and rape a girl because in his own mind he makes excuses for his impulsive lusts. You must have lived a very sheltered life to still buy into this misogynistic bullshit. Talking to a woman or a man does not automatically mean you are fucking them. Do you know what I think, Stacey? I think you are not only secretly wanting to fuck me yourself, but I also think you are the jealous one, not my Ginger."

Stacey gasped. "That is not true. Take that back."

I smiled evilly. "Oh I won't. I have recently been taught lessons about telling the truth, Stacey. I have decided to stop lying to myself. You should do the same, darling. It is okay. If you gave me one second of your time, I could rock your world." I winked at her.

She started to fake retch. "Oh my God, you are such a freak."

I laughed. "Oh you have no idea, darling, but I would love to show you. Let me have a talk with Ginger. One night with me, and I can change your religion."

"Shut up, Psycho. Shut up now. I mean it," she screamed nearly busting my eardrums.

I got close to her ear and whispered, "Okay sweetheart. Just remember the offer is there if you ever change your mind. Oops, I mean, if you ever want me to change your mind that is. I know what you dream at night when you think no one is around. I would take you there, but you must be ready to take that ride. Once you go, there is no coming back." I then grabbed her knee and squeezed it.

I felt her swoon, she really did, as sweat broke out on her forehead. "Cut it out or so help me find another ride you psycho motherfucker."

I laughed loudly. "Ah. You are so fucking right. It is about time you saw me for what I really am, Stacey."

She reached over blasting her radio top volume to drown out my insane laughter as we finished our ride to class.

Once we arrived CJ and Diane were hanging out in the parking lot waiting on me. They had been working hard to try to increase the sign up for their application on charter. I was not any good at getting new recruits but intelligent enough to help them navigate the legal speak of the college's application process. They had a question from the form they hoped I could answer.

Stacey got out of the car slamming the door and racing off in a hurry. I got out still chuckling at this dumb girl's homophobic overreactions.

"What flew up Stacey's ass," asked CJ as she and Diane approached me.

"Me, she hopes." I started giggling.

I suddenly realized that I maybe was acting a tad bit too giggly over this stressful circumstance. I started to worry I was starting a psychotic episode. My biggest fear was that I would have a schizophrenic blow up at school and get put back into the Snake Pit over it. This was a realistic fear since I was heading closer and closer to an assured complete break with reality from the acute cycle. The problem was, neither Mistress Ginger nor I had considered an emergency plan if such a terrible situation were to occur. This left me wide open to a serious threat since episodes are far more common when I am under stress. Nothing on Earth was as stressful as college. It was just a disaster waiting to happen.

NOTE: *I had been aware for some time that Stacey had a secret crush on me. Yeah, she did, and in time would admit to it. It is amazing how many people around me would eventually confess up to dark fantasies where I was the star. I am not that pretty, and as for anything else I may possess; it is somewhat of a mystery. The only thing I have ever been able to identify is that I have a strong sexual charisma (or did in my youth). It is possible that my lack of care about societal views, and appearance of strength may have driven some of it. Hard to be sure since I am not sure such a thing as charisma is definable. If we look at the actual definition: "compelling attractiveness or charm that can inspire devotion in others," and "a divinely conferred power or talent" it is possible that I have such a gift.*

The other possibility is that in a time and town of great repression of sexual expression, I represented to some the ultimate free love icon. That is again, due to a very errored perception of who I was and am based solely on the way I dressed (which wasn't even selected by my own damned hands) and by my ineffectiveness at hiding my Keyholder relationships (also not up to me). I had to protect the true nature of my situation with each Master, so on the surface it seemed that I was having a full-blown wanton sexual affair with others of the same sex. Okay yeah, I was but it wasn't quite what the normals thought, except for Mistress Ginger. That was exactly what everyone thought. She was happy to demonstrate our passionate interests for each other's unit in public as often as she could..

I tried going to class but the giggling was getting stronger. I politely excused myself from CJ and Diane assuring them I would get back to their question as soon as possible.

I took off back to Stacey's car terrified as I felt my mind beginning to crawl around inside my skull. There was no longer any doubt. Stacey's little confrontation had set off a chain reaction. I was going to take a trip to Mars, and there was no one around to help. The terror at being helpless in a strange town, with cops who would not know to 'not shoot' sent my disease into pure horror overdrive.

Thank the Gods, CJ had noticed my strange behavior as she and Diane had broken off to go to their own classes. She decided to linger just a bit by a window and saw my hurrying back to the parking lot by sheer chance.

This set off alarm bells in CJ who still didn't know about my disease. I was never in a hurry to divulge such information until forced to do so. It was pure instinct only seen in one who has true feeling of concern for the welfare of another. CJ told Diane she was going to see if I had just forgotten a book, or if maybe there was something more.

NOTE: *CJ was one intelligent girl. Well, CJ was not a gal to be realistic. She had discovered very young that she was born the wrong gender for her brain. At the age of twenty-five she had begun the process of fixing her birth defect by starting the long process of transition from Cindy Joe the female to CJ the man. Diane was his loving partner in all ways. She was a hard-core lesbian but for CJ she did change teams as the transition progressed. In the Fall of 1994, when I met CJ and Diane, the transition had only just begun. He had not even started the hormones yet. So, please understand currently CJ was still identifying as she to the world at this phase of the story.*

In another five years, CJ would be the man he was always meant to be. I only state this so you can follow it as CJ goes from, she to he. You will also note that I discuss this person in the past tense. Yeah, suicide. I know that doesn't surprise you. Since the incidences of suicide among those who are transgendered are so high. Sadly, poor CJ was not an exception to that rule. He couldn't ever find happiness and peace in a world just not ready to accept him as a fellow human being. All they ever could see was what was in his fucking pants, or not in this case.

I was still not completely gone by the time CJ reached my unit trying like hell to get back into Stacey's car. For whatever reason I believed if I could find a place to hide, I could ride out the episode without being caught, shot or hauled off to some jailhouse I didn't know.

The world was already shifting beneath my feet, and my brain was about to slid to the left. I couldn't swallow. Drool was pouring from my mouth in buckets. CJ came toward me asking what was going on. I saw her and backed up terrified.

"Get away from me," I yelled looking around wildly as the world began to flicker and constrict with psychotic flow.

CJ was stunned unsure what to make of the situation. "Psycho? What is going on? Are you having a seizure? Holy shit. What is happening?"

I looked at her terrified. "I am schizophrenic. Help me. Please God help me. I am having an episode. Please don't let them shoot me." I felt my brain slide falling too far to the left as the world went away and I floated into loss of memory and time.

I awoke in an emergency room, strapped to a gurney bed. Next to me was a very scared looking CJ.

I looked at her. "Where am I, CJ? Why am I strapped to this bed?" I began to struggle getting more upset by the second at this weird turn of events.

She backed up from the bed. "Psycho, calm down. You are in the local hospital ER. They had to restrain you. You were trying to beat the shit out of everyone. Including me."

I stopped struggling and looked back at CJ noticing cuts on her arms and knuckles. It was then I noticed my own unit aching from apparent blows, and my ass burned from what I assumed was a shot of sedatives. Apparently, it was Lorazepam, or I wouldn't have been conscious. I would have been off having a love affair with my beloved Prince Val had they given me the good stuff.

I noted there was no IV drip. It would appear they didn't intend to keep me. That made me a bit more than nervous. There are only two reasons they don't start IV drips when I show up in the ER like that. They are kicking me to the streets or they are about to send me to a mental hospital.

"How long was I out? How did you get me here? Did I hurt anyone bad? Are they arresting me? Are they sending me off again," I asked in a flurry of nervous questions.

CJ shook her head. "Uhm, okay. You went whacko about two hours ago. I brought you here after I knocked your ass out when you came at me screaming like I had tried to kill you. Sorry about that by the way. I think they are going to release you to your guardian. She is on her way they told me a bit ago. Good thing you had a wallet on you or I wouldn't have known to call your, uhm, mom?"

I looked at CJ hard. "Ginger is my lover CJ. If you called her my mom in front of her she would kick your ass."

She laughed. "Oh, okay. Well Ginger is on her way. You feeling okay now? I mean, you know who I am?"

I nodded. "Yeah, I guess I need to thank you once again. I am grateful you were there. No telling what would have happened if you, why were you there CJ?"

She shrugged. "Intuition, I guess. Look Psycho, I wish you had just told me about the uhm, well I just wish you had told me. There is no reason to be ashamed of a fucking disease. I already figured you were mentally ill or just weird as hell. I guess you thought I would judge you?"

I nodded. "Or not have any faith that I could be anything other than insane. Look CJ, I would appreciate if you kept this to yourself. I am glad you don't have a problem with it but others, well they use it to take advantage of me. I am not always right in the head. I have to be careful who knows about this."

She smiled. "You bet, Psycho. I get the name now. I must tell you it is cruel as hell that they call you that. I assume you have a real name? I just thought it was a cute little nickname but now that I know the truth I am not sure I can just call you that anymore. It would be like me having the nickname Dyke. It is not right you know? I am sorry I laughed about it too."

I chuckled. "Oh that is okay CJ. My name changes all the fucking time. Everyone has called me Psycho forever. I am quite used to it by now. Doesn't bother me anymore. Knocked me out you said? Damn girlfriend, was that really necessary? I think I am starting to feel it." I wiggled my jaw.

She laughed. "Yeah it was. You sure are strong for such a little thing. I don't think I broke anything on you. I have a brown belt in karate. I was careful as possible I swear it."

Mistress Ginger came running through the door appearing quite concerned just as CJ started explaining to me the basic moves of karate.

"Psycho, oh my poor baby." She ran up throwing herself across my unit as I stared at a very amused CJ watching the drama show.

"Did they hurt you sweetheart?" Mistress Ginger lifted off me and began to caress my face while trying to examine the rest of the unit for marks by pulling at my clothing.

"No Mistress, I am okay. Uhm, thanks to CJ here. CJ this is my Mistress Ginger," I said trying to get her to notice we had company.

Mistress Ginger looked startled that I had addressed her proper. "Psycho? Did you get hit in the head that hard?" She stopped trying to pull off my clothing while staring at me with concern.

I shook my head. "CJ knows about our lifestyle Mistress. She is with the LGBT group at the collage."

Mistress Ginger smiled then turned to CJ. "Oh well, then allow me to thank you for helping out my Psycho with her issue. You can go now. I will take it from here." She turned back toward me not even offering to shake the hand of the person who had saved me from jail or worse.

I raised an eyebrow at what I perceived was rude behavior. "Mistress, can you undo the restraints please?"

Mistress Ginger chuckled. "Oh I don't know. I am getting sort of turned on with you being all tied down like this. Maybe I could just tell the nurse to give us a few moments alone? Why waste such a fine opportunity?" She began groping roughly between my legs appearing not to care that CJ was still in the room or anyone for that matter.

CJ snorted. "Excuse me Ginger, Psycho just had a really bad fit. I am not sure if this is the time or place for that kind of, uhm, stuff. That kind of excitement probably isn't good for her. I think she needs some rest."

Mistress Ginger's face twisted into anger. "CJ is it? I think you need to mind your business. Psycho is mine to do with as I please. I will decide what is good or not you worm."

I almost fainted when she said that. CJ just snorted, "Yeah, okay. Psycho, catch you later, chick." She left the room in a hurry likely afraid she would say something that would cause a scene. I know I would have done the same damned thing had our roles been reversed.

Mistress Ginger looked back at me, her heels now cooled, "Okay what the fuck happened here Psycho? You threw a fit at school? Really? You could have been locked up you know. I am not happy that I had to drive all this way to bust you out of the fucking ER. I thought you said the acute wouldn't come until December?"

She began to loosen my straps. "It won't. I was stressed I suppose. I am sorry Mistress. I tried to get out of there, but Stacey had already gone to class."

Mistress Ginger glared at me. "Okay so let me see. You are trolling around with this Stacey bitch. Now I see you with another woman or was that a man? Psycho, I ordered monogamy you know."

My eyes went wide. "Oh no, Mistress. Stacey and CJ are not like that. I would never, never ever." I couldn't believe this shit. My Mistress was accusing me of fucking these two. What is wrong with everyone these days.

She snorted. "Oh your sexual appetites scare me sometimes, Psycho. I have a feeling if I didn't keep you on a tight leash you would fuck till you died, and with a smile on your face I might add."

Now that pissed me off. "Mistress, I must beg your forgiveness, but that assessment was unfair, unwarranted, and untrue. I only sleep with you and never betray my collar. I have never slept with anyone outside my collar that was not a forced situation or ordered by a Master. I don't choose my partners for pleasure. They are chosen for me. My so-called sexual appetites are dictated by you and only you." I sat up glaring at her as she removed the final restraint.

She growled. "Keep your eyes off me, Psycho. How dare you question my assessment? I believe you are the one court ordered a guardian not me. You can't even remember to take a fucking bath half the time. If I call you a horny bitch, then that is a fact. When we get home, I will correct your mistake in believing you have the right to an opinion unless I give you one. Do you hear me?" She grabbed my collar and shook my unit.

I looked to the floor. "Yes Mistress," I growled.

She had now severely pissed me off. I had not insulted her, yet she comes to my hospital bed after I just had a stress induced episode, to accuse me of betraying my collar. She had also essentially called me the whore even if she had just told June I was not. Worse still, I was going to be punished for denying her misconceptions. Just what the fuck. Equal service for equal service. I did pray she had not forgotten my warning.

I was released and sent with Mistress Ginger. She had to drive due to the amount of sedative they had popped me with. All the way home I listened to her bitch at me about her displeasure that I had not called her immediately when I noticed I was showing signs of psychosis. I didn't respond except, yes Mistress and no Mistress. I was still pissed off that she had told me I was to be punished over defending my honor.

However, when we got home, she didn't punish me as she said she would. For the first several hours every time she would make a sudden move, I would practically hit the dirt. When the first four hours went by without any signs of the Vampire Gloves, leather strap or shock collar being deployed, I finally started to relax. My Mistress had merely spoken out of anger. She had obviously thought better of it and changed her mind. She must have decided I was right.

I was about to learn lesson number three of the D/s lifestyle:

3. ***When a Master/Mistress say you are to be punished,
the time frame for said punishment is at their discretion.
While immediate punishment is often expected, it is not
always the case.*** A submissive should expect that if they are
informed a punishment is due, it will be dealt out without
failure **even if the Master or Mistress is in the wrong.** No
good Master or Mistress would ever make a threat then not
carry out the deed. Lack of consistency is more unforgivable
than being correct in the right to punish. If the Master or
Mistress punishes too often behavior that was not wrong,
there are other ways to compensate the submissive that are
permissible. To continually make threats of punishment but
not carry them out would erode the fear of correction. Over
time, it would lead to a loosening of the strict adherence to
all rules set down during submission. *In other words, it
makes the Dominate look weak to let perceived infractions
slide.*

By the end of the next day, I had already forgotten her
threat of punishment all together. She and I had been getting
alone very well despite the little spat at the hospital that
Monday.

Stacey and I had chosen to not speak to each other for a
while, so the rides were back to an uncomfortable but quiet
truce.

CJ and Diane did not mention my disease and appeared
to be willing to pretend that the whole things didn't happen.

As usual, I was not with reality in thinking that
everything had just magically smoothed over. It was just a

little episode, just a little argument, just a little disagreement, just a little insult, just big trouble waiting to boil over.

Wednesday morning before Stacey arrived to pick me up for class my Mistress asked if I was still off work from the funeral home Thursday night. I nodded that I was. She proceeded to tell me that when I got home to come dress her and myself for the dinner with her friends that had been chronically put off for the last two weeks. Apparently, the couple she wanted to show off to had finally gotten their shit together. I stated I would attend to my commands the second I got back home.

I got into Stacey's car that morning wondering why my Mistress would ask about my being off work Thursday if the dinner was that night. It seemed a bit odd, but then again, Mistress Ginger was often a secretive creature. I didn't always have access to what she had planned or was thinking. A fact that in the end would bite me right in my ass two years later. And on this occasion as well.

My mental health had been holding steady despite the little episode that Monday. Without serious drama or stress in my life, the disease was sitting quiet, waiting out its time to bust into its very active cycle. I felt like I was tip toeing through the tulips everywhere for the two days after the ER visit terrified me that I would have another episode in class or on campus or even during the ride in Stacey's car. It was my anxiety over anxiety that was making a very painful situation a bit more painful than it needed to be. However, I got through the Wednesday without throwing any more fits despite my chronic terror that every sensation felt by the unit was a signal that the end was near.

When I got home, I headed right to Mistress Ginger's room to get her dressed for the dinner. My children were already dropped off with Maiden Mary. My Mistress was asleep taking a likely well-earned nap. The kids could be quite a handful. I awoke her gently then proceeded to attend to her dressing and hygiene requirements. I was again irritated that her choice for my own clothing was the exact opposite of her very racy red latex catsuit. Mine was black and unzipped just below the beasts allowing for my very ample bust to appear almost ready to pop out any second. When my Mistress added my corset and bondage gear, I looked like an extra for some seedy porno flick.

PS: You know the one where the guy comes to the door to deliver Pizza but the whole thing ends up with extra toppings within only a few crappy, poorly written lines of dialogue. If you don't know what I am talking about, I must say this, you haven't lived until you have sat through at least one shitty porno from the 1980s or 1990s. You should do this just once before you take your journey to the Summerlands.

Mistress Ginger saw me pouting as I usually do when I don't agree with a command. "Oh stop it Psycho. You have a gorgeous unit. I am pleased to show it off."

I growled. "As you wish Mistress. However, you know we don't eat turkey eggs because we can't find them. We eat chicken eggs because when a hen lays them, she is quick to tell the world right where she left them." I stared at the ground angrily.

My Mistress began to laugh loudly. "Oh how I love you, Psycho. What a true joy you are. I swear I just can't get enough of you. Now, stop pouting and let's get going Christopher and Joyce are never late."

I nodded glad to finally hear the fucking names of these mystery friends of hers. I drove to the fancy restaurant that had been selected by this Joyce person. The moment I pulled into the parking lot I realized Mistress Ginger and I were not dressed appropriately. This was a swank eatery located in the same town as my college. Things such as caviar and lobster – the good kind not that shit from Red Lobster – were served by the pound. I would have assumed white tie, and ball gown would have been the protocol.

My confusion was evident. "Uhm, Mistress?"

She laughed. "Oh live a little, Psycho. We will give the blue bloods something to talk about for weeks." She commanded I come and let her out of her car.

I did as I was ordered taking deep breaths wondering what would happen in stir with me dressed like this. I doubted I would get bailed out without a few more forced affairs to add to my ever-growing list of them. I was certain that even the cops would be unable to pass up such easy access to my unit with that outfit on.

She got out of the car hand gesturing me to follow in high protocol until otherwise told. I nodded then fell in behind her the three paces to her left side. I did come forward to open the restaurant door but then fell back again always making sure she was front and center of all attention. I was more than happy to let her take that heat. We looked like two street hookers in a country club, and I was in no hurry to push my recent run of bad luck.

The hostess took one look at my Mistress and me and said, "Oh, your party is already here waiting in the back."

She didn't have to even ask the name we were there to see. She knew. That bothered me. Just who the fuck were Joyce and Christopher anyway? I didn't have to wait long. The hostess practically sprinted us to the very back rooms. Her rush through a semi-crowded dining area actually caused more raised eyebrows than our outfits did. It was as if the woman were training for the three hundred yard dash. She was in no mood to have the decent folks' meals ruined by the two trollops. I imagined she was wondering if we managed to save enough from our tricks to afford a nice meal.

We were shown into a back room that had a door for privacy. I sighed with relief realizing at last that we could be dressed that way because the main floor would never see us except in coming in and our departure. However, my relief was fast quashed once the door closed and I got a look at the two mystery guests.

Joyce was a woman near sixty dressed in a cat suit made of blue latex not much unlike my own Mistress. She had long white hair that was pulled up tightly into a bun. Despite her advanced years this woman was still very pretty with a well-defined face, thin lips and bright steel grey eyes. I immediately understood Joyce was also a Dominatrix.

Christopher who sat to her left was a man in his upper thirties. He was clean shaven with large brown eyes and a square jawline. His hair was brown and well-groomed in a spiky hair style. His long-sleeved shirt was made of dark golden color and his pant were black. Both were made of latex. I understood he too was a lifestyler, and to my extreme horror I didn't see a collar around his neck. That meant he was not a submissive. Mistress Ginger had brought me to show off to her Dominant friends.

Now the reason this was frightening to me was that it was hard enough to be judged by one Dominant but to have to sit through a dinner with three of these (sorry Master Jon) nightmares. Well beauties that was stressful. One wrong move and I had six pairs of eyes ready to call me out. My training kicked into high gear as I quickly pulled out the chair for my Mistress and took my place standing behind her with my eyes cast down, and arms behind my back. Looks like no dinner for this idiot.

Now most of you are aware of the lifestyle. Maybe you have read it in books. Maybe a couple have been around people involved in it. Maybe you don't have a clue. Let me say this, I doubt any of you have been in a situation as one in the role of submissive being forced to stand and listen to the conversation between Dominants. Oh my Goth beauties. I was glad I was wearing my high platforms. The bragging, the arrogance, the one-upping, the bullshit, it was sickening.

Now I am not saying all Dominants are like this. However, even my beloved Master Jon will tell you all Dominants are arrogant and willing to let you know all about it. That day, I heard it all in living color.

I just stood there, in my high protocol pose only moving to make sure my Mistress's glass stayed full, or to put a napkin in her lap. Otherwise, not a peep or stir came out of my unit. I never made eye contact with any of them. I was not on the same level, and according to the rules, lucky to be in the same fucking room with such royalty.

It was my understanding that Joyce was a long time, well celebrated Dominatrix in the small community around that area. Christopher had been trained by her in his twenties. They both bragged about how many submissives and slaves they now commanded, and how much scratch they were paid to attend these weekend kinksters.

My Mistress seemed to enjoy listening to these two blowhards. However, when her turn came to brag very proudly she announced her submissive was full-time and collared plus 'old school trained.' That seemed to impress the two very much. She informed them she had me 'completely under her thumb' and I possessed over fourteen years of training in all areas of service. That of course raised their eyebrows until she informed them, I was from a rogue House and raised illegally since childhood. They both informed her that despite their abhorrence at such foul misuse of any child she was very lucky to have one who didn't know any other life. I didn't have to look up to feel their eyes running over my unit as they listened to her describe my incredible training, and perfect service to her in all areas.

NOTE: *The difference between a Kinkster and a 24/7 or lifestyler. The kinkster will only engage in the lifestyle on weekends, doesn't live with their Dominant, and while often claims to be collared doesn't follow the Dominant's rules day and night without break. They usually have a normal job and normal life. They are part-time role players who often hide this aspect of their life from those around them. Many must pay a Dominant for the services they provide such as light thudding, or whatever fetish bullshit they are into. That is what Joyce and Christopher were, kinkster Dominants. It is also what my own Mistress had been before she collared her first 24/7 or lifestyler. That would be me.*

My kind is full time, lives with the Dominant, may even acquire employment with the Dominant, and all their funds go into the household income for which they serve. We do not hide our lifestyle status and this is no role play. The rules and punishments of the home are not for pleasure as it is for the kinkster. Such things are in place to protect and defend the submissive who is often incapable of doing such things for themselves due to disease, or personality defect. The 24/7 will create a hopefully lifelong bond with the collar holder. It is like a marriage without the legal papers, only with strict rules and roles for each partner. I am a 27/7 who always minds my Master. I am not impressed or turned on by the aspects of BDSM because unlike the kinkster this is not a fetish. Certain things such as thudding and bondage are indeed a part of my life and must be expected and accepted due to the nature of the usual personality type that becomes the Professional Dominant. The pleasing of my Dominant is my ultimate goal. I expect them to return the services (even tolerance of the above) by protecting me from myself, granting shelter, attending to things I am incompetent in, fulfilling my court ordered guardianship, and if I am lucky providing affection that I would never receive due to my serious impairments in the real world. My Master should be investing a lot of time in my care, so I invest just as much back. If he wants to thud, tie me up or walk me naked in the front yard, he gets it with a smile and "thank you for the pleasure to serve you Master."

Do you know why? Because of the constant psychotic cycling, the thwarting of at least one attempted kidnapping, the fact that I have not starved to death, have a Goth house all to myself, Simon can live with me in the open, Master Jon loves me, gave me fur babies all of my very own, a hundred other kindnesses, and love me (oh I said that twice, it is because I like that one the best.

Of all my Masters and Mistresses he has never raped, assaulted, stolen, used, or abused nor allowed anyone else to do these things to me. Now that you are reading my story, you are realizing how rare this kind of person really is in my lifestyle or in any lifestyle. Not all my Keyholders knew shit about my very service oriented world, all will attempt to learn, and all but Master Jon failed.

I will not get into what makes a Dominant a professional and worthy of a 24/7 role but will leave that to my own Master Jon if he cares to share such information.

143

Mistress Ginger's problem is she is still behaving as if she is dealing with a kinkster in many ways. This will result in much aggression, resentment and eventual retaliation from her very well trained so-called submissive. Again I provide service for service and yes this is a real thing. But again we get ahead of ourselves. Back to the show.

Mistress Ginger went on to brag a great deal about my talents, especially those in the bedroom. I stood there irritated at this silly fool. It seemed to me bad manners to discuss the personal aspects of my special services of the collar to those who she is not intending to sell my collar to, wait, was she? Oh shit.

Terror gripped me the more she bragged about all the things I could do, the potential things I likely could learn. I could almost hear those two wolves licking their chops across the table. She eventually had me kneel before her using only her hand gesture, then commanded me to fill the other two Dominant's glasses also using only her hand signals. The two were quite impressed. I could feel them both looking up and down my unit like I was on the menu.

"So, how much for the collar, Ginger," said Joyce while looking at her plate as if not that interested.

Mistress Ginger practically purred, "Oh my goodness. No way I could part with this most magnificent submissive for any price, Joyce."

Joyce looked up glaring. "Then make a note when you tire of your plaything you offer me first bid on it. I am sure I could make much better use of it than to parade it around like a show pony. Fine submissive flesh such as this should be training other submissive and slaves. You are wasting this opportunity with stupid tricks and wanton pleasures," she said sternly. I already hated this bitch

Christopher laughed. "Easy mother. Ginger can do as she pleases with her playthings. You are just jealous that old school teaching is out the window. No one wants to put up with stuffy, outdated old rules and protocols anymore. Get with the times." I also hated this guy right away.

Mistress Ginger snickered. "Oh you two fight it out if you like but I have to use the little Mistress's room. Psycho, you will attend your Mistress."

I pulled out her chair then, pushed it back in standing back and bowing as she passed. Taking my place three paces behind I followed only jumping in front to open doors in her path but then quickly dropping back to take my place behind her once more. I was aware this trip to the bathroom was designed for her to show off my abilities to know my high protocol behaviors to these two magpies.

Once in the bathroom, thankfully we didn't have to walk through the main dining hall to get to it, she turned and looked at me laughing. "Did you get a load of those too dipshits?"

My eyes went wide. "Mistress, I would not dare to call any Dominant such a thing."

Mistress Ginger laughed. "Oh, of course you wouldn't Psycho. At least not where anyone could hear it. But you are thinking it. I can tell."

I looked at the floor. "If you wish to believe I would think such a thing, then so be it Mistress." I dared not lie, because I was indeed thinking it.

She laughed while she stood staring at me. "We will stand here a bit to make this look like a real trip to the bathroom. When we return, I will tell them I have a headache, and we are going to get the hell out of here. Christopher is a hottie, but I can't stand another second of that fucking dust bunny Joyce. Not even to stare at that beefcake."

I was surprised. "I don't understand Mistress. If you want to be with Christopher than why not just meet him and leave her out of it?" I didn't get that at all.

Mistress Ginger had not ordered her own monogamy. She had kept the right to sleep with whomever she saw fit. Many of my Keyholders would do such a thing. I didn't care. They are not my spouses and if someone else is holding their attention it gave me the night off.

She wrinkled her nose. "It is complicated Psycho, but Christopher is off limits to me. Just understand his D and my D are not allowed to mix. That dry bitch Joyce is to blame, or I would have jumped his bones more than a year ago. Now come on, you ask too many questions. You are supposed to look beautiful and be quiet. Follow me and later I will find a use for that pretty mouth that is more pleasing."

I followed her out a bit perturbed that she had been so damned insulting about the special services of the collar. It seemed that such a thing should not be used to debase my worth like that. I provide many services, and that one always seemed to be the one that trumped them all. I would think always having someone around to get your remote control, tell you a story or joke, answer the fucking phone or even run your bath would be of more pleasure and usefulness. But what do I know?

As we started to leave the bathroom an older lady dressed in the finest of dresses, wearing very expensive perfume came in the door. She took one look at Mistress Ginger and I and about shit herself with disgust.

"Oh, my Lord. Who let the likes of you two in here." She said in a deep southern drawl while gripping her chest as if she were about to have the big one.

Mistress Ginger looked back at her, remember I was behind her three paces, then stopped. I went to open the door for her but she hand signaled for me to come to her immediately. I was confused but did as she ordered. She grabbed my unit roughly then pushed me into the bathroom wall with much force. Before I could recover, she covered my unit with hers in a lover embrace groping my crotch with one hand and sliding the other into my half open shirt exposing one of my breasts. She then forced her mouth to mine once again playing tonsil hockey with her tongue. I was in shock, but not as much as that old lady who had made the rude comment.

Mistress Ginger had her back to her, but I was stuck looking directly at the woman while my Mistress fondled me both through and under my clothing. My Mistress appeared so wanton I wondered if she had been slipped some Spanish Fly or something in her drink.

The woman's eyes were wide, but she didn't move a muscle as if she had seen Medusa herself and turned to stone. I tried to reach down to pull my Mistress off my uhm, who ha (LOL) but she grabbed my arm pushed it above my head then to my absolute shock put her mouth on my exposed breast loudly sucking the nipple. I swear, Kodak was made for the look on that old crone's face. I swear the color drained from her face and it turned at least ten years older in seconds. She let out a yelp then ran out the door leaving me still being molested by my own damned Mistress right there in the bathroom of a swank restaurant.

Once my Mistress heard the woman leave, she let me go. I stood there out of breath, warmed up from the very talented advances of my lover. I have to say, damn it was hot in that bathroom. They must have had a broken thermostat or something. I was not sure what to do, so I just stood there still half disrobed and panting.

My Mistress went to the mirror and fixed her smeared lip stick then looked at me. "Psycho, adjust yourself. You can't be running around with your boob hanging out. Everyone will have a heart attack." She laughed at her silly joke.

148

I pulled my parts back into their places not that there was much room it was so tight and tried to shake off the interest my Mistress has set on within by touching me like that. I was ready to finish that business, but she suddenly seemed distracted by her grooming. I shrugged a bit more than disappointed that she wasn't going to tell another of Aesop's Fables. I would have been happy to act out several of them at that point.

As we left the bathroom I began to realize that Mistress Ginger had a habit of grabbing me like that in public whenever she thought the behavior would upset the person(s) around us, and there was no chance of us getting caught. I began to understand this was a turn on for her, or at the very least a way to humiliate the person caught watching her enjoying her privileges to my unit. That epiphany sort of irritated me a bit. I thought she was just unable to control her urges for me. It sucked to know I was just a piece on her chess board game against society. She only wanted me at those moments because it stirred up the normals and because I was not allowed to tell her to stop. It was perfect for her to get a cheap thrill and would rarely lead to any orgasms for me. Since she was always the aggressor it would be my unit exposed not hers to some poor unwitting witness. What was I thinking anyway? I mean there was no way anyone would be so overrun with lust that they just couldn't wait for a better moment. I had been a stupid little fool to not see the obvious. Even the day in the ER had been for CJ's benefit not my own. Oh well, it sucks to be me.

As she commanded, we made our excuses and headed home. That night she thudded me much harder than she had been while appearing quite frustrated. I didn't understand but did my best to endure it. She ended up having to gag me to keep me from yelling out in agony loud enough to wake the neighbors. She had left the kids with Maiden Mary for the night. So, I had to put up with a lengthy session of her strange mild irritation behaviors. I didn't ask what had gotten her upset. I couldn't anyway, I had a ball gag in my mouth.

The next morning, I got up and ready for my lab as usual for Thursdays. She told me that she was leaving the kids at my Maiden's house for the night. My Mistress said she needed a breather from Barney and juice boxes.

I was unhappy to hear that. My ass was still flayed from the thudding that night. I would be sitting gently all day. I assumed with the kids gone she would be seeking more of the same. Her demeanor was off, but for the life of me, I couldn't figure out what was going on in her head. I am not supposed to read a Keyholder's mind but that morning I was tempted. Stacey showed up a bit early, so I never got around to it. I wish I had. It could've at least prepared me for later that day if nothing else.

School was uneventful, and Stacey was still sullen. I arrived home right on time. I no more got through the door that my Mistress commanded me to head for our bedroom. I groaned but went as I was told. I was just tired and sore. It seemed that surely, she had been stated enough only a few hours before. I was starting to fear she was a nymphomaniac like the beast who shall not be named.

Once in the room, I was told to strip down. After I was sky clad Mistress Ginger wasted no time binding my arms and wrists together, then she put a ball gag in my mouth. I watched completely confused when she retrieved a chain leash from her basket of BDSM toys in the closet. I hadn't seen one of those since the days of Master Julie. I was in no hurry to see one that day either. I tried to back up when she came to affix it to me. She grabbed my collar and pulled it hard locking it in place with a small padlock. I groaned recalling my long, horrid history with this kind of leashing.

She told me to stand up and follow her. I did as command completely confused at this very strange game she was playing. She pulled me down the hallway back to the living room. My Mistress took a seat on the couch then told me to kneel at her feet. She was still holding the leash like I was a fucking dog. I glared but did as told. Luckily the house was warm. She pulled out one of her romance novels and started reading completely ignoring my naked, kneeling unit.

The ball gag is not very comfortable. I was ready to have a cow at having to wear it for several hours while my Mistress pulled this weird ass shit on me. It didn't take long for the drool to start to flow. That made her giggle when she finally looked up to see me helpless to do anything about the rivers of spit rolling down my chin. My arms were bound behind me elbows and wrists. Even Dennis's handcuff couldn't have done a better job at keeping me from fighting back or at least wiping my fucking mouth.

After about an hour of this bullshit she put down her book then looked at the clock.

Stretching and smiling she said, "So, it is time to punish you for talking back to me in the ER Monday. I have decided to leash you to a male Master for the night. You will learn to appreciate the kindness I show you after you have had some experience with the harsher side of this lifestyle. I noticed all your Masters have been women so far. Well Psycho, I can't sleep with Christopher, but he can certainly sleep with you. I am using one of my leash privileges but only for this one night. You will obey him, but you are still mine. I will be there watching the whole time. It will solve two problems for me. One it will let me see if he was worth wanting in the first place since I will see his prowess in fucking. Second it will teach you to appreciate what you have. I won't let things get out of control, but I will join in and enjoy my own privileges with you when and if I desire it. I knew letting him see what I had would drive him bonkers. Well, Psycho baby, he is more than happy to help me keep my girl in her place with a little discipline."

I sat there looking at the floor feeling sick, terrified and betrayed. My Mistress had the right to leash me to another by submission contract, but it was not meant for this kind of use. She was aware leashes were for seeking new Keyholders, or for when she was ill or out of town. To use one not only for her own personal curiosity, to see if Christopher was a worthy lover, but as punishment, which was in my mind betrayal of the foulest kind. She wanted me to trust her to do what was best for me, but this is what I got for it. She was not breaking a rule since this man was being granted only this one-night privilege by leash right and was a Dominant himself, but still it was beyond cruel.

The beast who shall not be named had done a similar act, but she had made the mistake of demanding full monogamy. She had not demanded leashing rights during submission and ordered that her husband be minded as equal Master. Mistress Ginger was cleverer. She had demanded monogamy until she deemed it lifted, kept leashing rights (only three times per collar) and made it clear this Christopher was only a leash. She was maintaining control over the entire scene.

She had tricked me into bondage and the leash, so I was helpless to run away. She had gagged me so I could not voice my arguments that she was being unfair. All I could do is kneel there angry, hurt and broken hearted. Mistress Ginger didn't love me at all. I was just a plaything to her too, just like I was for everyone else. I had been daft to think otherwise. I decided right then and there if she was going to do this, I would make her pay for it the only route I had available. I would pretend to enjoy this Christopher's actions and make her watch it. I could not stand for another fucking rape, so I directed my attitude towards that of pure sexual drive without caring who was providing the pleasure. She was breaking my heart, now I was going to do my damnedest to break hers back.

Christopher arrived only a few moments after I was told of my fate. I was told to stay kneeling while she answered the door to let him in. I didn't even look up at his smiling face when Mistress Ginger proudly handed him my leash then gave him the news, she was not leaving him alone with me. He told her he understood, then thanked her for sharing her submissive with him for the night. She chuckled and said it was her pleasure.

Christopher tugged my leash then immediately demanded I follow him back to my Mistress's bedroom while the two of them yapped about the weather. I walked behind them wishing they both would catch fire and die. I felt the pain welling inside my chest. The helplessness, the sadness at this horror unfolding. I closed my eyes as Christopher told me to kneel and he began to remove his own clothing. My Mistress was closing the door while I reached deep inside to find the strength to endure this latest indignity of my shitty position in life.

This was something I would have to endure many more times in my life, many, many more times. When you are at the whim of others, their value of your person matters. If you are nothing to them, it is easy for them to put you in a situation where others can also use you for their own desires. No one cares you are a human, that it hurts, that you don't want to do these things. They only see their own needs. It was going to take one hell of an acting job to convince my hateful Mistress that this bullshit was not bothering me. It would take an even better one to make her think I was happy to be with this leash. Well, I should have gone to Hollywood. I would be dusting my awards on my mantel this very day.

When Christopher had removed his last article of clothing, he removed my ball gag and demanded I prepare him for carnal congress. I took care of business appearing more than eager to satisfy. I made sure to wink at my Mistress while making Christopher a slave to my talents. He almost didn't make it to the main event in fact. I smiled at Mistress Ginger evilly as he lifted my unit to take his pleasure intimately. I made as much loud, racket and loud moaning as I could without over doing it as he thrust madly like a man who had not been with anyone in years. That part was not so hard. The fellow was not a bad fuck at all. That was very lucky for me. It didn't hurt that like my Priest he was handsome to boot, and nicely endowed. I wasn't unsatisfied.

My Mistress on the other hand had realized too late, that her punishment was anything but that. I was faking it all at first but as the night wore on, Christopher did much to pleasure me. Since I was a new lover, even after he was spent quickly, he recovered and went for seconds. I was happy to oblige him. This really pissed my Mistress off. I saw jealousy flashing in her eyes. At first, I thought she was angry that I was getting to be with the object of her desires. However, after Christopher's second merging with me, he apparently was getting ready for a third helping. It became very evident at that point I was the object of her desires not him.

He went to try to kiss my unit's breast and she let out a scream, "That is it. Twice is enough, you pig. Get your clothes and get the fuck out, Christopher. Never come back."

He looked up at her surprised. "Ginger, what the fuck? I thought you said Psycho was mine for the night? I could do whatever I wanted. Psycho isn't complaining are you sweetie?"

I smiled at him pretending to pant in desire as he ran his hand down my unit toward my female parts, "No Master, I am here for your pleasure."

Mistress Ginger flew into a rage. She grabbed him by his hair demanding he get off me. He started cussing and she said she would call the cops if he didn't leave immediately. Christopher called her several nasty names but grabbed his clothes putting them on while bitching he was misled and he should own Psycho because he knew how to please a submissive better than she ever could.

All he did was piss her off more. In the end she kicked him in his backside out of her room. I was still bonded with my arms behind my back so I just laid there in the bed snickering as I heard my raging Mistress hurling insults at the Dominant she invited to defile her prize. I felt satisfied partly because Christopher had given me several orgasms. It was also very nice to see Mistress Ginger had gotten her equal service for equal service by the backlash she sent in motion with her own cruelty. She should never have tried to punish me by having me raped. I am the Queen of forced sexual encounters. I had learned how to make lemonade out of lemons. Okay more like orgasms out of sex I never wanted. She was dealing with a professional.

She returned after getting the now very angry Christopher out the door.

He had yelled out, "Psycho baby, you ever want a Dominant that knows how to treat a fine submissive call me.

I would never share you." Then I heard the door slam and my Mistress let out a roar of anger.

I admit it, I was giggling at it. I know I should have been very angry over that bullshit but fuck it. I was tired of being the victim. Mistress Ginger demanded I learn to take back my power and release my anger, well I did it. The fellow was a nice change of pace. Made me miss my Priest.

He was on my mind when my Mistress came into the room with her face as red as her hair. She was beyond livid. I saw her go for the closet to grab the shock collar.

"Uh oh." I thought as I immediately whipped up the tears.

"Mistress please, mercy. Why did you let him do that to me. Please, I need you to hold me. Please mercy," I wailed loudly trying to sound as miserable as possible. It worked.

Mistress Ginger dropped the shock collar. "Oh baby. I am so sorry. I don't know what I was thinking. You poor thing." She came over and held me tightly.

I continued to wail letting all my pain go. I had found a way to guard against the forced sexual encounter with Christopher, but her hurting me like that, well those tears were real. My heart ached. I wanted to love Mistress Ginger, but now it would never be possible. I would never forget that at least this one time she treated me like property, not the human she kept trying to tell me that I was. From that moment on, I never could trust her completely again. I would never had done that to her for a second. I often think of others even when they forget about me. But this was only half the equation that led to the arrest the next week.

Chapter 29: Fall Faster Disaster
Mistress Ginger

"Roses are red. Violets are blue. When Mistress Ginger listens to Psycho's screams of pain, the neighbors do too."
Psycho explaining 'romance' in a D/s relationship to CJ and Diane. September 1994.

Mistress Ginger held me tight now crying herself apparently having a bit of sellers remorse at having shared me with Christopher. It was too late. I would never be able to undo the memory of this forced encounter no matter how much she apologized. The entire event had lasted for well over five hours. In all that time she could have stopped it without my having to go into acting mode. However, she had sat there watching him defile me without even considering my feelings once.

I let her hold me, crying myself. I however was crying for a different reason than her. Her tears were selfish. She was sorry she had abused her plaything. Mine were because I realized she had never loved me. I had wanted her to love me more than anything in the world. I wanted to be loved by anyone more than you can know.

My children loved me that is true, or so I believed. Simon loves me because he is me. Zeppelin had loved me too. The emotion of love is the most wonderful thing in the world. It is the real purpose in life. When everything else is lost, it is the light in the darkness that falls. It will keep you warm on those cold nights, and it will make you get back up when you think you are done. More than anything else it will keep you fighting for another day when pain is all you can feel. I had come to understand if I wanted to survive, eating, bathing, taking my medications, and feeling loved were necessities.

Until Ginger only Simon was aware of the final one. He had encouraged my keeping the children because he knew what would happen if I didn't. If no one loved me, as a mirror, I would never love me. It was disabling enough to have no true inner self, but without self-love I would eventually end my existence no matter what he said or threatened. The children were a temporary solution for him. In time, they would grow up and no longer need us. When that day came, we were doomed.

Our unit would only be young and attractive for a short time. He was in a hurry to find the one who could find love that was not based on responsibility. The kids are an example of responsible love. We needed love for no reason other than because someone cared deeper than just a need to fuck or use us. Looks, youth, strength, only mattered to get someone to see us. Holding on to them would require much more. Since those things are fleeting if we didn't move quickly, there would be less a chance every year.

We were already significantly injured, diseased and terribly scarred up inside and outside. We had almost nothing to offer other than our undying loyalty and service to another. We gave Mistress Ginger and all the others everything we had and it still fell miserably short. My tears that night were very bitter and well earned.

I was just not enough for her, she needed more. I couldn't give more than I possessed. Our relationship was already over before it had even begun. As she lifted my still bonded unit helping me to the bathroom to wash away Christopher, I hardened my heart to her lies of love. There was no longer any doubt in my mind that Mistress Ginger would eventually toss my collar. The only question left was how long did I have before the next nightmare Keyholder came to claim another piece of my soul?

She ran the bath water still refusing to untie my arms. I begged but she wouldn't listen. Once the bathtub was full, she picked me up and put me into the water ropes and all. Mistress Ginger washed my unit roughly with her own hands and a wire Brillo pad. Yeah, you read that right. The water was unreasonably hot, and her cleaning method cruel in my most sensitive parts. I screamed in pain, but she continued as if trying to scour the foulness of Christopher by taking off layers of my skin and mucus membranes. This resulted in heightening my serious PTSD reactions plus it hurt like hell.

I began to freak out, screaming, thrashing, kicking, gnashing, biting and spitting with all I had. Mistress Ginger ignored my obvious signs of complete melt down. She held me down in the water while she continued to almost literally scrub me to the bone. I was bleeding from my intimate places when she finally was finished, scraped raw by her cruel techniques.

She then lifted me from the bloody water and laid me on the floor drying me off then wrapping me up in a big towel. I sobbed feeling tired, frightened, helpless and burning in places where one should never feel such a nasty sensation. I really wanted to just die. I thought I may die, my heart hurt so bad. It was pounding irregularly and fast. Too much, too soon, too bad.

NOTE: *To this day I am unsure what that little scene with the forced scouring bath was about. I wondered, even at that time, if Mistress Ginger was doing that to wash away all evidence of the rape, so I could never go to the cops and report Christopher's and her crime, and that was a crime. I was tied up and it was against my will. This is rape, plain and simple, no matter how much I tried to ignore that fact at the time.*

The other possibility was she was just that upset over her permitting that man to defile what she believed belonged to her. For whatever reason she felt the need to erase all traces of his essence from my unit in one of the most painful and torturous bathing experiences of my entire life. Yeah, I said one of. I have had a rough life. Lots of things that should never hurt or have bad experiences associated with them have been both in my past. Even the normal act of bathing.

She hauled me back to our room and laid me in the bed. Mistress Ginger spooned my unit while I wept myself to sleep. She didn't say a word just held me tightly. My final thought before I feel asleep that night was if this was what love is about I was not sure it was something I wanted.

The next morning she finally undid my bonds. My arms were almost useless from hours of being tied behind my back. I couldn't even take notes, much less sit down thanks to the shenanigans of her and her boy Christopher. Neither of us spoke while I had gotten ready for class. She was quite probably feeling sheepish. I was feeling confused and unsure of what to do to prevent her from further harming my unit. Stacey showed up and I nearly ran out the door. To be honest I was afraid of my Mistress.

That Friday I had a lot of trouble paying attention in class. I was plagued with thoughts about where I was going in life. I had been so busy struggling to survive, to find a Master, and reunite my family I had somehow lost sight of the reasons any of it mattered at all.

Once years before Simon had told me that a college degree would give us the documentation to prove we were someone of worth. He had wanted a family so that we could have a place to belong. The Master was there to help us stay on the path to normalcy or at least the appearance of such a thing.

However, what I had found was a series of persons who were helping make my life more insane than even I could have done without aid. I had been raped twice in less than two months, nearly murdered by one, the other ordered by someone who claimed to love me. This same lover had me unable to sit down and wearing clothing that marked me as a freak in a place that was usually more liberal in acceptance of different. Just what the fuck had gone wrong.

These facts were trapped in the Looper's reports in my ears. The next day I was due to run a religious meeting with hundreds of people there counting on my wisdom to help them find their path to faith. I no longer felt that I deserved such a role since I seemed to be the last one on Earth with any valid answers about anything. I was just a crazy, unreliable, unstable, schizophrenic fool. I was becoming more convinced that in the great game called life, no matter what Mother Delleh tried to tell me, I was going to fail miserably.

This internal feeling of insecurity was eating away at my deeply ingrained need to continue fighting to live like a deadly cancer. Mistress Ginger's attempts to break down my defense mechanisms was the sole culprit of this undertow of self-doubt. She had told me I needed to learn to trust and to be loved. She then began to slowly unravel my complex web of walls. This had kept me insulated from feeling the brutality of other's exploitation of my compromised position in life. Now that my Mistress had been successful in creating a few holes, I was feeling it alright, but it was not the security of trust and love she had promised me. It was fear, insecurity, and helplessness which are the reality of life as an unsupported disabled person.

Good job Mistress Ginger. The notoriously psychologically well armored Psycho was now wounded to the quick. An old delusional process rushed in to try to fill in the gaps of the cracked defenses. **<u>The belief that the hands and tongue attached to my unit are not mine.</u>**

NOTE: *This delusion had been created by Julie during her attempts to force me to admit that I had schizophrenia many years before in 1988. Julie's ignorant and mean forcing me to face facts I was not ready to accept had hurt my faith in myself. You may recall this situation developed in the chapters entitled "Feeling so Schizophrenic" and "Radar Love" back in the earlier parts of this story.*

I have been told, by the psychologists and psychiatrists, an errored belief that my own tongue would never have betrayed me by saying such a lie had developed in response to her cruel forcing of my admission to disease. My hands were also viewed with suspiciousness since they had not found that radar or been capable of keeping Julie off me. Therefore, these items had betrayed my own best interests. My own unit would never due such a thing. Ah, so, then the tongue and hands were clearly not my own. That had to be the answer. My own tongue and hands must have been stolen, and these foul replacements were here to help others hurt me. So they need to go.

My belief (still have this one by the way: I know, I know. I struggle with it constantly. It sounds crazy but then again did you know I have schizophrenia?) is that once these fake or Judas parts are removed from the unit my own will be returned to me. Until they are cut away, I am unable to be sure that they will not betray me to my enemies. They often have in fact. Had it not been for my prime directives from the Masters I would have already completed this mission. I would rant about this one all day if I could, but people are watching. This belief is what has gotten me incarcerated in the past. Okay back to the story.

It was around my last class of the day that I began to obsess on how to rid myself of the offending tongue and hands. My thinking was that if I could just get my own parts back, everything would be alright again. I could stop the aching in my chest caused by my Mistress not loving me as she had promised. I was so damned sure it was because I had said or done something to make her change her mind about what she wanted of me. Well, not me really, it was the alien tongue and hands that did this. They had to go.

This thinking set off the Looper into planning mode. I started feeling less lost and more sure of myself. We believed we had discovered the problem that was causing these epic failures. My mood immediately improved. All I had to do was wait for the blueprints and do what needed to be done. Then Mistress Ginger would love me and never hurt me again. It all made perfect sense if you are a schizophrenic slowly becoming psychotic.

Stacey noticed my odd, preoccupied behavior on the ride back home that day. She seemed to be willing to speak for the first time since I had called her out on her weird crush on me.

"So, I was thinking about how I have been so judgmental towards you, Psycho. I just want you to know I am sorry. I know you are not like those other people. You have always been very fair and cool to me. I had no right to say it was your fault those boys tried to rape you the other

166

week. You are right. No one has the right to rape or hurt other people," she blathered to me.

I shrugged. "I don't really care what you think. Your apology is unnecessary Stacey. I know who you are. I know you will never change because you don't have to. That's fine. Not my business."

She narrowed her eyes. "I am trying to be nice, Psycho. I may not approve of your lifestyle but as long as you keep it to yourself, I suppose it is not for me to say anything. I just know if you keep hanging out with people like that CJ dude and Diane, someone is going to kick your ass eventually. I was trying to be a friend. I guess I went about it the wrong way."

I laughed out loud. "Trying to be a friend? Hmmm, recently I have been told a lot of lies. This one is the biggest yet. I am impressed because believe me I have discovered some real whoppers. Tell you what, let's never be friends, okay? I will sit here quietly, you drive, and we will be acquaintances. I don't think I have enough on my cosmic credit card to afford you as a real friend Stacey. You are too expensive, and the interest rate is fucking insane. Plus, what I'd get isn't even worth a penny. Thanks, but no thanks."

Stacey snorted. "Okay I didn't understand a fucking word you just said Psycho. You are so God damned weird. I don't know why I keep bothering to try to be nice to you. I am beginning to wonder if maybe your crazy is catching."

I just looked out the window ignoring her as she continued to rant about my strange behaviors and insanity. I knew she was just jealous of Mistress Ginger. She had to be aware I would never want to love her. I didn't even find her physically attractive. Stacey was just ugly right to her shitty soul. Besides I had more important things to occupy my thoughts, such as how to make a clean cut of both hands since it would take time for them to grow back. Once I got one off, how would I remove the other smoothly? I had decided to use scissors on the tongue, but an axe would work for the thicker wrists.

When I got home, I noticed my Mistress still had not brough the kids back from Maiden Mary's care. I felt a bit nervous since the night before this had signaled her misuse of her rights to my collar. It didn't take long for me to realize she had every intention to enjoy her full privileges in another way. Mistress Ginger bound me tightly then thudded every inch of my safe zones. She didn't stop until every single spot of my unit was either heavily bruised or striped. My Mistress ignored my cries for mercy giving me no quarter or kindness. When she tired of my wailing, she gagged me so she could continue her art without the irritation of my attempts to get her to lay off.

It was around the time she began to work over my forearms I realized this was not a normal turn on session for her. Mistress Ginger was doing this for a purpose. The next day I was to be Sky Clad running the circle and initiations of the Green Rings at Springfields as the High Priestess. She was aware everyone would see my naked unit, thus her handiwork.

I groaned realizing that she was marking me up the way a dog pisses on a favorite toy. My Mistress was making it clear I belonged to her. More than anything else, this was her way of reminding me – and anyone else who looked at her obvious injuries – that no matter how powerful I was in the Coven, she was still the Dominant over me. It could have been a way to try to humiliate me in front of my Priest and Queen, or it could have simply been a way to stir drama. Either way it was sure to cause eyebrows to raise and tongues to wag. Branding me in this way is its own special type of cruelty.

Once I understood what was going on, I stopped trying to beg. I also did my best to stop crying about it. This was going to happen whether I liked it or not. Mistress Ginger was always hell bent when it came to get what she wanted. I endured it the best I could hoping that by the next day I could come up with a very good excuse to offer anyone brave enough to ask about it.

After she had finished rendering me black and blue she demanded I take care of her own sexual pleasure. I was left that night without a single bit of relief. Not that I could have taken any. Her Brillo pad had left me less than interested in any kind of sexual congress for several days to come. Her leaving me without orgasm was the only mercy I was granted that night.

The next morning, she removed my collar after I begged her for almost an hour reminding her of her submission promise at least fifteen times. The red van driven by James pulled up by eight. I was ready to get the hell away from my

Mistress for a while. She had been most unpleasant to be around for days now. I did desire she love me once again, but for now I needed to get away from the moody bitch. There is just so much a person can take.

She followed me to the van. Maiden Mary had slid open the passenger door to let me in when my Mistress grabbed me by my waist. She pulled my unit close to hers and kissed me deeply holding my head tightly so I couldn't pull away. She made sure everyone in the van saw that as she sucked half my face off. Irritation at her gross public display of fake affection made me nauseous. Mistress Ginger no longer fooled me into thinking she really wanted me. She was just trying to elicit embarrassment. She finally let go saying she would see me at Springfields shortly.

I just glared at her while I got into the van. My Coven members were all snickering. They actually thought Mistress Ginger was sad to see me go and that was a passionate farewell kiss. I wanted to kick the false look of woe right off her pretty face. What a liar. Besides, she was planning on driving herself down on her own anyway. Not like we would be apart for long.

Everyone started teasing me about my ability to break a heart as we left the red-headed actress behind still standing in the yard appearing grief stricken. Whatever! I just sat there ignoring their jeers and ribbing trying hard to maintain my temper.

Truth is all I wanted to do is scream at them that my Mistress was a drama queen and that they were all playing into her mind games. However, I maintained my dignified decorum eventually getting them to re-center to the Mabon Sabbat business.

We arrived right on time thanks to James's willingness to break the posted speed limits. My Priest as usual was there to help me from the van. He looked stunning that day. It may have just been an aura of happiness that caused his extreme beauty. We were about to initiate more Coven children all at one time. More than ever seen in the history of the Green Rings. He wore pride very well.

It could have also been the recent awakening of interest in the male unit caused by Christopher's forced encounter or even just because My Priest did appear to be honesty fond of me, unlike the false affection granted to me by my Mistress. Whatever the reason, his touch, look and closeness caused my inner drives to nag me. It didn't even matter that my shop was temporarily closed for business thanks to Mistress Ginger's cruel cleansing techniques. It was very clear that my unit wanted to engage in the "Great Rite" with Roary once more.

This horror caused me to do my best to try to avoid him for a bit until I could get my overzealous sex instincts under control. I hid out in the bathroom washing my face repeatedly with cold water trying to think of anything but his, well everything. I have often wondered if this strange interest in my Priest that day was just a rebound need to engage in sexual congress willingly in some stupid effort to negate the previous forced situations. It seems silly to think

I could have believed I could un-rape the unit by sleeping with Roary on purpose.

Yet, there it is. I was thinking that way at the time. As I got my urges under my thumb, I also got my errored thinking to stop acting stupid too. Slowly, I got my shit together and snuffed out the need to rut like a woman in heat with my most gorgeous Priest. *Good thing he never knew how close he got. He would be super pissed if he knew that he could have been intimate with me that morning if he had asked. I never betray the collar but since I felt Mistress Ginger had, well service for service and all.*

I came out of the bathroom feeling a bit more settled. It was then I spotted Circe across the room sitting at the Elders' table. My insides burned with a fury demon that demanded I set it free on her head. It took all I had not to run across the hall, grab that bitch throw her to the floor, then stomp a mudhole into her ass. This was all her fault. All of it. Mistress Ginger, Tammy, even just standing there as the High Priestess had all been because of her efforts to punish me for granting her what she had asked for. That vile creature was exiled from the Coven but sat there like the arrogant shit she was as if nothing had ever happened. That was it. She had asked for it. I immediately went to seek out Mother Delleh. Circe had not listened to my warnings. It was now time to put an end to her bullshit once and for all.

Mother Delleh was in her room meditating. I waited by her door patiently until finally she emerged looking very tired, thin and her pallor was greyish. There was no longer any doubt, my Mother was not long for this plane. For a moment, I forgot my anger at Circe while despair at losing the object of my intense adoration overcame me.

"Mother, you look very tired," I said as I rushed forward taking her arm to aid her while she walked slowly toward the hall.

She smiled at me sweetly, "I am Daughter. I am very tired. But there is plenty of time for rest soon. Today I have come to see all my children raised. It is too fine a day for sleeping."

I nodded. "Well, I hope you don't sleep for a long while, Mother. Selfish of me to say, I know but the truth." I shot her a weak smile trying not to tear up at how bad she looked.

That made her laugh till she coughed. "Oh Daughter Arodia, you are such a joy. I will sit with you and your Husband during the feast and draw from your youthful energies. I want to be more awake today than ever I have been in my life."

I looked at the floor in reverence to this great spirit. "Mother, you are welcome to take all you need anytime. We are all here for you."

She nodded. "Thank you, Daughter. You have seen Mother Circe I believe? I can see it in your eyes that her being here has upset you. That is why you came to see me, right? Surely it was not to just help a dying woman to her table?"

I felt a bit of shame at that correct assumption. "Uhm yes. I am sorry to admit it, but I came to speak with you about her. She has been officially exiled from her own circle. I have her chalice with me to give to you at the Coven request. She was dutifully informed of this action and was there when they voted. Yet, she boldly sits at the table of the Elders taunting those who have spoken out against her abuses of her station." I sighed while wishing I didn't have to sully up Mother Delleh's final days with such bullshit politics.

Mother Delleh stopped walking then looked at me hard. "Daughter Arodia, Mother Circe is exiled, and she is forbidden being here today, she knows this. She believes that no one will make her leave with my poor health and this large initiation due to begin. It is her thinking that none of the Elders would want to cause a scene by escorting her off the grounds in front of those who are unaware of her status. Now that she is no longer capable of being elected the next Green Queen the obvious choice will be Mother Thalia. She is not a bad heart, but she is not one who will seek growth. Nor is she strong. It will be up to you and your Husband to keep the Green Rings in motion. With that understanding, I would ask you, what would you suggest I do with Mother Circe today?"

I understood exactly what Mother Delleh was saying. She was alerting me to the fact that Mother Thalia would not perform her duties in protecting our Covens from inward threats such as Circe. She was preparing Roary and myself to take on this role by offering me the chance to make my very first decision about how to manage a rouge witch in our mists. I also realized that if I let my emotions, my personal hatred for Circe, blind me to what was right in this case,

Mother Delleh would go to her death believing she had chosen her Priest and Priestess incorrectly.

I closed my eyes and pushed down my fury demon. "I believe we should allow her to sit at her table and ask all the members to actively shun her. If she doesn't stir any trouble, she can stay. However, we should have a Summoner keep an eye on her constantly. This is the initiates day, and we should not allow her to steal that from them by giving her cause to stand up and publicly bad mouth that which she had already abused enough. When the feast is over, and members leaving I would pull her to the side and inform her that if she comes to Samhain she will be removed before she gets out of her car. I would go further to tell her that she is now exiled from all Wiccan circles in the region and would call and inform all the Queens and Elders of her most grievous behaviors here today." I opened back up my eyes to see Mother Delleh's eyes bright and shining with laughter.

She hugged me tightly. "You are going to make a fine Queen yourself one day Daughter Arodia. I will watch with pride from my place in the Summerlands when that glorious days comes that you take the Green throne. I know in my heart, with you and Priest Roary, my children are forever safe. Blessed Be."

I hugged her back savoring my moment in the arms of a real Mother. I could have held her for the rest of my life it was so wonderful. However, it was only brief. The good things in life always seem too rushed compared to the bad. She pulled away from me, then directed I aid her to find

Johnny the Summoner. She went about putting the plan I had given her to rid herself of Circe into action.

In the end, the power struggle of that bitch and the Queen overshadowed my precious time with someone I truly valued above all others. I would only have one more Sabbat with this great spirit, my time was running out. My ex-Mistress had already taken so much, and yet here she was to attempt to steal even more. I thought of what Mistress Ginger said about never bringing the corpse of the past into a wedding bed. My Mistress was very wise in that statement. It was time to bury my dead.

Circe did not know it but she had just been officially black balled from all honest Covens within the entire region and would no longer be viewed by any self-respecting Wiccan with anything but contempt. I watched as Mother Delleh instructed all the Elders that Circe was to be shunned, and to spread the word of her fall from the position of power. I didn't say a word as all of them agreed to cut her cords, break her chalice, scratch out her name in the Book of Shadows and burn her robes. She was now more than exiled from the Green Rings. Circe was now erased, excommunicated for those who understand that term better, from the memory of the God and Goddess, viewed as a deceiver, and liar.

I had warned her to leave me and the Coven alone. She did not listen. Her hubris that she could bully her way back into the Green Rings had sunk her. Now she would be banned from starting up her own circle or joining another Coven. Mother Delleh was going to remove her titles of

Crone and High Priestess. The Elders would spread the word to every Coven in the land. She wouldn't have anywhere to hide or play Priestess.

This was the worst thing that could happen to any Wiccan that worked among the organized branches of the faith network. It still boggles my mind to this day how bad that dumb woman fucked up by showing her exiled ass at that Mabon Sabbat. I guess she really thought I would be afraid of her, or that Mother Delleh would be too sick to strike her down. Whatever reason she did it and then we did it back. Remember the Wiccans believe in balance. Circe had called down the thunder so Mother Delleh answered by washing her ass away with a storm of ultimate destruction.

NOTE: *Now you must be bad to be exiled, but you must be pure evil to be stripped of lifelong titles or erased. In many ways, I felt my own position of High Priestess was tainted by the fact that the only person ever in the whole history of the Green Rings to be stripped and shunned was my own mentor. This fact would continue to bother me for many years to come.*

Mother Delleh and the other Coven Elders would never question my amazing rise to power in their circle, but I would always know I was forced into it by the very creature they now were about to destroy. It was this weakness in my reign that I never could justify in my own mind. It is also the reason I eventually stepped down and handed over my Triple Crown to a new High Priestess. Though I had become a devote and wise leader who loved her children more than anyone can ever know, I was never called to lead.

In order to be a true Wiccan High Priestess, or any religious leader, one must feel they are called to such a burden. In my case, it was the greed of Circe and desperation of a dying Queen that put me in the black cord. I was called only to heal and cleanse the Green Rings, not to rule them. I spent over a decade fulfilling my destiny as I understood it. Once my task was completed, I raised a True High Priestess who had heard the calling. Then I quietly walked away from all of it.

Mother Delleh told me just before her death she had raised me uncommonly young for a High Priestess with the hopes that one day I would become the Queen of the Green Throne. I am aware I could have easily taken this title in time. All I had to do was stay with my Coven and in another seven years and thirty days (I will be fifty-five and qualify for Crone status) if the throne were open for a vote I would have been Queen at some point. She was aware I would be a guarantee to succeed with so many years under my triple cord, and so many children raised by my own hands. However, I let her down by owning up to the reality of my rise through the circle ranks. I was never called to be High Priestess, and sure as shit was not called to be Queen of the Green. I am many things, but I am not a liar. Such power is not something I ever wanted, needed or could tolerate.

To this very day, I honor the wheel faithfully. I have never opened a circle, called the Watchtowers, led a Coven, presided over a handfasting or even held Esbat since I

*handed over my crown. I am still an official ordained High
Priestess of the Green Rings in good stead, but I no longer
claim the religious preference of Wiccan. When forced to
claim a religion I say Pagan only. I kept the basic beliefs
in my heart but shucked the politics and organization.*

I kept a baleful eye on the brooding Circe and the other
eye on my Mistress Ginger who had just arrived. I aided my
Queen to attend all her Elders. My Priest followed close
behind never taking his eyes on me. I could see a lustful look
there. I would catch him smiling and watching me. He would
quickly turn his gaze trying to appear embarrassed he got
caught eye humping. Normally, I would have exchanged
playful sexually tinged humor at his boyish behaviors but on
this day, I had serious problems preoccupying my concerns.

I honestly can say I will never forgive Circe nor
Mistress Ginger for making that Sabbat (one of the
potentially best next to the Great Rite Beltane Sabbat) one of
high anxiety and dread. My Queen still was ruling, my Priest
was in fine form, I was raising twenty-seven children, spirits
were high, and I was young and in my prime. Thanks to the
greed of two evil women in my life, I enjoyed none of it.

I was having to guard against a blow out by Circe, keep
from running into an overzealous Mistress, and was covered
in bruises, wire burns and cuts. My stress was at such a level,
I was almost sure I would fall into an explosive psychotic
episode. Luckily, I managed to hold it together, for a bit
longer anyway.

When my High Priest Roary and I began to remove our robes to prepare for the circle cast, he let out a gasp of sheer terror as he saw my branded unit. I looked at him. His eyes told a tale of a mix of pity and anger.

"My Priestess, who did this shit. I will kill that son-of-a-bitch," He breathed out.

I smiled bitterly. "No my Priest, it was me who did this. My schizophrenia has been heading for acute phase. Self-abuse is common. Pay no mind. It looks worse than it feels," I lied.

He shook his head. "Arodia, my Priestess, you need to be in the hospital where they can help you, not here today raising initiates. This is not okay. I am worried." He continued to look over my unit with pure sadness.

I nodded. "Soon my Priest I will go. It is not quite time yet. Please try to ignore it. It is the price I pay. Mother Delleh has explained this to you."

He nodded back and tore his eyes away. Our circle was cast without another word regarding the marks. Everyone stared, many gasped but no one dared question me about it. Mistress Ginger had been unsuccessful in ending my ability to rule completely. As we began the initiations, I started to feel a bit of relief. She had failed instead of me. It all went without further incident or hitch. When my Priest and I re-opened the circle, we had raised our children well. Many tears of gratitude and pure overwhelming of their spiritual awakening were shed. Everyone there that day thought it was the most beautiful thing they had ever seen, next to the Great

Rite of their beloved High Priest and High Priestess. Johnny the Summoner had blocked Circe at the ritual room door. She never got to see the children she had forbidden entry receive their white cords. It was justice as far as I was concerned. She had never wanted them, now she would never have them.

Linda came up to me after the ceremony. I already knew she had come to voice her concerns at my appearance. Yet, I smiled as she approached trying to appear in good humor.

"My Goddess, how are you so beautiful?" I hugged her while we were both still Sky Clad realizing this would probably throw her mind elsewhere. I did that on purpose by the way.

She giggled, "Oh damn. I do love these rituals Mother. I could hug you all day." She wiggled as she said this into my ear.

I laughed. "And night I am sure. What can I do for you Daughter," I said as I released her and pulled away.

She pretended to pout. "Well you could hug me again. I just wanted to know, well it is not my business, but you seem to be, uhm, in a bad way. Is this new lover of yours causing a problem?" She looked down appearing unsure how to approach me as her Priestess rather than just plain old Psycho.

I feigned ignorance. "I don't understand what you mean, Daughter Linda. All is well. You should go join the feasting.

I believe a bard is going to tell a story. He is good I wouldn't want to miss that if I were you." I smiled at her.

She frowned. "I suppose this can wait till a more appropriate time. I will be back in touch Mother. I want to know more about your new living situation."

I nodded. "Another time Daughter. Now get going before Will and your Father eat all the food. You know those menfolk are greedy bastards."

She chuckled then headed away. I felt an arm going around my waist. I turned around surprised only to be held tightly while my Mistress locked me into a deep kiss. I tried to pull back, but she was not going to let go. This behavior in the ritual room was not permitted. Luckily, no one was around to see it yet.

I finally struggled loose from her octopus hold. "Mistress, you know better. This is sacred space. Not okay. What do you think you are doing. What if someone had seen that."

She smiled then said in an almost purring voice, "Well I couldn't help myself. You look so damned hot standing there. I mean I see you naked and I go stupid with need. Oh, and that Priest of yours. I have been fantasizing this entire time. Seeing the two of you together makes me practically wet my pants with excitement. Tonight when I come to your room, you should bring him too. We could share him Psycho. Just think, you, me, and that hunk of beefcake makes three."

I glared at her angrily. "You are not fooling me, Mistress. You want me to bring Roary so you can have two powerful leaders under your thumb. Not going to happen. Not ever. He is off limits to you and to me too. I must work with this man for my entire reign as Priestess. If we start having sex it will cause difficulties between us at some point and you know it. I will not tolerate your interference with this part of my world. You agreed to this at the submission. If you persist in breaching the contract, I will have Johnny remove you. I am not kidding."

She looked surprised. "Psycho, how dare you speak to me like that. I am still your Dominant. You can't remove me or tell me what to do."

I took a step toward her and she stepped back realizing the seriousness of my rising aggression. "You listen to me Ginger. In this place you are not my Mistress. You are not even a member. You can punish me as you see fit tomorrow but today, I will have you removed or even arrested if need be to protect my Coven from the drama you have come to set about causing. Do you hear me? If you wish to stay, then you had better be so fucking quiet I can't see or hear you. One more peep and see if I am bluffing."

Her eyes blazed with anger. "I will punish you tomorrow for this insolence. You will be sorry, Psycho."

I smiled with fire in my gaze. "I will punish you in return for your betrayal of our contract. You, my love, shall be just as sorry. Why don't you ask my previous Mistresses what happens when they abuse the gifts I granted? They forgot that I gave my obedience honestly, but I could also take it back when they were dishonest with me. I am not a slave, nor mindless. I am, however, just crazy enough to pay back ill favor with my own brand of correction. Want to find out what fucking with me in my circle will cost you Ginger? How long can you keep me tied up so I don't come seeking my equal service for the service you stole?"

She suddenly looked frightened. "I didn't betray, I mean yeah I agreed, but I haven't, well, I mean I am staying out of your business with the Wiccan stuff."

I looked around the room. "Are you? Hmmm, glad to know I am hallucinating. For a second I was sure my Mistress was invading my ritual room, standing in Springfields, and demanding I bring my Priest to her bed. If I were you love, I would leave now before I start to believe my hallucinations."

She nodded then quickly left, not even looking back. My Priest came through the door at that same moment. Luckily, he was dressed in his High Priest robes. She nearly knocked him down but didn't stop or apologize. He stood there watching her scurry off appearing mildly amused. I went over and grabbed my own robe to re-dress.

He rushed forward to aid me. "What was that about? Isn't that the woman who helped when you had that seizure back at Lithia?"

I pulled my robe down as he grabbed my cording then began to tie it around my waist. "Yeah, she was lost. I told her she needed to leave since she is no longer thinking of initiating."

He frowned. "Just not for her huh? Oh well, you can't get them all Wife. I came to see if you would sit with me at the long table. I miss holding your hand." He took my hand then kissed my knuckles.

I glared at the Judas wretched hand hating it will all my being. "My husband, I will be happy to sit with you. However, I would ask you hold my wrist today or even around my waist. My hands are sore from work this week." I pulled the hand away from him.

He smiled. "I would hold you anywhere you would allow me to hold. Tonight, the Moon is calling for lovers. Are you free to call down the Gods with me in the woods while the weather is still warm? I would be honored to worship my Priestess as often as she would allow me to." His eyes spoke of the many forbidden pleasures he would indeed heap upon my alter.

I felt the stirring of agreement deep within that such adoration would be welcomed. However, I was not just being an asshole to Mistress Ginger. She had granted permission to have sex with him if I counted her in of course. I am sure if he had known the opportunity to sleep with his Priestess and a beautiful red head was right at my fingertips he would have gotten on his knees and begged if front of the whole Coven. No way he would have turned that amazing offer down.

However, I believed and still do sleeping with Roary, no matter how tempting, would eventually lead to emotional difficulties. If I left the memory of our one great moment intact without further sexual interactions, it would continue to grow in his mind as the greatest sex, he had ever had. Partly because it was spiritual, partly because of the stress, and a bit because we didn't even know each other's name.

NOTE: *Our one sexual encounter had been socially forbidden, spiritual, mildly dangerous, and definitely scary. We both had massive orgasms just from the situational environment, rather than the actual act itself. I never wanted to sully that beautiful moment with the dirty reality of casual love making.*

I did want very badly to be with him one more time. Yet, I knew in the great scheme of things, it was best to leave The Great Rite as our only measurement of our sexual abilities and desire for each other. Over the decade to follow my handsome Priest would continue to pursue me with vigor. I continued to play the card of 'maybe.' The Covens viewed us as the greatest romance they had ever known. No one knew we were not fucking each other. They just assumed our passionate speaking and obvious deep attraction for each other was based on reality, not the fantasy it really was.

His words were always filled with sexual innuendoes and promises of eternal love. Mine were always of the grateful lover, who could never doubt her husband's prowess. We managed to keep that spark between us lit because we never risked putting it out. Only those who live on a memory could have held that truthful a lustful wish for so long.

I had learned well by now that often when someone gets what they think they always wanted, they often take it for granted over time. Roary has never been able to take me for granted, because he never got what he wanted, and neither did I.

I smiled longingly at my Priest, then lied through my teeth, "Oh my dearest husband. I am still not free for such a delight. One day, the planets will once again align, and we shall visit the God and Goddess in their own lands once more. I am counting the days my Priest. Until then, I beg you allow me to see your face when I call down the Goddess and enjoy my own ritual."

He nearly shuttered with desire at those words. "Permission granted, so long as you allow me to see your ritual in my mind's eye when I engage in my own."

I allowed him to put his arm around my waist as we began to walk from the ritual room. "I would insist that you watch, my Priest. I would find it easy to reach my apex if I knew you were there in spirit adoring me."

Hahaha, we just agreed to masturbate while thinking of each other. Damn, too much information. Fucking Pagans are always such lusty creatures. The don't even let a little thing like no partner around stop their sexual antics. Nurse, medication over here, now.

187

I noticed when Roary and I went to the head of the long table the seat that Circe had occupied was empty. I was told she left the grounds in a huff when she was not allowed entry to the ritual room. That made me chuckle. She had lost her final bid to bully the Covens. I knew I would never see her face at the Springfields again.

At least now I could finally relax knowing the first of many cleansings had been finished. I would have started to finally enjoy the Sabbat, but I noted that my Mistress was sitting a bit too close and speaking a bit too often to Linda in the hall. I didn't care much for her sticking her nose in yet another weak link in my chain of support. Try as I might, I couldn't keep my eyes off the red-headed Mistress.

She would often flash me an evil smile while she appeared to laugh, speak intensely or even as she whispered in Linda's ear. A few times Linda would look at me as if surprised. I sat there next to my boisterous Priest while he told lies of his greatest hunting conquests while I wanted to strangle my Mistress to death. She was aware of what Linda meant to me. I should have known Mistress Ginger would find a way to irritate me without directly attacking. This was exactly why I had made her promise to stay out of my Green Rings Coven business. I was too vulnerable to her cruelty and in no position to tolerate more stress. I decided after the Sabbat I would have to punish my own Mistress to assure this bad behavior was not repeated in the future. Otherwise I would need to drop my crown now and walk away. I could not serve and lead at the same fucking time, and she had no business trying to make me.

Many of the revelers decided to stay the night. I opted to leave with my Mistress for home. We verbally argued the entire way back. I was not backing down no matter how much she threatened punishment. I even went so far as to tell her I would take back the collar as I had done to Circe and the one before her if she ever showed up at another Sabbat or at the Green Temple. Both of us were beyond angry by the time we pulled into the driveway of home.

Once in the house, my Mistress stormed to the bedroom then returned with my collar demanding I kneel so she could re-submit me to her authority. I refused her until she agreed to keep her original promises regarding my High Priestess activities. This time I said that if she did not verbally state that breaching of this promise would result in termination of her rights to my collar, I would refuse to provide any service from that point forward.

Mistress Ginger was beyond livid at my most fair demand. She fumed and kicked, then finally said she would keep the promise and understood the punishment if she broke it again. Once she had given in to my demands I knelt before her to receive her collar. The sound of the click still sent me into a moment of despair even though this was not a true collaring. She noticed my momentary wincing at her locking the damned thing. My Mistress flew into a fresh fury accusing me of secretly hating her.

I did my best to calm her down even falling into a prostrating pose before her promising that I adored her. She continued to accuse me of lying to her until eventually she got me to the point of promising her anything to get her to

189

stop behaving so erratically. It was setting off my own mental issues to be honest. Had she continued to flail, scream and throw shit like that I would have attacked her just to stop all the damned drama.

"I swear I adore you Mistress. What can I do to prove that to you? Please you have to stop accusing me of hating you. It is not true," I begged on my hands and knees at her feet truly miserable.

She stopped yelling. "Psycho tell me you want to be thudded. Tell me you want to make love to me and only me, anywhere I wanted you to do it. Say it and I will believe you." She stomped her foot almost stepping on my head.

I was near tears with frustration at this insane woman's constantly shifting mood. "Thud me all you like. I only want you. I will do whatever you want, wherever you want. Please Mistress you have to believe I want you to love me like I love you." I didn't want to be thudded, especially since I had not healed from her last session with me, but I was ready to promise anything to end the arguing.

She suddenly smiled. "Get up. Get dressed. I know just where I want you to prove you love me."

I looked up at her now feeling quite terrified that perhaps she had set me up again. She took off towards her room to select my outfit to wear for her pleasure. I followed her feeling I may throw up. I wondered if she would make me sleep with another man or woman for that matter. Something was just too smooth about this entire situation. I suspected she planned the whole thing. Her mind games knew no boundaries.

She playfully groped and fondled me while I quickly dressed in the black tight outfit she had selected. I noticed it unzipped all the way down the front in a single jumpsuit fashion. She then directed me to dress her in a red latex suit built in a similar fashion. These outfits I noted would allow for ease of access to the important parts of a woman's anatomy when engaging in carnal congress. My Mistress than directed me towards the car. We were apparently going for an outing. I worried it was going to be a very public outing if you catch my drift.

I drove us to an address she had given me. It was a small white A-frame home in a modest neighborhood. I did not know the name on the mailbox. My stomach was doing flip flops as I began to think that she indeed intended to betray me again as she had with Christopher. I followed my Mistress to the door. Her spirits were now chipper and she even hummed happily while we approached the porch of this house.

Mistress Ginger knocked on the door and a middle-aged woman answered. The lady was very masculine looking. She seemed to know my Mistress. They smiled and hugged. I was introduced to this woman named Rebecca, then we were led inside. I realized with great horror there was a party going on. All the people there were quite obviously either lesbian or gay males. Couples of both genders were sitting around on couches and chair drinking, holding hands and folk music was playing in the background. Rebecca offered me and Mistress Ginger a drink. My Mistress was not a drinker and of course neither am I. She took a coke and directed me to sit next to her on one of the couches after Rebecca gave her the beverage.

I don't care for gatherings of people in general. Too much noise and movement. I could barely get through my job as Priestess thanks to my sickness. Sitting at a party with a bunch of strangers was my nightmare come true. I worried that Mistress Ginger was planning on having me sleep with someone there later, maybe this Rebecca person. My Mistress continued to yap with her almost ignoring everyone else in the room, including me.

I sat there quiet and nerve wracked waiting for the punchline. My Mistress was not too hard to figure out. If we were there, there was a reason for it. Whatever was coming was sure to be something horrid, public and likely painful. However, after about an hour, still nothing other than sitting, listening to music and discussions about mundane things. No one had done anything terrifying. Nothing sexual or obscene was said. I finally started to relax just a tad. The doorbell rang and Rebecca excused herself to answer.

To my utter dismay it was Linda. Mistress Ginger had drug me to a LGBT party that Linda had told her she was attending after the Sabbat. I suddenly realized with great sadness this was Mistress Ginger's payback and punishment. She would surely flaunt our relationship in front of my love-sick Goddess, and likely everyone else there that night.

I just glared at my Mistress with contempt that she had chosen to be so cruel. Linda knew I was with someone, but she had not known who and certainly had not been tortured by being forced to watch me in the arms of another. Thank goodness my beloved Mistress was ready to change all that. I truthfully wanted to beat her half to death over this latest indignity.

Linda saw Mistress Ginger and I immediately. She ran over to hug us both excited to know someone. It was then I discovered Linda was the one who invited us. Mistress Ginger had told her that we were lovers at the Mabon Sabbat. For a moment I started to calm down thinking that Linda must have handled the news very well to invite us to meet her at this party. Again, I say that reality is not my strong point.

Mistress Ginger had me scoot over so Linda could squeeze in beside me on the over occupied couch. They talked over my head while I sat there wondering how I managed to get into these predicaments every time I turned around. It was boring and irritating but nothing was sinister about the conversation they were having. Linda was unusually cold and quiet, not even offering to try to bring me into the discussion. I was actually glad for that mercy. I didn't like this obnoxious display by my Mistress to rub our relationship in Linda's face.

After a bit, my Mistress reported she needed to use the restroom. She was directed that the privy was down the hall to the left. She stood up then glared at me using a hand gesture that meant, follow me. I nodded, then rose to do as commanded. Linda scooted into the space left by our now absent units. I was ready to follow my Mistress if nothing more than to ask her what the hell she thought she was doing hanging out with Linda and friends. She knew I wanted to keep her at arm's length.

I was working out what I was going to say to Mistress Ginger when half-way down the hall she turned around and slammed me into the wall. She began to unzip my clothing reaching into my very raw nether region, while doing her signature oral stimulation on my breasts. To my absolute horror she was going to fuck me right there in the damned hallway with Linda sitting only inches away.

I fought to get free of her grip, but she would not let go. Like it or not I was going to have to endure her affections. Of course, Rebecca the hostess, came to see if we found the bathroom alright. To her amusement she walked upon the scene of my Mistress fondling my unit under a picture of her favorite dog Princess in her hallway.

The open-minded lady just chuckled saying, "Oh my. Okay I see you girls found what you were looking for. Pardon me." She exited the hallway quickly to allow for our privacy.

Mistress Ginger looked at me smiling. "I am not stopping until you orgasm, so get on with it or we can do this all night."

I was not in any mood or condition for such pleasure. "Mistress please, I am still not well from your bath service. I beg you to stop this. I cannot reach an orgasm right now. It hurts too much." I was not lying. Her attempts were only setting me on fire, in the wrong way I may add.

She looked at me feigning pity. "Ah, poor Psycho. You shouldn't have had sex with Christopher. Men always land a girl in hot water." She giggled at what she believed was a clever statement regarding her cruel bathing techniques.

I closed my eyes groaning at her continued rough probing of my sore genitals. "Please Mistress, I beg you to stop. Mercy, please," I whispered loudly into her ear.

She roughly doubled her efforts then said into my ear, "I will stop, but only if you get on your knees right here. I want you to fuck me with that skilled mouth of yours until I am satisfied."

I was now wild with agony at her harsh treatment of my injured areas. I must admit I would have agreed to anything to get her to stop. I usually handle pain very well, but this was pure hell. I nodded that I would do as she asked, no longer caring where the fuck we were doing this intimate act. I just wanted her to stop hurting me.

She laughed while she removed her offending hand then undid her own zipper. Mistress Ginger leaned back into the wall pulling my own unit in front of her. She pushed me down to my knees by grabbing my shoulders demanding I get to work attending her desires. As usual I did as told hoping that Rebecca would warn everyone to give us a few minutes without interruption.

However, Rebecca may have or may not have warned everyone. It didn't really matter. No one needed to enter that hallway to know what was going on in it or who was involved. My Mistress began to moan loudly while I began my efforts to bring her to ecstasy. I tried to pull away, but she grabbed the back of my head holding me tightly to the object I was to attend.

"Oh no you don't. Not till I get an orgasm. Now get to it, Psycho. I mean it. I can hold you like this all night if need be, but you are doing this," she said angrily.

I understood she wasn't kidding. So, I went back to my job of pleasing her. She again began to moan loudly and bang her head into the wall lightly making as much racket as humanly possible without causing injury.

Finally, to cap off the total humiliation of this situation she began to yell out in a near scream, "Oh Psycho, oh yeah. Oh baby, I am going to cum. Oh my God. Oh yeah, Psycho, that is the spot." She then wailed as she did indeed reach her orgasm nearly twisting my head off in her spasms.

I was grateful she had reached it so quickly because to be honest, I needed air. The woman was holding my head to her so tightly it had nearly cut off my air supply. She let me go as she loudly announced her pleasure to the entire household.

I had been pulling back with all my might to try to get free. When she released, I fell backward gasping and coughing only to look up and see my Goddess standing there wide eyed at the end of the hallway. She told me later she had witnessed the sorted scene. Linda never told me why she rushed to that hallway knowing full damned well that Mistress Ginger was obviously engaging in carnal congress with her beloved Psycho. She was yelling my fucking name. Part of me believed, and still does, she just couldn't pass up the chance to see me in action. I had teased her for years about such things. Well now she was very aware it was not a jest. I could please a woman just as I had always boasted.

However, curiosity has killed many a cat. My sweet Linda was heartbroken. I could see the intense jealousy in her eyes that it was Mistress Ginger and not herself swooning, panting and sweating against the hallway wall in the afterglow of my affections. I stared at her trying to apologize with my gaze, but I could see only pain in her own.

She mumbled, "Oh pardon me ladies." Then they turned and left not only the hallway but Rebecca's house.

Apparently, she had enough partying for one night.

I glared back at my smiling Mistress who also saw the hurt in Linda's eyes. "Wow, some people are just so sensitive. Did you see that look? I bet she is crying right now, Psycho. You'd think she just caught her lover with another woman. Guess that will teach her to keep her fucking hands to herself," she said as she zipped her clothing back into place.

Her statement surprised me. "Linda and I have never been together, Mistress. You set this up so she would catch us. Why would you do that? What has she ever done to you?"

My Mistress laughed. "It is what she wanted to do that got her burned. Now she knows what she is missing and what she will never have. Serves her right for wanting what is not hers." She grabbed me by my collar pulling me back to my feet.

She kissed me hard pulling my Judas tongue into her mouth then said, "Don't speak and stop trying to hold me back. Just keep doing what you just did. No matter how mad I get you always manage to keep me coming back for more." She smiled at me evilly.

I glared at her thinking to myself, "*Tomorrow I am going to fix the problem. Then I won't be saying the wrong things or pushing you off. I won't have a tongue or hands to do either one. Then you will finally love me for real.*" My mind was beginning to shatter from within.

Chapter 30: Handheld and Tongue Twisted
Mistress Ginger

It looks like the reign of Mistress Ginger has its ups and downs, mostly downs. That's okay. We are not worried. We have been through much worse than this in our past. This is just another bump in our road to nowhere. Twenty-five more years to go of amazing sights, epic fails, and nightmares so sublime even the devil is jealous of our memories.

When we remember Mistress Ginger many words come to mind; red, hot, sex, pain, cruelty, public, private, and unstable. The one word we have wished to include a million times is: love. Of all our Mistresses and Masters this was the one who defined that forbidden feeling for us. Her definition was much like her, twisted and wrong. However, in our youth she was everything we ever wanted. Too bad we were not enough for her.

Mistress Ginger needed the world to fall on their knees to beg her mercy. She was deeply angry and horridly lonely even in a crowded room. Her inner numbness led to an inability to feel warmth no matter how high the fire. In her rush to find what she had lost, she managed to shatter her toy. Her sharp tongue and greedy fingers were mirrored through the cracks she created. We will pay the price for her expensive tastes, and in many ways so will she.

Circe is like a plague of biblical proportions. No longer a respected witch she only had a month to stop the coming darkness. She will make one final bid, by trying to recapture what she had so carelessly threw away. She has forgotten that in our world there are no second chances. We only play for keeps. A loser is always a loser, we should know.

The Lord of Misrule has come to take his black throne. The Pagan New Year is here. The world is growing cold, the snow is on the winds of the north. The circle lights the way to a world of white once more. Psycho will sleep with the demons of schizophrenia, hibernating until all wounds have healed. The time is acutely felt as everything slows down to a standstill. The winter is a time of restraint, electrical storms and lost moments of youth. Will new life bloom in the season of birth or will it just be another Strawberry Spring?

Ready to see what is on this chapter's menu? It is exotic, and rare we promise. You may not enjoy it at first but give it some time, you never know till you try it. We know we didn't like it at all ourselves. It is one of those things we acquired a taste for.

> *"I can't breathe without a lung,*
> *nor find warmth without the sun.*
> *If I lose my legs I can't run.*
> *My heart is broken; do I still have one?*
> *I must be dead because I have none.*
> *Cut off my hands and my tongue,*
> *I can put an end to Ginger's fun.*
> *An ax and the scissors will get the deed done."*
> ---**Psycho clanging to Dennis during her arrest on September 24th, 1994.**

Mistress Ginger appeared quite proud of herself when we both emerged from the hallway. The small group of people gathered for the party were smiling coyly at us. A few even stood up and clapped. My Mistress took a false bow in her most dramatic fashion. Her smile nearly cracked her face in half. I kept my gaze to the floor angered at her atrocious misuse of her special services of the collar.

I began to compulsively wipe my mouth repeatedly while chewing on my tongue viciously. It was my Judas parts that had betrayed poor Linda. My tongue and hands would never have agreed to such a gross display in that hallway. They had to be stopped before they turned on me, maybe even murdering my unit in the night. They could not be trusted.

It was my wish to leave that place immediately, but Mistress Ginger was enjoying the new notoriety that was being lavished upon us. Many there found the entire situation quite erotic. A few couples even disappeared. Within short order moans, and groans of pleasure emitted from the walls while others attempted to re-create our tryst by engaging in their own. The homeowner, Rebecca, began to chuckle telling my Mistress she had started something amazing.

I had to agree with that sediment. Amazingly stupid if you ask me. It has always baffled me why some people feel the need to follow bad examples or exalt poor manners to a lofty height by replicating them. The more the others disappeared, the louder the screams of coitus, the sicker I got to my stomach. The blood from my chewing began to roll out of the corners of my mouth. I was unaware of it, merely believing I was drooling (I tend to do that). I had been wiping my mouth madly already. This caused the sanguine liquid to stain my chin and sleeve.

At first, no one else noticed it either, but finally, Rebecca tore her undying attention from my Mistress to ask if I desired a beverage. She let out a yell of terror. I was bleeding heavily from my attempts to chew off the offending organ before the symptoms of my stress behavior was discovered.

"Jesus Christ, Ginger, Psycho is bleeding like a stuck pig. What the fuck," yelled out Rebecca as she ran to the kitchen looking for towels to clean up my gory mess.

My Mistress turned to look. Her face immediately drained of color. Everyone in the room was staring. I couldn't understand why they were all so concerned. It wasn't even my tongue. Why should they even care? I glared back at them working harder to chew that fucker off.

Mistress Ginger realized what I was doing, "Psycho, stop that right now." She reached out and grabbed my lower jaw holding it tight yelling for Rebecca to hurry with the towels and to bring ice as well.

I tried to knock her hands off my face, but she shook my head by the jaw. "Get your hands down. Hold still now. Do what I say, or you will be sorry Psycho, I mean it." She again yelled for Rebecca to hurry while the blood poured out in rivers from my mouth.

Everyone was whispering and watching the drama unfold. Some of the couples were returning from their very public adorations of each other. They would sit down and those who were already there were filling them in on my insane antics calling it a seizure of some kind.

Rebecca finally returned with ice and towels. My Mistress forced several cubes into my mouth then held it closed using a towel to cover the opening.

Mistress Ginger growled, "Hold those ice cubes, Psycho. Let them melt, don't you chew them. Damn it, what are you doing to yourself. Rebecca, do you have some rope somewhere?"

Rebecca stated that she did. My Mistress asked her to cut her enough to tie my mouth open until she could get me home and suppress my mouth properly. Everyone snickered at that revelation when Rebecca rushed off to find the item requested.

While my Mistress held my mouth closed on the ice cubes the other couples began to discuss their desires to quiet down by gagging various people such as bosses and their significant other's extended family members. One curious woman asked Mistress Ginger what she would use on me to stop my chewing of the Judas tongue.

"A ball gag should stop this shit. Psycho has schizophrenia and a seizure disorder. She does shit like this all the time. It is hell on Earth keeping an eye on this idiot sometimes. I can't take her anywhere," roared my irritated Mistress.

The woman raised an eyebrow. "You poor thing. Well, I hope Psycho appreciates how lucky she is you look after her. Most schizophrenics end up on the streets or mental institutions."

Mistress Ginger smiled at that, "Psycho knows that. That is why she does whatever I tell her. She knows what will happen to her if she gives me too much shit. Don't you, Psycho?" She looked at me her eyes dancing with delight at my compromised position.

I glared but nodded. She knew I couldn't speak or defend myself. My mouth was full of ice cubes, held shut and worse still was filled with an alien. I could almost hear it laughing at me. I wondered what the fucking hands were up to. They had not even tried to break Mistress Ginger's grip with any effort. They too were against me. I would have to figure out a way to trick them into destroying their brother the tongue, then each other just as soon as I could get a bit of time away from prying eyes.

I could hear the couples calling me names, taunting me. A foul song was playing that was broadcasting my disgusting deeds to the rhythmic beat of a folk tune. The electrical grid was rushing louder and louder above my head making it hard to see through the flip book flashing of the tapestry.

It was then I realized I was losing time and space while everything constricted faster around me. The Earth was groaning, shifting below my feet. I could feel its heartbeat. I watched in amazement as the words of the now strobing people around me left their mouths and lingered in the air like fireflies on a summer night. Each word got trapped in the webs that holds the universe in place. Then to my complete horror the Looper came running out of the kitchen right into the room. He stood there staring at me with hellfire eyes.

The Looper's head was as big as a beach ball. His eyes were black a night and he had no nose. His mouth was full of razor-sharp teeth built for chewing up the soul. He was tall and thin with charred up, leathery skin. I knew it was him because he had just told me he was coming to kill me. I had been waiting many years for this showdown, but I never thought he would be so gruesome. I screamed tearing free of my Mistress like a mad woman. He came running for me, and I took off running for the door.

He grabbed me just as I went to rip the door open. I turned and spit the bloody ice in his face, but it didn't stop his clawing my back. My screams of terror could be heard for miles I am sure. The Looper was beyond nightmarish. His hissing and thousand voices were flooding my senses to blow out.

I couldn't get out the door, he was dragging me back inside to finish me off. I fought him by kicking, biting, punching and headbutting. I wasn't going down easy. Suddenly three or four of his shadow demons joined into the battle. They were trying to restrain my arms and legs. One was trying to put a rope in my mouth to keep me from ripping out their spy the tongue. Somehow, I managed to knock them all off me. I got into the kitchen and saw the scissors sitting on the table. Just the tool I had been seeking. I knew it would only help a bit, but maybe if I got the Judas out of my mouth it would slow them all down.

I grabbed the weapon and stuck out the offender. I had just laid the blade on the surface when screams filled the air all around me. The Looper grabbed my arms, crushing my wrists. I tried to hold on, but I felt the sorry ass betraying hand let the scissors fall. I saw the blood pouring everywhere. I had injured the demon in my head.

I began to laugh maniacally over its wound. "I got it. I got that sucker. I got it," I yelled as I filled with relief that it had been punished for its crimes against us at last.

I broke free of the shadow once more then grabbing the scissors went for the left wrist cutting into it deeply trying to severe as much of that bastard as possible. Now, I would only have the one creature still attached. Sooner or later I would get that diabolical right hand too.

The noise around me was deafening. The shadows were most unhappy that I was killing their brethren. That made me laugh. I hated the shadows more than I hated the Looper. They wailed and begged me to stop cutting off the hand thing sticking off my wrist. I ignored them. Then the Looper showed up once more this time he hit me in the shoulder hard. I dropped the scissors from his force. That pissed me off. I turned screaming and plowed right into the big-headed creature.

I hit him with all I had and tore at his hair. He had fallen backward onto the floor. Nothing would stop me from ending this son-of-a-bitch. For over eight years he had plagued me day and night with his constant prattle, taunting and derogatory statements. I unleashed all my pent-up anger and frustration on his swollen head trying to kill him once and for all.

Yet, something was wrong. I felt very tired, and weak. Each breath seemed to be draining me of my strength. The need for sleep was suddenly overwhelming. I begin to lose interest in killing the Looper. I got off his unit and staggered into the center of the kitchen then sat down with a thud. I need a nap, just for a second, then I would finish off that rat bastard. I laid down noticing the floor was wet with cool aid. I must have knocked over a pitcher of it. It was sticky, maybe too much sugar? I didn't care. I laid in the thick tacky red liquid watching the shadows help the Looper back to his feet. I figured he would maybe kill me while I slept, but honestly I couldn't get up to fight anymore. The sandman was coming. I felt my lids growing ever heavier with his magic grains as they weighed me down. I closed my eyes ready for a long rest.

I was being lifted and shaken hard. Something sharp hit my cheek. I could hear someone talking in the distance. They were not allowing me to rest. I moaned but didn't try to wake up. That is what they were saying, wake up.

I ignored them. Something cold was shoved into my jumpsuit. I stirred and tried to tell them to stop it, but nothing came out. The demon tongue had swollen up. I chuckled remembering I had cut it out. I opened my eyes to see Dennis standing over me looking scared and beat to shit too.

His face was covered in scratches, his hair was disheveled. I groaned but couldn't understand his words. He was slapping my face and putting ice in my clothing. Mistress Ginger was holding a towel over my left wrist. She had been crying. Her face was red and scratched up too. I wondered if she had been in a fight.

I saw lights flashing across the ceiling, red and blue. A wailing was in the air. I wondered who was being sent to the hospital. Surely, that was the sound of an ambulance or least it sounded like one to me.

I saw shoes. I looked up it was Boyd. He too had been fighting. His eye was black, his lip busted. I assumed they must have had to take down a criminal. I felt bad for them, but I would send them a get-well card right after my nap. I was tired. My eyes closed too heavy to keep open another second. Someone, a young man was forcing a mask over my face. I tried to get up to get out of his way. He must have made a mistake. I didn't need that smelly thing on my face. Dennis pushed me down telling me to hold still.

I felt the bite of a needle in my arm. I saw the IV bag. That didn't make sense at all. I tried to rip that away. Why would they be bothering me with such bullshit. I just needed a fucking nap. I became angry again. I tried to get up, but the young man and Dennis were strapping me to a board. I couldn't get out of them. I could hear the Looper laughing and taunting me. He had won. He had called the fucking cops on me. I was being taken to the hospital. That motherfucker. I tried to sit up, but they had me tied to that board. They were lifting me up. I began to yell, but the alien tongue wouldn't work. All that came out were repeated words, and rhymes.

"Damn, damn, damn. I think maybe I am having an episode, something is wrong here." I thought but what came out was, "Damn. Sam. Ram. Ham. Lamb. Yam. Pam. Damn."

The sedatives shot into my IV began to work quickly. The world whirled for a moment suspended in time and space, then imploded into the darkness of the void taking my consciousness with it. I gone off to La La Land.

I was taken to the local hospital and admitted inpatient treatment in the psychiatric wing for 'attempted suicide, homicidal and self-injurious behaviors.' Apparently that had not been the Looper, but Mistress Ginger I beat up, then the second time Dennis. Poor Boyd got smacked around trying to pull me off his partner. I was quite a bad Psycho this time. I used a chair from the kitchen table when my fists were not working while assaulting the attending officers. Thank the Gods it was Dennis and Boyd. Other police officers likely would have shot my raging ass.

My own injuries were also grievous. I had cut my tongue significantly and opened my left wrist. The blood loss had led to my losing interest in the battle with cops and my Mistress. They forced a blood transfusion, stitched up the tongue, and closed the wounded wrist too. The many bruises and injuries on my unit caused by Mistress Ginger were catalogued as previous self-injurious behavior and didn't make me look reliable in my own defense.

NOTE: *I lucked out in that Mistress Ginger did not file charges and Dennis and Boyd didn't push it either. My lawyer got the charges chalked up to insanity and I ended up with enforced psychiatric treatment committal for two weeks to stabilize my condition. They kept me out of my mind with sedatives for the first four days. I have few memories of much of this inpatient treatment thanks to intense antipsychotic medication and heavy Benzodiazepines. I was later informed this was the most violence that I had demonstrated to that date. Ah hell, I can beat that in no time promise. In the end, four of us went to the ER. Dennis, Boyd and Mistress Ginger were all treated for cuts, contusions, and Mistress Ginger had a slight concussion. Guess she shouldn't have been fucking with me hmmm?*

Amazingly no one questioned from that party seemed to report the likely reasons for my extreme violence that night. Not even my beloved Linda, who when questioned told her fellow officers I was fine when she left. Thanks for the help there Linda. Everyone believed I just went off without provocation. You all know the real reasons behind it. I did try to tell the psychiatrist I had been under a lot of stress, but I was told it was my prodromal kicking into acute phase, and nothing more. Whatever. We all know better, now don't we.

I didn't say a word about my discovery of the Judas unit parts. The psychologist asked me why I had tried to cut out my tongue. I continued to deny I had any memory of doing such a thing. Eventually, the entire subject was dropped. The psychiatric folks chalked it up to just another of my psychotic episodes set off by oncoming switch in my cycle. No one doubted that at some point I would require longer care, but for now, they cut me loose with only fourteen days in the white room.

NOTE: *It may seem strange that they didn't keep me longer. I mean I did try to cut out my tongue and a hand. However, I only had shitty old Medicare insurance. There was no money in holding me for months so long as I appeared docile and compliant. I was quite experience at the inpatient game. I had learned to keep my mouth shut about delusional process and never reported hallucinations. Only my most serious symptoms such as Echolalia and clanging were obvious. Those often disappeared rapidly with heavy increase in meds. So often I was released while still psychotic as hell.*

It may piss you off to hear this but the hospitals are not there to cure people like me. They are only money-making machines. Long term illness is avoided unless there is a ton of cash to be made. Schizophrenics are some of the poorest and least decently insured people on Earth. They are also the ones who need inpatient the most often and for the longest time. However, they are likely the most underserved of all the mentally ill. I was referred to by the inpatient staff as state trash because I had Medicare and was a chronic case.

While smaller hospital psych floors, and private mental hospitals tended to be more attending to my poor health, they too treated me different than the paying or insured persons. I often was put into straight jackets for days on end, hosed down rather than bathed, and never once did they check my vitals when not in a physical hospital. If I complained of physical problems, and often had them, I was ignored and even strapped down and shot up with sedatives to shut me the hell up.

So, it is kind of like being at home with the Mistress or in jail when I go to the hospital. This time is not much different, except they have Master Jon watching like a hawk. Suddenly, I am being treated better. They really hate it when you have someone advocating for you. I mean having to do your fucking job must blow right?

I was grateful to find I was not fired from my funeral home job nor kicked out of college. I did have to do some serious catching up, and sadly I was not even close to well. Somehow, I would manage to do both, but the severity of my psychotic episode during early prodromal was worrying me a bit. It was rare to have a near miss on a felony when I still sort of had my wits about me. It didn't bode well for the coming winter storm of acute phase. Even my hard headed Mistress was now a bit afraid of what may be coming down the road shortly.

She visited me often while I served out my time inpatient. My Mistress brought flowers, love notes she had written me, and even lovey, dovey cards covered with hearts and glitter. She brought my children to see me with Maiden Mary and Delilah's aid a few times. They were now old enough to grasp that their mother was sick but still too small to understand the brain sickness I have.

It did help keep me from falling into depression believing there was something to come home to. The visits didn't stop my errored belief about my tongue and hands. Mistress Ginger put a stop to my attempts to remove those items by giving a prime directive to leave the tongue and hands alone. She further sanctioned my threats to these parts by stating that any perceived aggression towards any parts of my unit would be treated with immediate commitment by her own hand to the Snake Pit. She knew that would make me think twice before trying that trick again.

A guardian can sign me in against my will without even going before a judge if the hospital agrees to take me. The hospitals are always on the side of my guardians even though I didn't always agree that anything was wrong with me.

For now, at least, I would have to call a truce in my war against my alien organs. It pissed me off to no end, but I didn't have a choice. Sooner or later I would get them, I swore it. I had healed up quickly from my thwarted self-abuse. My Mistress was most pleased when she picked me up to bring me home to find my unit unmarked, unscoured and ready for her to continue with her enjoyment of it.

She didn't waste any time either. She picked me up from the curb in the wheelchair, pulled into the first backwater dirt road in a secluded area and demanded I pleasure her immediately. I didn't argue about the fact that we would have been home in fifteen minutes.

Mistress Ginger liked to get her jollies where there was an element of danger involved. Didn't matter my ass would go to jail right next to her if we had been caught. What she often perceived as eagerness in my efforts to send her to climax was actually anxiety. I was merely trying to get the deed done quick as possible before we got arrested.

Once I had given her what she demanded, she pawed at my unit demanding I allow her to adore me. I pushed her off saying I didn't feel up for such affection. This angered her.

"What the fuck is wrong with you. Psycho? You have been distant and cold. I would think you don't love me anymore." Mistress Ginger pouted while I straightened out my outfit from her attempts to defile me.

I shook my head. "I just got out of the fucking hospital Mistress. I am behind at college, full of antipsychotics, and to be quite honest a bit pissed to be asked to fuck you in the God damned woods like an animal," I growled not willing to play her stupid games.

She snorted. "Oh, animal. That is what you are. My pet, I love the woods, the open air. Stop worrying so much and live a little. Relax and let my kiss you all over. You just need a little release is all." She grabbed at me trying to slide her hand down my pants again.

I grabbed her arm holding her off. "I just told you I cannot, Mistress. The medication numbs my unit. I cannot orgasm and I am not sitting here for hours while you rub me raw trying the impossible," I yelled feeling my heart speed up with the aggression.

Mistress Ginger looked at me angrily. "You have been fucking someone else haven't you. You little whore. I should just sell you back to Circe. You have been worthless.

Nothing but trouble since you came into my life. Well, who is it. Who are you slipping around with? I will find out so you may as well confess now, you whore." She slapped me across my face.

I glared with true fire in my eyes. "You should sell me back to Circe? Who the fuck do you think you are? I have about had enough of your shit, Mistress. Keep fucking with me, and I will do more than bust your noggin." I slapped her back hard.

She jerked back frightened into the door. "How dare you. I swear…"

I interrupted her, "Go ahead, swear. I will finish you, Mistress. I am tired, overmedicated, and to be honest there is not a lot keeping me from killing every motherfucking one of you bitches that ever got in my way. I want to go home. Leave me the hell alone. I won't warn you again. You wanted to be fucked. Now do you want to be fucked up too? Keep pushing me and it is about to happen," I said through a toothy smile, angrier than I had felt in many weeks. (*NOTE: my prodromal is more likely to result in homicidal rage than any other cycle. I am often irrationally irritable and easy to set into outbursts of fighting. You'd think she realized that since I just got out. Sheesh*).

She wisely decided not to test my resolve. Mistress Ginger started the car and took me home. For the rest of the afternoon she avoided me. I was left alone to rest on the couch unmolested. I needed time for the medications to exit the bloodstream if she was looking for amour.

NOTE: *Antipsychotics at that level will destroy the sex drive and cause extreme fatigue. My irritability indicated the flowing psychosis roaring just under the surface. There was plenty of indication this acute phase was going to be extraordinarily severe. It is unclear what causes one break to be deeper or more significant than others, but stressful environment, and lack of care have been implicated along with lack of loving social support. In this case I had two of the three working against me.*

The rest of the week my Mistress made sure I followed the doctor's orders. She complained loudly to anyone who would listen that she was unloved and mistreated by her live-in girlfriend Psycho. I ignored her attempts to gain attention. I was far too busy trying to catch up on my exams, notes and chapters missed while I had been convalescing in the nuthouse.

I dropped out of the LGBT group from school. CJ and Diane tried to argue with me about that, but with my grades in trouble and Samhain coming, it was too much to add to my schedule. They finally let me be about it when I promised to regroup and re-join during the spring semester.

At work I was given every shit case they could find. It was partly because June had switched to the dayshift. That put Pat in the shift before my own graveyard one. Pat was a lazy fucker, so I ended up working almost every night without any extra time to study.

My grades suffered slightly as I dropped from straight A's to include a couple of B's on the make-up exams. That irritated me immensely. I knew I could do better, but not even I could catch up without proper time to do so.

At home only one week away from the Samhain Sabbat, my Mistress continued to pout and mope about. She apparently didn't want a schizophrenic, workaholic, maternal, student as her only lover. She began seeing other people.

I didn't care. I knew her claims to love me were always false. Once in a while she would bring some idiot she was sleeping with home. Always a young male or female, always dumb, and usually they had no self-respect. Only someone who thought very little of themselves would agree to fuck another person with their live-in lover sitting right there growling at them.

I never bothered to do more than caste them a foul look or two. My Mistress would lure the poor fools into our bedroom, while I would sit in the living room trying to study. I only had a few hours before heading to the funeral home to work like a dog.

Nothing beats being forced to hear your Mistress and some stranger moaning and groaning in passion from the bedroom the two of you slept together in. I would just roll my eyes and sometime put rolled up toilet paper in my ear holes to drown out their grunts and thumping headboard noises.

My apathy about her trysts really made my Mistress angry. She viewed my lack of concern as evidence I didn't care about her. Truth is she was right. I didn't care for her. It is hard to give two shits about someone who cared so little for you they allowed another to rape you, force you to fuck them in front of people you love, and rip half your clitoris off with a Brillo pad. Yeah, you could say I was soured on the idea of ever having that red-headed bitch near my nether part again.

Now that she soiled herself with an endless stream of one-night stands, I added her playing with the potential for disease onto a growing list of reasons not to fuck her ever again. If you throw in massive environmental stress, the prodromal cycle and increased medication you could safely say I had the sexual appetite of a nun. It wasn't too hard to turn down her feeble attempts to try to get me interested in carnal congress with her once more. She and I had not slept together since the fight in the woods and it was looking very unlikely it was going to happen again anytime soon.

To make matters worse, I managed to snag a phone bill. To my extreme irritation I saw she had been conversing on a regular basis with my old nemesis Circe. When I confronted her with the evidence she admitted the old witch was calling constantly offering cash for my key and collar. That sent me right to planet pissed.

"What the fuck Mistress. You can't sell my collar back to her. One chance only," I yelled.

Mistress Ginger's eyes blazed. "I could take her money then drop you off, you tell her that and come back home. We could have the money, and you won't go anywhere. See it would pay her back for being such a shit to you. Think on that, Psycho."

I rolled my eyes. "Are you stupid? Go ahead try to sell my collar, Mistress. Then you are out too. One chance only. We are done with this conversation. You talk to Circe if you like, and I will punish you for bringing a corpse into our bed. Aren't you the one who warned me about that shit, Mistress." I stormed off leaving her there stuttering and stumbling trying to come up with more excuses to speak to that demon.

I knew why Circe was trying to bid to re-collar. She was attempting to snag me back in the hopes she could stop the exile from happening that weekend. If she could hold the High Priestess hostage, she thought she could hold back the tides of destiny.

Even if she had been successful in such a bullshit plan, she continued to misunderstand how all this works. The Coven had exiled her, not me. I was powerless to stop any of it, just as I had been from the start. The Coven voted her out, even if I had been killed, she was still a goner. For being as smart as she was in many areas, Circe was truly ignorant when it came to Circle politics.

Circe's pathetic pursuit of Simon's Key and my Collar were not so farfetched. I sort of expected that heartless woman to do anything to try to keep her tentacles in the pockets of the Green Rings. However, my Mistress Ginger's stroking Circe's desires was outrageous and unforgivable. She was quickly falling down the ladder of my respect for her authority. I would have demanded she hand off Simon's Key had I not been compromised by my damned shifting cycles. The night I found out about her conversations with Circe behind my back, I decided to dump Mistress Ginger the second I was finished with my madness in the spring. I assumed she would do her best to drop the collar anyway, even without my refusal to serve.

NOTE: *The Master or Mistress can toss/sell/trade the Key and collar, but I can also demand Simon's Key be traded/sold/tossed as you have seen twice already. I can also refuse all service and even cut off the collar and abandon the Key if the infraction is bad enough. Mistress Ginger was on the verge of being failed Keyholder number three. In her first sixty days of this occurred from September 3rd to October 30th with most happening in September alone, she had::*

1. Broken a promise to the collar by showing up at Mabon, thus interfering with Wiccan/circle work.

2. Bonded me, then had me raped on her command.

3. Punished me for the very rape she ordered.

4. Forced me into sexual congress that threatened my weak support system and in front of Linda.

5. Failed to protect, even injured my unit without just cause (Brillo pad scour bath and severe thudding before Mabon).

6. I had been committed by the state, not my Mistress due to a violent psychotic episode, that she had set off.

7. Flaunted her lovers to cause stress and brought these strangers to our home thus endangering my own and the children's safety. Who the fuck knows what those people could be up to.

I could have been killed and nearly killed myself in my horrible response to her bad treatment. Even the beast who shall not be named, and Circe had not managed Simon's Key so poorly so rapidly. For a so-called professional Dominatrix she was doing everything wrong. I had begun to believe I had made a terrible mistake. She was very structured and excelled at making sure all my daily adaptive functioning needs were being met. However, she was causing so much drama in the environment that it had negated all her good deeds in comparison. This is because making sure I eat, take a bath and take my medications does no good when the Masters don't protect and defend me from myself and the stresses of exploitation, disease and, let's face it, abuse of my own dangerous desire to serve the one who holds the Key without ability to say no.

Then two days before Samhain, my Mistress brought home a male named Matthew. This man was twenty-eight, at least six foot five or six with long straight dark blond hair. He had deep set pale blue eyes, and a strong jawline. He was well formed appearing to be without an ounce of body fat, and one could say uncommonly handsome. Matthew appeared to be of Scandinavian or German descent by his phenotypical makeup. This is only a guess since he didn't really know himself. Interestingly, he was dressed from head to toe in black.

He proved to be a credit to the masculine side of the species with exceptional manners, was soft spoken and completely in control of himself. Matthew was not like the other lovers my Mistress had brought in off the streets. This fellow was college educated, not addicted to some substance, not incredibly young, and he was introverted as hell. He also didn't appear to be interested in my oversexed Mistress in the carnal sense. This was a rather big shock since my Mistress may have been a bitch, but she was uncommonly beautiful herself.

She had met him at a local bookstore and coaxed him into coming home with her with promises of an exceptional book collection. Once he arrived and looked through her many novels of erotic subjects, bondage and other taboo subject matters, one could say he was completely turned off. I could tell he was only being nice hanging around for a bit longer after realizing he had fallen for a trick to get him to follow her home. I assumed he must be either married or otherwise taken. No way a guy was going to turn down the obvious free, wild sex my Mistress was practically throwing into his lap.

I had a big exam coming up the next week so as usual I sat on the far end of the sofa trying to ignore this latest of her attempts to conquest an unwitting fool. I watched using my peripheral vision, with some humor, as my Mistress did her very best to tempt this quiet giant. She was hell bent to get him into our bedroom for a viewing of her etchings. Matthew wasn't falling for anymore of her bullshit. He seemed rather annoyed he had made the trip to her couch and was less than interested in seeing her boudoir.

I tried not to snicker when she made immature statements such as "You are so big. I bet you could just toss me around like a little dolly" and "Oh my goodness what cologne are you wearing? It is making me feel so warm."

Matthew saw me hiding my smile with my hand. I was dressed as usual like a BDSM slut with my signature makeup. I had noticed he raised an eyebrow when he first saw me. Like most people he likely was wondering what my damage was. I looked like a female backup singer for KISS wearing huge platforms with a white face and blacked out eyes. He had offered his hand to shake but I just looked back at my book ignoring this latest victim. He would be gone by morning. No sense in getting too familiar with the help after all.

Now that he had figured out Mistress Ginger's game and my obvious approval of his actions, he was interested in finding out just exactly what my role in this whole fiasco was.

"I introduced myself earlier, but I suppose you were busy studying. I am Matthew." He stood up offering to shake my hand again when Mistress Ginger left the room to pee.

I didn't even look up from my book at the gentle giant, "You can see I am still studying Matthew."

He snickered. "That you are. I apologize. It is just, well, your look is far out. And I have a passion for Science. I see you are studying Advanced Genetics. I am fascinated by the recent discoveries of the human DNA geom. I realize it is quite rude to interrupt but finding someone around here that can read much less understand more than air is made up of oxygen is just too tempting to pass up."

I looked up at this strange fellow from my page to see his face showed honesty. He was not trying to come on to me. He obviously was much brighter than the average bear. I could understand his pain. Most people in the area were not very smart or were poorly educated. I softened my irritation slightly.

"Well Matthew, they call me Psycho. Before you get comfy, I dress like this because Ginger, the woman you followed home, she is my Dominant. You see this collar? (I lifted my collar) This means I do whatever she says. I belong to her, so that makes me her lover or I was. You look like the poor sacrifice for tonight. I thank you for taking my place. She is quite the lover, but you see I am unable to reach ecstasy because of all the medication I take for my disease schizophrenia. I hear voices, run my head into walls and try to cut out my tongue. When I am not busy doing all that Mistress Ginger forces me to my knees. It is usually my job to eat my Mistress's…"

"Psycho," my Mistress came out and interrupted my attempts to frighten Matthew away.

"Oh my God. Look Matthew, my little sister here is right, she has schizophrenia. Don't listen to her. She is cracked you know. Now, if you would just come with me to the back, I have other books you may be interested it." Mistress Ginger tried to grab Matthew's wrist.

He pulled away "Let go. I wanted to hear what else Psycho had to say." He looked back at me smiling.

That was very confusing. 'Uhm, I guess I was done. Mistress, he is not interested in you. I would suggest you show him the door. Looks like he is smarter than you pegged him for. Good thing he figured you out before you pegged him for real." I snickered at my nasty sexual reference.

(If you don't know what pegging is then look it up. Nurse, I need meds over here).

To my shock Matthew started laughing too. "Holy shit that is funny. Ginger, I adore your little sister Psycho. She is great."

My Mistress blew out her breath appearing frustrated. "She isn't great, Matthew. She is sick in the head. I told you she is mentally ill. Psycho is a pain in the ass once you get to know her. She should be locked up and the key thrown away."

He suddenly stopped laughing then turned to her glaring. "That is very small of you to say. My favorite Aunt had schizophrenia, Ginger. If I were you I would read a fucking book or two on the subject. She is not a pain in the ass to anyone. We are the pains in the asses to people who have this illness. You should cut your sister some slack. She is smart, funny and creative. How lucky you are to have all that right here in your life. I loved my Aunt Maggie more than I can ever say, and when she died from suicide, it nearly killed me. She was the greatest heart I had ever known, and the most tortured. Thank you for the look at your book

225

collection. Thank you, Psycho, for the laugh. Today, I needed one. You ladies have a wonderful evening, I need to be on my way." He bowed just a bit at the waist then headed for the door.

My Mistress shot me a look of panic then took off after Matthew, "Wait, Matthew. Stay for dinner. Psycho is an amazing cook," she nearly screamed.

Matthew stopped at the door. "Really? What's for dinner?" He smiled.

Mistress Ginger smiled. "What is your pleasure, my Prince. Psycho can make anything you want. Right Psycho?"

I groaned. "Yes, Mistress." I put down the book, then headed for the kitchen pissed I was being pulled into the wooing of a potential lover for my own damned Mistress.

This was low even for me. I didn't care how many dicks she sucked or women she fucked. However, I was not her matchmaker and forcing me to help her bag Matthew by offering a meal and conversation was just undignified. Not just for me, but for my beautiful girlfriend. She needed not resort to tricks, lies and schemes to get laid as far as I saw it. If Matthew wasn't playing ball, then forget him. He was lucky she even bothered to give him a second glance. A girl should have more respect for herself than that, at least that is how I saw it.

However, when the Mistress orders you to cook, and join the conversation you do as you are told. At least she was asking for services I was much more peaceful about providing her. The special services of the collar were still being withheld due to reasons already stated. She was providing for all my daily adaptive functioning needs, so in the end, I justified this bullshit (when I really needed to study instead) as my return for her very stellar services in those areas.

Once Mistress Ginger got off the topic of sex or anything about carnal congress, Matthew began to yap pretty much non-stop. He actually was very intelligent, well rounded in interests and a great conversationalist. The three of us were able to engage in interesting topics for almost the entire three hours I had left before work. I made a lovely pasta-based meal which made both my Mistress and her guest eat with gusto. While I cleaned up the mess, and attended the children, Mistress Ginger continued to wow Matthew with her grasp of Greek Philosophy.

I put the kids to bed then returned to the budding love birds to announce I would have to leave for work very soon.

Matthew looked down at the table. "That is too bad, Psycho. I was hoping you could stay and talk some more."

My Mistress practically leapt from the table. "She can call in sick. Call in sick, Psycho, now."

I glared at the horny Mistress. "Really Mistress, even if I did, I have the test coming and Samhain to get ready for. I do appreciate the conversation; it has been a breath of fresh air. However, you must forgive me Mistress, I am just too overwhelmed right now. I am close to losing my GPA as it is." I was not lying about any of it.

Mistress Ginger growled, "Psycho, you do what you are told now. I said call in sick. You are staying home to visit with us and that is final."

I rolled my eyes, trying to calm my anger demon. "As you wish, Mistress." I sighed loudly while I began heading to the living room to make the ordered call.

Matthew looked up stunned. "Wait a second, then it is true? What Psycho told me in the beginning? She isn't your little sister. She is your submissive and your lover? That collar is real?"

Mistress Ginger shot me a look of irritation/ "Well, Matthew, it's, uhm, complicated."

I chuckled. "My Mistress means, yes I was telling you the truth. See you another time Matthew. It was a pleasure. Don't forget to write."

I walked to the door to grab my coat. I needed to get to work. It was best to end Matthew now before I lost any work hours to this farce anyway. I knew my Mistress would kick my ass for telling him the truth, but this guy was smart. He was going to figure it out soon enough.

I already realized he was not the kind of guy who wanted one-night stands. This man was looking for long-term. He had admitted he was neither married nor taken. Only a gay man or one who was super picky and looked like that would still be single. If he was picky, then he would never fuck my Mistress then just walk away. If he was gay, well that would come out in the wash sooner or later too.

I actually thought Matthew likely was a romantic – just for the record, so is Master Jon, he is this kind of man. These kinds want to get a ring on the finger. I got on the Motorpsycho, feeling a bit better about humanity now that I knew men like Matthew existed. Maybe there was hope for the world after all. I am sure my Mistress would not agree that his kind was the best of them all. She would go to bed alone that night. Oh well, she would just stop bringing home decent folks.

The next two days were a blur of studying and a bit of anxiety. I was very afraid that Mother Delleh would cancel the celebration of Samhain. There were rumors in the Green Temple that she had started to develop seizures from her brain tumor. Only the Queen could exile Circe and exiles usually only happened during the Samhain Sabbat since it was the holiday of death and new beginnings. I practically held my breath for the next forty-eight hours, jumping every time the phone rang confident it was Maiden Mary or Summoner Johnny calling to say the ritual was cancelled. However, the call never came. That fine Saturday morning James pulled up in the red van to take me and the children with my Coven members to Springfields. This time, Linda had decided to join her circle elders by accepting a ride in the Temple vehicle. I am sure James was not too happy. Since Linda was a cop, he would have to slow his happy ass down just a bit.

My Mistress was sullen, bitter and angry when I came to have her remove my collar earlier that morning. She had not successfully managed to gain any new lovers in her bed for over four days. I am sure she was feeling unsatisfied. I was still refusing her access to my own unit but was attending her needs when pushed hard. She was not allowed to thud at all. The doctors had warned her to keep me from self-abusing. Of course that was her not me, but the doctor didn't know it. The thudding tended to stress me out. Stress would send me deeper into the pit of whackoville. My Mistress was forced to stay her hand or be guilty of not protecting or defending her property when it was at its most vulnerable.

She had been so angry at her lack of being about to abuse me as she had been the night before the Sabbat, she had lost her temper. Mistress Ginger said that only being allowed to have me pleasure her without her usual fun was as boring as masturbation. What she was really saying is that not being about to torture, thud, humiliate, or otherwise touch my unit, straight sex without fetish or BDSM, was not her thing. It was my assumption that when the time came, we would both be ready for the Key to pass hands. She was obviously unhappy with my service as could be provided at that time and I certainly was unhappy with hers. A nice clean toss was in the air. All I had to do was get through the winter.

The ride to Springfields that day was pleasant. I had not spoken to Linda since that infamous scene in the hallway she had walked in on. To my surprise she asked me to join her in the very back of the van for a private discussion almost immediately after leaving my house. Chuck was kind enough to join the others and provide a bit of space for me and my Goddess to work out our hurts.

"Uhm, Psycho. I just wanted to say, look I had no business coming into the hallway that night." She looked at the floor appearing embarrassed.

I chuckled. "Well, you must have known what was going on. No matter. It shouldn't have been happening at all. I suppose Ginger and I got a bit carried away. I apologize you saw that."

She smiled. "Oh well, I can say I have had a lot of dreams about it. Only it was not Ginger against the wall." She blushed.

That made me smile. "I am glad you are more mature about it than Ginger or I were. Just do me a favor, never invite my girlfriend to a party you will be attending again. Also, if you hear someone moaning out my name best to stay seated. I can promise you they are not asking me to pass the salt or grab them some toilet paper."

She began to laugh wildly. "Well, I can see why she was yelling your name. Tell you what, you ever decide to ditch Ginger, I always have a place in my bed for you. Now that I have seen the advertisement I am sold."

I winced realizing that her catching us like that only made her desire to bed me deeper. "I will keep that in mind, Goddess." I gave her a hug then we rejoined the rest of the members.

I felt better than she was not too heartbroken over seeing me like that. However, it nagged at my heart strings that she still only saw me as a potential lover not just as a friend. I didn't need more people wanting to fuck me (over is more like it). I needed support and friendship without the dirty grim of sexual tension. It seemed to me that normals allowed the act of lovemaking to complicate things. Once it happened, they never could just let it be that one special time or in the past. They either wanted more or felt they were owed something more in a relationship. It seemed to me the intimate act itself should be payment enough. It is a hard thing to do, isn't always clean or beautiful, and opens one up to complete discovery by the lover. To expect more after submitting to such a thing is just greedy if you ask me. No one usually did.

The weather that day was uncommonly hot for that late in the year. Yet, the second the sun would set the night would usher in downright cold temperatures. Everyone was ready for the wild ride Mother Nature surely would bring us on this last night of the Pagan year. We arrived on time despite James foot being a bit lighter on the pedal. I was grateful to see most of our new children had already arrived. The grounds were alive with hundreds of Wiccans all bustling about to read their fortunes or collect wood for the bon fires later. The long table and table for our honored dead was decorated with many a picture, amulet, or other special item that once belonged to a member of the Covens in their time here in this plane.

I was told my Priest's Coven vehicle was held up in traffic, but he and his members were rushing to make the sundown deadline. I wasn't worried. I knew my Priest. He would never let his family down. I walked over to the table honoring the fallen. So many smiling faces, so many items that no longer had an owner laid there. It made me feel forlorn. You could feel the grief radiating off each thing there, the tears of those who were left behind.

A hand reached out and touched my shoulder. I turned to see my beloved Queen. She was very thin, ashen and disheveled. She had to walk using a walker now. Her time was upon us. I could see the Summerlands reflected in her eyes. I felt a tear fall down my cheek not even realizing how deeply affected I had been by the death that surrounded me in that place.

She smiled. Many of her teeth had fallen out in only thirty days since last I had seen her. This beautiful woman was withering away, becoming a spirit right before my very eyes. My rush of sadness was not for her, it was selfish. I didn't want to see her go away. I feared being left alone to help her children find their own way till they too ended up on the table for the dead. As usual, she could read my mind.

"Ah, Daughter Arodia, my Necromancer. You feel the death near, don't you? You know it is my last Sabbat with all my children. I can see it in your tears. I understand. I once was you. My Queen was leaving me and I had to take up the heavy crown alone. I cried till I thought I would die of dehydration, but I knew I had to carry on. You and your Consort will do the same. It is the way of things. The Wheel turns from the birth of Spring to the Death of Winter for us all. I am not afraid. The Summerlands will see me healed and beautiful once more. I will come back again and next time I will do it right." She chuckled.

I shook my head trying to buck up. "Mother if you didn't do it right this time, none of us have hope of ending our own cycle of rebirth. I doubt I will ever see you again. I must say it has been an honor."

I felt I may break down realizing this was goodbye. We would not have another moment alone this Sabbat. Whatever I said now would be the end of it.

She smiled as she watched the tears begin to roll despite my best efforts. "We all do our best with what we have in this life, my Daughter. Only the Gods can decide if we were balanced or if we took more than our fair share. I would like to think I lived a life of pure love and trust, but I know I didn't always. Somedays, I was human and not the deity everyone thinks I am. I will be reborn when my time comes and I hope I get the honor of seeing you in the next life. If not, then know that it was my honor to meet one so loved by the Gods before my time was done."

That confused me. I was not loved by the Gods, which was for damned sure. However, I would never get the chance to ask her what she meant by that. Right after she said that we were both overrun with questions and circle business. I would never get another chance to be alone with my beloved Mother. I like to think of Mother Delleh that way. She would have to leave early from that Sabbat, and she was right, she would never return to the Springfields again.

Over the years I finally decided the wise woman meant that despite what my life journey looks like, I am most beloved by the Gods because I am still here. No matter what came, no matter how bad it looked, no matter how much I lost, I came out on the other side. Not that I didn't bleed, fail, cry, suffer, or even scream. I did all those things and more. She meant that the Gods always seem to send just enough or catch me just before it is too late to turn back. I may be the unluckiest person you have ever met, or maybe just maybe I am the luckiest. It is really up to each person to look at a life and make that decision based on their own perceptions of what is luck, what is balance, and what is it they expect from the viewpoint of natural laws. Mother Delleh viewed my existence as evidence of the divine. Who am I to say this amazing soul was wrong?

My Priest arrived just in time to help me begin the Dumb Supper. That night no one reveled at that table as they normally did. We could all feel the veil was thinning and opening for our Queen. No one dared to even make a sound. It was as if everyone thought if the Lord of Misrule forgot we were there he would forget to take Mother Delleh with him to the other side. No one could keep their eyes off her. I could see the wetness in many eyes and many plates were sent back barely touched. It seemed most had no stomach for this ritual of honoring the fallen. Everyone knew next Samhain, Mother Delleh's beloved Green crown would lay next to the last Queen's on that table and her throne would be empty.

Our tradition dictated that when a Queen died, even though a new Queen was elected, she would leave the throne empty for one year and one day in honor of her that gave her lifeforce to the Covens. In all the years I ran the Green Rings, no Samhain was more bitter, cold, sad than that one. I was told by the Elders after the death of Mother Delleh that no other Queen of the Green in the Coven's memory had been so beloved or so missed as she. I can understand why, and I for one would not have wanted to try to fill that throne next. Circe had been an idiot to even consider such. Those people, including me, loved their Queen Delleh. Her death broke everyone's heart.

After the supper was done. Mother Delleh rose from her throne and with great dignity, reverence and silence she took Circe's chalice into her hands. She called upon the Covens to approve the exile of the Crone from the Green Rings. The members all raised their hands. It was unanimous. Only us Elders could not vote. Roary and I sat with the other High Priests and High Priestesses with our cowls up and heads down. We didn't say a word. Mother Delleh, with Summoner Johnny's aid, walked past all us Elders showing us the chalice warning each of us to remember that a cup is to be drunk from by our members. A cup doesn't drink from its own as Crone Circe had done. We were reminded that our Coven's raised us and they could lower us too. Each of us knelt before our Queen as she took the chalice to the hearth. It was laid on its side along with the triple cords, triple crown, and Priestess robes that had been confiscated from Circe. Our Queen cut the cords with her own ritual knife. She tossed them into the blaze. She picked up the robe and threw it in after. Then she took a ritual mallet and smashed the cup and crown tossing both in to be licked up by the cleansing elemental of fire. No one dared to speak or breath as she opened the Coven's Master Book of Shadows. She scratched out the name Circe in dragon's blood ink. The exile and erasing were complete. Circe was forever banished, banned and forgotten in the great history of the Green Rings.

This would be the last official act of Mother Delleh. She left just after this ritual exile, never to be seen again. She did not officially die until late December, but she went into a semi-coma, not more than a few weeks later. I got the call just a few days before the calendar of man turned to 1995. Our Queen had died in her sleep, peacefully swept away to the world of perpetual Summer. I admit, I fell to my knees in grief. It took many days for my recovery from the blow I already knew was coming. She meant a lot to those who loved her. Even now as I write this I grieve over the loss. Believe it or not, even my normally cold hearted Mistress Ginger broke down shedding tears.

Losing her was my first real loss in life. I had grieved for Zeppelin, but he didn't die, he just went to live somewhere else. I grieved for Master Anita, but again, she had hurt me more than I even knew at the time. Mother Delleh, that was true death, pure and simple. The Springfields were never the same without her. I put her crown on the table for the dead with my very own hands the next Samhain, just as she had predicted to me. I broke down crying as I did it even though it had already been a year. Maybe it was the reality of knowing Mother Delleh was leaving, or maybe it was the ineffectiveness of my attempts to catch up that caused my early break from reality only one week after the Samhain Sabbat. It is hard to say, however, that break did show up early, it was deep, and the changes it caused would vibrate my plans for the future in ways I could have never seen coming.

So, there it is. A sad end to a beautiful person. We all have lost that one or two people in our lives that we would do anything to just have a few more hours with. Delleh was mine. Sadly, she is the only one I would desire to see again if I really could speak to the dead. However, after she left us, I never heard nor saw her in dreams, visions or other to this very day. I like to believe it is because she was so wonderful, she never had to be reborn. She didn't believe that, but maybe she really had earned the right to stay in the Summerlands forever.

Now we still have many surprises left in Mistress Ginger's reign. I also have an acute phase to suffer that is almost as epic as the one that led me to kick in church doors. Is everyone ready to take that wild ride?

Chapter 31: My Girlfriend's Boyfriend
Mistress Ginger

What is that title all about. What has Mistress Ginger done now. This insane woman seems to know no boundaries. Why can't she seem to be satisfied? That is the way it was with this hot-blooded Mistress. We will say again, you were all warned. Mistress Ginger was a woman of her time, the 1990s.

The nineties were a time of exploration into new territories. In the last moments before the invasion of the computer and the infancy of the World Wide Web, women were coming out of the home into the workforce in mass. Marriage was on the decline. New definitions of what comprised a family unit were evolving. Some were pushing the borders of human sexuality. Being straight and married was no longer viewed as the end all be all. Even the males of the species were seeking once forbidden pleasures when the lights went down. Mistress Ginger was beautiful, in her sexual prime, talented, and ready to face the final decade of the millennium with an open mind. So were Psycho and Matthew.

In this historical period of upheaval, rapid change, and shucking of old traditions, Mistress Ginger, Psycho and Matthew are going to hit the ground running. Twisting what is accepted was the game, and finding affection was the prize. Three in a triangle of trust, maturity, and discovery of the collective consciousness that all people share. When the economic environment no longer favors the monogamous pair, what is a couple to do? Well let's see if we can answer that for all of you.

Ready to take a walk down yet another path of the different? Ah, well, that is the spirit. Now, for this chapter, you may want to call all your very closest friends. Makes sure all of you are ready to join in the fun and games. No worries, there is plenty to go around here in the memories of our past. Shuck off the shackles of what you thought you understood and find that your heart really is bigger than you thought. In fact, we can assure you it is vast in its capacity to adore. All you must do is stop being so damned selfish. That lesson about sharing you learned as a child, well let's see if you really took it to heart.

"You should have run away when you had the chance. Not like I didn't warn you. Geez I thought you were smarter than this. There is still time, if you hurry, but once you take this step there is no coming back. I should know." **Psycho's warning to Matthew: January 1995.**

After the Samhain Sabbat I returned home to find my Mistress still moody, pouting and appearing on the border of depression. It seemed she had not found what it was she needed in our relationship. The trouble with Mistress Ginger was enough was just never enough. Her need for attention were far too great for any one person to fulfill. I often would think that is why she missed the big city so bad. She desired to be adored by the world. My Mistress seemed only happy when her name was being dropped from every mouth around her, no matter in what capacity.

Our own situation was deteriorating rapidly. We no longer slept together, and it had only been two months. Since I refused to submit to thudding and her attempts to bring me to orgasm, she had lost interest in the special services of the collar. That was fine by me. I had too many problems for such bullshit anyway. I was grateful to see an end to her public antics to humiliate me or those around unfortunate enough to witness her loud attempts at drama. She still provided constant monitoring of my daily adaptive functioning needs and I still provide all other services. However, when a couple's sex life goes to hell, the relationship is going to tank shortly thereafter. That is just natural law for you. When you have healthy adults, with, errrr, healthy sex drives, not getting any in the bedroom heralds the coming break up louder than an emergency alarm.

Both Mistress Ginger and I were aware our time was going to be horridly short. It was too bad, but I have schizophrenia and couldn't handle stress. She had Borderline Personality Disorder and she needed constant stress. It was a match made in the pit of Hades. The fights were more epic than our wild trysts had been. Neither of us wished to continue with the farce. Just a few days after my witnessing the erasure of Circe, she and I met to discuss passing of Simon's Key.

The November day was raw, and gloomy. My Mistress asked me to put the kids to bed early and meet with her in the kitchen to discuss issues. I was happy to follow that command. Though I wanted to wait until after my acute stage had passed, I knew it was best to just get this all out in the open. I, like Mistress Ginger, was tired of tip toeing around the house hoping we wouldn't run into each other and be forced to interact. That is just no way to live.

She was already waiting when I entered the kitchen. My Mistress was a beautiful creature to her credit. Despite my distaste for her cruel treatment of my collar, I couldn't help but look at her longingly. If only she had been half-way, well normal. Yet, neither was I. So, I just shrugged off my strange urge to give into her amazing glamor.

She looked up appearing bitter. "Psycho, grab a seat please. It is time to discuss what to do about your Collar. This is just not working for me. I don't think you are very happy either."

I sat down nodding. "I agree Mistress. We are a bad fit no doubt. Whatever you decide to do is alright with me. Just remember there are no second chances. Circe is not eligible. I assume you will want to sell to the highest bidder. Maybe get some of your money back or maybe get enough to go back to LA?"

I looked at the table somewhat saddened that this relationship had failed so quickly. I doubted the next holder would be any better. I had given up all hope of ever finding a decent Master at this point.

My Mistress smiled appearing a bit sad. "I suppose that would be the thing to do. I don't want you to think I don't love you, Psycho. I really do. If I didn't, I would have already tossed your Collar. I know it is not working out, but I don't want to let go. I can't win. I can't handle the trouble without more from you, and I know you can't give me what I want. At least not now. There is no telling how long I will have to wait till you are well enough to be the Psycho I thought I was getting again."

I chuckled. "Look Mistress you knew I was ill when you took that Key. I apologize you just got unlucky enough to catch the disease in the Prodromal cycle. It is likely I won't be well before summer, and it is likely I will only turn around and start a new cycle quickly. This is what life is like for me and always will be until they cure it or I die. I imagine the second is more likely."

She nodded "Yeah, it is bullshit. I am so sorry Psycho. I know you suffer. I know I have been a super shit to you too. The Christopher thing was, well I won't apologize since that would just be words. I made a mistake. We both know I made a few already. I know you have paid for them. I feel I owe you by holding your Collar till your acute phase is over. If I do that and take care of the children, until you are residual again, can you forgive me for the stupid shit I did?"

I looked up in utter shock. "Mistress, are you saying you will keep me through acute, attending the issues that come with it to make up for Christopher?"

She began to tear up. "Yes, if you will say that makes us even. Everything was wonderful with us until I fucked up like that. I am not stupid. I realized that what I did to you was not much different than what that man in the van did to me all those years ago. I don't know what got into me, Psycho. I sometimes just hurt people I love, and then it is over. I have broken so many hearts, but in the end, it is me who ends up alone. Now I have lost the greatest love I had ever known. I would try to make promises it will never happen again, but I won't insult your intelligence. I will hurt you again and again. I can't stop myself. You are too sick to handle it. I also think to be really honest that you deserve better." She broke down sobbing at this point.

I stared at the table unsure what to say. My Mistress was right. She had destroyed something that could have been beautiful. I would never trust her again, and she also had just admitted what I already knew. She would do it again. Mistress Ginger was ill just like me. Like for me, there is no cure or good treatment. She had at least been kind enough to face the reality. We were like fire and oil. We wanted to love each other, there was serious attraction between us, but we had symptoms that were incompatible with a sustainable love affair. So, there it was. A lover I wanted would have to be sent away. That is life. We don't always get what we want even when we really need it.

I stood up and went to her, holding her while she cried. "It is okay Mistress. I will accept your offer to help me and the children through my acute phase. If you do that, know that you are forgiven. I made mistakes too. We are human after all. No one is perfect. When I am in residual, sell Simon's Key and go home. You don't belong in this world of rust. Your engine burns too hot to ever find happiness here."

She held on to me tightly weeping like a little girl. I wanted to cry too, but I didn't dare. I noticed my brain was

244

feeling a bit dizzy and tilting just a tad too far to the left. I dared not allow any emotions to well up or I would have an episode. There would be time for my own tears when the acute wore off and I was left in the arms of another. A Master I did not know, nor likely would feel anything for, would replace this Mistress I was deeply enamored with. I was going to lose the one I adored. It was indeed breaking my heart, but I was helpless to stop it. I sat there holding her for a good hour, finally leaving her with a box of tissues while I headed off to work.

That night I tried to keep the feeling of despair away. It was futile. Despite all her faults and cruelty, I had fallen for my Mistress. It was so difficult for me to find affection for another person. The thought that this was indeed a fail was eating at me like maggots in my brain. I didn't even go home that morning after work but took a nap on one of the slabs. I couldn't deal with seeing the object of my desire knowing I could never have it. It was just too much. I walked home in just enough time to catch a ride with Stacey to my classes.

She noticed I was wearing the same outfit from the day before. Stacey also noticed I was in no good humor. That means she was going to open her fucking mouth. She like my Mistress tended to like to kick a person when they are down.

"What is the matter Psycho? You and the wifey having a lover spat again?" She chuckled thinking her attempt to insult clever.

I glared. "Uhm yeah actually we are. She thinks I have ringworm, but I say it is scabies." I began to scratch as if infectious.

Stacey's eyes went wide. "Are you fucking serious. God damn it Psycho. Don't spread that shit in my car."

I smiled. "Oh Stacey stop being a baby. I was kidding. It is head lice." I started scratching my wig.

She realized I was fucking with her at that point. Even she knew I had no real hair. "Very funny asshole. I was about to bleach out the entire car you idiot."

"I know Stacey. Now, do me a favor and shut the fuck up." I leaned back and closed my eyes to pretend to rest.

My brain was still tilted too far to the left. Something was just not right. However, as long as I didn't stress, I was sure I was going to be just fine. The acute wasn't due for another thirty days, or more. I would just make it through the semester, and hopefully inpatient would be brief enough I could still make the spring semester without trouble. I hoped anyway.

My first class went alright. Except the guy behind me kept mumbling throughout the lecture. I finally got tired of it. I turned around and told him to stop making all the racket. He just stared at me surprised I called him out on his bullshit. Some people are just so rude. When the class ended, he ran from the room as if I may beat his ass for interrupting my education experience with his need to babble on like that.

My next class was a General Psychology course. I found the subject boring and droll, but it was a requirement for my Major. The instructor looked like a doppelganger for Jim Varney, the 'know what I mean Vern' dude. He was in his mid-fifties at that time and awful full of himself for a guy who was uglier than homemade soap. I really hated this professor because of his rambling, arrogant, and often misogynistic lecturing style. His courses were allegedly some of the toughest on campus.

I discovered quickly that it was not because he was intelligent. It was because he sucked as an instructor. His exams all came from the book, and if you learned the five to six chapters per test you could ace his class no problem. He had noticed I pulled perfect scores.

Now the other issue with this idiot was he also had a reputation for easy A's if you were female, pretty, your skirt was high enough and you met him after hours for a drink, if you catch my drift. I really hated the guy big time. He was and is everything I hated about human males. A bigoted, racist, homophobic, chauvinistic pig who thought himself smarter than everyone else.

He had indeed noticed my grades were blowing his perfect score at failing most of the class, women in particular, and I was not blowing him to get the A. He had attempted several times to get me to answer questions in class. I would just glare at him saying nothing. Sure, I knew the answers, but I didn't like him, so I didn't speak to him. I know, I am such a sweetheart.

That day, I was having an issue. The static was lingering in my peripheral vision, and I noticed everyone was mumbling like the fellow from my last class. This was starting to piss me off. I could not for the life of me understand what was so damned important everyone felt the need to speak under their breath about it.

The professor started the lecture by handing back our MMPI-2's (Minnesota Multiphasic, Personality Inventory 2nd edition) that he had requested we all take so he could score them and give us a run down on our personality types. He said it would be fun. I had been a bit more than skittish since this test was well known to me. I had taken it over twenty times already in my many psychiatric evaluations since I was first diagnosed at fifteen. I had no idea at that time how fucking reliable and valid that test is. It never misses. Unbeknownst to me, I had just handed over my diagnosis to this fucking asshole just by taking that stupid diagnostic test.

When he walked over to my desk to hand mine back in red pen he written, "See me in my office after class."

He walked on to the next student not saying a word. This got me very upset. I noticed unlike everyone else, my work did not have a typed-out assessment of my results. Just that demand I see him after class. This started to stress me out a great deal. I sat there ignoring his lecture trying to figure out what he knew and didn't know about my disease. Other psychologists had used this type of instrument to glean out my alleged schizophrenia. Surely this asshole had figured it out too. Until now I had managed to keep my sickness on a need to know basis. I didn't think this monster needed to know my weakness.

Then suddenly out of the blue, his name was re-called to me by the Looper, Doctor Shree. Shree, this was the name of the psychologist that had been handling my case since the days of Debbie. This name was on all my records as the overseer of all my foster placements, and psychiatric records. This guy was the asshole who approved Mary and then the Sloans as my foster guardians. He had also set me up with Doctor Commisso. Holy shit, that bastard was solely responsible for my fucking delusions and shitty life since my escape from Debbie.

Anger began to burn as the Looper taunted and laughed at my stupidity. I had been sitting in a classroom with the very motherfucker who had been the designer of my destruction and I had not realized it. Now, I was more than ready to see this fucktard after class. I had a few things to discuss with him too.

I felt the homicidal rage growing with each second of the clock while I watched this arrogant prick pick on the students. He stood up there lording over them like he thought he was a God. He made cruel jokes when a student got an answer wrong. I saw the room constrict and pulsate with red flashes of light all around. I was having an episode and I didn't even fucking care. All I could see was blood. I wanted this man dead.

Then he made an error on the board but didn't seem to notice it. He had put down the wrong name of a theorist of a psychological ideal. I watched as the students all wrote down the errored information thinking he couldn't be wrong. However, he was wrong. I had read that chapter and Erikson was not the correct answer, it was Carl Rogers. I tried to ignore it, but my anger demons took over. I felt my unit stand up while Doctor Shree had his back to all of us writing down more errored information across the board.

The other students watched in shock as I pushed his scrawny ass out of the way and erased his bullshit. I turned to them and informed them all that on page 255 they would find that Carl Rogers was responsible for the theory of self-actualization, and that Doctor Shree was a fucking moron.

They all sat there gasping unsure what to do as I then took over the lecture begin with Rogers and working my way to Maslow and the truth about Freud's boy Erikson. Amazingly, after a few checked the book, they all began to write down what I said, even nodding in agreement. Then a few even began to ask questions. Doctor Shree just backed himself against the far wall silently watching as I took over his class teaching his students about the important theorists in the history of psychology. Why he didn't call the cops is beyond me.

The hour finished and I released the students as if I had been doing this for a lifetime. I turned to see Doctor Shree still standing there watching the very amused students leaving. He motioned for me to follow him. I went and grabbed my things. I had every intention of getting to the bottom of this matter. I could hear the chalkboard rattling out the equations and codes from 'they' as I walked out after the idiot professor.

NOTE: *For the record, the other students in class that day were well aware I was a four-point student. Many told Doctor Shree later that my lecture made more sense than his did, and my teaching style was more interesting and structured. So, no one was complaining once they realized I did indeed know my shit. Many thought I was his teacher's aide and this classroom take over was planned. So, no one freaked out like they did in high school when I did this very same damned thing when I took over Algebra class.*

This little scene actually caused other instructors to notice me as a potential teacher aide and eventual adjunct Professor. I was contacted the very next semester by several professors and instructors and asked to stand in to lecture when they were called away for illness or other reasons. This began my career in lecturing and teaching on the college level. No kidding. A psychotic episode resulted in my becoming a sought-after instructor. Only in college.

I stormed after Doctor Shree ready to kill this man with my bare hands. The walls in the hallway were heaving and breathing with the burden of years of dusty lectures. I felt my brain fall too far to the left just as we stepped into his office.

He sat down in his desk looked at me and said, "So, you are child X. I will be damned. I can't believe you are in college. In my class. How the hell did you manage that." He looked at his desk.

I followed his eyes and saw a folder with my name on it. He had figured out who I was just by grading my MMPI-2. That really pissed me off but before I could verbalize my irritation, he interrupted my errored thinking.

"In all thirty-five years working in this field I have never seen a psychological profile like that one I scored yesterday but once. It was child X back in 1987. I pulled the file and compared the scores. An exact match. There can't be two of you in this small area. I had forgotten the name, and I notice the names don't match. I did some checking and it turns out the courts have changed your name a few times young lady. I never thought we would ever meet in person but here you are taking over my class and doing a fine job. Quite amazing in fact. However, I think maybe you are psychotic. Your test says you are acutely ill. I have a friend down at the mental health center. Let me call him. I think you may need some help. When you are feeling better, I would love to talk to you about your history, disease and what happened here today but for now I think you need to be in the hospital." He reached for his office phone.

I let out a guttural growl. "Get your fucking hands off that phone, you monster, or I swear I will kill you right here and now." I grabbed one of the books from his desk and hit his hand hard with it. He retracted it, his eyes wide in terror.

I smiled full of venom. "Now that is more like it. You fucker, I want you to know how much I hate you. You ruined my life, you never checked or sent anyone to watch those cunts you sent me to live with. Who fucking approves a foster home relative placement with my mother's mother knowing what she did? You are a fraud, a phony and a bastard. Do you know how I got here to this college? I had to do things you can't even imagine, you motherfucker. I am leaving now before I end you and go to prison. You are not worth it. If you call the cops or even touch that phone, I will burn your office and this fucking school to the ground. You may get me put away, but they will let me out. They always let me out. You remember that fucker. I will remember you. Accidents happen you know." I then realized what I was saying, loudly I may add, in a crowded college office full of other students and professors.

I panicked at my verbal threats. Without another word I turned and ran like the Devil himself were chasing me. I knocked down every student in my path, scattering books and nearly tore doors off their hinges. The terror was fueling my flight into overdrive. My heart was thumping like a jackrabbit. I plowed out of the building into the bright sunny day. The light seared at my brain like a red-hot poker thru my eyes. I had to get out of there. Surely, Doctor Shree would be on the phone calling the cops by now. They shoot schizophrenics. I had to get home to my Mistress or die trying.

I saw Stacey's car and as luck would have it, not lucky for her by the way, she was sitting in the driver's seat studying for a test between classes. I ran to her passenger's door, practically ripped it open then crawled onto the floorboard trying to hide from the helicopters they had sent to find me. Not sure why I thought helicopters, but hey that is why they call it psychosis right?

Stacey stared at me stunned by my odd behavior as I screamed at her to start the car and get me the fuck out of there.

When she didn't move, appearing unsure what to do, I came out of the floorboard. I reared back and punched her right in her nose hard. "I said get me the fuck out of here. The cops are coming. Drive, damn you. Drive now. Get me home." I then retreated rolling up on the floor trying to keep anyone from seeing me in her car.

This made Stacey wake up, she started the car and took off like a shot racing for home just as I had told her to do. She didn't ask me why or what happened. She appeared to be aware I was damned dangerous. The smack to her beak probably told her that.

NOTE: *Later Stacey told me when I first got into the car I was clanging and not making any sense. She was scared to death by my strange actions. I appeared upset, scared and angry. When she didn't move unsure what to do, I hit her. She told me that then suddenly I started speaking in coherent sentences. Once she understood what I was wanting she didn't dare say no. She took me home like I demanded.*

I am known for my clanging. When acutely psychotic I have an inability to know I am not making sense, so she is likely telling the truth about what happened that day. Maybe she would not have gotten swatted had I been capable of making my needs known more rapidly. As it was, she wasn't too injured, and she was aware I could be violent. Her doing what I told her was the smartest damned thing anyone could have done given those circumstances. She likely saved her own life by just keeping her mouth shut and getting me home.

We pulled up in my driveway. She didn't have to say a word. I got out of her car running for the front door like the yard was on fire. Stacey didn't stick around she backed up and tore out of there squealing tires ready to be shut of my insanity before I came back to finish her off. I practically kicked the door in finding my Mistress in the living room floor playing blocks with my children.

I looked at her in panic then back at the door. I was certain the cops were hot on my tail. I didn't know where to run, but I knew I had to get away. Mistress Ginger grabbed the kids and rushed them to their room. Something in my eyes told her I was not there, and the one who was would not be kind if those children tried to rush up to hug their mommy.

I rushed from window to window looking for the signs that the swat team was closing in on me. I paced and babbled feeling terrified. Voices of every gender, nationality and pitch began to speak all at once. I swore they were driving me mad. I grabbed my ears trying to drown out all the fucking noise. The lights began to pop as the world shifted nearly sending me to my face on the floor. I wailed feeling my brains were melting inside my head. The pain was unbearable.

"Psycho, listen to me. I will help hide you. Come with me, I can help you." I heard a voice call out behind me. I turned to see a red-headed woman motioning me to follow her.

I needed to hide. The police were coming. I remembered that suddenly. I kept my ears covered but took off following the woman to a place of safety. She led to a dark room and closed the door. The flashing stopped but the noise was killing me. I continued to groan as I fell to my knees unsure who this person was, who I was, or where I was. Everything was so damned confusing. I knew I should know, but I couldn't recall anything. It was all jumbled up and tangled like a blown fishing line.

A shadow grabbed me from behind and began forcing a straight jacket on my unit. I fought it but the thing was too strong, the room too dark and I couldn't breathe. The thing was fastening me up keeping me from fleeing any further. I saw the room light up red and blue. I watched the dancing colors fascinated by the gracefulness of the art. I giggled when the blue took the red and curtsied. That was silly, only the red would behave that way. I realized this was not an opera it was a comedy. Or was it. What was it? I had lost my place, something was wrong, but I couldn't recall it.

I saw Dennis and Boyd. They must have come by for that get-well card I was supposed to make for them. They had been beaten up by some criminal I think? I smiled at Dennis.

"You are not the one that is the general because of this was it," he said to me still smiling.

I just giggled. He wasn't making any sense. I wondered if he may be drunk, though I didn't recall him being a drinker. His face looked sad suddenly. I became upset, what was wrong?

I felt he and Boyd lifting my unit. I tried to shift in the jacket, but I couldn't get my arms out. I tried to kick them, but they knew my tricks. They kept me from reaching them. I tried to speak, but I couldn't remember how to make the words right. Something was wrong with my, oh yeah, the tongue is a Judas. It was refusing to do the job. Everyone is against me, you know. No one believes me but even my tongue and hands are working for those who want me dead. Well, no worries. One day I will get rid of those rat bastards. The shadow people can't watch me forever.

NOTE: *Mistress Ginger had me committed to the local psych ward. She had managed to get me into a straight jacket safely, then called Dennis and Boyd to pick my insane unit up. Once examined in the local emergency room, I was diagnosed officially acutely psychotic on November 5th, only a week after my return from Springfields. Doctor Shree had never alerted the authorities and Stacey never reported my strange behavior either. No one had even tried to warn Mistress Ginger I was dangerously ill. I will never forgive either of them to this day. I could have killed my kids, or Mistress Ginger, or myself.*

My cycle was a full thirty days early, deep and I really have almost no memory of the next six weeks of my life. I was told I wandered, paced, babbled, giggled, and clanged even with two series of ECT and heavy atypical antipsychotics. The hospital eventually resorted back to Thorazine in a last-ditch effort to bring me back from the land of the dodo bird. Only then did they start to notice improvement in my severe symptoms. On the seventh week after Christmas Day I was released with a diagnosis of schizophrenia, acute phase, controlled: prognosis guarded. This means if stressed, I would get psychotic rapidly).

My Mistress had to disenroll me for the semester to prevent me ending up with Incompletes for my coursework. I had lost another half a year of college and was now a full year behind my original graduation dates. Luckily, I still had my job with the funeral home. Since I was just an extra helper, my job was flexible, and my boss owned the mortuary business outright. He knew I would have many periods of time where I may be hospitalized when he hired me. Therefore, Julius was very understanding when I couldn't hold off the disease any longer. I was grateful for that one mercy. I was not allowed to return to work until February if I passed reality testing that was ordered on a weekly basis through my psychologist that is. He told me to take it easy and he would see me when I was back up and running again.

I was only home about a day when the news came of Mother Delleh's death. It was very bad timing for me, the Coven and of course for her too I am sure. For over a week I wouldn't even get out off the couch since I was in deep mourning over the loss of the only Mother I had ever known. Even if only for a couple of years, it was better than I had before her. My Mistress was surprisingly understanding and allowed my grief reaction without pushing me to just get over it as I had always assumed she would.

To be honest I was miserable. I cried almost all day, every day on that couch the whole week after my release. I didn't want to see my children or anyone. I was in depression hell. Not just from the loss of Mother Delleh, though that was a big part of it, but from all of it. My semester was blown, my Mistress was going to toss my collar, I had lost more time of my life to only the devil knows where. I didn't see any reason to keep trying to survive. It was the depression that sometimes follows a deep psychotic break threatening to take me under.

By the next week when I still didn't get up, my Mistress called the psychiatrist and demanded I be put back on antidepressants before I did something stupid. She could smell suicidal ideation like a dog can smell a rat through the walls. Depression was one mental disorder she knew well herself. I met the new year of 1995, wishing for death, after surviving the hideous 1994.

After serving eight Masters, being raised to High Priestess, building a Temple to the Gods, being kidnaped and raped twice, helping to exile a wicked witch, sleeping with a strange man in front of Wiccan Elders, saying goodbye forever to a Mother figure, confronting the orchestrator of my ultimate destruction and taking over a college classroom,

I can safely say I was not sorry to see that fucking year go away.

However, only two weeks into the new year I was finding nothing but endless despair. To Mistress Ginger's credit she had kept her word. My children were safe and lovingly cared for while I suffered the ravages of my disease. They were brought to visit me when I could be trusted to know who they were and interact safely. She took care of all the household finances and bills. She made sure I was treated fairly by the inpatient staff. My Mistress was actively involved in my psychiatric treatment and even forced them to switch to Thorazine once she realized in the past it was the only medication that had ever done shit to calm my disease. She had effectively advocated for my medical forgiveness at having to drop out of college again. Mistress Ginger had even noted and step in when the signs of Major Depression started to rear its dark head.

On more than one occasion I had awaken in the night to catch her sneaking into the living room to put a blanket on my unit or check my forehead for fever that sometimes would outbreak with the use of Thorazine at that high a level. She had redeemed herself as a caring, loving, attentive Mistress despite all her drama and diabolical behaviors in the early days of her reign. I was beginning to regret being so hasty at asking her to sell Simon's Key. I don't know what would have happened if she had not been there during this most catastrophic acute cycle. When it came down to the serious business, she had done the job she was supposed to do as Keyholder perfectly.

As the third week of January began, and the antidepressants finally started to kick in, I wondered if maybe I could find a way to work out the wrinkles in my relationship with my Mistress. I wondered if putting up with having sex with her in public or possible surprise lovers in the bedroom were really so much to tolerate when compared to her remarkable ability to keep my attempts at a future on the straight and narrow.

It also was not lost to me that I had only done six weeks with one of the most severe breaks since the Hebephrenic attack in 1988. That was because my Mistress had done her homework and made the hospital change the meds just in time before I went so far it would have taken months to drag me back from outer space.

I went with Stacey the day before the spring semester was to begin trying to work out a plan to speak with Mistress Ginger about how we could both find peace without her selling off Simon's key. Stacey of course ribbed me about my little incident but she was careful not to push me too hard. I was still a long way from residual, so episodes could occur rapidly with very little stress. I had warned her and for a change the dumb thing heard me. She kept her discussions neutral, and cheery. I was able to sign up to repeat all the classes I had lost in the fall. I made sure to select a different profession for General Psychology. I never wanted to see that asshole Doctor Shree again.

When I got home, my Mistress was alone in the house. She had called the Maiden Mary and requested she keep the kids for a few days. I put up my backpack and books unsure what was going on, but my stomach was in knots. I worried she was about to tell me she had a buyer for Simon's Key. I was likely too late to stop the inevitable. She asked me to join her at the kitchen table to have a discussion. Walking into that room that day must be what it would feel like to walk in front of a firing squad. I kept my eyes to the floor trying not to break down crying. I knew this was coming. It seemed I should try to be adult about it. It was her right if she was unhappy with my service. Since I had been sick most of her reign, I couldn't blame her for wanting me out of her life.

I sat down taking slow deep breathes as I prepared for the bad news. She looked at me with what seemed like pity. That made my heart skip beats. I was now sure this was the end. Why else would she feel sorry for me?

Mistress Ginger asked me to look at her. "Psycho. I have been thinking a lot about us, our problems. I admit when you got real sick, I almost sold your Key to Joyce just to be rid of the constant strain."

I winced upon hearing the name of that horrid Dominant I had met the day at the restaurant when she introduced me to the rapist Christopher. The woman Joyce didn't even refer to me as human. She called me it. I started to open my mouth to beg her to reconsider. I would serve anyone but that foul woman.

Mistress Ginger raised her hand in a silence signal. I sat back keeping my mouth closed realizing that angering her now was not smart.

"Well, I almost did it. I just couldn't imagine being without you. It was just fatigue and frustration talking. So, then you started getting better. I had to decide what to do about this mess. I want to be with you and hold Simon's Key, but I keep hurting you. That is not going to change. You are not going to be cured. I was stuck, still without an answer. Then, call it luck, call it divine intervention, an answer to all our problems called me up out of the blue." She paused and a smile broke across her face.

She was just so damned beautiful. I smiled back despite myself, more than a bit confused by her words. I hoped she was saying what I thought I was hearing. She was going to try to keep Simon's Key, she had found an answer?

I shrugged. "Okay Mistress, I am all ears. How can this be fixed?"

She smiled even wider. "The question I ask you Psycho is do you want to fix the problem? Do you want to stay with me? If so, how badly?"

I sat back in my chair then crossed my arms thinking on her inquiry carefully. "Of course I want to fix the problem. Yes, I want to stay with you. There is no doubt I adore you, but what do you mean by how badly? I am willing to tolerate your public displays, rejoin you in your bedroom and even put up with thudding if that is what it takes to receive your perfect service and adoration. Is there something more you are asking me to accept?" I narrowed my eyes. My Mistress didn't fool me, there was indeed something more or else why this meeting.

She chuckled appearing quite pleased. "Yes there is something else. I have found another submissive. I want to add a collar to our household."

My eyes went wide and my mouth hit the table it dropped so low. "What? You want to add another fucking submissive in this house. Are you insane?"

Mistress Ginger laughed out loud. "Yes that is what I want. With two of you it will keep me from picking on you, and you will only have half the stress. Plus, the added income will allow the family to thrive. More than anything else it will add more dimensions to the bedroom. When you are sick and cannot serve, there won't be a break in service, and a second pair of hands to aid me in my care for you too. It is a beautiful solution, Psycho. I can keep you, my love, and have the bonus of another beautiful face kneeling at my feet." She looked proud of her ability to solve this issue.

I still was in shock. I knew other people who claimed to be submissive existed. I had never encountered, much less had to tolerate them in my world, house or share a Master with one. My mind went immediately to Joyce. Mistress Ginger had said she spoke to the woman. I recalled Joyce had said she had several submissive and slave kinksters. She also said she didn't know of any other 24/7 lifestylers. Now I was very confused. If the Dowager Joyce didn't know of any, where the fuck did Mistress Ginger find one. Of course Joyce didn't know about me either did she, hmmm.

I frowned. "I am not going to be okay with some drugged-up kid playing kinkster living in this house around my kids, Mistress. I love you no doubt. I want to stay under your collar, but this may be too much for me to accept. You haven't said, but I am assuming you have someone in mind for this plan of yours. How long has this sub even served? Are they a lifestyler? Who was their last Master?" I started asking questions flying like angry bees around a bear raiding the hive.

My Mistress sat there smiling appearing very smug waiting for me to stop asking questions. "If you are done?"

I nodded that I was finished.

She leaned on the table using her elbows. "This person has never been a submissive. I want you to train him."

I sat up straight. "What the fuck? Not even trained. A he? Hell no, Mistress."

Her smiled melted into a look of irritation "Psycho, I am trying to be nice about this. You really don't have a choice, you know. I am still your Mistress. There are no Key rules about you being the only submissive under my control. I wanted to add to our family with your blessing only because I love you like I do. I wanted this to go smoothly. However, if you push me, I will order you to accept, comply and teach this new collar the ropes. This is what I want. I am going to submit him tonight. You will be there to make sure he knows what he is doing and is made aware of his rights, and make sure he can never say I took advantage of his youthful ignorance."

My eyes almost bugged out on this new information. "Seriously! This was decided how long ago Mistress? This surely didn't just happen today. You knew this and I am just now finding out that there is going to be a fucking stranger in my house and bed."

Mistress Ginger laughed appearing to blush. "Oh, you are a clever one Psycho. Yes, this has been going on since the week after you went into the hospital. I will now officially rescind my order for your monogamy, which is my right by our collar agreement. You are to remain monogamous with one exception. You can and will sleep with the second collar on my command. You will train the new submissive to serve his Mistress, tolerate thudding, and bondage. He will learn all domestic duties and remain monogamous to this house unless I otherwise command."

I was now angry. "Oh, is that so Mistress? Hmmm, and if I don't agree to this shit?"

She smiled hatefully. "Then I will sell your collar to Joyce plain and simple. Serve me or serve that old dust bunny. I have given you the choice just like I promised. So, what is it going to be, Psycho?"

I rolled my eyes not believing this utter bullshit. "Does this want to be submissive have a name Mistress? Or do I just call him fool?"

She roared with laughter. "Well Psycho, you will be thrilled to hear his name is Matthew. You met I believe."

I felt the room spinning. "Did you say Matthew? That big guy from the bookstore? He wants to be collared. What the heck?" I got up and wandered out of the kitchen feeling I had been struck in the head with a mallet. I was so confused.

Mistress Ginger got up and followed me as I sat down on the sofa feeling sick. "Mistress, please don't do this to him. This is all my fault. If I had not been trying to be ugly, if I had not told him the secret. I made a mistake. He is a nice guy, don't bring him into this horror." I trailed off feeling like a monster.

She stood there glaring at me. "Matthew is a big boy, Psycho. This is his choice. He knows what he is getting into. I spent the last several weeks telling him what the life of a 24/7 is like. He is aware. You act like I brainwashed him or something. I am offended."

I looked up at her feeling I may start crying. "He cannot know what he is getting into in only seven- or eight-weeks Mistress. This life sucks. Was sleeping with him not enough for you? You must put a fucking collar on him and make him get on his knees. Mistress, just role play him or something. This is serious shit. You could break his spirit. It is not right."

Mistress Ginger chuckled diabolically. "Oh Psycho, I haven't even seen that beautiful creature naked much less fucked him yet. Not until he is collared. Then I can do whatever I want to him, and to you. I will have one of each. You will have each other. It will be amazing. So, he must learn to kneel or take whatever pleasure I chose to take out on him, in return he gets to live with two beautiful women who adore him. He can worship one and serve at the other's side like a partner. Matthew will be the luckiest submissive on Earth, hell luckiest man. Why do you hate your station in life so much. That is your problem Psycho. You never learned to appreciate the power of your role. Unless you don't like Matthew? Is that it? You don't find him handsome? Or intelligent enough to serve by your side?"

I dropped my head into my hands feeling sick. "Mistress, please don't do this to him or to me. I am begging mercy. Role play him, have your fun then send him away. Or fuck it, marry him, but don't put a collar on him."

NOTE: *I am not completely sure why it bothered me so much that Mistress Ginger was going to collar Matthew. He was old enough to choose his own way, and smart enough to make his own decisions. I think it was the fact that often what a person thinks sounds good on paper is not what the reality of that thing is. Matthew seemed like a sweet guy, kind, gentle, and a good heart. Yet, my evil Mistress would take that most rare of humans and make it beg, grovel, scrap and suffer like I did. I didn't have a choice, or I sure as shit would not be on my knees. Matthew still had the freedom I coveted so much. It was this and the fact that my attempt to run him off had opened the door for his ultimate submission to her dark desires that stuck in my craw.*

I will be honest and say it could have also been jealousy on my part. No submissive wants to share the attentions of a Master with another submissive, any more than any Dominate would like to share their submissive with another Dominate. Let us not forget how angry Mistress Ginger got over my acting like I enjoyed Christopher's attentions as an example here. I want to believe my misgivings and horror at the collaring of Matthew were purely selfless interest in his freedom of spirit and choice. Yet, it could have just been plan old villainous greed on my part. You can decide that for yourself. Matthew will be with us for the next year and eight months as our partner collar, equal, lover and I dare say friend (at least sometimes).

Mistress Ginger would not hear any of my pleas. She was hell bent to collar this poor fool. In the end, I was told to either prepare for his collaring or to get packing for Joyce's house. I, of course, chose to get ready to accept Matthew as a brother collar. At least with Mistress Ginger I only had to train one submissive. Under Joyce's control I would be worked to death training ungrateful kinkster half-wits. I likely would not receive any serious service in return and in the end, who knows who would end up with my collar next. Like it or not, right or wrong, Matthew was going to be a part of my dark world now. In this lifestyle, there are always choices. Just often not the ones you want.

My Mistress had already received a specially made collar and Key for Matthew. She showed me a pretty streamlined silver ring that looked just like the one she gave me, only larger for his much bigger neck. She had also already been shopping for him. To my utter amusement she had picked out nearly disgusting see through mesh black shirts and tight leather pants for this poor fellow. I told her he would be mistaken for a club kid or a refugee from the gay clubs wearing that overly BDSM advertising stuff. She glared at me not finding my statements as humorous as I did. I asked her if he had seen his uniforms yet. She admitted he had not. I rolled my eyes trying not to snicker and piss her off further.

Oh well, if Matthew wanted to be submitted, he was going to find out the hard way once you belong to one of these Masters, they often will enjoy your pain. He was surely in for more than he had expected if he expected any at all. It then suddenly occurred to me that maybe Matthew was one of those masochistic types. I asked my Mistress, but she verified he was not. Usually, the 24/7er is more intelligent than average, very specialized (geared towards service) and often not into pain or humiliation but is aware of all of it and bondage comes with the territory (so they all learn to tolerate it).

NOTE: *You would not last long in this daily life if you wanted to be hurt on purpose. Too many Masters would beat the shit out of you until there was nothing left. Usually masochistic types stick to kink and fetish where they fucking belong. You must be capable of learning fast, adaptability, tolerance, patience, meekness, and temper control to survive as a lifestyler. Matthew fit the bill in all those areas on the surface. Only time would tell if he was submissive material for real or just a close facsimile thereof.*

A submissive must learn to endure, serve, be silent, look as beautiful as possible, compliant, gentle, kind, adoring, carry on intelligent conversation and take orders swiftly with little to no argument, just to name a few of the duties. They are works of art, capable of a large array of talents, and intelligent enough to learn even more upon request. Like the Geisha of old legends, the lifestyler submissive is not a whore, but a master of the art of entertainment and pleasure. While sexual congress does play a role in what we do, it is very strictly controlled just like every other aspect of our daily existence. Everything has its place, a rule and protocol. Not many can truly do this job well, fewer still do it perfectly. It takes a lifetime to learn the role properly and even then, there is always room for improvement. That is what Matthew was about to walk into at the age of twenty-eight, without any previous experience of this kind of life. Poor thing, he was in for a rude awakening.

I dressed my Mistress in her favorite red latex cat suit, the one she wore when she collared me, and handed her signature crop to her. She had me carry the collar meant for my soon to be partner submissive. In dramatic style she even had put the blasted thing on a black pillow like a damned oversized wedding ring. I tried not to snicker at this pomp and pageantry. She informed me that since this was Matthews first collaring she wanted to make it special. I noticed she lined up all her favorite thudding tools in preparation for Matthews consummation later after he was duped into being submitted to her. I just rolled my eyes. Poor fool.

"Psycho, you roll your eyes one more time, I will dust off the shock collar," she growled then threw a black cat suit and red cuffs at me ordering I get dressed.

I did as I was told. I then followed her down the hall carrying his collar on the silly pillow. She sat down on the sofa ordering I attend her with a glass of water then get the door when he arrived. I had only just handed her the liquid when the doorbell rang. I couldn't help but sigh as I walked to the door.

"Psycho, I mean it. Keep your thoughts to yourself or pay the price. You will not sully this moment for your brother. Now get the fucking door. Hurry up," She said to me.

I opened the door and there stood the tall, handsome, future submissive. He was dressed in a simple black shirt and black jeans with black tennis shoes. I looked him over realizing he would not be too keen on the elaborate boots and black latex or leather outfits he would soon have no choice but to adorn his handsome frame with. Amazingly, I was feeling more pity for him than awe at his bravery to take such a step. This life is just not for most.

He stepped in keeping his eyes to the floor. At least he had that natural. I closed the door behind him suppressing the urge to tell him to run for his life. I really didn't feel like taking his place in her honeymoon bed that night. I understood it would happen if this idiot ran away now. Better his ass than mine.

I took my place behind my Mistress crossing my hands behind my back while Matthew stood there appearing unsure what to do. My Mistress pretended not to notice him.

She looked at me smiling. "Psycho baby, what should I have Matthew here do to prove he wants my collar?"

I grinned back at her. "Well Mistress, I think you should give him Mistress Ginger's Bath Service, then make him crawl for it. I seem to recall that is how it is done." I just knew that would end this nutjob's bid for a horrid collar.

My Mistress smiled diabolically. "Ah. You are correct. That is why you are the head submissive in this house and Matthew here is just a little baby. Babies, crawl. Take Matthew into the backyard Psycho, have him strip down and bring the hose. I will be out in a moment. Make sure he doesn't try to run away or it is your ass." I nodded motioning Matthew to follow me out the back door.

We lived in a neighborhood but lucky for old Matthew our backyard was private. I had only recently begun to build a privacy fence so my Mistress could sun in the backyard without prying eyes. He would be viewable by those who were looking hard, so the humiliation of public nudity was there just as much as it had been for my own collaring back in September of the year before. He followed me out without argument or bitching that I had given the Mistress the idea of stripping his ass out in broad daylight or making him crawl like a baby. I truly expected some ribbing or complaint, but true to his desires he was silent as death.

Once outside I told him to get to it, strip down to bare unit. He began removing his clothing without argument. I went to fetch the hose, then turned on the facet. I returned to find him completely without garment standing there staring at the ground.

He was indeed handsome and fit. His clothing didn't hide some horrible detail or secret. In fact, Matthew was the picture of male beauty in perfection. Once again, I had to shake my head wondering why the fuck he was doing this to himself.

The Mistress didn't order we not speak, so I took that moment to ask him myself and to warn him. "Matthew, why? Do you have any idea what is about to happen? You are handsome, smart, you have so much going for you, why throw it away for submission?"

He looked at the ground. "Because I knew the second I laid eyes on Ginger and you I was in love. This is where I belong. I worship Ginger, and I adore you. It is in my soul to be at the feet of a beautiful Mistress. You are the added joy as my sister."

I snorted then warned him to turn back. No love was worth the pain, the loss, the utter humiliation of no freedom. Nothing I said reached his lovesick brain. He was a natural submissive, there was no longer any doubt. He was doomed to a life of servitude just as much as me, only for a different reason. It was in his soul to serve. He would never feel whole unless he found one worthy of his adoration.

I realized Mistress Ginger was indeed the luckiest Dominatrix on Earth. She had found one of each gender. Both Pansexual, both trapped in their role and both deeply in love with her.

I saw Mistress Ginger standing at the door. I rushed to it and opened it for her. She walked by me and took my place three paces behind her.

"Is he ready, Psycho," she asked even though she could obviously see he was standing there naked and ready for her bath service.

"All is as you requested, Mistress," I said making damned sure to follow high protocol. Failure to play ball would get me a nasty punishment no doubt.

She used a hand signal command for me to bring her the hose. I did as I was told, then knelt dropping my head to look at the ground while handing it over.

Mistress Ginger smiled then patted my head. "Matthew you would do well to watch your sister Psycho. She is well trained, with many grueling hours of servitude to glorious Masters. She will help you learn and you will obey her when I am not around."

Matthew looked at me then nodded, "Okay, Ginger."

I looked up at Matthew startled by his lack of knowledge. "Kneel fool. Mistress Ginger to you," I yelled, glaring at him hatefully.

He jumped at the deep sound of my voice but at once fell into the same position I was in and repeated, "Okay Mistress Ginger."

That made the Mistress laugh loud and deep. "Oh my, looks like my two loves already have worked out this pecking order. Very good, Psycho. Now see Matthew that is why you want to watch her. She knows her shit. Hmmm, speaking of things that are foul, I believe someone has to be bathed." She turned on the sprayer hitting Matthew full force with the freezing water.

He immediately tried to cover up his face while yelling in surprise. Just as the Mistress did me, she demanded he hold still and allow her to spray him everywhere. She made him jump like a flea on a hot plate as she spent a great deal of time torturing his male parts with that frigid stream. She persisted until his manhood shriveled up and ran back into his unit to escape the cruel Mistress. Matthew eventually quit trying to fight her spraying just as I had many months before. He knelt there shivering, looking straight ahead taking her punishment. She finally killed the water and handed the hose back to me to turn off and roll back up.

I returned taking my place behind her with my submissive stance as usual. Once I had returned she looked at Matthew who now resembled the biggest drowned rat I had ever seen quivering in the January cold.

"You want my collar, Matthew? Then you will crawl to me for it. You will beg me for it, and you will admit that you hate yourself for needing me to love you so much." She ordered then turned allowing me to aid her back into the house.

When we got inside the Mistress told me to watch him through the window to make sure he crawled the entire way without cheating. I did as she told me to do. I watched this big guy crawl across the yard and up the steps. I opened the door for him. He looked up and mouthed 'thank you.' I mouthed back, 'idiot.'

I followed behind him as he crawled across the floor finally sitting in front of his soon to be Mistress Ginger. She told him to kneel as he had seen Psycho do. He quickly took his position. I watched from the kitchen doorway wondering if he would wake the fuck up before she got that collar around his neck. He didn't, of course.

After he told the Mistress he hated himself for needing her love so much, she began the collaring process. Mistress Ginger made her promises to protect and defend him, to serve him as he was to serve her. She ordered monogamy with one exception, his sister collar Psycho on her command. Oddly, she did not keep the right to rescind this order, she ordered chastity unless she deemed otherwise (no masturbation without permission), and he was to address her as Mistress Ginger from there on.

Mistress Ginger finished her promises then looked to me "Psycho, come kneel next to your brother and aid him in understanding his promises. Make sure he understands his verbal agreements and right to negotiate the terms."

I came over, knelt next to Matthew and told him to repeat the words of promise to serve with the understanding of choice. To refuse commands resulted in punishment at the Mistress's pleasure unless the order would result in damage to the unit or family. He repeated the words, stated he understood the terms, and swore unwavering loyalty to his collar.

I stood back up not willing to be anywhere near that collar coming at Matthew's neck. I watched as he closed his eyes. Mistress Ginger placed then locked her silver submission band around his neck. The clicking made my stomach flip flop. It was done. Matthew now belonged to Mistress Ginger just like I did. She had one of each. A brother and a sister. Her smile was magnificent. She wore pride well.

Matthew looked at me a bit confused. "Now what?"

I laughed bitterly. "Time for the honeymoon, fool. See you tomorrow, maybe, if you survive it."

Mistress Ginger shot me a warning look. "That will be enough out of you Psycho, or I will have you in there demonstrating the ropes tonight, you hear me?"

"Yes, Mistress." I backed up to the wall shutting my mouth immediately unwilling to push my luck.

"Come with me, my love.," aid Mistress Ginger as she grabbed Matthew's collar pulling him to his feet, dragging the big moose down the hallway to his awaiting surprise.

I watched them leave then took my place on the sofa to start reading the chapters for my upcoming courses. Poor Matthew, apparently when Mistress Ginger was explaining the lifestyle to him, she forgot to talk about bondage and thudding. Too bad for him. He was just about to get his first lesson in enduring.

You have been reading about this kind of lifestyle relationship for some time now. With the knowledge you have gained take a guess, what will the interaction between Psycho and Matthew be like? Let me give you a selection. Over the next several chapters you can gage if you were right or not. It will be fun. Will it be 1. Loving 2. Kind 3. Helpmates 4. Jealous 5. Hateful 6. Adoring 7. Cruel. 8. Sidekicks. You can pick as many as you like because no relationship is just one thing now is it?

Chapter 32: I Beg to Serve; Your Wish is Mine
Mistress Ginger

There is nothing wrong with enjoying a little peek into the forbidden, taboo and downright weird. Those words sum up my life experiences. Just when I thought I had seen everything, there was always something new to horrify and disgust. While most of my strange journey can be chalked up to the Queen mother of all mental illness, schizophrenia, some of it can't not be explained away that easily. Matthew was one of these enigmas that to this very day I am still left saying, "What the fuck happened there."

Mistress Ginger is having the time of her life. It was a two for the price of one sale at the old submissive discount store. She couldn't be happier. One handsome male, and one pretty girl both wear her silver bands around their necks. The Mistress no longer needs to be left wanting. All her darkest desires are now met. With two practically begging for her attention right at her feet what could possibly be wrong in her world of plenty and perfected pleasures? Oh, well only that she never bothered to consider the hearts of her collars. Her adoration of them, and theirs for her, does not mean they adore each other. In fact, they despise the competition.

The red-haired Mistress forgot that aggressive needs to win are not solely the property of the Dominant. Her submissive brother and sister are behaving like the children she claims them to be. If only she had created a structured understanding of expectations in the beginning, she could have avoided this countdown to extinction. However, the impulsive woman was only thinking about her desires and not with her brain. A battle has begun, that will threaten to tear the triangle of trust into tiny bits. Can she step in and stop this sibling rivalry before it is too late?

Ready to watch one of the strangest relationships morph into something even odder? For this chapter, bring all your immaturity, petty hurts, and selfishness along. This is the domain of the Dominant. Everyone wants to be Prince or Princess submissive in the Mistress's playground. To obtain that coveted title you will need to play dirty, kick sand in eyes, and pull hair like a pro. Make sure to stick out your tongue, and do you remember your childish taunts? Oh, let us help you recall: "Mattie, paddie, pudding and pie, Kissed the Mistress, made Psycho cry. When the thudders come out to play, Mattie, paddie runs away." Mattie paddie is a wussy.

"This is going to stop. Do you two hear me? You are behaving like little brats. Well, I know just what will fix this once and for all."
--Mistress Ginger during correction of Psycho and Matthew: March 1995

The night of Matthew's collaring is one that stands out in my mind as a true example of the cruelty Mistress Ginger could be capable of. I had only just begun my chapter reading when I heard the first yells and pleading of my brother Matthew echoing through the walls.

At first, I admit I giggled, a lot, because I thought him stupid for letting the red-headed Dominant talk him into this shit in the first place. Every thud was followed by a very upset yelp from Matthew. I began laughing so hard my sides hurt when he began to ask her to stop after only three whacks. This guy was a real lightweight. I assumed any second he would turn tail and tell Mistress Ginger he had made a mistake submitting to her authority.

Yet after several more minutes of her work over he still had not taken back his oath. I was not laughing as hard but still was chuckling that he was whining loudly. I knew the Mistress. He was in for a real bad night if he was already in agony less than ten minutes in. She would go for hours.

At the twenty-minute mark, I stopped all mirth. His sounds had become very desperate. Matthew was clearly in a lot of trouble now. As a very experience 'thudder submissive' (which means I have lots of experience with being thudded which you all already know from Debbie and Julie) I could tell by the pitch of his voice he was in terrible pain. This was not good. Matthew had a low tolerance for discomfort. He would never survive at the end of Mistress Gingers crop, much less be capable of handling her cat o'nine or any of the red-head's floggers.

I started grumbling to myself calling him an 'idiot,' 'fool,' and 'novice.' However it was clear, based on what I could hear and believe me half the neighborhood could, he had not been aware of thudding or bondage. His begging turned rapidly to wailing and tears. Much more rapidly than it should have.

At the thirty-minute mark, I began to worry. Apparently, the Mistress had gagged him but still his sounds of torment were seriously atrocious. If he wanted to change his mind, the ball gag would keep him from voicing his second thoughts about this obvious mistake. Matthew was too tender for a collar under my thud loving Mistress. Thudding is not something one just gets over or used to. You can either do it or not, period. Your pain tolerance must be high and your ability to control the urge to fight stronger. He had neither. I heard the headboard of the bed groaning from his frantic attempts to break his bonds. I couldn't understand why Mistress Ginger wasn't realizing this guy was freaking out.

I got up and walked into the hallway. I stood silently trying to decide if I was willing to incite the anger of the Mistress by interrupting her defiling of this idiot. It seemed to me she should stop and at least offer him a chance to toss the collar now before traumatizing him beyond return. Part of me wanted to help Matthew get away, part of me thought if he was this dumb he was getting what he deserved. It was a tough call. I certainly didn't want to take his place. He had asked for it. I did try to warn him. He ignored me. Then again, he didn't know he was going to be thudded and tied up. Oh decisions, decisions.

Luckily, I didn't have to step in. I heard the Mistress stop thudding the wussy. She began to speak to him softly. I could hear him weeping. She had gotten his ass good. I smiled assured that by morning this guy would be running for the door. The Mistress would get a good fucking, and Matthew would not soon forget to stay out of dark places without checking the territory carefully next time. I went back to my sofa to study.

I was only a few pages in when I heard the thudding begin again. I almost dropped my book. I couldn't believe it. Mistress Ginger had stopped to talk with him about his behavior, but he had agreed to continue. No way. I listened as again the wailing, crying and begging started all over almost immediately. This was more than I was willing to take. I went into the bathroom and got toilet paper to plug up my ears. His pleading was hurting my feelings for goth sake. How could she be so cruel? The man was terrified, and this was no act.

Now with his sounds muffled, I went back to my books. It was not that I didn't pity Matthew. I did. It was just that some people must learn the hard way. I knew if I stepped in he would never get the full effects of what the Mistress could dish out. If he was going to run, I assumed he would, he could do it in the morning. Mistress Ginger could bring on the pain, but she would not leave permanent damage. He would heal and maybe get away before it got any worse for him. It was his cross to bear not mine. I didn't have a choice. If I didn't take those thuds, the bondage, the crushing life of servitude, the result would be death. He could walk. I must be honest, it pissed me off he had chosen to throw that away. All I could think is how much I would have given to be in his place. I already had started to hate Matthew. There was no way I was going to help him learn to be a loser by training the fool. He could forget it.

The next morning I awoke on time despite forgetting to set my alarm. I needed to get ready for class and provide wake up service for Mistress Ginger. She had not ordered this service cancelled but she also didn't provide any

284

protocol for how to approach her while with her new lover. I stood at the bedroom door listening to make sure I wasn't walking in on the two of them in the middle of lovemaking. When I heard only the light snores of the Mistress, I realized it was safe to say they weren't in the middle of anything but sleep.

I opened the door and quietly went inside. I saw Matthew wide awake tied by his arms the way she tended to tie me. He was kneeling on the floor at the end of the bed leashed up like a dog. I snickered but then realized I had been there thousands of times with this one and other Masters, so I stifled the taunt. He was gagged. His eyes looked red and swollen from crying. Pity for the poor bastard washed over me, but he was not my problem. I looked away knelt next to my sleeping Mistress and began to awaken her softly.

She opened her eyes smiling at me. "Ah, Psycho, aren't you a beautiful sight first thing in the morning."

I handed her coffee and then informed her I had breakfast ready. I inquired as to where she wished to eat it.

She sat up with her cup then stretching looked at Matthew. "We will eat at the sofa this morning. You and your brother can eat at my feet."

I nodded then went to her closet while she directed which outfit she wanted for the day. She ordered the scared looking Matthew to watch this dressing service being performed. He didn't take his eyes off the two of us as I dressed and groomed the Mistress preparing her for the day. I went to the Master bathroom and prepared her toothbrush and waited till she was finished before quickly cleaning up any mess left behind. I didn't even bother to look at the untrained submissive nor did he cross my mind.

My tasks were so deeply engrained in my head by now, I did and do them without thinking. I had by that time been servicing a Master almost non-stop for almost fifteen years. I wasn't even twenty-four yet. I did really know any other kind of life. I wanted nothing more than to be free. Even if I didn't know what it was to be such a thing.

Once the Mistress was satisfied with her service, she ordered I dress, while she finally unbonded Matthew. He was told to dress as well. I had to cover my smile while Mistress Ginger got his outfit then laid it out on the bed directing him to put it on. She handed me the usual black cat suit with her red cuffs. I was rather used to her obnoxious dressing style by now. I didn't even raise an eyebrow to her selection. Matthew on the other hand was purely unhappy with his new uniform. Mistress Ginger told us to hurry up, then left for the living room to wait for us to attend her.

He stood there staring at the black mesh shirt and leather pants with disgust but didn't say a word. I smiled at him when he looked at me appearing to question with his eyes if Mistress Ginger was serious. I shrugged then started to remove my old clothes to start putting on the new. It was then I noticed Matthew was staring at me. I didn't like that one bit.

I glared at him. "Turn around and keep your fucking eyes to yourself, idiot." I had not uncovered anything yet, but I would be damned if he was going to get a peep show.

He snorted. "You got to see me naked. Not fair."

I growled. "You are a dog. Untrained, stupid, useless. You can't even take a light thudding, you baby. You belong to the Mistress and so do I. She didn't give permission to look at me, did she." I looked at his backside and thighs.

Mistress Ginger had made her marks well. The man was stripped, bruised and cut some. She didn't hold back on his unit. I imagined she thought him tougher since he was so big. However, I heard him crying like a child. He was not a bad ass at all.

He narrowed his eyes. "I didn't know I needed permission to look at other subs. I didn't want to see you naked anyway."

I glared. "Good pervert. Now get dressed stupid before you get us into trouble. The Mistress is waiting. Keep your fucking head turned and eyes to yourself."

He blew out his air but did as I told him. I assumed he would march straight out the door as soon as we both headed to the living room after getting dressed. I had decided this moron was just a want a be who made a serious mistake. Now that he knew it was not just getting to fuck two horny women he surely would be on his way.

He watched as I put on my makeup and boots. His dressing was much faster since fellows didn't have all the bells and whistles us ladies have. I watched him from the mirror try to sit down on the bed. I chuckled when he winced then stood back up.

"Hurts doesn't it. You won't be sitting down for a while, big boy. Hope you have a good back. It will ache from all the standing you will be doing." I chuckled while I applied my lipstick.

His refection glared at me. "I suppose you could do better? That shit hurts."

I finished my look. "I have been doing it for years little man. You better get used to it. Mistress Ginger can't get off without thudding for at least one hour. That was your first, so she was going easy on you. Wait till tonight." I turned and headed for the living room.

I heard him gasp at what I had said. I just knew that was the end of him for sure. So, I was shocked when he knelt at the Mistress's feet waiting for me to serve everyone breakfast. He didn't rush for the door as I had suspected he would. I sat down with my own paltry meal on the other side of the Mistress looking at Matthew. I was now sure he was crazier than me. Only a nut would stick this out when they had the freedom to run away. Oh well, his funeral. I had more important things to worry about.

Stacey showed up just after I finished my meal. I started to gather up the dishes, but the Mistress said that Matthew would handle that task. I could go. That was nice. I didn't have to be told twice. I ran out the door forgetting my backpack and books. I was getting into the car when I saw

Stacey's mouth fly open and her eyes go wide. Following her gaze, I saw Matthew coming out of the house carrying my things.

He rushed over to me. "Psycho, you forgot your books. I hope you have a wonderful day." He reached out grabbed the back of my head and forced his mouth to mine kissing me deeply before I could stop him.

I pulled back hard trying to push him off, but he finally let go, then trotted back to the house. I watched him then noticed Mistress Ginger smiling from the doorway. Ah, she had ordered the fool to do that to humiliate him and myself in front of Stacey. I just smiled bitterly and waved at her while I got into the car.

"Asshole," I mumbled as Stacey sat there staring at me still stunned.

She finally found her voice. "Who was that."

I smiled then said in a mocking voice. "That other team you told me I should play for. Can we go now?"

She smiled widely. "Holy shit. You have gone straight. This is wonderful news, Psycho. He is sexy. Damn. Where did you find him?" She took off down the road appearing happier than I had ever seen her.

I looked at her angrily. "I met him at Church this last Sunday. I was there worming orphans and getting baptized. He just got back to the states from the Peace Core after treating lepers for the last five years off the coast of Wisconsin. We are getting married this June by Anton Levey at the Church of Satan. Elvis is going to be his best man. I have chosen red and black as my wedding colors. I am already pregnant with his child through Immaculate Conception. It is okay though because the Pope blessed our unholy union. Oh, I am registered at the dollar store if you want to get us a gift. I am good on paper plates, but I can always use plastic forks and spoons. You'll just love him. He has a PhD in bullshit to go with my propensity for lying." I crossed my arms then looked out the window to see if she wanted to play this game any further.

Stacey sat there obviously not understanding a word I said. "Okay, so you are dating or what? I mean he must have stayed overnight, right?" Damn this girl was stupid.

I growled, "Stacey, wake up. That is Ginger's boyfriend. He is not mine."

She shook her head confused. "Wait, I don't get it. I thought Ginger was your girlfriend? Her boyfriend just kissed you like a bride to be? I don't understand."

I forced a laugh. "Neither do I, Stacey. When I figure this shit out, I will be sure to let you know."

That day I had a lot of trouble paying attention in class. Matthew was on my mind. His being in my house with my Mistress was getting to me. I just couldn't understand why I cared so much. He was taking the thudding I hated and saving me from having to provide special services of the collar. It seemed perfect. Yet I couldn't stop thinking of hurting him, running him off, sending him to the garbage bin.

I was not back on shift at the funeral home for a couple of weeks so I could be around the house more than normal. I decided maybe I should keep an eye on this weirdo. I couldn't stop ruminating on how arrogant it was of him to stick his nose into my relationship with Mistress Ginger. I mean sure we had our problems, but with him there those issues would never get resolved. He would take over the house, and eventually she would get tired of my antics, then she'd sell me off to Joyce. So, there it was. I feared being replaced.

The anxiety that my Mistress would slowly fall for Matthew and dump me sent me into submissive hell. I could barely wait to get back home. I would beat him by being overly attentive to Mistress Ginger, and she would tire of him instead of me. It was a simple plan. This guy wasn't even trained. If I never taught him, he couldn't take over anything but her sexual appetites. I could do much more than he could for her. Surely, she wouldn't throw away the submissive that did the most to serve her.

The first day of school was thankfully uneventful. I was not in the mood for more difficulty. If Mistress Ginger's plan was to put a fire under my ass to try to please her, she had been successful. Instead of viewing this second collar as a helper or teammate, I saw him as a threat to my continued existence. This gentle giant I had once thought was a credit to the masculine side of humans was now viewed as a danger. He was targeted for immediate destruction.

Stacey did her best to wrangle out of me the identity of the tall good-looking guy who had kissed me that morning.

I was silent the whole way home. I refused to discuss anything about my home life with her before. She seemed a bit too interested in this asshole. I started to think maybe she should just fuck the guy like Mistress Ginger did and get it over with.

I could not help but to think: What was wrong with these women? Hell, he was just another dick attached to a man. They acted like he was Adonis dropped from the fucking heavens. I had never seen so much hub bub over a stupid guy. Apparently, they just didn't know the male of the species as well as I did. No man is to be trusted. Wherever they are, they are sure to destroy all they touch. Men had no control, no respect and everything is about taking advantage of the weak.

I had a plan. What needed to happen is Matthew needed to have his collar removed. A submissive without a collar is just a normal. I would get the bolt cutters and cut his off, then send him packing. Then Mistress Ginger would see I would do whatever it took to please her and not send me away. This was just a test. Of course. That is why she was tolerating an idiot that couldn't even handle a light thudding. All I had to do was prove my love for her by chunking this moron. I was feeling better already. Again,, not in touch with reality, just saying.

I nearly jumped out of Stacey's car before she was completely in my driveway. I was on a mission. She left with me storming across the yard. I went to the back of the house to find the toolbox. Once I had found it, I took the bolt cutters from it. Now, I went looking for Matthew. Time to hunt me a subby wannabe.

When I came inside Matthew was kneeling by the sofa. I looked around and didn't see my Mistress.

"Where is Mistress Ginger? If you hurt her you are a dead motherfucker," I growled at the now surprised Matthew.

He looked up seeing the small handheld bolt cutter in my hand. "Uhm, she is taking a nap. She told me to stay here until she released me. Psycho what is that in your hand?"

I held the tool up. "Your eviction papers, asshole." I ran at him.

Matthew tried to stand but I plowed into him too fast. We both went sprawling into the floor. I nearly dropped the cutter but recovered then went grabbing for his collar. He saw me coming while still trying to get off his hands and knees.

"Hey, what the fuck," he yelled as I caught him by his silver band with my left hand then began trying to cut it off with my right.

I held him tightly, but he grabbed my offending hand holding me back from chopping off his submission.

"Let go, idiot," I roared.

He grabbed my collar in his free hand while holding me back from cutting his off with the other. We rolled and struggled in the floor knocking over the coffee table, and

Mistress's lamp. Both of us were trying to rip the other's collar from our units. He was strong as hell but I wasn't budging either as I hung on to his wedding band with a death grip.

Our racket woke up Mistress Ginger who came down the hallway to find her submissive pair locked in battle rolling around on the floor, red faced and swearing at each other. She stood there laughing for a few moments watching the fight. Until she noticed the bolt cutting tool.

"You two stop this shit now. Put down the collar cutter, Psycho, or so help me," Mistress Ginger roared out angrily.

We both immediately let each other go. I dropped the tool. Matthew and I knelt panting, disheveled and scratched up from the fray before our Mistress. She stood there glaring at us.

Then she walked over and picked up the offending item. "Psycho and Matthew, I now give a directive: no removing the other's collar. If you get caught even touching my property, I will show you just how nasty I can really be. Understand me."

"Yes Mistress," we said in unison shooting go to hell looks at each other.

Our obvious irritation towards one another made Mistress Ginger howl with laughter despite our busting up the living room furniture and trying to remove her submission symbols.

"Oh, this is better than I could have hoped. You two are riot together. To think I worried you would adore each other. I should have known better. Jealousy makes you both more beautiful to your Mistress. However, you can't be breaking up the house. Psycho, you will take Matthew to the bathroom and teach him how to provide bath service. After you both clean up this mess. I am going to relax and watch television. I had better not hear anymore fighting. Don't come back until he knows how to provide it properly. I mean it, Psycho. Don't test me." She looked at me hard.

I snorted. "Yes, Mistress. I would prefer to be punished. Thank you very much for your mercy," I said glaring back at her.

Matthew looked up startled. "Are you fucking nuts? You are taking punishment."

I growled at him. "Shut up stupid. I would rather fry than help you wash your ball sack, asshole."

Mistress Ginger didn't expect that answer either apparently. "Psycho you had better think on that a moment. I have the shock collar ready and waiting or the Vampire gloves."

For a moment my heart skipped a beat, but I steadied my resolve. "Either works." I wasn't helping Matthew replace me, God damn it, no matter what the cost.

Mistress Ginger growled then flopped down on the sofa. "Go get the Vampire gloves. I will beat your ass with them. Then every time you refuse to teach your brother what I ordered I will beat you for it. When you are immune to the bite, I will get the shock collar. Then the strap, and we can start over again from there. I don't mind, we have all night. You up for that kind of abuse, Psycho? Do you want to test my resolve?" She stared at me hard.

I let out my breath. "No Mistress." Damn, she had me. I was aware she would beat me all night to get her way, shit.

She smiled. "That is better. Now, do what I told you to do, or so help me I will beat your ass just for the fun of it. Hurry up. You need to make dinner and I want Matthew spick and span for special services of the collar tonight."

I looked over to see the look of fear in Matthew's eyes. Apparently, he wasn't too keen to share the Mistress's bed anymore (hahaha). That made me feel a bit better. If I was supposed to be cleaning his skank ass up so she could thud him some more, I was happy to help.

He and I cleaned up the upturned room, and luckily the lamp wasn't broken. Then I told him to follow me to the bathroom. Once inside, I closed the door and told him to strip while I started running the bath water. He did as I told him appearing preoccupied. I realized he was worried about his upcoming thud session. An idea popped into my head. I would get rid of him another way.

"So, how are you and the Mistress doing in the special services of the collar Matthew," I said pretending to check the water temperature while he watched me gather the items for a proper bath service (rag, soap, razor, towels).

He looked at the floor. "I didn't know she was going to tie me up and hit me," he whined.

I looked up appearing concerned. "She hits you. Oh my. Well, that is because you are not pleasing her you know."

He looked at me surprised. "Really? She doesn't hit you?"

I shook my head. "Oh hell no. I know what the fuck I am doing, idiot. She only hits when you can't make her happy the way she likes. Gosh you are so damned ignorant. Didn't you even read up on the lifestyle before you rushed in?" I told him to get into the tub.

He got into the water as I showed him how to lather the soap properly and where to start the bathing process. Matthew watched appearing to do his best to remember the steps.

He then asked the question I had set him up to ask. "Okay, so what can I do to please her so she stops hitting me?"

I smiled. "Thudding, Matthew. Thudding is the proper term. Why should I tell you? You have come here to replace me. I am not stupid. If I help you, you will see me thrown to the streets. I was here first." I was washing his feet, so I grabbed and twisted one of his pretty toes.

He winced. "I did not. I swear it. I wanted to join you, not get you thrown out. Please Psycho tell me. I can't take that hitting, thudding business."

I laughed. "Sure you swear. I know better than that. I will tell you when you admit you are a pussy who thought he was getting easy pussy." I twisted another of his toes.

He groaned. "No I didn't. I swear it."

I twisted another toe. "Yeah you did. You are a man. Men lie. They try to fuck and hurt girls that is all they do. You thought you could take advantage. Well surprise, not so easy is it, pussy." I smiled evilly at that.

Matthew narrowed his eyes. "Please tell me the secret, Psycho. I swear I wasn't doing any of that. I love Mistress Ginger, and I want to love you too, but you are fucking mean as hell."

I really started laughing. "Ah, you have no fucking idea how mean. Didn't Mistress Ginger tell you the Devil is my mother? Well, now you know, pussy. Best not ever fuck with me, Matthew. You got that?"

He nodded. "I swear it. I will never bother you ever. Now, please tell me. I am a pussy. The thudding is going to kill me."

I looked at the door to make sure Mistress Ginger wasn't there then leaned in close as if sharing a big secret. He leaned in too so he wouldn't miss the answer to his question.

"Mistress Ginger loves a rim job. You see if you do that, she will never hit you again, but you must really go deep. She won't ask for it either. You must take the initiative. Also, slap her ass when you do it. She will go wild." I leaned back pretending to work on his calves smiling knowingly.

He leaned back in the tub. "Really? It is that easy?"

I nodded. "Yep. She loves it."

The truth is Mistress Ginger's ass was off limits. If you even accidently got to close, she would whop the shit out of you. She also would not give a blow job under any conditions. Matthew was just set up for big trouble if he dared to put his mouth anywhere near her bottom and if he slapped her anywhere, holy shit. She may kill him. I suppose I should have felt bad that I just set this idiot up for a major thudding, but I really am that hell bent to survive. I truly believed he was there to replace me. You would do whatever it took to get rid of a rival too if your fucking life depended on it. Mine did or that is the way I saw it.

The idea was he would piss of Mistress Ginger to the point she would unleash her fury. Since I knew Matthew couldn't handle her loving thudding, he surely would throw his collar over a hateful one. I viewed this as a win/win situation. I would win the competition, and Matthew would save himself from a lifetime of nightmares at the feet of this red-headed Dominate. See, I was doing a good thing, right, hahaha.

He looked at me appearing truly grateful. "Thank you for the help Psycho. I won't forget this."

I laughed out loud. "Damn right you won't. Now wash your own fucking dick. I am not your submissive." I threw the rag and soap at him.

Matthew demonstrated he got the technique down. I then had him get out and show the proper way to dry off a Dominant and wrap them. I hated kneeling and scraping before this asshole but now that I had him set up for failure, I thought I could get over it. He wouldn't be there by morning anyway. He watched as I cleaned up the mess in a structured fashion asking a lot of questions about why it was done this way or that way. I answered him honestly. I assumed if I correctly did this training he would be more likely to believe the so-called secret to get out of thudding later. I did my best acting job yet. He really thought I had just suddenly become his helper and trainer. Whatever, I still hated his guts.

That night dinner went without a hitch. The dumbass had to follow me around everywhere. His presence was more than annoying. I kept tripping over him. For a big guy he was not very graceful. I informed him he needed to start trying to learn to be less clumsy. I told him to take belly dancing lessons when he asked me how to improve his balance. He started snickering but Mistress Ginger heard him. She had been coming into the kitchen but neither of us saw her because we were busy cooking.

"Oh, you think Psycho is being funny. She isn't. She is very good at it and her balance is perfect. Psycho, loan him your belly dancing tapes and make sure he does a thirty-minute workout a day. Good eye to see he needs work in that area." She walked into the kitchen and sat down waiting to be served.

Matthew glared at me angrily. I just smiled and shrugged. "Yes Mistress. I will see to it."

I leaned in close to him then whispered, "Hey asshole, you wanted that collar. Well suck it up, butter cup." I snickered.

He growled then whispered back, "Not cool, Psycho. I am not going to fucking belly dance. Fuck that shit."

That made me snort as I said quietly, "Take the punishment then. I am sure the Mistress will love to thud you some more."

He rolled his eyes. "Shit."

Mistress Ginger looked over at us. "What are you two whispering about? Plotting against your Mistress already," she cooed.

I looked up as if startled. "Oh my goodness no, Mistress. Matthew was just saying thirty minutes a day isn't enough. He thinks an hour a day is more appropriate."

Matthew's eyes almost bugged out of his head as he started at me unable to grasp my throwing him under the bus.

She nodded. "Matthew is correct. Make it an hour. Good job, Matthew."

I smiled diabolically at him while he scowled mouthing, "I'll get you back for this."

We both served her dinner, then stood behind her, me to the left, him to the right while she ate. The submissive is not supposed to ever eat at the table with the Dominant unless special occasion or invited. Neither of us received either exception so we just waited. I heard his stomach growl which made me grin again. No doubt he really was a pussy. I was feeling sure he would be gone in no time.

After the Mistress finished, we cleared the table. Mistress Ginger was feeling vigorous. Matthew's ass was grass for sure, literally. I smiled as she told him to hurry up and eat something then join her in the bedroom. I handed him a plate of food to eat while he stood by the table. We also rarely sit down to eat, we don't usually have the time. Food is consumed on the run.

He started shoveling it in while I washed the dishes. I could tell he was feeling anxious. One thing I can say about Matthew is he was a super-fast eater. I had barely started cleaning the pots when he dropped his plate into the soapy water. Then he began to help by drying the washed dinnerware.

I stopped my task. "Uhm, you are supposed to be headed to provide special services of the collar fool." I snatched the dishrag from his hands.

Matthew cleared his throat. "I don't think I can go in there. She is, uhm, scary as hell."

That sent me into spasms of laugher. This giant was afraid of five-foot six Mistress Ginger. Now that was funny.

"You don't have a choice, butthead. The Mistress has called for your favors. Get to it stud. I thought you loved your Mistress," I mocked him.

He glared. "I do love her. I just, I can't take the thudding."

"Deal with it. You can't then I suggest you toss that collar right now, fucker. It only gets worse from here pal." I said now baring my teeth.

Matthew grabbed his silver band as if afraid it had fallen off. "No, I will learn to get over it. Okay, rim job, right? That will make her happy you said?" He looked at me for assurance.

I nodded trying to look sincere. "Oh yeah, that'll do it for you, I promise."

He flashed a quick smile. "Wish me luck?"

I looked at him harshly. "Never. Bye Matthew, Mistress Ginger is waiting." I waved him away.

I had just finished the kitchen when the walls trembled with the screams of anger from Mistress Ginger (uh oh). I heard her strike Matthew several times till the big moose was yelling for mercy. Then I heard Mistress Ginger yell out loud enough for the neighborhood to hear it:

"You stupid son-of-a-bitch. You ever do that again I will fucking kill you. You stay away from my ass."

I started snickering realizing he had gone for it. Oh man was she mad. I heard her thudding him with all her might

303

and he was not happy trust me. She was so awful I even started to feel a bit bad about setting him up like that. However not that bad. I wanted him gone. Surely, he would leave after the beating he took that night.

Mistress Ginger was merciless. I finally plugged up my ears again. I couldn't take all the noise of his screams, begging, pleading, and wailing. Wow, she must have skinned him alive. I wasn't in there so I can only guess. She likely did to him what she did to me before Mabon, marking every available inch of his unit with every tool she owned. Now, that is something an old hat like me can take and function fine the next day. For a novice like Matthew, I figured he wouldn't be sitting, laying down, or maybe walking for days. She was still whipping the shit out of him when I finally fell asleep on the couch for the night. Mistress Ginger was a no if, ands or butts kind of gal. Seriously, Matthew really fucked up going there, and I fucked up telling him to.

My problem is I was not recognizing Matthew's bravery and resolve to do this. Had I not been so hell bent to get rid of him, I wouldn't have been so blind. He did go to her bedroom even though he knew she was going to thud him. He had not left the day after his consummation where he found out thudding was going to happen. Matthew had put on the clothes she picked, done everything the Mistress told him to do, and even though angry he accepted an order to belly dance an hour a day. I was such a dumbass I never respected any of these facts.

Matthew wanted that collar. He had decided no matter what, he was sticking this out. I just assumed that since I hated the collar everyone else would hate it too. My lack of empathy was going to be punished harshly. To be honest, I had it coming. Normally, I didn't deserve what I got in life. This time I did maybe worse. I was being an asshole and it was time I got taken down a peg. Thank goodness Mistress Ginger was going to see to that.

I awoke the next morning to find with astonishment the ground was covered with snow and ice. Classes had been canceled and everyone was told to stay home. This was the south, so any amount of snow or ice was crippling. They just didn't have the equipment to deal with it, and people didn't know how to handle icy roads. It happened so rarely. Maiden Mary had called, which woke me up, to tell me all school and most workplaces were closed. We had gotten a rare three feet of snow and more was coming. I hadn't seen snow there since that horrid snowstorm of 1988 when I first started living at Darlin. I looked outside realizing I was trapped at home with a likely pissed off Mistress Ginger and a very beaten up Matthew.

I made coffee then went to awaken Mistress Ginger. I went into the room to find poor Matthew just as he was the morning before, but this time, he was indeed black and blue all over. I winced at the sight. She had worked his ass over. He was kneeling but half asleep. He heard me come in and just sat there glaring at me. I did my best not to return his gaze. Matthew no doubt realized I had fooled him. I hoped he would have left despite the snow. If not, he surely would want revenge. I sure as shit would. No reason to worry, he would leave, right?

Mistress Ginger opened her eyes then smiled as I handed her the coffee. "It has snowed significantly. Nothing is moving around today, Mistress. I am not going to class. It was cancelled."

She sat up appearing pleased to hear that. "Wonderful, I need to have a talk with you anyway. I thought it would have to wait till this afternoon but since you are here for the day. We can talk over breakfast."

I nodded as I got up heading for her closet while avoiding the brooding Matthew. She waved me away from it. "Just a robe today. No need to dress. No one will be coming over I am sure."

She sat up as I helped her into her favorite red silk oriental decorated robe. The Mistress looked over at Matthew still bound and gagged appearing irritated.

"Psycho, untie your brother and meet me in the kitchen. I will attend to my own hygiene later today." She got up and left the room. Uh oh.

I looked at the sullen submissive for a moment but then did as she commanded. He stood up looking very angry. "You tricked me. She got really pissed, Psycho. Look at me. She beat the stuffing out of, shit look at me." He was examining his welts, stripes and bruises.

Looking at the floor I responded, "Well you must have done it wrong. It always works for me. Sorry about that.

Guess you will be heading out now right? Told you this is a tough life. Not for everyone." I tried to look apologetic.

He chuckled much to my surprise. "No way. I love this. I have never felt more alive or more adored in my whole life. Everything has a rule. Even bathing is an art. Yeah, the thudding sucks, but shit I will get used to it. It has been teaching me to stop being afraid all the time. It is like the worst thing you can imagine happens but the next morning you are still here. It is eye opening. Mistress Ginger is a fucking Goddess on Earth. I would die for her if she asked me to." He looked up with a dreamy look.

My mouth was hanging open. "Are you fucking serious? This is a mind-altering experience for you? Okay, man, I have some extra Thorazine. You may want to be tested for mental illness…"

Matthew interrupted me. "Please don't make me laugh. My ass is killing me, and I think even my bones are bruised. Your humor is just too much. It is one of the things that drew me back to this place. I have decided to move in like Mistress Ginger asked me to. This is the thing that has been missing from my life. Last night, when she was wailing on me, I realized how much I belong. I need this. Thank you, Psycho, for helping me learn it. You are amazing."

My mouth was gapping but now it was floored. "Mistress Ginger told us to hurry. We had better get moving. Put on a fucking robe, will you? I can't talk to you if you are going to stand there naked. Your welts are blinding me."

I turned around and headed for the kitchen feeling I may throw up from anxiety. Matthew was moving in. Surely that meant I was moving out. I no longer was thudding or sleeping with the Mistress. There was no good reason to keep me as soon as I got Matthew trained. I assumed as smart as he was, I had maybe three months at best before she could sell my Key to Joyce and be shut of my loony ass. I had bid to remove Matthew and lost. Too bad for me.

I found my Mistress sitting at the table waiting. I assumed the talk was of making new arrangements for Simon's Key. I sighed trying not to get too upset. I guess the better, uhm, man won. I can't compete with a male, I didn't have the right parts and if Mistress Ginger was in the mood for steak, she was never going to settle for sushi. Yikes, nurse meds. That was one foul reference, eh?

She smiled sweetly at me. I looked down rapidly grabbing her plate of food. Matthew walking in taking his place to her right. I grimaced, feeling the icy hands of death reaching down my spine while I served the Mistress. She reached out and grabbed my wrist.

"Sit down for moment, Psycho. We need to talk." She pointed at the chair next to her.

I took a deep breath then glared at Matthew who smiled at me appearing either ignorant of my dismissal or happy about it. Either way, I hated him more.

I sat down as the Mistress began speaking. "I have now received the special services of the collar twice from your brother Matthew. You are aware." She looked at me.

I looked back. "Yeah, so is the whole neighborhood, Mistress." I felt my lips quivering expecting her next words to be, 'so you are no longer required.'

Instead she chuckled then said, "Your brother is exceptionally gifted in the areas of penetration. However, in the art of pleasing me orally he is terrible." She wrinkled her nose.

I looked up at Matthew startled. He looked back appearing confused.

"Mistress is this over the little incident last night? I was assuming you would like that kind of thing," Matthew said looking at me with desperation in his eyes.

Mistress Ginger shook her head. "No, Matthew you suck at oral sex period. It has nothing to do with last night, but I will remind you, make that mistake again and you know what will happen."

He nodded appearing hurt by her cruel words regarding his performance in the bedroom.

She looked back at me. "Maybe the problem is I am spoiled. No one knows her way around a woman like you do, Psycho. So, from now on I am calling on your special services of the collar. No arguments. I want my rights to receive pleasure from you that is final."

I almost let out a breath of relief. "Oh, okay Mistress. I just thought for a moment, well you have Matthew now. I thought you didn't need me any longer? That kind of thing can be taught."

I hated myself for being honest, but I no longer fooled myself. If she was going straight, I was finished. If she wasn't, then Matthew was. Besides she likely was going to order I teach him anyway. She wanted me to teach him everything else.

She laughed hard at that. "Yeah it can, but I prefer your softer more experienced touch. No one can rev my motor better than you can, Psycho. You can start my engine, touch me in all the right places to get me to ecstasy. Then your brother Matthew can send me into orbit with his specialty. I can have the best of both worlds. That is why I wanted one of each."

Matthew and I looked at each other openly aggressive now. "Wait Mistress. If I can't have some familiarity with your beautiful form, then how will I get excited," he said appearing angry that his ability to pleasure a woman was reduced only to his ability to thrust.

Mistress Ginger glared at him. "You will keep your hands off me except to do what you do best. How you get ready to do your job is not my problem, now is it?"

He appeared confused. "What?"

She growled. "Get yourself up. I also think you should masturbate before sex with me. Your coming to orgasms before I even have time to say how do you do."

Matthew turned bright red blushing. "Mistress I don't understand. Masturbation? If you would help me arouse that wouldn't been necessary."

Mistress Ginger turned around looking right at him. "I don't give submissive assholes blow jobs, Matthew. You will masturbate so I can have you for more than two damned seconds. You are a man so if I can get a couple of shots a night, I am damned lucky. I need your attempts to do more than piss me off. The only thing you are good for is thudding with my crop and a couple of weak thuds in return. You are too damned eager, Matthew."

I looked at the table stifling a snicker. Mistress Ginger was essentially calling Matthew a 'two pump chump.' I knew better but I couldn't help it, the giggling erupted like a volcanic burst.

Mistress Ginger turned back toward me with anger flashing in her eyes. "Finding this funny are you, Psycho? You enjoying Matthew's failures? Hmmm?"

I stopped laughing realizing I had just fucked up royal. Matthew was near tears from the Mistress's complaints about his performance. Men get upset easy over that shit. You never laugh when the Mistress is correcting not you.

"No Mistress. I am not finding this funny. I apologize for my most inappropriate behavior. Mercy please." I got ready for the back hand sure to follow.

Mistress Ginger had started to rear back her hand but paused mid-air. "No, wait, hmmm. I forgot about you, Psycho. I don't know why I didn't think of this before. How silly of me. Mercy denied. You will make sure Matthew is spent before lovemaking. You will get him prepared too. Yes, this is perfect. I could even watch for added fun."

311

I looked up horrified. "Mistress, no, I choose punishment."

She growled. "Are we going to do this again? You know I will just punish you until you relent."

I nodded. "Yes, you will, but I won't relent. I am not doing this. I never agreed to sleep with Matthew and you have no right to ask me. I am not touching him."

Mistress Ginger looked at Matthew. "You feel the same way too? You going to deny me my rights to command you to receive blow jobs or sleep with Psycho?"

He looked at my disgusted face. "Yeah, I agree with Psycho. You are the Mistress. I would prefer to keep it to you. She is trying to get rid of me. She wants to see me gone. No way I want to sleep with that bitch."

I got up and plowed into him knocking him into the wall. He pushed me off him, but I came back at him grabbing for his collar again, he grabbed mine. We were pulling each other like a human tug of war rope trying to get one of us out the door. Mistress Ginger watched the show appearing to enjoy our anger, jealousy and frustrations at each other. She allowed it to go on for a bit, finally appearing to tire of our cursing and pushing.

"Enough you two." She got up as we both disengaged from our stalemate battle.

Mistress Ginger told us both to kneel. She then left and returned with the shock collar. We both got punished for grabbing collars until I was sure smoke was coming out of our ears. She reminded us that we were directed not to do that.

Neither of us argued that point. She was right. We had broken her directive, but to be fair she started it by making fun of Matthew's sexual abilities, then trying to bring me into their space. Now, Matthew hated me as much as I hated him. The war had begun.

I continued to take punishment rather than comply with her demands to 'spend' Matthew for sustained carnal congress with her or to prepare him for it. I did, however, return to her bedroom for her requested pleasures. I refused to do so unless she made the interloper Matthew leave the room first. I refused to be anywhere around him or service her if he had been with her first. I am not a submissive and even if I were one, they have the right to refuse and should when a Master is crossing the line. A good submissive stands up for themselves and is no doormat.

Weeks passed as the animosity between he and I grew to epic and property busting proportions. Almost no day passed without one of us throwing something at the other. Somedays we make a connection injuring the other one. Somedays we missed and broke whatever was thrown.

At school I had started to guest lecture in several classes a couple of times a week. My grades were stellar and I had finally returned to work. On the surface I was looking good. Straight A's, a respected teaching assistant, an employed well-adjusted mother of two. My kids were healthy and growing up strong. They were well mannered and loved by five. Me, Maiden Mary, Delilah, Mistress Ginger and yes even Matthew adored them. No kid on Earth received more affection or attention than mine did.

The Green Temple was doing well. The new initiates were devout, and each month the circle grew in strength as its members continued to build and plant with their own hands, funds and wills. No one was expected, everything was free, but everyone pitched in to make it an amazing place to mediate, fraternize with other Pagans, and perform ritual. I didn't make it to the Imbolc Sabbat thanks to my acute illness, but I was looking forward to Ostara to finally set our fallen Queen free and hold the election to raise a new one.

Everything on the outside looked bright as the March winds blew in like a Lion that year. At home however, the battle raged on. Matthew and I jockeyed for the attentions of Mistress Ginger. We fought over who gave bath service, who cooked, who cleaned, who offered wake up and bedding service but most of all who got the Mistress for special services of the collar daily. It was coming to serious sabotaging of each other's services, blows and huge cuss out fights. We both were getting punished almost every day as well. It was pure hell to live D/ss in that house unless you were Mistress Ginger. She was loving all the attention, and our jealousy over her affections.

Honestly, most of it was being caused by her tendency to favor one and neglecting the other. It was her borderline personality disorder symptoms showing its ugly head. Matthew and I must have known that on some level, but our long-term bickering had led to bad blood between us.

Finally, just a week before my twenty-fourth birthday, it had gone too far.

The Mistress had been out in town to enjoy a moment away from her now smothering submissive pair. We were left to clean the kitchen and living room. I took the kitchen, he took the living room. I was washing dishes when he came by and dropped a dirty spoon in the sink.

"Missed one, bitch," he said laughing as he splashed the soapy water by throwing it in hard.

I turned and flung a plate at his head like a frisbee. He ducked and the plate shattered on the wall.

I yelled out, "I missed a bitch again." Then began to laugh loudly back.

He grabbed Mistress Gingers ashtray and flung it. I moved, it shattered. I grabbed another plate, the same results. Glass was quickly spreading throughout the kitchen floor. He flung another curio from one of the coffee tables making connection with my head. I was bleeding and now pissed. I grabbed a kitchen chair aiming for his head. He moved I shattered the living room window but kept wildly swinging the chair. He grabbed another curio, threw it and made a direct hit. Only, it was into Mistress Ginger's head, not mine. She was clocked good and hard. She staggered forward then fell on her ass knocked senseless.

Matthew and I stopped fighting both running to attend our fallen Mistress. She had started to come around, and she was mad as hell. She stood up pushing both of us off.

"Kneel, God damn you fucking brats," she roared.

Matthew and I fell to our knees as she walked around the busted-up house surveying the damage we had wrought. Her boots crackled and crunched in the tons of shattered glass from our game of dodge whatever the hell I can throw game. Mistress Ginger walked back into the living room and stood before us barely able to contain her rage.

"I have fucking had enough. This is going to stop today. You both will clean up this mess, patch that window then meet me in the kitchen. If you are not done in two hours, I will toss both your fucking collars in the gutter where you both belong." With that she went back out the front door and sped off squealing her tires.

I looked at Matthew. "Your fault. You hit her. You can leave now. She hates you and so do I."

He growled back. "Fuck you Psycho. You need to go. She told me she hates you and I have never hated anyone more."

We sized each other up flames burning in our eyes, but we heard the Mistress. If we chose to fight, we both were doomed. So, we got up and worked together to clean the mess. We barely finished when she came back through the door. Her face told us we were in big trouble. She had not calmed down a bit. I noticed she had a big bandage on her forehead. Damn, it looked like the strap tonight. Fuck!

Matthew groaned too realizing as I did we were in for a wicked punishment on this one. We again glared at each other while the Mistress directed us to the table, telling us to sit down. We did as she commanded still hatefully stealing glances at each other while she came in and sighed.

"Here is the deal. It was funny to watch you two fight for a while but now it is getting out of hand. I am going to divide up the services in this house. Psycho you will do your half, and Matthew you will do yours. Not crisscrossing, no trading and no fucking arguing." Mistress Ginger handed us both a sheet of paper with our service lists.

We both groaned. Mistress Ginger's eyes lit up with rage. "Shut up. I chose these services based on who does them the best. You both have amazing abilities. You are both beautiful, intelligent, witty, creative and wonderful submissive in your own right. You both love and adore me. I have never known such pampering. I can't complain in the service department. If I had switched the lists, it would not matter. But you two hate each other. Your fighting is tearing up the house, interrupting service and to be honest is getting on my last fucking nerve."

Matthew and I looked at each other still glaring threats at the other. "Mistress, maybe if you sent one of us away," said Matthew.

I nodded in agreement. "Yes, send him away."

Matthew growled and I got ready to attack him again.

Mistress Ginger put up her silence hand command. "I said enough. No one is going anywhere. You both belong to me. I own you both. I love you both the same. The problem here is you don't love each other. I have decided to fix that today. You are both owed a punishment. I have decided on what it will be. Like it or not, you will accept the punishment or get on your fucking knees now and I will toss your motherfucking collars."

Now that had our attention. She looked at us hard. "You both willing to accept whatever punishment I deal out? No questions asked or else."

We nodded, then in unison said, "Yes, Mistress."

Neither of us was willing to risk our collars over an unknown punishment. We did hit her, so we both knew it would be horrible, but then again, what punishment isn't? That is why they call it punishment.

She smiled cruelly. "Follow me you two, now."

We followed her to the bedroom where she told us both to kneel and be still. I don't know about Matthew, but my heart was racing a mile a minute in terror as she went to her closet and got out rope and a single chain that was only about 8 to 10 inches long. She also got out two small padlocks. I caught Matthew looking at me confused. I shrugged not understanding this punishment either.

She turned to look at us after laying out her rope, locks and the chain on her bed. "Okay you two, strip down now. Everything off."

I grumbled, while Matthew snickered. I had been very careful to never be naked around the douche bag. Now I had to strip so the pervert could get a look at my unit.

Mistress Ginger grabbed her crop and slammed it down on the bed making a popping noise. "Shut the fuck up now, both of you. Strip quietly."

Once we were both Sky Clad she told us to kneel again. We did and waited to see what weapon she planned to use to thud us with. Instead she walked over to Matthew telling him to stand and follow her. She had him sit on his ass legs out as if to row a boat. She then came back for me. I was told to sit on his lap my legs straddled around his waist. I shook my head no.

"Then kneel and let's get that collar off you." She glared at me.

I grimaced but got in the position she told me to get into straddling Matthew having to sit with my parts and his parts, yikes touching. He began to stir unable to take his eyes on my large breasts. Mistress Ginger had very nice breasts, but they were not large, so this was the first time he'd seen mine without clothing. Shouldn't have been so harsh on him I guess.

"Don't you fucking dare," I growled at him.

He looked up from my boobs. "I can't help it sorry. I will try harder, I mean to think of something else." He did seem apologetic.

Our Mistress laughed at our banter. "You see that is the problem here. You two have never slept with each other. So, here is what is going to happen. I am bonding you collar to collar until you two give in and fuck. I am ordering it in fact.

319

You can do it all night if you like. There won't be anything else to do. You will be together until tomorrow when I feel like dealing with your bratty asses again. I will know if you completed the act, because Psycho, I am going to check. Now on your lists you will notice I did not include special services of the collar. That is because after tonight you both will join me in this room at the same time. Psycho you will handle what I wanted in the first place by spending, then prepping, Matthew. Matthew you will allow Psycho to attend my pleasures then do you own properly without excuse. We are a team, a family now. We will all eat, sleep, work and fuck together like a well-structured D/ss family should. Everyone will know their role, got it. If not, let's get those collars off and end this shit." She looked us both in the eyes.

We both looked away. Even with this latest indignity, both Matthew and I had too much invested to just throw it away over structure and enforced carnal congress even if we did hate each other.

She smiled. "Good. Let the games begin." She then did as she said and tied my arms behind his unit and his behind mine in an embrace. She secured them so we could not slide out by securing his wrists to my waist and mine to his. Our legs were left free in case we decided to follow orders and copulate. She took that piece of chain and locked our collars together with almost no space to pull away from nearly being forehead to forehead. Then she walked out and locked us in.

I have to say, I have had some very uncomfortable moments in my life. This makes the top five. We stared at each other angry and struggling to get loose from those ropes for a good while not saying a word. I guess we feared biting each other's noses off. This was not fun, no matter what you may think. No matter what we did, even working together, we could not get out of her knots the ways she had us. We were stuck like that. I couldn't get off his lap and he couldn't get enough space to get from under me. She had only left enough wiggle room to have sex if we decided to follow directives.

We gave up then sat in silence for quite a while.

Finally, Matthew looked at me and said, "You know I don't really hate you."

I snorted. "I don't hate you either. I fear you."

He nodded. "Yeah same here. I thought she would ditch one of us."

That made me laugh. "I am surprised she hasn't ditched both of us."

Matthew tried to blow some of my wig hair out of my eyes. "You know I always wanted to tell you that you have the most beautiful eyes in the world. They say you can see into the soul through them."

I chuckled at that. "How romantic you are Matt. I mean you take a girl to all the finest places. Then try to seduce her by talking about her eyes. I don't think it is my eyes that are turning you on right now." I again felt him stirring.

He took a deep breath. "I am trying to think about puppies, kittens, and babies, anything but that gorgeous woman sitting naked on my lap. God help me I am going to die I swear it. I am so sorry Psycho but it just, God help me," he said starting to try to take deep breaths and look up towards the sky.

I sighed too. "Matthew, you may as well get this over with. Mistress Ginger isn't kidding. If we don't do what she says she will toss our collars."

He looked at me then said, "I didn't want it to be like this. I would never do anything against your will, Psycho. This is completely wrong. If you don't want me to be with you, I respect that. I will let her toss my collar before I force myself on you. I mean it. Whatever comes, I want you to know I have loved you from the second I saw you reading that Advanced Genetics book. You are the reason I called Mistress Ginger back. I admired you so much, I wanted to be like you. Now I am and it feels right."

I looked at him feeling an aching in my chest. "You have just said the words I have waited a lifetime to hear."

He looked confused. "That I wanted to be like you?"

I maneuvered my unit until he was in position then allowed him to enter me. "No, you said you would let her toss your collar before you would force yourself on me. You gave me a choice. I choose to be with you." I kissed his neck as he closed his eyes shuddering.

We made love the entire night, slowly, softly and beautifully. He was very gentle, and we shared many climaxes quietly to not disturb the Mistress. Despite the situation, it was very fulfilling for both of us. Mistress Ginger found us the next morning sleeping off a night of ecstasy cuddled up in the middle of the room smiling.

She had been smart to force us to deal with our fears. We were not jealous of each other in the sense of normals. We feared the favor of one over another would send us to the streets where neither of us could survive for long without our collar and Mistress.

Chapter 33: My Brother, My Lover, My Friend, A Triangle of Trust
Mistress Ginger and submissive Matthew

Mistress Ginger finally has calmed down her home. By restraining, then breaking two wild spirits she has created a single heart that beats in sublime unison. The submissive war has ended with both sides able to claim victory. The spoils have been divided equally. Matthew has found his soul and Psycho has established her reflection. The triangle of trust is complete, perfect and unbreakable. The two circles will hold up the Top. The Top will shelter the bottom. Nothing is more of a dream come true than the peace found in this home of D/ss. However, the greedy Mistress will never find satisfaction that easily. Peace is not what she wants. Chaos is her King. Her collars will work together to bring her the drama she wants. No worries this time, the battle is for entertainment purposes only with one insignificant exception.

The Green Rings has been in black mourning robes. The most beloved of Queens has taken her journey to the Summerlands. The darkness has reigned for a season. It is time for the Wheel to spin. Spring has bloomed. Renewal, growth and new life is breaking through the gloom. In the East the sun is rising. Will the summer be hot or will it be unusually cool? Nothing is worse for a period of growth than the neutrality and indifference of a farmer who doesn't tend the fields.

For this most unusual chapter in our life, bring your appetite for the delights of the flesh. No worries, there is a buffet ready and waiting, no matter what your desires, it is on the menu. You may consume until you can handle no more, then come back for unlimited helpings in this world of plenty. The spring and summer of 1995 are a time of abundance, of all things that can bring pleasure to the senses.

"I think she is trying to get another submissive Matt. We must stop her greedy shit or before you know it there will be a fucking army of Mistress Ginger's idiots. Don't you think two fools in her collar is plenty?" ----**Psycho plotting with Matthew against Mistress Ginger, May 1995**

Mistress Ginger made no noise until she was standing over our sleeping units. "Well, well. Looks like my little brats have come to an agreement to get along at last or am I mistaken?"

She reached down between my legs seeking the signs that Matthew and I had followed her order to copulate. I laid there quietly staring at the Mistress. I didn't struggle to stop her. Matthew was also awake and watching her to see if she would finally be satisfied. I could feel him hold his breath like I was. We both were hoping she agreed we had done as she asked. Then, surely, we would be cut loose from our bonds.

She smiled as she found what she was looking for. "Ah, looks like my collars were greedy little piggies. My word Matthew. For a brother who hated Psycho so much you sure enjoyed her favors quite a bit. I think you shall have to provide bath service for your sister and clean the mess you made up. However, first you shall service your Mistress and let's see if this plan of mine to have you spent first will make any difference."

Matthew nodded. "As you wish, Mistress."

I winced at that realizing if Matthew was unable to hold back his moment of ecstasy with Mistress Ginger after an all-night fuck-a-thon with me, he was doomed. I felt his heart speed up, we were bonded so tightly his chest was on my own so yes, I could feel his heartbeat. He was also aware of this possibility apparently.

I no longer desired to see his collar tossed. If I had, the Mistress would not have found my unit full of his seed trust me on that. The sad truth was he could have forced me to have intercourse, we were practically there already the way we were bonded. Instead, he held back his carnal drives and submitted to my judgement as his senior submissive. That was not all he had done. He had gone the extra step of voicing his beliefs about forced sexual congress and said he would not do it even at the risk of being punished by dismissal.

His nature was that of a true gentleman, an independent thinker, and a good heart. When commanded to go against his beliefs he had stood up to his Mistress by refusing to blindly obey the way a stupid slave would. He had proven he was no one's doormat. He was worthy of his submissive collar. I had been the real fool all along. When I am wrong,

I admit it. I was wrong about Matthew. I was now honored to call him my brother and truly shamed I had ever thought of him as anyone other than my own kind.

Good thing I knew just how to make it up to him. If he was able to fulfill the Mistress's request because of our own intimacies, I would aid him from that point forward every day to continue to please her. In other words, I would be available to cause him orgasm however he needed it done so that he could obtain an erection and would no longer be a 'two pump chump' with Mistress Ginger. I had nearly cost him, and myself, the collar. It was a proper penance to repay my debt to him and allowed me to satisfy the desires of my Mistress by proxy.

NOTE: *In our world, sorry doesn't cut it. Those are just words. Only fixing by a repayment deed is acceptable. My behavior had hurt him, and now I would have to help heal the wounds I had created. Luckily, it was a payback I was all too happy to provide. Matthew had proven an excellent lover. I couldn't wait to see if he was not bonded he could do even better.*

Mistress Ginger began the process of untying Matthew and me. We held still as both were needing to piss worse than you can ever imagine. It had been twelve hours since we were last able to get a call in to mother nature. I held my breath. I felt my brother collar do the same. She was mercifully quick about it. Matthew and I almost knocked her down running for the bathrooms to relieve our tensions.

Mistress Ginger yelled after us, "Hurry up brats. When you are finished both of you get back in here at once."

"Yes Mistress," echoed in one male and one female (okay deep but still female) voice from down the hall.

My heart was pounding like a dog's hind leg when you rub his belly just right with worry that Matthew would not be able to make the greedy Mistress happy. She had not reported to either of us just exactly how long would be long enough to make him worth keeping for stud. I finished my task then ran down the hallway back to the bedroom almost running into Matthew who was also rushing to attend our Mistress. We stopped just outside the bedroom door which the Mistress had closed for some reason.

He looked at me seeming frightened. "My apologies, Psycho. I thought you were already back in there."

I looked at the floor. "Matthew you have to relax, or you are going to fail at this. Take a breath, then go to the place you go when she thuds you. If you do that, you can outlast her."

Matthew smiled at me. "Or I could just give her a rim job and have her take me there right now."

We both started laughing at that. "I am sorry brother for setting you up like that," I said with true apology in my voice.

He chuckled harder. "Nah, it is okay. It is funny as hell. One day I will tell you about the look on her face when I did that. Totally worth the thudding I got." He winked at me.

We walked in together trying to wipe the smiles off our faces. I couldn't stop thinking how much Matthew really was like me. He found dark humor in that most awful whipping he got when I tricked him. He said and did what I would have had the situation been reversed. In many ways, we were mirrors to each other. I have never been sure if he was just naturally the same personality type, without schizophrenia, as me or if he had picked up the mirroring while I was training him.

NOTE: *I would like to believe he was a brother from another mother. Since he had so many qualities prior to his collaring that I found refreshing, it is more than likely he was being himself in the hallway that day. In time, I would find more and more in common with him till eventually I began to wonder if he was indeed blood kin somehow. I* hope not because that would have made our lovemaking pretty, ah, well in my family normal I guess. Okay that was dark, sorry. He wasn't related, I did check.

The Mistress was already on her bed naked and ready to receive her adoration from Matthew. He looked at me still appearing nervous. I smiled then led him by taking his hand to stand in front of her. I quickly attended him, and he quickly responded. New lovers you know. I watched as he mounted the Mistress then began his job of pleasing her.

I would have left them alone, but the Mistress did not give me an order for release. Watching the lovers in carnal congress did nothing for my own interests thanks to my fears that Matthew would fail, then be tossed to the streets. He must have been feeling that same anxiety because despite his best efforts I could tell he was losing his, uhm, interest in attending Mistress Ginger. She was no longer moaning in ecstasy. Oh shit. He was about to flop.

Without hesitation I jumped on the bed quickly deep kissing the Mistress with my own backside at the faltering Matthew. I then reached down and began to manually stimulate Mistress Ginger never moving my hind side from his view. This function was to arouse his interests by giving him something carnal to look at and to distract my Mistress by forcing an orgasm even if Matthew was unsuccessful in his own efforts. This may sound very kinky, and it was, but that was the point. The way to keep Matthew safe was to make her reach climax. No matter what Matthew or I had to do to get her there. That is what special services of the collar are all about.

It worked. Matthew regained vigor and proved he could hold it together until his Mistress found pleasure from him. Mistress Ginger reached several screaming orgasms. Everyone was kept safe under one roof. For a change, my behaviors had succeeded rather than failed.

When Matthew was finally spent, the Mistress required I attend her a bit longer until she was finally sated too. All in all, the first team effort to please her had been a hit. Pardon the pun since no one got thudded for a change.

She sat up in the bed looking at us with the glassy haze of satisfaction in her green eyes. "Very nice. Just the way it was supposed to be. I love how you both have learned to work together to meet my demands. I think you can both stop worrying about being sold off or tossed so long as you keep that amazing work up."

I looked at Matthew who flashed a smile at me. I smiled back. Both of us let out a sigh of relief. We had been scared out of our minds since his collaring back in January. That was well over thirty days of fighting, clashing and terror. We were ready for it to end and grateful it finally had with no one getting their collar tossed.

Mistress Ginger stretched. "Now both of you get out. Matthew you have bath service to provide to Psycho, then you both have chores to do. I am going to take a nap. My subs have worn me out." She giggled in happiness.

Matthew and I got out quickly closing the door behind us. We headed for the bathroom so Matthew could do his ordered task. Once inside I told him I could handle my own bath.

He looked at me slyly. "Oh? Are you suggesting I cheat and not follow my Mistress's command? That could come back on me when my trickster sister tells on my insolence later. I don't feel like a thudding, Psycho."

I smiled back mischievously. "Now Matthew whatever made you think I would do that? Don't you trust me?"

Matthew laughed. "Sure I do. I trust you will submit to my attempts to follow my Mistress's orders that I clean up the mess I made of my sister." He reached out and grabbed me by the waist.

He lifted me like I was nothing but a feather and placed me on the sink countertop. I let out a yelp of surprise. He looked at me smiling like the cat who ate the canary while putting his finger to his lips.

"Hush don't wake the Mistress Psycho. I have a secret to show you. Just remember, shh." He grabbed my ankles and pulled my legs open as he knelt before my, uhm, unit.

I almost fell off the countertop as his mouth made electric connection with me. His abilities at oral congress sent me into spasms of ecstasy within only mere moments. He didn't stop until I felt I may die from a climax induced heart attack. Matthew was fucking amazing at oral sex. I had to cover my mouth to keep from alerting the neighborhood of his secret.

When he finally felt he had bathed me properly he stood up then helped me off the countertop. I stood there leaning on him, my blood had rushed from my head so I was swooning a bit, to keep from falling down.

"I don't understand Matthew. Mistress Ginger said you suck at oral sex. You are like a God. What the fuck." I was starting to return from planet 'hell yeah' as my senses began to sharpen once more.

He smiled then looked at the floor sheepishly. "The first night I was so freaked out by her thudding me, I guess I was distracted by the pain. The next night you told me to rim her and once I did, she beat the shit out of me again. I was pissed and to be honest she doesn't shave. I hate a hairy bush. I did a shitty job both times. Then she never gave me a third try at it. So, now that she has said I suck, fuck it. I happen to love doing it so I will do it to you, and she can just lump it."

I looked at the ceiling feeling more upset than ever. "Matthew if she knew you could do that, she would no longer need me. I think you should be honest with her. You are just as good as I am. It is not right to keep such a secret." I thought I would die fessing up to that truth.

He held me tightly then kissed me deeply. "Your oral sex is amazing. I nearly lost it before even getting to her. Plus, I would like to go with you now. That sex we had last night was fucking incredible. I have never enjoyed it more. You are like me in the sack. Mistress Ginger is too straight laced for my taste. I need more to be interested. I think you can give that to me, and I can give you what you need too. When Mistress Ginger commanded you to spend me, and get me prepped to screw her, I noticed there was never any mention of your needs. I also noticed she demanded you attend her orgasm but refused to give you yours in return. The Mistress doesn't care about our sexual satisfaction. So, we have each other to keep our frustrations down and still do our duty to her. So, keep my secret Psycho. I am begging you." He got down on his knees.

I smiled. "Hey, while you are down there cup cake, just so you know your plate is still full." I teased while winking.

Matthew looked at me laughing. "Does that mean yes this can be our secret?"

I nodded. "Yes, you are right Matthew. She tossed you without considering the stress. Her loss my find."

That made him smile. He was very handsome when he smiled. Hell when he frowned, yawned, puked, whatever, the dude was handsome period. Matthew stood back up then began running the bathwater. Bath service was on my list and to be honest other than the Brillo pad incident and the hose in the back yard, or the many submersions to drown me by Master Julie I had never had bath service of my own.

When the water was ready, I looked at it then insisted Matthew get in with me. After all he was filthy too. He laughed but agreed. We started bathing each other, and one thing led to another.

Mistress Ginger opened the bathroom door to find her two collars going at it like wild animals in the bathtub knocking down all her wall ornaments with our thudding.

Turns out he was right. He and I were wild in the bedroom. After years of dealing with many Masters, Mistresses and rapes nothing was off the table with me, and just like a reflection and a pansexual, Matthew was a truly twisted fuck too. When you got us together our lovemaking was animalistic, loud, and aggressive on both ends. We both had suffered years of sexual frustration with our needs not being considered or even close to met. We had a lot of catching up to do.

Mistress Ginger was not even sure what she walked in on when she opened the door. Her tastes were just straight sex, nothing kinky if you ignore her thudding and bondage issues, other than her not caring if it was either boy or girl. With her collars, it was truly insane with shit often getting broken in whatever room we picked to play. Perhaps too much information but there it is.

NOTE: *Quick example just for laughs. Matthew and I often employed toys and other items in our wild trysts. Even bondage was not out of the question sometimes for fun (yeah you wouldn't think so given our histories but hey if it was weird, we likely did it at least once, okay twice, okay often lol). I am not kidding when I say he and I were matched as twisted in the bedroom.*

One day he came to our appointed meeting place with a package of Roman Candles. I took one look at him and said, "Really?"

He smiled and said, "We could do it once."

I made him take them out of the room. So, do you know why I had him take them out rather than just leave them and do what we set out to do? Because I knew us too well. If they were within reach likely it would have been Independence Day in that room before we were done. I couldn't afford to have the temptation available. Yeah, we were that crazy together.. Therefore, you never allow subs to be lovers without a referee present. No holds barred. Oh, and by the way, now you know why Master Jon always has that huge smile on his face.

We didn't even notice she was in the room for several minutes while we continued our scratching, pulling and wild tryst. Matthew saw her first. He almost dropped me (yeah, he was holding me up, use your fucking imagination, damn it) back into the tub. When he stopped, I followed his look of terror to see her standing there smiling at us with her head cocked as if she was confused.

"Uhm, sorry Mistress. Did we wake you," asked Matthew still in congress with me as I closed my eyes expecting one hell of a beating over this little oops moment.

She laughed loudly. "Yes you did. However, I am glad you did. This was worth seeing. What exactly are you two doing?"

I silently mouthed, "Shit, we are so dead," to a very scared looking Matthew.

He looked back at our Mistress. "Getting ready for tonight as you ordered Mistress."

Mistress Ginger came into the bathroom and took a seat on the commode never taking her eyes off us frozen in our odd position.

She cocked her head again looking us over. "I assumed that, Matthew. I meant what or should I say how did you get into that position?"

I snorted trying to stifle a giggle. "Belly dancing lessons, Mistress." I said looking at Matthew who started giggling too despite himself.

He looked back at her. "Yes Mistress, belly dancing lessons."

She nodded. "Damn. Well I will be joining the two of you from now on when you practice. This is pretty cool looking. Psycho I never knew you were so limber."

I groaned. "I should have said so Mistress. My apologies. I beg your mercy."

That made the Mistress laugh till she almost couldn't breathe. "You two are more than I could have ever hoped for. I will leave you to it but hurry up. Psycho, I am ready for lunch." She left while we finished what we had started (without losing any steam by the way).

Things were always peaceful with Matthew and I after that night and day until the day we said goodbye. Our lovemaking was epic, and the one thing we both looked forward to when our work and chores were done. With him, it never got boring. Each time it was like an adventure in that we never knew if we would make it back in one piece or at all. Sort of kidding. As the weeks started to pass, we developed a closeness only lovers can share. However, we were not lovers. We were not even friends. We were Mistress Ginger's submissive pair.

NOTE: *In the world of the normal we would have been viewed as 'friends with benefits.' Neither of us was jealous of the other's favors for Mistress Ginger, nor would we have been jealous had either of us been leashed to another. That is what it is like for a submissive. We are not allowed to feel territorial about that which does not belong to us. Sadly, it is not only are sexual partners that are not all our own. Our hearts don't belong to us either. The hearts, like our units, are the property of the Mistress/Master.*

So, you may be asking did Matthew and I love each other. Sure, in a way that is often hard to understand. He and I adored each other. We were partners sharing the same burdens and pains. We were intimate daily. He and I were also confidants to each other. No one could understand what our lives are like unless they are submissive as well. Therefore, Matthew and I could speak to each other in a way that was deeper than that of a best friend. If we divulged what we told each other, it could result in severe punishment for one or both of us. That made our relationship closer to that of siblings in some ways.

However, our truest desire was for our Mistress. She was the one we really loved. That is the confusion that a normal (or vanilla) can never complete grasp when it comes to the submissive in a lifestyler relationship. It was her love, affection and attention we both desired above all things. What we had for each other was minor in comparison. Mistress Ginger was our world. She made he and I possible. Without her, we would be lost. Whatever she wanted, we would almost die to get her. Mistress Ginger was a fool to not ever truly appreciate what she had. I sincerely hope all of you can. In the end, I think she did indeed realize it and it is the loss of this beautiful world that I believe is the second most important reason she did what she did in October of the next year. But we are getting ahead of ourselves. So on with Spring of 1995.

Ostara was coming. The Spring Equinox was of super importance that year. Our beloved Mother Delleh had passed away just before the New Year. I had missed the important

Sabbat of Imbolc thanks to the acute stage of my disease, so the Covens had held off the election of the new Queen until my return. My Priest didn't feel comfortable with running the vote without his Priestess by his side. My Mistress kept her promise and she and Matthew were staying out of my business with the Green Rings. That morning I kissed them both goodbye before the astounded eyes of my members waiting in the red van that included Linda.

When I got inside and we were down the road, all eyes were on me. The Coven was unsure how to ask about the strange sight of seeing their High Priestess passionately engaged with two people. It was no longer something I could keep secret. No one in that van had missed the sincerity of that farewell custom I had just engaged in with Mistress Ginger and Matthew. Of course, my Mistress had set that up to cause exactly this kind of reaction. What I could not understand is why she would do that when obviously she would not see the behaviors it elicited firsthand. Mistress Ginger was just a universal shit stirrer I suppose.

Lisa shifted appearing a bit uncomfortable, "So, Mother, who was that guy with you and Ginger?"

Tracy, Linda, and Mary nodded in agreement while Chuck and James leaned to hear the answer I would give.

I laughed. "Oh well you all know I am not normal. That guy is Matthew. He is uhm, well, I like variety what can I say." I smiled coyly.

Linda let out her breath. "Damn Mother, just damn. Are you going to join a commune next?" She appeared irritated (likely because she realized that now she would have to wait till I went through every woman and man to get to her now, just kidding).

"That is the plan, Daughter Linda. I am working on building my own. Want to join," I teased her.

Tracey smiled. "If that guy is in it, count me in." James growled fake indignation from the driver's seat at his wife.

Everyone laughed, even me. Spirits were high though everyone dreaded having to be at Springfields without Mother Delleh. They all hoped a good Queen would be chosen, but I knew what the great Queen had predicted. Crone Thallia would win and there would be a weak throne. My Priest Roary and I would be stuck dealing with the heavy issues if that old bat did in fact rise.

I knew Crone Thallia well. She was a tongue wagger, but often did not follow up on her promises. She missed more Sabbats than any other member. She tended to shirk her duties as Crone. What I couldn't wrap my mind around is why she was predicted to win. My only clue was that she had been around a long time, longer than any other Elder. Her senior status and long memory of the Coven should not have been the only factor but trust me it was. There was nothing else outstanding about her. In fact, she was completely forgettable as an individual.

When we arrived at the grounds, my Priest as usual came running. I allowed him to help me from the van while all the maidens and young maids ogled and fawned over the alleged great romance he and I shared. For a change, thanks to my brother collar, I was feeling less frustrated. I even was able to carry on with him sounding more like the proper Priestess than ever before. My quick wit and his unbelievable acting skill made for quite an imaginary affair indeed.

"My Priest, you look worn and thin my Husband. You must sit at the long table with me and sup tonight. Tell me of your worries." I said my eyes dancing with promises of forbidden pleasures while looking at Roary.

He smiled and puffed up. "My Priestess, I have lost weight from my pining for your affections. It would be my honor to sit with you tonight. My only worries Wife is that I will only have but a few hours in your arms this Spring night." He looked at me adoringly.

I let him take my hand and kiss my knuckles. "Ah, my Priest, I shall have to feed you amply. You may of course have all you like because I have hungered for you as well Husband. You shall be the picture of perfect manhood when I am done nourishing you back to fit health. I would only ask that you never love another as you would have me love you."

He grabbed his chest as if in pain. "You know I am your slave, my Priestess. I would be a happy sacrifice in the Beltane Wickerman if the order came your full red lips. I am but a helpless babe against your charms. Your wish is always my command. I shall never love another like I love you."

I curtsied him, then he took my arm as the young women swooned, all of them wishing to be me. Even my own Coven members appeared taken in by these most false promises

Roary and I made to each other of eternal love. They knew better, but that was and is Roary for you. The man should have been a Hollywood actor. He was handsome enough for it no doubt.

We entered the hall to find Crone Thallia. She of course had been told that the vote was tallied, and she was about to be announced the official new Queen of Green. Our votes were taken by mail out to the four Covens. Each Coven High Priest and High Priestess, if there was a pair, then took the vote during the Esbat prior to Ostara. The winning Crone's name was mailed to the hall. Since there were only four Covens, me and Roary would have made the tie-breaking vote if there had been one. This time, it was unanimous. Crone Thallia was now Queen. I felt that Mother Delleh was with me in spirit as I walked to the Green Throne. It would be empty for the year.

The Great Queen had sat on the throne for her entire Crone life, fifty-five till her death at 69. For fourteen years, the Coven had been stable and peaceful under her crown. Now, the laziest of all the members of the Green Rings was taking her spot. I prayed to Mother Delleh that nothing significant would arise until this Queen too took her own journey to the Summerlands. I was tired of drama. However, I was ready to block it from disturbing all that Mother Delleh had created.

My Priest walked up behind me. "I miss her too Arodia. I swear, I can't stop crying every time I hear her name. I owe her so much. She gave me this life, you, the world. I pray she is finally at peace. No one deserves it more."

I felt a tear fall down my cheek. "I agree Roary. She was a great woman. Crone Thallia is going to be a problem. She told me this herself before she passed on. Are you ready for whatever comes Husband?" I turned to see he too had tears in his eyes.

Roary stood up tall as possible. "For Mother Delleh, for the Green Rings, I would gladly die if that is what was required."

I chuckled despite my tears. "My Husband, I swear you keep talking of dying today. I am glad that Mother Delleh was wise. She chose my consort well." I placed my hand on his chest.

"That heart of yours beats only for the Green Rings. Woe be it to the woman who truly falls in love with you. I doubt she will like always being second fiddle." I winked as he smiled with honor at my most true words.

As I have said, Roary is a devout Wiccan and true Pagan. He no doubt would happily lay down his life for the Covens. Mother Delleh knew that when she raised him as High Priest when he certainly didn't qualify. He was not a third year student and had only served as Summoner for three months when he was asked to be my Consort Husband. He had just finished his third year when this event happened and I wasn't third year until Yule. She had chosen us not because we were the oldest, most experienced nor even met all the requirements. She chose me because she thought she saw someone who could rally the people and Roary because of his lion's heart.

At that time of upheaval, we were the best suited for the leadership roles to pull a struggling Coven from the brink of oblivion. Since he and I were indeed successful, one can say she knew her shit. In the coming decade, the internet came, and then social media. Roary and I were no longer the best suited for the new problems this created. He and I were relics of the past when people had to send letters snail mail and you could go to Sabbat or Esbat and never been hailed by a cell phone. That day he and I had a serious discussion about the changes we both saw coming of speed of communication, and the social fabrics of our culture.

It was on this Sabbat we wrote into law that all Elders would give up the seat of power in their covens. This transfer of power would happen every decade after raising a new generation of High Priests and High Priestesses to keep the circles from ever stagnating again. Roary and I did this before the lazy Crone Thallia took power. We knew she would sit on the law never sending it to a vote if we did not force the Covens to see it soon. It was a very clever move. Queen Thallia never allowed a single law to pass her entire reign, no matter how badly it needed to be voted on. In fact, the woman never lifted a finger for the very Covens she ruled. Roary and I were often frustrated, angry and in the end ready to give up our seats thanks to the foolish indifference and pure laissez faire attitude of this most useless Queen.

That day my Priest and I witnessed the raising of Queen Thallia. He and I were only third levels and a fifth level Priestess could only be raised by fourths. I was not impressed by the ceremony. Later Roary said he wasn't either. It was pomp, droll and boring.

We chuckled when we both said that at the same time. "Now being raised to High Priest and High Priestess, which was wow!" Totally worth seeing but better being.

The ride home was quiet and subdued. No one was happy about the new Queen. She had given a speech that was idiotic, rambling and long. The truth is Queen Thallia was really the only choice. The other Crones all had made sure to let everyone know they didn't want the throne. Those ladies deserved it more. They realized what following in the crown of Mother Delleh would be. That means they cared. Queen Thallia cared about herself. She may have been useless, but like Mother Delleh predicted she was not destructive thankfully. She would reign the entire decade Roary and I were the Leader Elders, dying one year after he and I raised our replacements. I know nothing of the Queen raised after because by then I was forced to move on. That again is another story.

My children were now five and three. My daughter had started kindergarten and my son was attending pre-school. They had grown up strong and good natured. Maiden Mary and Delilah adored them, and Mary's children were like their own siblings. My kids were staying the weekend with Aunt Mary so the van dropped me off alone.

I went into the house to find Mistress Ginger thudding the hell out of Matthew. He was screaming in pure agony. I sat down on the sofa not daring to interrupt. I was unsure if this was a correction thudding or if she was feeling vigorous. Luckily, she heard me come inside. She stopped her applications and came into the living room for my report leaving my brother bonded awaiting her further pleasure.

I filled her in on the happenings of the election, the disappointing speech to the Covens and of the new law my Priest and I enacted. She listened nodding her head in approval. I wanted to ask her about Matthew but feared inciting her anger. When I finished my retelling of the day's events she seemed satisfied I had not left out anything she needed to know. Mistress Ginger told me to follow her to the bedroom to be recollared. Remember she had to remove it when I did Sabbats or Esbats.

I saw poor Matthew welted and bruised. He was in a lot of pain and gagged. No matter how hard he had tried he could not adjust to the art of thudding. My heart pitied him as his sad eyes told me this was a pleasure thudding not correction. Mistress Ginger must have been bored.

She went to her dresser retrieving my collar. I knelt while she relocked me in.

I smiled at her seductively. "I missed you Mistress. Roary was there. He asked about you. I told him I was going home to run my hands all over your milk white skin. His manhood nearly broke off with the thought."

Mistress Ginger suddenly smiled wanting to hear more. I knew this would work. One needed to stroke the Mistress Ginger's ego more than any sex organ to make her happy. I very carefully acted out the bullshit I never told my Priest on my Mistress's now very excited unit. Within short order I had her engaged in carnal congress with me. She had forgotten her thudding of Matthew. I made sure to wear her out by bringing her to ecstasy until she could take no more.

Once she was sated, she told me to untie my brother and leave her so she could sleep it off. I untied Matthew who was stuck watching my seduction of our Mistress. We left in a hurry before she changed her mind.

Matthew got a robe to throw on and I closed her door following him down the hallway back to the safety of the living room.

I sat down on the sofa and he sat down next to me. "What happened Matt," I said as I took up his now very bruised forearm to check him for cuts that may need attending.

He shook his head. "I don't know Psycho. She was watching TV and I was cooking her dinner when suddenly she got in the mood to thud. I thought she would kill me for sure this time."

I nodded. "Okay, yeah that sounds right. She was bored, Matt. We are going to have to try to keep her busy. When she is bored she will thud the shit out of you."

He looked at me. "She never thuds you? Why?"

"Because you are afraid of it and I am not, that is why. I am an old thudder so I will yell and cuss but rarely cry or beg anymore, Matt. She gets a kick out of your terror." I told him to stand up so I could check his other parts for cuts.

He shook his head. "I can't help it. I try, but I just, it hurts too much. Thank you for saving me today. I know that is what you just did. You never said any of that shit to your Priest."

I laughed. "Okay big moose, you are cut on your thighs and backside. Follow me to the bathroom for treatment. How dare you accuse me of lying brother." I smiled impishly.

He sniffed, he'd been crying again during the thudding. "Well I know that is what you did. I guess I owe you a favor back. What can I do for you to make us even?"

"Follow me to the bathroom, my fool. I think I need Matthew's bath service." I took off sprinting for the bathroom.

He laughed out loud sprinting after me. "That sound completely fair."

After my 'bath service' and picking up all the shit we knocked off the walls, counters and sink, he and I had a serious discussion about thudding and Mistress Ginger's tendency to get bored easily.

"Matthew, I think I have figured something out about our Mistress," I said while cleaning up the tub.

He was scrubbing down the sink. "Yeah? What? That she is mean as a snake?" He laughed.

I snorted. "That too. I was thinking she loves drama. Remember how much she would laugh when you and I would beat the shit out of each other?"

He stopped then looked at me. "Hey, you're right. She loved that shit." He stopped and leaned against the sink but then winced when his ass reminded him it was bruised to hell.

"Well, I was thinking, she didn't thud as much when we did that. So, what if we pretended to fight or argue occasionally? You know, not throwing shit but just the old wrestling and insults. Like we used to do. I think she'd believe it, and maybe it would save your ass a bit?" I looked at him noting he was nodding as if agreeing with me.

"Just one problem, Psycho. She used to punish us for it too. I am not too keen on the fucking shock collar or that damned pair of Vampire gloves either." He shuddered just thinking about them.

I snickered. "You are such a pussy, Matthew. Yeah it will get us punished but we could take turns. The shock collar and Vampire gloves are a one-time thing. Your thudding sessions can go on for hours. Just think on that. A quick punishment every other week versus daily thudding pal."

He nodded. "You have a point, Psycho."

I laughed. "What that you are a pussy?"

Matthew smiled playfully. "You are what you eat. Look at me, Matthew the Psycho Pussy."

He plowed into me knocking me to the floor. He straddled me demanding I call him Matthew the Psycho Pussy by torture tickling until I nearly pissed myself laughing. Then we agreed to pretend to argue once a week with topics to be agreed upon during our trysts.

Finally, he got off my unit claiming himself the ultimate victor of our past battles. I called him an idiot to have ever allowed himself to be collared in the first place, then pull him back down into floor with me. This time, our wrestling quickly turned into our daily rough carnal congress. I have to say this time he could not deny I was the victor of that little battle.

The very next day we put our plan into action since the kids were at Mary's place. I pretended to be incensed that I thought the Mistress was paying more attention to his foot massages than to my bath service. Matthew and I made damned sure she was just around the corner to hear us bickering.

"Yeah, well I can rub a foot, what can I say," Matthew barked at me from the living room where he was dusting tables.

I turned around from cleaning the dishes. "I can say you smell like a foot. If you learned to rub a clit like you rubbed a foot maybe the Mistress wouldn't have had to call me in to do your fucking job."

Matthew almost choked trying not to laugh. "Oh yeah. If you are so fucking good at oral sex, then why can't you give a blow job worth a shit? Didn't anyone tell you that you are supposed to spit not swallow?" He started clearing his throat as if something were stuck in it.

Quick Note: *Okay yeah, we were nasty like that because back when we were really fighting, we were really foul just like this. We had to make her believe it, didn't we? Besides, like me, Matthew could talk like a trucker when he wanted to do so.*

"Fuck you sloppy second" I said trying not to smile while I saw Matthew making faces at me.

He snorted. "You have to fuck me, don't' you. How's that for a punishment? I can do whatever I want and you have to grin and bear it," he yelled trying to sound angry as he made humping motions while slapping the air.

I walked to the kitchen door my hands on my hips trying to look indignant. "You call what you do fucking? Shit, I had better sex with a needle full of sedatives jammed in my ass."

The Mistress came into the living room. "What is this happy bullshit. You two are at this again? Get in here, Psycho. Kneel both of you now."

I came in and knelt next to Matthew as ordered. I noticed a look of satisfaction on the Mistress's face. "Who started it?"

Matthew and I had agreed I would take the punishment this week since he had been thudded the day before.

"I did, Mistress. You favor Matthew more than me. I was only saying the truth." I said wincing while hoping it would not be the shock collar.

Mistress Ginger purred. She always did it when very happy. "Oh? Is that so? Well Psycho, I am in the mood to do some thudding today. I think I can make you realize you are incorrect. Matthew is just as loved as you are. Not more and not less. I suppose you need a little pampering to prove it though. So, march your ass into the bedroom. I will be there shortly to give you some extra attention." I got up headed to the bedroom groaning.

I heard Mistress tell Matthew his punishment was to take on my chores of cleaning the kitchen while she attended his sister's jealous streak.

As I walked back to the room, I winced realizing this was more serious than we had considered. Mistress Ginger had chosen to thud over all punishments available which meant she was in one of her thudding moods. Our arguments were not going to stop her from attacking Matthew. He was too easy a target. I normally was not a selfless kind of person. However, my brother was not cut out for the art of thudding.

This was my first session since before my acute onset back in November of the last year. I decided to do something extraordinary for the submissive I had once set up to be beaten half to death. I would find a way to take over as the sole thudded submissive in the house. This was going to require I pull out all the stops in my acting abilities. I also would go out of my way to incite her to hit harder in the hopes that at least some of my terror could be real. I could handle the thud and keep going unlike my brother collar.

Right or wrong this was what I was going to do for Matthew's comfort. He would pay me back. I knew that. He was always fair in service for service. I consoled my heavy heart with ideas on what I would ask him for in repayment for this gift if I was successful in literally saving his ass.

I waited patiently for Mistress Ginger. She came into the room and ordered I dress her in her favorite red cat suit first. I was right, this was a mood, not boredom. I would have to really work hard to get this service all to myself. Matthew was like a fucking sugar-coated candy to the thud loving Mistress. He would be a tough act to beat without over doing it and giving away my bullshit.

She bonded me quickly going on and on about how excited she was to finally have me under her crop again after so many months. I pretended to be afraid which seemed to really excite her. Step one, success. When her first blow came, I didn't have too much trouble yelling and pleading because it fucking hurt, damn it. This led to her sending more my way. I waited until she got to her fifteen-minute mark (counting in my head by Mississippi, you know one Mississippi, two Mississippi, etc.) then turned on my tear maker. This surprised the Mistress, but she kept thudding appearing more thrilled every second. At the twenty-five mark I began to beg promising anything and throwing a ton of 'mercy please' in there for good measure.

This was just too good to be true for the Mistress. She untied me and demanded special services of the collar before getting to her floggers that I saw waiting in the wings. I did as command by aggressively attending her as if afraid that if

I didn't do it properly she may thud me again. Now all of this past the first three swats was mostly act. I had learned how Matthew was behaving by listening through the walls. All I did was replicate his behaviors, then time them just right. When she was sated of her desires, she tied me up and began to sensually torture my unit like she used to in the beginning of our relationship. Now this time it was no act. That shit hurts no matter how long you have been doing it. It is kind of like electricity, there is no way to gain tolerance for it.

I had forgotten she had a need for this kind of torture. Now she could do this with Matthew, but it would not be as dramatic and there was a limit. With a woman, it could go on all night non-stop. She had stopped employing this type of torment due to my illness, but I was now almost residual. My stress level tolerance was much higher. I took my punishment. Once she was finally done making me miserable, I was unbonded.

Unlike Matthew, I had earned bed privileges now that I had returned her sensual sadism behaviors. She held me tightly spooning practically cooing in my ears at how much she had missed that treat. Yikes, for her maybe

I cleared my throat. I had been yelling. I told you that shit hurts. "Mistress, I would beg your favor on something I have been thinking about. I am sure your glorious person has as well."

She sat up on her elbow to kiss my neck. "Psycho, you only talk pretty when you want something big. Out with it, baby girl."

I closed my eyes hoping I was doing the right thing. "I would like you to separate out the thudding and torture like you have the other services Mistress."

She snorted. "What? Why? Thudding and torture are part of the special services of the collar."

I sat up, then turned to her keeping my gaze down. "Mistress they are, but I want them for myself. I know it is greedy of me to ask, but Matthew doesn't appreciate them like I do. He is bigger and can't do what I can do for you. I reached out and ran my hands down her unit seductively." I tried to look as if I were pouting about it.

It worked. I still can't believe it did actually to this day. She said, "Yes, you are right. Matthew is great at other things, but his thudding stance sucks, and sensual torture is just a too much of a pain in my ass to bother doing to him. I will let him know at dinner you are to be the thudder in this house. You will now have full bedroom privileges so that I can have what I want, whenever the mood strikes me." She began to kiss me deeply demanding I attend her yet again. The woman was damned insatiable sometimes, fuck.

I did as she requested feeling queasy that I had just talked myself into a fucking nightmare all to save my pussy brother's lily ass. Had anyone told me even just a month earlier that I would sell myself into torture and thudding at Mistress Ginger's spontaneous request to save another from

355

a couple of swats occasionally, I would have called you a liar. So, I asked myself why the hell did I do it? Because while the Mistress was beating the piss out of me, I suddenly realized, Matthew had given me the gift of choice. So, I repaid him with the gift of mercy. He had earned it and for just once in my ugly dark world, I wanted to make sure something was fair.

When I was finally released to make dinner, Matthew came to assist me. The Mistress was back taking a rest after her rigorous work-out.

"You okay, Psycho? I was freaking out. It sounded bad. I admit, I was so scared for you. Maybe we shouldn't have faked her out like that. I will need to look you over for cuts," he said keeping his voice low.

I smiled then turned to him and said, "Matthew, you can look after I make dinner. You will be happy to know, Mistress Ginger will not thud you anymore, unless for punishment."

He looked at me confused. "What? How can you know that? She does what she wants, Psycho. I just have to learn to buck up is all like you told me."

I shook my head. "No Matthew, you are in the clear. I had the Mistress give me exclusive thudding and torture service. You are home free now unless you fuck up and get punished for something stupid. Still, that is occasional thing. She won't get you anymore. Promise." I went back to cutting up potatoes.

Matthew stood there staring at me in surprise and awe. "You did that for me? Why?"

I laughed out loud trying not to cry. "Because you are a pussy Matthew and because I adore you."

His eyes filled with tears. "You can never know how much this and you mean to me, Psycho. Thank you. You already know I have adored you from the start."

He reached out and pulled me close embracing me as I did my best not to let my emotions overwhelm me. Stupid big moose. If only he had been less of a baby about a little thud, sheesh.

I swatted him on his bruised ass making him yelp. "Get off me. You already got your service today pussy. Stop trying to double dip." I began to laugh deflecting the despair from within.

He laughed too. "Well how about one of those horrid blow jobs of yours then?"

I hit him in the shoulder. "Fucking liar. If you hate them so much why are you always begging for them?"

He shrugged. "Just offering you practice, babe. You know you should be on your knees practicing right now."

That earned him a full kick right in his welted ass, he returned one of his own onto mine which sent us both into laugher as we finished the Mistress's dinner.

We continued our plan of pretending to get on each other's nerves once a week when the kids were off at Mary's or we were home from work or school just to keep the Mistress happy. Good to her word, I was the only one thudded or tortured in the household. Matthew was very attentive to all my bruises, welts or stripes after every session. He must have thanked me a million times. His affections made it worth the pain. Mistress Ginger had gotten closer to both of us because of it too. That was the bonus. For the first time in my whole rotten life I was dare I say, content, at peace and full of hope.

Simon had promised one day this would happen if I did what he said. Now I had the proof he was right. Following the Key and Collar was the answer to all my problems. There were always little problems, dramas or bullshit, but all in all, I had everything a person could want. A loving Mistress who took care of what I could not. My disease was in remission. I had a glorious and wonderful lover on the side who could keep pace with me. My children were doing great in school and pre-school. The D/ss household was flush with cash from Matthew's job as a computer tech, and mine as a mortician.

Our Mistress managed all the money and she loved being able to spoil herself, the kids and well, buying us more horridly obnoxious clothing (yuck). She even bought a new car with all the bells and whistles. She didn't have to work so she watched the kids. Mistress Ginger was great with them, and since she never had any of her own, she seemed to enjoy the role as Aunt Ginger a great deal. I was making all A's in college again, and Matthew was a great study buddy when I could keep his hands off my unit, not that I really tried that hard to be honest.

Things were going wonderful the entire month of April. Then came May, and the phone call that would send me and Matthew into a tag team long game against Mistress Ginger, submissive style.

NOTE/WARNING: *Had things continued this way forever, I would be ending my story here. There would be nothing to write since my life would be so great, I would dare never brag about it. However, I will give everyone a single warning. Things with Mistress Ginger and submissive Matthew were indeed utopian. There are events that are funny, chaotic and worth telling. Just be aware this story obviously didn't stay beautiful.*

I will continue with Mistress Ginger's reign sharing the fun, the laughter and the adoration while giving you the knowledge that tragedy ended this union of three. I will do my best to tell it as it was without sugar coating the facts. I am still so upset over this that I am having to take it very slow. I have never spoken about the ending of this D/ss relationship or August of 1996 to anyone. I have also always forbidden the Looper and Simon from discussing it. I am reliving it for the first time since this all happened, unlike most other events in my life.

Why would this beautiful life be something I have kept away from my memory for all this time? Well we are still in the heyday of Mistress Ginger's reign and I often catch myself sobbing knowing what is coming in such a short time from now. A year is never enough when you had the world and lost it.

As we get closer and closer to the darkness that came to claim my beloved lifestyler family, Mistress Ginger and submissive Matthew broke my heart into dust. One had no choice, the other left me with no answers. In the end the triangle that appeared unbreakable, in the end there was only one.

There will be no other time in my life until 2013 like this one, where I can openly discuss with a smile on my face the pleasures of sexual congress that is of my choosing.

To be continued in Book Five of the
"27 Masters" series entitled "Triangle of Trust"

About the Author: Alexandria May Ausman

Alexandria May Ausman in her 16th year was diagnosed with Schizophrenia. She was quickly abandoned by her foster parents. While still only a teen, she was forced to battle this devastating illness alone.

Alexandria has struggled with lack of a support system, numerous psychotic episodes, exploitation, homelessness, and an uncaring mental health system.

Alexandria raised two healthy children. After obtaining her bachelor's degree in psychology she worked as a child abuse investigator and became a diagnostic psychologist while acquiring her Master's in psychology. Alexandria never forgot the experience of 'slipping through the cracks.' Her life's goal is to help people suffering abuse and/or mental illness have access to necessary services. By accident, she became a model of 'gothic attire' and the World Goth Queen.

She began writing a fictionalized account of her life experiences after a catastrophic return of psychotic symptoms. Today, Alexandria is retired, and homebound due to crippling symptoms of Schizophrenia. She currently lives in Tallahassee, Florida, with her loving husband and a loyal support dog.